The Land Where Horror Dwells

Deathrealm

SPIRITS

The Land Where Horror Dwells

Deathrealm SPIRITS

Edited by
STEPHEN MARK RAINEY

SHORTWAVE
PUBLISHING

DEATHREALM: SPIRITS

Cover illustration by J. Edward Neill.
Interior formatting and design by Alan Lastufka.

First Edition published October 2023.

10 9 8 7 6 5 4 3 2 1

Library of Congress Control Number: 2023914818

ISBN 978-1-959565-17-8 (Paperback)
ISBN 978-1-959565-18-5 (eBook)

CONTENTS

INTRODUCTION

STEPHEN MARK RAINEY

The year was 1986. Originally a denizen of Virginia's dark, rural shadows, I had moved to Chicago and, by day, held the position of product manager at one of the world's leading manufacturers of computer-based typesetting systems. By night, I wrote scary short stories, several of which I'd sold to some nice small-press publications. At the time, the late, great author, editor, and collector of all things horror, Mr. Bob Weinberg, sponsored Sunday morning "mini-cons" once a month at the Americana Congress Hotel in downtown Chicago, and I had become something of a regular. These mini-cons consisted only of a dealers' room, but what a room it was! By way of Bob's table, I discovered a trove of horror-themed small press periodicals, such as *Crypt of Cthulhu*, *Dagon*, *Eldritch Tales*, *Etchings & Odysseys*, *Whispers*, and many others.

If the titles don't immediately ring a bell, these publications were (and remain) gems of rare quality, and upon picking up bunches of them, I found myself bitten by a bug. I thought: how cool would it be if I were to try my hand at producing a magazine of my own, something new and hopefully different? I had some publishing experience by way of *Japanese Giants*, a long-running fanzine devoted to Godzilla, kith and kin, which I had created over a decade earlier. And, as you might have noted in the first paragraph, I worked for a company that manufactured typesetting systems. One of my daily tasks was to test the tolerances of these multi-million-dollar machines by typesetting and printing hundreds upon hundreds of dummy pages.

So why not typeset and print *real* magazine pages?

My magazine pages?

In today's world of digital publishing, some may not grasp the sheer novelty in the mid-1980s of being able to produce a fully typeset publication. Most semi-professional magazines consisted of pages of typewritten text and physically cut-and-pasted artwork or photographs, usually offset-printed (or photocopied, if the publisher was working on the cheap), and saddle-stitched (sometimes by hand). With the graphic resources at my disposal, including the excellent printing company I'd used for *Japanese Giants*, I felt confident that the physical attributes of this new, potential product would prove unique for its time.

Still, however sweet a magazine's appearance, it was the contents that would make or break it over the long haul. I already knew a couple of accomplished writers—Wilum H. Pugmire and Jessica Amanda Salmonson—from whom I immediately solicited work, and my friend, former roommate, and *Japanese Giants* co-editor, Bill Gudmundson, recommended I contact one of *his* friends, a certain Jeffrey Osier, who had written a horror story titled "The Encyclopedia for Boys." I did so, received the story, and promptly exploded with joy, for Mr. Osier's story was nothing short of brilliant.

And so, *Deathrealm* magazine was born. The first issue

appeared in early 1987, and it didn't take long to grab a sizable audience. Once opened to submissions from the masses, the issues filled up quickly, and although I could only afford to pay a pittance, at least early on, the quality of the stories I received rivaled many of those in the field's best professional publications. Mr. Osier's work frequently highlighted *Deathrealm*'s pages, and I credit him as much as anyone for putting *Deathrealm* solidly on the map. (Sadly, Jeff has retired from writing, though he remains an active and accomplished artist.)

Names such as Douglas Clegg, Richard Corben, Christopher Golden, Joe R. Lansdale, Elizabeth Massie, Billie Sue Mosiman, William F. Nolan, Tom Piccirilli, Wilum H. Pugmire, Jessica Amanda Salmonson, Jeff VanderMeer, Karl Edward Wagner, Manly Wade Wellman, and many others illuminated *Deathrealm's* contents pages. Many tales from the magazine went on to appear in the various Year's-Best anthologies of the day. In the early 1990s, *Year's Best Fantasy & Horror* editor Ellen Datlow named *Deathrealm* and Richard Chizmar's *Cemetery Dance* as the two most influential magazines in horror. And *Deathrealm* won several nice awards, including the International Horror Critics Guild Award for Excellence.

While I edited *Deathrealm* for its entire decade-long run, in 1993, Tal Publications took over the publishing duties, which increased the magazine's circulation ten-fold; in 1995, Malicious Press—a new partnership between author Lawrence Watt-Evans and screenwriter Terry Rossio—assumed the helm until the final issue (#31, Summer 1997).

It was during those last couple of years that drastic changes began sweeping through the publishing business, with the ages-old traditional publishing model giving up critical ground to what would eventually become the digital and independent publishing landscape that today is commonplace. Myriad newsstand and comic distributors, who owed Malicious Press many thousands of dollars, went bankrupt, altered their payment practices (as in gave up on them), or simply disappeared.

After its long and very successful run, the gentlemen of Malicious Press and I decided the time had come to retire *Deathrealm*. It went out on a high note, its final issue scheduled in advance, and all debts paid.

That was damn near three decades ago.

Still, even now, the epithet by which I was once commonly known—"Mr. Deathrealm"—lingers in the horror community. In 2004, I edited a limited-edition reprint anthology, titled *Deathrealms*, for Delirium Books, which included fifteen stories from the magazine's pages. For many years after the magazine's retirement, regular queries and submissions from anxious authors appeared in my mailbox, the most recent being in 2019. (My friend, please catch up with the times!) I can't count how many writers and artists who have built illustrious careers have expressed to me how significantly *Deathrealm* contributed to their success. At various conventions over the years, the number one question asked of me was "Are you ever going to resurrect *Deathrealm*?"

For a long time, pretty well burned out by the intensity of maintaining the magazine schedule, I always answered "Never." (Never say never again, eh?) Over the years, I did occasionally float the idea of editing a new, standalone anthology bearing the *Deathrealm* title (hey, look what you're holding!). A couple of times, the project appeared destined to fly but for various reasons did not (and with the benefit of hindsight, I'm glad of this, since it's clear the timing would *not* have been good). Eventually, though, after long, hard consideration, I—and Alan at Shortwave Publishing—felt the stars had come right again.

Some months ago, this particular monster began to take shape.

It's fair to say that today's horror lit field wears a different face from the one that spawned *Deathrealm*, not to mention countless other publications of that time. The content creators' names and faces have rightly changed (and far too many of my generation have passed to the Great Beyond). The remaining big publishing houses tend to be less open to new, experimental voices than in horror's "Golden Days," opting to support and promote only the tried-and-true; the once-prominent midlist, where so many working authors resided in those days, is a ghost of its former self. On-demand digital publishing more than rivals paper-and-ink books ensconced in brick-and-mortar bookstores, and self-publishing—once anathema to most accomplished professionals—has become not only accepted but commonplace.

Mind you, I'm not complaining. This is all part of the creative world's cycle—and evolution. "Different" is not synonymous with "worse," though to hear the voices of what I might call stagnant mindsets, you might not know it. The greatest challenge I see is mitigating the sheer volume of voices struggling to be heard amid so many more who now have opportunities that never existed just a few decades ago. For creators, it's always been hard, believe you me, and to my mind, it hasn't and probably never will get easier.

I'm not sure it should.

In *Deathrealm: Spirits*, you will find voices old, new, traditional, experimental, quiet, and chaotic. For all the shifting features of the horror world's façade, the heart beating beneath it, as it always has, sends the darkest blood through its pulsing arteries, some carrying dark shadows of the past, others blazing with new and very intense fire.

Whether this volume proves to be some new beginning or a crown on a long legacy, I do hope the stories here appease your immediate cravings but leave you longing for more.

As ever....

—Stephen Mark Rainey, editor

The Land Where Horror Dwells

Deathrealm SPIRITS

GHOSTS IN THE CELLS

JOE R. LANSDALE

The night was clear, and the three men could hear the river roaring nearby. The air smelled damp, like rain was on the menu, but still the stars could clearly be seen. There was a slight wind. The trees rustled their needles and leaves.

A large log campfire crackled and popped, and white smoke drifted into the night. Logs in the fire slowly shifted position, flaked ash, and fell apart. There was a pile of cut firewood lying nearby, along with an axe. The men had found deadwood and chopped it to suit.

They had cooked and eaten fish they had caught and cleaned, and now they were full and relaxed, drinking weak coffee. Two of the men, Bill, and Harry, sat on a large flat rock, cups in hand, while Jim lay on the ground. He held his head up with his hand, elbow pressed into the dirt. From time to time, he would sit up and pick up his cup, sip from it, set the cup aside, relocate his elbow to its spot, and again rest his head in his palm.

"It's been a good day," Bill said.

"It has," said Harry. He held his cup with two hands and blew on it to make the coffee cooler.

Jim agreed.

"You know," Bill said, "I'm out here in this wilderness, I think about God. His incredible works."

"It's nature," Jim said. "Not God, Bill. One does not need the other. Nature doesn't need God."

"I can't say I can embrace that idea," Bill said.

"God or Nature," Harry said. "We carry the past, even the distant creation of the universe inside of us, and that's what intrigues me."

Jim said, "How do you mean?"

"I am not a believer in God," Harry said. "But I believe we are all part of the past and the future, and that nature is not merely what we observe, but it's us as well."

"That's because you're a scientist," Bill said. "You have been taught not to believe in God."

"Not at all. I know several scientists who are religious. But perhaps it is the sort of work I do that makes me see things differently."

"Genetics?" Jim asked.

"My work in genetics is peripheral. I am a cog in the scientific wheel. There are far greater scientists than me who I have learned from. A couple of them being men of faith. Genetics looks back centuries, not just four thousand years, the age a lot of hardcore Christians assign to the age of the earth. That idea is not sustainable. The world is far older. I find it odd that most Christians I know believe in genetics when it convicts a person of a crime, but not if it disagrees with the age of humankind. That conflicts with their view of the Bible."

"How does it prove the age of humankind?" Bill asked. "I don't get it. Come on, Harry, how?"

Harry said, "Well, there were a lot of ancestors before

modern humans, and at about the time we rose to prominence on Earth, there were other humans, different lines of humans, sharing space with us. We have discovered in the genetic line, in our DNA, not only Neanderthals, which are provable, but Denisovans, a less-known offshoot of humanity, also provable. Most curious to me is the discovery of an unknown ancestor that exists in most of us. A line of humans that ended up extinct. They lent their genes to us. But they are a strange group, these Unknowns. A less-identifiable distant ancestor. There is only a ghostly whiff of them left."

Jim said, "Ghosts?"

"Ghostly. Loose term, meaning we know very little about them, but we know they have found their way into the depths of our DNA, our primitive brains, buried in our cells. My job is part of an experiment to get in touch with our ancestors. These ghostly ones seem the easiest for us to connect with, which is odd, considering the others are more obviously apparent."

"Connect with?" Jim said. "What's that mean?"

"It's research," Harry said. "I really shouldn't talk about it."

"It's me, Jim. I've known you since we were kids. We both have. Come on. When it comes down to it, me and Bill hardly know what you do, beyond research. I was thinking about this the other day. What the hell does Harry actually do? Talking in that formal way of his. What is that all about?"

"It is called education, Jim."

"Kidding. Tell us about this ghost in our genetics," Jim said.

Harry leaned back and looked to the night sky. Like a warning shot, a shooting star streaked across the skies.

"All right," Harry said. "It is not like you plan to call me out for revealing the research. Besides, I am only discussing the tip of it. Best that way, so you can understand. And when I say that, I am not insulting your intelligence, just the fact that I am versed in this subject, this discipline, and you are not."

"Fair enough," Bill said.

"Yeah," Jim said. "Let's hear it."

"According to genetic studies, there was a lost ancestor, and the remnants of that ancestor's genetics are in us, because numerous human species shared those genes."

"They had relations," said Jim.

"They had sex, yes," Harry said. "We use a method of statistics labeled Bayesian Inference. It reveals a third introgression. Meaning that what we think of as modern humans interbred with this populace as they moved out of Africa."

"Statistics lie," Bill said. "You can bend them anyway you want them."

"Sometimes that's true," Harry said. "But frequently, they tell the truth, and sometimes it is a hard truth to swallow. But there is something else, and in my view, it proves this third population."

"What's that something else?" Bill said.

"Neuroscience, and a bit of quantum physics. And what may sound like voodoo. Much of what I am doing is provable. We have made investigations into the depths of the mind. I have heard and seen things that have made me feel that we may be tapping into something best left untapped. The bottomless pit of who we are, and where we came from."

"Vague," Bill said.

"This ghost ancestor may be the one that left us with that part of our brain that is most destructive, if for no other reason than it is self-serving. Early humans, those more like us, may have killed that human line off, and if they did, they may have had good reason."

"Doesn't that prove the killers who killed them off are destructive too?" Jim said.

"I think it may have been done more as a means of survival, and because those darker genetics are inside of us to begin with.

But this ghost ancestry I am referring to, that is all they are about. They were perhaps so self-destructive they did themselves in. Reptile thinking is all that mattered to them. Eat, have sex, kill. For them, whatever happens in that pursuit happens."

"You can't know that," Bill said.

"Not with exactness, no," Harry said. He picked up a stick and stirred it in the fire. Red embers popped and sparked. "But we damn sure know some things. We can use drugs and hypnosis to investigate those ghosts in our genes. There is a strong theory that ghosts, what people claim to have seen, are not being seen with the eye. Instead, the brain is transferring images to the eye."

"Seeing what it wants to see?" Bill said.

"I am not sure we always choose it. These ghosts in our genes reveal themselves now and then, in some people more than others. It is like inheriting high blood pressure, heart disease, so on. Except this inheritance leads to darker problems. Mostly in men, I believe. Talking about the guys with dead kids buried in their basement. The ones who leave a trail of dead women, or men, across the country. This ghost ancestor is the Hyde part of our species. The raw reptilian factor in what we call the reptilian brain. The fellow next door who was babysitting your child beats the mailman to death with a garden rake, and everyone says, 'but he was so quiet.' The genes can lie quietly dormant for a long time before manifesting themselves, like heart disease, working away at clogging your arteries, and then one day, they are clogged."

"You said you have communicated with ancestors," Jim said.

"Through one particular clinical trial via one particular volunteer," Harry said.

"Hypnosis and drugs, you said," Jim said.

"That's right," Harry said.

"Couldn't someone tell you something under hypnosis they

believe to be true, and it could be nothing more than their brains creating a story?" Bill asked.

"When I started this research, that was my first thought. We had a very compliant research volunteer. He would go into a hypnotic trance effortlessly. Easier than anyone I have ever seen."

"You don't know me, then," Bill said. "I am highly susceptible. I was hypnotized to lose weight. Lost twenty pounds. Hypnotized to quit smoking. Stopped immediately. I was once hypnotized at a party and told I was a rooster. They said I strutted around and crowed. I don't remember. I'm an easy subject, like your guy."

Harry stirred the fire with his stick again.

"After a few sessions, he dropped out," Harry said. "Found the hypnotic trips too disturbing. Said it got so he couldn't sleep at night. Said he had strong and uncomfortable urges, like someone being possessed by a Wendigo. You know, that ravenous monster of Native American legend?"

"The one that is always hungry and is constantly looking for someone to eat?" Jim said.

"That is the one," Harry said.

"He was a Wendigo?" Bill said.

"No. He used that as comparison to explain how it felt to connect with this prehistoric ancestor. I suspect our belief in monsters may come from deep primal memories of those lost and gone folk. Bottom line, it was too much for him, and he dropped out of the trials."

"Have you followed up?" Bill asked.

"Yes. He was doing better. But I do not know if he will continue to do better. This ghost of an ancestor is buried deep in his brain, but it is there, and it is strong. I think it wanted to connect, this ghost. And it did, and I gave it the tools to do so. Hypnosis. Drugs."

"Rubbish," Bill said. "He's still the same person."

"That is my point," Harry said. "Who knows how strong this thing is in him? This ancestor, in my view, has everything to do with the sociopath, or psychopath, that exists among us. But in varying degrees. Depends on how strongly we inherited those genes."

"Hypnotize me," Bill said.

"What?" Harry said.

"Hypnotize me. Prove what you're saying."

"That would be unethical."

"It would prove you are full of it," Bill said.

"Hardly. If you do not have those ancestors as strong in your genes as my former patient, then you may not connect with them. Probably would not. And that would be for the best."

"Hypnotize me once, just so I can see if I can get in touch with those ancestors that you say existed."

"Still exist, even if it is just your greedy relative at Thanksgiving that takes the best cut of turkey, the largest slice of pie. You could have it in you slightly, or to put it in unscientific terms, muchly."

"Come on, Harry," Bill said. "Prove it."

"I do not feel compelled to prove it," Harry said.

"Because it's unprovable," Bill said. "I mean, hell, Harry. Call it a party trick. I see Alley Oop in my hypnotic journey to the past, I'll tell you. I don't intend to bring him back with me."

"But it, them, ghost or ghosts, want to come back with you," Harry said.

"If it were in me in any truly negative way, we would know by now. Right? I'm thirty-eight years old, a church goer, have kids. I haven't gone off my nut and left a trail of bodies in the wilderness, so I'm unlikely to now. I guess I've had moments of anger and disappointment, but I haven't killed anyone."

Harry contemplated the idea for a long moment.

"Very well. A touch of it, and then out. And remember, you might encounter something you wish you had not. It is on you."

"Agreed," Bill said.

"I do not have any drugs, but you say you hypnotize easily, so that is all we have."

"I have a muscle relaxant in my bag," Jim said. "I got them for my sciatica. Would that help?"

"It just might," Harry said. "Let's have it."

Harry was into it now. Bill took the muscle relaxant with a slug of water from his canteen. It was not like the more powerful drugs Harry was used to administering, but if Bill was as compliant to hypnosis as he claimed, it might be enough.

Bill stayed seated on the rock, as did Harry. After a few minutes, Harry turned and looked at Bill. In the firelight he could see the muscle relaxant was starting to kick in. He could tell by Bill's eyes, the swollen pupils.

"Ok," Harry said. "We'll give it a try."

Jim was no longer lying down. He was sitting on the ground, watching carefully.

"Listen to me, Bill. I want you to relax. Think of nothing right now but the sound of the river. Can you do that?"

"Yes."

"Now you are listening to the river. You are in a boat, and you are rolling gently with the river. You are in no danger whatsoever. You are friends with the river. It is carrying you along down the center of the river with the moonlight on your face. Now close your eyes. Listen intently to the river. There is only the sound of the river. It is carrying you back, back, back. Reach deep inside yourself. Think of the river as flowing back in time. Imagine that. Flowing backwards in time. All the way back. As far as you can remember, and then beyond what you personally remember. Can you do that?"

"Yes."

"Good. Now, in all of us, Bill, there are ancestors, and they remain hidden behind the curtain of time, but you are going to remove that curtain. Imagine a curtain hanging down in front of you. Can you see the curtain? Behind that curtain are all your ancestors. Remove the curtain slowly. Gently push it aside."

Bill reached up, grasped an invisible veil, and moved it aside.

"What do you see?"

"The river."

"Yes. Anything else?"

"I see people. They are naked. No clothes. It is night and the moon is bright and they have a fire and they are sitting there, talking. I can't understand what they are saying. I can't understand the language."

"You are no longer floating along the river?"

"No. I'm walking alongside it."

"Keep walking farther into the past."

This went on for an hour or so, with Harry making suggestions, and then Bill started to sweat. The sweat on his face popped bright in the moonlight.

"Okay," Harry said. "Now relax, and just let yourself feel what is inside you. Go deep into that part of your brain where you keep little things that bother you. Any insecurity. Do you have those, Bill?"

Bill, eyes still closed, said, "I suppose so."

"Now think of anyone that might have wronged you."

"My wife. She's having an affair with one of my best friends."

"How long have you known this affair was taking place?" Harry asked.

"For some time. Six months."

"Do you feel betrayed?"

"Yes."

"But you haven't said anything to either the betrayer or your wife?"

"No."

"Why?"

"I need them both. My wife. And Jim."

Harry put his fingers to his lips as he turned his attention to Jim. He gently shook his head to keep Jim from speaking.

"Do you feel inadequate when you think of Jim and your wife, Blanche?"

"Yes. I've never felt adequate sexually. I try. I just don't have the drive. She says I don't find her attractive, but I do. But she's not living a Christian life."

"Let yourself think about that inadequacy. Her failure. Your friend's betrayal. Let everything you feel negative about, let it all boil. It is okay to be mad. Get mad. Maybe you are inadequate. Maybe you are a failure in your marriage. Think of Blanche in bed with Jim. Think of what they might be doing to one another."

"Hey," Jim said.

"Bill," said Harry. "You only hear my voice. No one else. Do you understand?"

"Yes."

"What else makes you mad?"

"My friend Harry."

Harry paused. "How is that?"

"He thinks he's so smart, so superior."

"Could it be he is?"

"I don't know, but if you could sell him for what he thinks he's worth, you would be eternally rich."

"Okay," Harry said. "Jim is a better lover, and Harry is smarter and superior to you. How does that make you feel?"

Bill had begun to vibrate slightly, as if he were boiling inside, heating up to explode. He was gripping his fists so tightly a bit of blood ran from between his fingers where his nails stuck into his palms. His eyes remained closed.

"Let yourself feel all those things that disappoint you about yourself, and understand, there are good reasons you feel that way. Bill, you are inferior."

"Yes. I am. And it makes me angry."

"Furious?"

"Furious."

"You are not normally a man prone to anger, are you?"

"I am, but I try not to show it. Sometimes I break things. On a Christian mission trip, I paid a woman to come to my room. I beat her after we had sex. She left and didn't report it. The filthy whore."

Harry paused, surprised. He looked at Jim. Jim shrugged. Harry turned his attention back to Bill.

"What is it that makes you feel this way? "Not your feelings, but the deep source inside your primitive brain. What is it?"

"Guignal."

"What's that?"

"He is him, and he is them," Bill said. "And he is hungry. I am hungry."

Bill's body vibrated slightly.

"Bill, you are now going to come forward in time, slowly, not too fast. Okay?"

"Okay."

"Are you coming?"

"Yes. And Guignal is coming with me."

Harry paused before saying, "I want Guignal to stay there."

"He doesn't want to. He's real mad. He wants to hurt something. He wants to eat."

"Bill. Leave Guignal there, where he lives in the deep recesses of the brain. And you Bill, you come slowly and gently back to us. Slowly, slowly."

"Okay."

"Is Guignal with you?"

"No."

"That's good. You are among friends here, so you want to come back to us."

"Do I?"

"You do."

Bill took a deep breath, but he didn't open his eyes.

"The sound of the river, Bill. You can only hear the river. Come to us Bill. Listen to the river. The river."

Slowly Harry brought Bill's consciousness forward, out of the past.

When Bill was awakened, he was sweaty and weak. "Things I saw," Bill said. "Killing and cannibalism. Guignal is a horror."

"Who is Guignal?"

"He is him and them. Us."

"What does that mean?" Jim said.

"I have to lie down," Bill said. "Oh, Jesus, everything that's wrong starts there. Must lie down. I think he may have come back with me."

"No, you are alone," Harry said.

"We are never alone, Harry. All those ancestors, they are there. Always there. Exhausted. So exhausted."

"You are safe now," Harry said. "Forget all of that."

Harry and Jim helped Bill to roll out his bedroll, left him to sleep by the fire.

"Exactly what happened?" Jim asked. "What is Guignal?"

They had seated themselves on the large flat rock and were looking at the fire. Bill was sound asleep.

"Harry?" Jim said. "Are you trembling?"

"Guignal is the same thing the research patient said he met on his trip back in time. That solidifies it for me. Two people on mental time trips, and they both came back from those trips mentioning Guignal. Guignal may be a singular person, but I suspect that when someone opens the primitive brain and dismisses all else, Guignal becomes a representative, a ghost, of all that branch of humanity that is the worst in us. I thought my former patient could have been making it all up, not on purpose, but due to my suggestions as a hypnotist. But now I've lost my doubts. It explains people who hear voices that tell them to do atrocious things. Explains belief in demons. Ghosts. A lot of things."

"It creeps me out," Jim said.

"Bill wasn't kidding when he said he was susceptible to being hypnotized. I let my ego run rampant. I connected Bill with Guignal. I used his anger, stirred it, provoked it. The thing that makes it easier to connect with Guignal. That was a mistake. I knew better. Bill is angrier than either of us suspected. Going to a prostitute, and then beating her, are two things I would never have suspected about Bill. Jim, are you having an affair with Bill's wife?"

"I'm ashamed of it, but yes. I had no idea Bill knew. I'm ending the affair. I'm going to ask Bill for forgiveness."

"And perhaps I can stop being such a pompous ass," Harry said.

"He'll sleep and be okay, I bet," Jim said. "The other guy, the research fellow. Was he okay later?"

"As far as I know. But I only know so far."

Harry and Jim rolled out their bedrolls near the fire, and soon Jim was asleep. Harry found it impossible to sleep. He got up and wandered away from the fire and to the edge of the woods to pee.

He stepped into the forest and let the limbs of a spruce drop dark shadows around him as he relieved himself. He was about to step out of the woods when he saw that Bill was on his feet. In the firelight and moonlight, he could see that Bill had the axe in his hands. Harry watched as Bill walked over to Jim, who was still sleeping, and swung it. The blade came down with a wet smack and black shadows jumped up in the air and settled down with a plop. Jim's legs twitched and shook, and Bill screamed a satisfied scream, like a war cry. Bill kept swinging the axe. As he did, Harry could see the silver-white shape of something ghostly around him, like an aura.

The axe was rising and going down rapidly now. The sound of the axe blade burying in clothes and flesh and dirt made Harry's backbone throb. He stepped backwards, even deeper into the shadows.

Bill paused to dip his free hand into an open stomach wound and jerk free loose strands of intestines. He paused to chomp at them like fat spaghetti. Bill's face and mouth were coated in blood.

After an especially vicious swing of the axe that sent Jim's head rolling toward the river, Bill turned his head and looked in Harry's direction. It was as if he could see through limbs and shadow and know Harry was there. Harry could sense this as firmly as if Bill had called out his name.

"I see you in there," Bill said, and the voice sounded as if it were coming through a pipe that went all the way back through time and into the source of Bill's murderous rage. The voice of Guignal, and it sounded like thousands of voices in angry harmony.

Harry ran into the woods, limbs hitting him in the face, thorns poking through his clothes. He tripped over a root, went down, scrambled to his feet, and kept running.

Glancing back, he saw that Bill was pursuing him, waving the axe like a semaphore flag, his bounding shape outlined by that glowing silver-white aura.

Harry broke out of the trees and onto an animal trail that led to where they had parked the car. The trail was too narrow and the woods too close for the car to reach their campsite, but it was not that far away. If he could just make it to the car.

Behind him, Bill, spinning about as he ran and making a noise that was somewhere between a chuckle and a death rattle, was still coming.

Harry was almost to the end of the trail. He patted his pants pockets for the keys. Yes. He could feel them. Good. He wouldn't even have to take it out of his pocket. Just being near the car door would cause it to unlock.

When he was at trail's end, the last of it sloped down. He could see the car below. As he started down, he slipped on damp leaves and took a ride on his butt, down, down, down. He heard a strange noise as he slipped. Working himself to his feet, he looked back and saw at the top of the leafy slope, Bill. He was trying to pull the axe head out of a tree.

That had been the sound. A swinging axe, and if not for him slipping, it would have implanted itself in his head instead of a tree.

Harry touched the car door. It unlocked with a click. He hurried inside, pressed the button on the dash, and the car came alive. He threw it in gear, backed out onto the driving trail, put the car in Drive.

Bill leapt onto the hood. He had the axe cocked, and his smile was so wrong, too wide, dripping saliva and showing a lot of teeth. The blue-white silver glow surrounding him stood out in the moonlight, quivered as if Bill were coated in transparent jelly. Bill's eyes were penetrating, and for an instant, Harry could see deep into them. His very essence was falling into those two deep pits. Falling all the way down, and inside of Bill was the sensation of every despicable thing one could imagine, and those beyond imagination. Harry screamed. It was long and loud, and it brought him back to reality. It was as if he had somehow managed to leap out of a pit. He was exhausted.

Harry pushed the gas pedal as if he were stepping on a poisonous bug.

The surprise jolt sent Bill tumbling over the roof of the car and then down the back of it. As the car moved on, he could see Bill was on his feet, running after him, illuminated by the red rear lights and the silver-white aura.

Bill caught up with Harry quickly, unnaturally. Bill slammed the axe into the back of the car. It hung in the skin of the trunk, and Bill was pulled along by it. His feet were practically flapping in the air.

Harry jerked the car left and right, but nothing caused the axe to come loose, or caused Bill to let go. Harry decided to go off path, down another. He knew the path from former fishing trips. It was just wide enough for a car, with lots of low-hanging limbs jutting into the trail.

A sharp turn, and Harry had the car bouncing along the nearly washed-out trail. Limbs slapped the car, took off a windshield wiper, scraped the roof like a can opener.

Glancing back, Harry saw the silver-white glow. Bill was clawing his way across the back of the car. He had let go of the axe, but somehow, he was moving forward, clutching into the very construct of the car. He raised a fist, struck the back window. The rear windshield popped with stars of shattered glass but held.

And then a limb scraped over the top of the car, caught Bill in the teeth, and knocked him off.

Harry saw Bill in the rear-view mirror, in the fire-red glow of the taillights. He was rolling along the ground.

Harry slammed the car into reverse, backed fast, hit Bill. There was a bump and a gushing sound. When Harry had passed over him, he saw Bill trying to rise from the ground. He drove forward, feeling Bill's body thump beneath the tires. Back again. Forward again.

And then it hit him. He was doing what the primitive brain wanted him to do. Survive. He too was in touch with Guignal.

Harry drove on. The narrow trail looped off into a wider one. Harry followed it all the way to the highway. He hadn't gone far when the car became hard to drive. Something had come loose.

The car began to coast and rattle. Harry guided it onto the side of the highway. He opened the door and got out, leaving the motor running, the lights glowing. There were no other lights on the highway. He was alone.

He stood there hoping for someone to come by. Hoping someone might stop. And then he saw a silver-white glow from under the car and Bill crawling out from beneath it. He had been hanging onto something under the car. Bones popped through Bill's flesh. Blood made his clothes soggy. His hair was matted with it. His face stained with it. He stood up awkwardly, came toward Harry dragging one leg, paused, and changed course. He went to the back of the car and pulled out the axe that was still imbedded back there.

Harry bolted toward a pasture next to the road. It was contained within a barbed wire fence. He ripped his pants scurrying over it. When he was in the pasture he started to run, looking back just in time to see Bill's glowing form leap the fence like a track star, land on his good leg like a flamingo, then come quickly toward him. His dragging leg wasn't slowing him down much.

Harry was breathing heavily. His lungs burned. He began to fade. He was no longer able to run. Even walking fast was difficult. Then his body quit on him. He fell forward into the dirt, taking in a mouthful.

With difficulty, Harry rolled on his back. There was Bill, or what was left of him. He was coming apart. The silver-white glow sputtered, like a bad bulb about to go out. He stood over Harry with the axe.

One of Bill's arms fell off. Now he was holding the axe with one hand. And then the bad leg gave out altogether, and Bill went to one knee. His guts poked out of a rent in his stomach. The shirt was gone, and there was a tire track across his lily-white belly.

The glow moved off Bill. It settled on Harry. Bill's body collapsed, and as it did, bones popped, and teeth fell out of his mouth.

Harry took a deep breath. He found strength he didn't know he had. He realized the drugs, the muscle relaxants Jim had given Bill, had not allowed the power of the ghosts in his cells to have full rein.

He came to his feet, bent, and picked up the axe.

What was it Bill had said about Harry thinking he was superior? I am superior, you idiot. Vastly superior. Harry began to chop wildly at Bill's body, cutting off the head the way Bill / Guignal had chopped off Jim's head.

Harry picked up Bill's head and drop-kicked it. It sailed a goodly distance, bounced, and lay still.

Harry looked at his hands. They were bloody and glowed silver-white. The glow ran up his arms. It covered his entire body. He felt so angry. He had never felt this angry. It felt good. He bent, tugged out Bill's intestines, and ate his fill.

Harry started back to the highway, hoping someone might stop.

He was so angry. So full of violence. So hungry again. He needed someone to stop. He was no longer Harry. He was legion.

He was Guignal.

AS BELOW, SO ABOVE

LINDA D. ADDISON

for Michelle Renee Lane

The endlessly repeating dream:
brilliant sunlight caresses
sweet air with each inhale,
blanket of warmth dissolves tension,
I smile at the possibility of new love.

Alone, from here to the horizon rolling
hills:
saguaro stretch arms into blue sky,
arms crowned with red-purple pods,
all fruit pods split open at once,
dark red oozes down to sandy earth.

In a blink, endless red surges into the sky:
chaotic pulsing covers the cactus,
the ground, me with thick liquid,
a blanket of warmth, I lick my fingers,

salty, sweet blood, not fruit juice.

Memories of an unlikely place returns:
I open my mouth, inhale each drop,
tension gone, I smile at the taste
of my fear suckled from old desires,
desires we foolish humans crave.

I look down, a reflection floats in a dark
puddle:
an animal stares back, hungry, sad
red rimmed eyes, it stops lapping,
falling to my knees, reaching to it,
my fear, my animal, my oblivion.

No love will spring from earth:
soaked in the blood of lost hope,
lives shattered each time my heart
twisted love in the direction
of my desire, my awful desire.

The dream ends & begins again, again:
each time a different animal consumes
dreadful beliefs I cannot release,
the hunger, lies like a secret told
again, again, whispered to no one.

Waking aches more and more, oblivion:
feels more intimate with each night,
daylight becomes the dark dimension,
a false land, mimicking actual life,
night terrors uncover my foolish truth.

The endlessly repeating dream:
arms pump blood into blue sky,
each inhale, each blink a memory,
I am the animal staring, emptied
of false belief, I am night terror.

TO FEAR AND TO RAGE

TIMOTHY G. HUGUENIN

Ain't nobody knows where they came from. Some said they sprung from the trees like termites come out of a log when it's set on the fire. Other folks said they done come right up out of the Augustus River at night, shed their scales and fish-slime and whatnot and there they were in the morning when the town woke up.

I live up on the ridge overlooking the little town of Augustus Valley, West Virginia. I was asleep when they showed up, so I can't say as to where they came from. But I seen 'em with my own eyes—good Lord a-mercy, with my *eyes* I seen 'em, and ain't a night I shut my eyes and *don't*, their faces so full of anger like the damned Devil hisself.

I'd driven my pickup down to town to buy some steaks from Pop's Market—my boy's birthday, see, and what better way to celebrate but some nice charcoal-grilled ribeyes? I remember the sky was bluer than the cotton candy from the state fair in Lewisburg, and I remember thinking it was gonna be a good day.

Rolled into town and there they were, all over the street,

roaming back and forth like they was drunk. I didn't know what to think—they all looked the same: long straight black hair, dark as an unlit mineshaft, heads bent down with one palm held up below their downturned faces. They wore long black dresses or robes or something—real spooky—and you could see that their bodies was slim and straight, like tall young boys'. And the way they walked—slow, aimless, not quite a stagger, more of an amble—to and fro all acrost the road, all over the sidewalks, everywhere and going nowhere. At first, I reckoned maybe they was all kids playing some practical joke. I honked and revved the engine, and then one just outside my window looked up at me.

I *say* looked up, though it ain't looking in no sense of the word. But what else can I call it?

I scrambled back from the window, half off my seat. The truck lurched as my foot left the clutch and the engine stalled.

Its mouth was open in a horrible silent scream of hatred, its nostrils flared—but there weren't an eye to be seen on its twisted mug. It faced me like that, the not-looking, horrible hating mouth and nose and blank space where the eyes was missing, and I couldn't look away. God knows I would if I could have, for a sight like that ain't nothing a man wants to ponder. I'd trade my own soul to never have gotten the image of them eyeless wanderers branded onto my mind's eye.

I never did get them steaks from Pop's. Just started my truck back up and reversed outta town, pulled a U on the county road, and sprayed mud all the way back up the hill.

When my boy got home I was inside, rocking on my worn-out chair and looking through the wall, still seeing that eyeless rage where it weren't.

"Dad—what's going on?" My boy's voice was soft and like to breaking. He stood there in the open doorway, his hand still trembling on the rusty knob.

"Come in and shut that door before the flies get in."

He did, and he set down on the couch acrost from me, looked down at the floor. He was breathing real heavy, and I could tell he was trying to hold it back.

"It's all right, son."

Then he cried, and I cried with him.

* * *

A few days later, even more eyeless wanderers roamed the town. Some had even spread out into the woods. I could see 'em from the house, and from time to time I saw a few on my side of the river, where the valley starts to get steep.

The mayor called a meeting. About everyone in town was packed into that tiny courthouse. It was a hot July evening, and though the sun was low, there weren't no AC in that crummy place. It got to smelling something foul right quick.

The mayor banged a gavel. "We're here to discuss the uh, *situation*, with, the eh, *interlopers* we find present in our streets."

Yells from the mob came all at once, so nobody could hear what the other was saying, but I think it was all the same sentiment: anger, fear, desperation.

The mayor again gaveled us all into order and continued. "Now, I think it is important to uh, be cognizant of the fact—er, to *note*, if you will—that while these um, *visitors* may be quite terrifying in appearance to some of you, not yet has one of them harmed or taken any sort of, um, *offensive* action toward anyone . ."

More yells from the mob. More bangs from the gavel. I looked down at my boy. His eyes were fixed dead set on the mayor, though I couldn't say if he was angry or just anxious to hear his next words.

"Now, I'm quite *aware*, of course, that we are all quite

perturbed, and I want you all to know that I myself am, uh, a bit *unsettled,* so I sympathize with your anxiety, and um, I also understand that many of you find yourselves quite, uh, *irascible* in our present, hum, *predicament.* But let us not, er,"—he held up his fingers in air quotes—"*lose our cool,* as it were."

This time the crowd's response was a little quieter, but you could still feel the tension in the air ready to bust, like the time I tuned my grandpap's banjo up too far until the catgut snapped.

I looked around the room. Every here and there someone was looking down at their lap, like maybe they was either crying or hanging their head for a nap. I figured it was likely the first, but later I found I was wrong on either guess.

Right then, though, all I knew was that something was starting to smell awful rotten in that room, and more'n just the sweat and summer stuffiness. I asked my boy if he thought the same.

He nodded, but he didn't take his eyes offa the mayor, who was looking down at his notes, now, like he was trying to figure out what he was supposed to say next but couldn't read his chicken-scratch writing. An awkward quietness settled amongst the people. One or two coughed. A small, despairing whine leaked out from someone acrost the room.

The mayor looked up, all squinty-eyed. "All who, um, decide to er . . leave their babies on the courthouse steps, and—yes, if you would, *eschew* your love of these morsels for a greater *existence . .*"

I ran a finger through my ear. Surely I was confusing whatever he really said with some bizarre, unsettling talk that didn't in no way make sense. Then I rubbed my hands over my eyes—for it looked like the mayor hadn't any eyes left of his own!

He was quiet for a moment. Then he looked down at his palm and slowly wandered off the stage.

"We gotta go," I said to my boy. He nodded and we hustled

toward the door. All around us, others were either getting up to flee with a look of the sickest terror, or they was getting up with no look at all but a mouth of spite and no eyes to speak of.

We shoved our way outside to the truck and hauled ass outta there. My boy and I slept in the same bed that night, held to each other tight like my dear wife and I did when we'd lost our little girl to a bad birth.

* * *

We stayed up in the hills after that, and never went down. You might call us a couple cowards, but then I'd say you never known a fear like that, and you couldn't unless you seen one a-them slow ones, face-to-hellacious-face. And what did we need from town, anyways? We had food. And like I said, it was summer, and my boy didn't need to be at school.

I reckon it weren't more'n four days before we saw sign of their roams spread halfway up the hill. They had stopped coming in the daylight as much. But we could tell where they wore down flat dead paths in the woods that they still came out at night and had made it clear up to where the maples and tulip poplars thinned out and became pine and hemlock.

As we noticed them coming closer and closer, we slept less and less. But we didn't dare step outside—the sight of an eyeless wanderer sends your stomach to feeling like a block of ice, and you feel a scream choking your throat in such a way that you can't release it to breathe. But then you find yourself in this terrible near-insanity until something in you *wants* to see more. Something perverse is born and starts living and breathing inside of you, and it turns your mind inside and out so that somehow you *crave* the fear. And once this starts, it's the beginning of the end.

How do I know all that? I seen it in my boy.

We thought somehow the slowness spread to a man like a cold, by a touch or a sneeze. We thought we were safe, in these hills—but they weren't yet a quarter mile from our house as the crow flies before my poor boy said he thought it was happening to him.

"I don't know, Dad," he told me over beans and cornbread—my boy's favorite, but this night he didn't do nothing but push it around his plate. "I . . I . . this . . I don't . ." He stuttered like this for a minute and then started to cry. I walked over behind him and put a hand on his back. He wiped his eyes with his sleeve and stared into his mushed food.

"I don't wanna stay locked up like this, always hiding," he finally said. "I'm afraid, though. But it feels . . it feels . ."

I rubbed his back. "It's okay, boy. It's okay, son."

He looked up at me, his eyes all swollen and squinty from the crying. "I *want* to be afraid," he said in a thick voice. "There's something comforting in being afraid." He looked back down at his plate. Then he said something, just under his breath, that made my hand stop rubbing and my lungs stop breathing:

"I wonder if we oughta just go back to town. With them. Maybe it ain't so bad."

God no, I prayed. *God, not my only son.*

* * *

We both decided it was best to keep him locked in his room for a while. I'd come in to bring him meals and sit and pray with him, but he didn't pray much hisself. Didn't talk much, either. Each day I brought back more and more untouched food. Each day I heard back less and less word from the Almighty. And each day them slow walkers wandered closer and closer to my property line.

Sometimes at night I'd sit at his bedside, just watching him toss and fluster, his blanket twisted all around him in a sweaty knot. He'd mumble things I didn't understand, some of it like to be in another language—some godawful, unholy tongue—other things in English but still with no lick of sense. He muttered strange things of firstborn babes, of righteousness and defilement, of cleansing, of being clothed in fear and wretchedness. Sounded like that ol' Baptist preacher we used to go listen to when my wife was still dragging us along with her each Sunday, before the cancer ate her away. Except, with the preacher-man, there was always salvation in the light, an escape of the wrath to come. The things my boy was saying, there weren't no salvation to be found lest ye *embrace* the shadow that draws nigh.

The night came when my boy said nothing at all in his sleep. Didn't turn, didn't struggle. He slept there so still I thought maybe he'd died.

Would to God he had.

That morning he got up. His eyes, again, were swollen to narrow slits. He scrambled back from any sunlight shining through the windows. And he didn't say nothing. I could see some times he would try to speak, he'd open his mouth to me—but it was like his throat was stuffed with cotton balls. Ain't nothing but confused and terrified moans come out. I felt a cold lead ball weighing down deep in my stomach when I seen him and heard his groans, and I was forced to turn away my face from his.

* * *

The woods all around the house are full of 'em now. In the day, they rest. But in the night, I hear 'em rustling all around. I keep the door locked, but I don't know for how long I'll go on. Now that it's just me, I don't know what's the point.

I wonder if these creatures will spread to other towns, or if they'll settle for Augustus Valley as their home. So far it looks like they mean to spread their bounds. Slowly, but surely.

At least I done right by my boy—I gotta believe it, even if most hours I ain't sure. But I just thought, *What would I want him to do if the situation was switched on us?* The Golden Rule, as Christ taught us all. I did learn *that* from the ol' Baptist preacher. (I think I seen the preacher-man outside my window last evening, when they all awoke to their ambles. Sometimes, I'll admit, it fascinates me to watch 'em roam.)

I made it quick for my son, and as much as a living man can tell, I don't reckon he felt any pain. I closed my eyes, but I held the twelve-gauge steady, and I didn't miss.

Oh God, but I'm afraid! Of what, now I'm not sure—at first I was afraid of *them*, but it ain't like they have tried nothing on *me*. My boy turned, and who was the killer between us two?

I don't sleep well, though none of 'em have yet tried to break a window or bust in the door. I close my eyes and see my boy's eyelessness—the rage, the furious, defensive fear! Yes, I was right to erase that look from his already half-erased face. He woulda done the same for me, I'm sure.

Maybe the fear I carry ain't a fear of them, but of—of what? It's a fear without object, a bullet shot acrost an empty field. Just the feeling itself: pure, simple. Spotless. Maybe soon that bullet will land; I'll find something or someone I can be properly afraid of. Until then, it's just fear itself that I wrap myself up in, fear that soothes me and keeps me going. You know, you can get to a point where you embrace the fear. Then it ain't so bad; it's like a familiar flannel shirt, something you can trust to be there for you when nothing else makes sense—because right now, don't nothing make sense, except to fear and to rage.

FORT LONELY

MEGHAN ARCURI

"Mommy! Mommy! Look at me!"

I tighten the screw on the doorknob to the new fort. Well, new-ish. Its Frankensteinian qualities (yeah, yeah. . . the monster) are on full display: mismatched shutters, shingles from three different architectural eras, and the slightly too small door. My summer project.

"Mommy!"

Impatience joins the excitement in Robbie's voice.

I drop the screwdriver in the grass and sit on my haunches. "Whatcha got, Bud?"

"I'm a Stuka dive bomber!" He extends his arms and makes a loud *neeowww* sound.

Someone recently got into his grandfather's Smithsonian coffee table book on military aircraft.

"Who flew Stukas?" I am woefully ignorant of history.

"The Germans."

Hoo boy.

"Wouldn't you rather pretend to be a good-guy airplane?"

"The good guys' airplanes didn't sound like this: *neeowww*!"

He zooms around the backyard, hopping over the boxwoods and seagrass that separate the patio's paving stones from the lawn.

Occasionally he swoops by the bouncy seat where his baby sister sits. Jessie kicks her feet, curls her toes, and smiles. My heart melts a little. Robbie can always make her do that.

"Just like Snoopy," I say.

Robbie jolts to a stop, arms dropping to his sides like a lifeless puppet. He looks at me like I killed a puppy. So dramatic.

"Snoopy was the World War *One* Flying Ace, Mommy. Stukas were used in World War *Two*."

Schooled by a five-year-old.

"My apologies, Herr Robbie."

He answers me with another Snoopy sound.

Jessie giggles.

Robbie stops for a second to tickle her feet. She erupts with laughter, every atom of her body vibrating. He takes a quick sip of his juice box, grabs a fistful of cheese crackers, then goes back to battling the Allies. And I'm left to wonder if I've accidentally raised a Nazi-sympathizer.

Before I go too far down the *I'm a bad mommy* rabbit hole, my phone vibrates in my back pocket.

Yuck.

I close my eyes, inhale for five and exhale for five. Repeat.

Am I the only person in the world who is physically repulsed by a ringing phone? My stomach drops, my heart flutters (not the good kind), and occasionally, a wave of heat washes over me.

It vibrates again.

I open my eyes to my husband's name scrolling across the screen. Not his name, per se, but the word *Awesome*. He added his info when I first got the phone and decided to be Mr. Funny Pants. ("More like Mr. Awesome Pants," he'd countered.) I never got around to changing it.

My body calms: he's the only person I ever want to talk to on the phone.

Another vibration.

I tap the green button. "Hey, Louden."

"Took you long enough."

"It only buzzed two times."

"Three."

Jessie whimpers; Robbie buzzes by, taking aim at the Matchbox cars-cum-Allied forces. I really need to have a chat with him.

"Two and a half; I picked up on the third."

"I started going gray, Margot."

"Started?"

"I'll let that slide since it sounds like the beaches of Normandy are being stormed."

"Why does he have to like the bad-guy planes?"

"'Cause they're freaking awesome."

"What is wrong with you?"

"Have you ever seen one?"

"No. . . yes. . . maybe. . . I can't even remember yesterday. How the hell am I supposed to remember seeing a Stuka?"

"Green plane. Yellow tip. Kinda looks like it's smiling."

"You're weird."

"But you know which one I mean, don't you?"

As stupid as it sounds, I do. "Whatever. I just finished putting the fort together."

"Did you put Old Biddy's knob on?"

"My grandmother was not an old biddy."

"Okay. . . Satan's Mistress?"

"She wasn't that bad."

"She was that bad. Sucking on her clove cigarettes, doling out judgements like a Pez dispenser. Saved her wrath for your mom, too, especially about the way you were raised. Not your uncles, though; they were perfect. Good thing she died when Robbie was a baby. Who knows what she would've said about us."

"Louden. . ."

"You sure you wanna put that knob on the fort?"

It was the cool, old amber glass one from the basement door of my grandmother's house.

"Why wouldn't I? It's so pretty. It's got a neat history, too. Gramma's father was a glazier. He found the stone, turned it into the doorknob, and gave it to her when she first moved into her house. Isn't that sweet?"

"I don't know that I'd use the word *sweet* to describe anything about your grandmother."

"Anyway. . . it took a sec, but I figured out how to make it work. I should have my own TV show."

"I'd tune in," Louden says.

One of the shutters slides to the ground, its corner piercing the dirt.

"Or not," I say, explaining about the shutter.

"Easy fix for a miracle worker like you."

"What's up with the compliments? You feel guilty about leaving me for a week to go to London?"

"Can't a husband compliment his wife?"

"I'm rolling my eyes. . ."

"It's not like I want to be here. SEC rules and regs say I need to physically be in all of our offices at least once a year."

"I hate the SEC."

"Me too."

"When does your flight get in?"

"Friday afternoon. I'll be home by dinner."

"Oh, my God. . ."

"Just a few more nights."

"I can't wait."

"Me neither." His office phone rings. "I gotta get that."

"Okay. Love you."

"Love you, too."

As I return my phone to my pocket, I drop the last screw in the grass. Dammit.

I can't stand this.

I don't want to be here.

Welcome to my mantra. Cute, right? Not quite like the ones they tout in self-help books. But it's the one I retreat to when things get tough. Always had it, although it comes more frequently these days. Am I a bad mommy for admitting it got worse once I had kids?

I'm sure I am. Mothers aren't supposed to have thoughts like these.

Ha.

I find the screw and secure the doorknob.

Robbie's by the house, back against the filthy siding, pretending to be a spy? A sniper? As he slides along the side of the house, his shirt cleans the mold that's been building up for the past few years. I was supposed to power wash that today, but finishing the fort became more important. Now I'll need to soak his clothes.

"Hey, Robbie! You want to come play in the new fort? The doorknob finally works."

I jiggle it, test it out. It does what it's supposed to do. Exciting, too, since a home improvement expert I am not. I probably should have bought a new one, but I'd always loved this amber one. When I was a girl, I'd spend a lot of time staring at it, fascinated by its various imperfections: tiny bubbles and flecks of dirt.

"You like that, huh?" Gramma had once said to me.

"It's so pretty."

"Sometimes amber has stuff inside it."

"Like what?"

"Wasps, bees. All sorts of angry little creatures. It's a shame this one doesn't have any of that, though. I like the way amber traps things."

It had fallen off while hospice had been caring for her, and I snagged it after she died, avoiding the notice of my mom and uncles and all their *I-want-this-ing* and *You-take-that-ing*.

I'd been holding onto it until the exact right moment. And the fort was that moment.

Sure, it had never worked well, and the old screws had mostly been stripped, but I was feeling crafty and decided to give it a try.

So far so good.

Robbie runs to the edge of the patio and stops short, about five feet from me. Arms and face drop again, but with less drama than last time.

"What is it?" I say.

He tilts his head like a dog hearing a faraway sound.

"Is it the doorknob? I know it's kind of. . ." I'm about to say, *girlie*, but I stop myself. With my luck, he'd repeat that shit on the playground and I'd have myself a kindergartener who'd been canceled and would never get into college or find a job and would live in my basement for the rest of his life, wearing stained, V-neck undershirts, bellowing up to me about "gimme another Hot Pocket, Ma" (even though he's never called me *Ma* and I haven't bought Hot Pockets since college).

So I say, ". . . sparkly. It's from my gramma's house. Silly. I know. We can change it, if you want."

He still stares at the fort, lips now parted, and without blinking takes a small step back.

"Robbie?"

The baby starts crying, but Robbie is transfixed, unmoving.

The cries turn to screams. The baby has managed to get her

legs twisted in the safety belt on the seat. She struggles, face scrunched up and turning purple from the screaming. Tears and snot flow freely.

In the split second it takes me to run to Jessie, a billion thoughts explode in my mind, but the dulcet tones of *I suck* are louder than the rest. This is one of those double-edged sword situations no one mentions as they're gushing about how wonderful it is to have children, especially more than one. *Oh, you're pregnant again? Good. I'm so glad. Now Robbie won't be lonely. You'll be able to apply what you've learned with Robbie. You'll be so much happier.*

The way I see it, I'm a bad mother no matter what: in the end, I've either ignored one kid's wacky behavior or the other's imminent physical danger.

But instinct took me to Jessie and now I'm holding her and bouncing her and *everything's all right-ing* her, and she's stopped crying.

Robbie hasn't moved.

I run back to him and tousle his hair. "What's up, Bud?"

Nothing.

I kneel next to him. He smells like sweat and mold and cheese crackers. His hands tremble. I squeeze one. Jessie reaches for him and squeals.

"Bud?"

"Is someone in there?"

He's staring right at the fort, but I still say, "In where?"

He points to the fort. "There."

A billion more thoughts: Has he lost it? Maybe he's joking. His hands are shaking—not a joke. Do I even look inside? There's no one in there. Is there? Look. Check. Reassure.

I follow my own advice.

"No one's there, sweets. Look. . ."

I tap on the window, knock on the door.

"Knock, knock? Who's there? Mommy. Mommy who? The coolest mommy in the world!"

I open the door (knob works perfectly, thank you very much). I stick my head in.

"See?"

I close the door and walk back to him.

Robbie laughs and squeezes my leg. "You're funny, Mommy!" Then another *neeowww*, and we're back at Normandy.

Before I have a second to process Robbie's *Changeling* moment, my phone vibrates again.

The word *Dad* pops up on the screen.

Another eyeroll.

He probably needs help with his laptop. My father loves the gadgets but has little patience for learning how to use them properly.

But I can't deal with him right now. I mean, what the hell just happened?

I hit *decline*.

* * *

"Do you think he's like the kid that sees dead people in that movie? I forget what it's called... *The Five Senses*, or whatever?"

I told Louden about Robbie's episode with the fort that afternoon.

"First of all, it's called *The Sixth Sense*..." I say.

"You don't have to get all snotty about it."

"Honestly, who would watch a movie called *The Five Senses*?"

"A health teacher..."

"Second of all, smartass, can we be serious about this? You weren't there. It was totally freaky."

"I believe you. But I also know how active that kid's imagination is. He was probably caught up in his war games and got lost."

"Maybe. But it was really odd. What if there's something wrong with him? What if he's seen too much war stuff?"

What if I messed him up?

I can't stand this.

I don't want to be here.

"Margot?" Louden says. "Where'd you go?"

"What do you mean? I'm right here."

"It got real quiet for a minute."

"A literal minute?"

"Actually, yes."

Weird.

"I'm worried about Robbie," I say.

"I'm worried about you."

"I'm fine."

"Fine enough to not help your dad with his laptop?"

"He called you? You're a million miles away."

"He said he tried to reach you four times."

"I didn't realize it was that many times. I was distracted. I'm sorry."

"It's not a problem. I was able to help. But I won't be available for the next few days, between client meetings and dinners with the London crew—"

"You'll be drunk off your ass and sleeping off hangovers."

"Har har. But yes," Louden says. "I'll call you in a couple days."

"Please be careful."

"You too."

* * *

A few days later, we finish our snacks and Robbie—surprise of surprises—wants to set up World War II battles in his bedroom.

"Why don't we go out and play in Fort Lonely?"

Like the new name? That's what I started calling it the second day Robbie wouldn't set foot in it. I worked my butt off on that thing, but he hasn't gone near it since I put on the finishing touches.

He slurps the last bits of his juice box, shakes his head, mumbles something I can't decipher—but the tone roughly translates into *Hell, no*—and runs up to his room.

"Maybe you and I should go play in it," I say to Jessie, who sits in her highchair.

She spits up a little.

As I wipe her face, a *thud* comes from the back yard. I walk outside toward Fort Lonely, half expecting to see another shutter on the ground. But it's not a shutter.

A bird lies in front of the door, wings askew, eyes lifeless. Gross. I grab one of Robbie's toy shovels and flick the body over the fence, proud of myself for not whimpering.

Hoping for no more birds, I turn the doorknob and stick my head in the fort: clean, quiet, and empty. I shut the door, my fingers trailing over the smooth surface of the amber. It doesn't seem as bright as it had before. Are there more flecks of dirt?

I go back inside, grab Jessie, and head up to Robbie's room. He's already pulled out all the blocks and vehicles.

"You build the towers; I'll set up the trucks and tanks."

"Sir, yes sir!" I say, with a salute. He's too busy with the Panzers, but I laugh at my joke. Someone has to.

I set Jessie down on the floor and hand her some blocks. She puts one in her mouth and within seconds, starts drooling. I build about three towers before she starts with the thousand-yard stare.

"I'm going to put Jessie down for a nap, Bud. I'll be right back."

"Okay," he says before knocking over all three towers with his tank.

Punk.

Jessie's room is already dark since I forgot to raise her shades this morning. I trip over the mound of clean onesies and jammies I forgot to fold from yesterday's laundry. Or the day before's. Does it really matter at this point?

I can't stand this.

I don't want to be here.

I just want to die.

Huh... that's new.

Jessie sneezes, a string of snot connecting her nose to my shoulder. Her big eyes flash surprise as they meet mine. She kicks her feet and giggles.

I can't help but giggle back.

I press her nose into my shoulder to wipe that string of snot away. The shirt's already ruined anyway, isn't it?

I kiss her forehead, the scent of sweet baby sweat filling my nose. Then I change her diaper (not so sweet) and put her in the crib. Fortunately, she's not too fussy and I'm able to exit the room without having to wait for her to sleep so I can crawl out of there on my belly like some French soldier in World War I.

I close her door and walk back to Robbie's too-quiet room.

He stands, back to the door, staring out his window, facing the back yard.

"I see you didn't rebuild my towers," I say.

He says nothing.

I walk next to him and put my head next to his. "Whatcha looking at? Is the fox out there?"

We'd been seeing a family of foxes roaming the neighborhood all summer.

He doesn't answer me.

"Bud?" I kneel next to him. He seems to be staring down at the fort.

"Do you see it?" he says.

"See what?"

He points at the window, down at the fort. "That."

"The fort? Yes, I see it. Are you as surprised as I am that it's still standing?"

At least he's not talking about the dead bird.

"Robbie?" I nudge his shoulder.

He doesn't move. Doesn't blink.

His mouth hangs open. His skin is pale. He still points. "Do you see it?"

"See what, Robbie?"

"The shadow."

"What shadow?"

"There's a shadow moving in the window over there." The fort is in direct sunlight at this time of day. "It's moving in the window. And it's scaring me."

His arm flops to his side. His head tilts.

But the windows are empty. They sparkle in the sunlight... although the doorknob looks even grungier than before.

The fort is still. The air is still. Robbie is still.

I turn his body toward me, his head the last part to move.

A tear rolls down his cheek.

"Buddy..." I pull him into a hug. "There's nothing there."

"Yes, Mommy. Yes."

I hold his face in my hands, wipe his tear away. "Do you want me to go out and check?"

"No, Mommy."

"I don't mind looking."

As I stand, his little fingers dig into my arms. "No! Don't go. It will hurt you."

"What will hurt me?"

"The shadow."

"A shadow can't hurt—"

A piercing cry from Jessie's room.

Shit.

Robbie blinks, uses the back of one hand to wipe an eye, uses the back of the other to wipe his mouth.

"I thought Jessie was sleeping," he says, the tone of his voice back to its cheerful self, the color back in his face.

"Are you okay, Buddy?"

"Yes," he says as he kneels by his tanks. "Can you please build another tower?"

What. The. Hell.

I don't want to build another tower. I don't want to deal with the screaming baby. I want to draw my curtains and curl up under my covers.

"Mommy?"

The baby screams again.

You'll be so much happier with two kids.

Right. . . number one is having a break with reality and number two is trying to break glass with her screams. Couldn't be happier.

"Another tower, Mommy. Please?"

I sit next to him and grab some blocks. I need to be close to him right now. And even though the *crying it out* method isn't always popular or easy, that's what I do with Jessie. I've done it before, and it's worked.

Eventually she stops crying.

I'm in the middle of building another tower when my phone vibrates.

The screen reads: *Awesome.*

I hesitate. Then I hit *decline.*

* * *

Jessie's five thirty a.m. screams wake me the next day. Louden usually deals with the super-early / super-late baby events, but he's three thousand miles away, sipping tea with the London gents, so this one's on me. Thank God he'll be home tonight.

I stumble down the hall in a sleepy stupor and scoop her up from her crib. But she doesn't stop crying.

The wind whistles outside. I lift one of her shades. The branches of the maple tree creak, the white-green undersides of the leaves show themselves—a sharp contrast to the dark green needles on the shuddering pines.

There's also a *smack-smack-smacking*. An erratic, annoying sound that pairs nicely with the screams.

The door to Fort Lonely swings on its hinges, slapping the frame at will.

Robbie hasn't even played in it, and the stupid thing is already falling apart. What was the point?

"Mommy?"

Jessie's head whips toward her door. Her screams stop.

Robbie's rubbing his eyes, his hair pointing in all directions, his jammies twisted around his little body.

"Why is it so loud?" he says.

"There's a storm outside. It woke Jessie up." I guide him back to his room. "I'm sorry it woke you, too. Why don't you try going back to sleep?"

"Okay, Mommy." He climbs back into his bed and pulls the covers up to his chin.

"I'll come get you in a little bit." I smooth out his spiky hair.

As we walk out of his room, Jessie looks at me with big, bright eyes. This child is not going back to sleep, and if I try putting her down again, she's going to resume her screams.

I didn't even get to throw on a bathrobe or brush my teeth.

I go back to my room and put her in the center of my bed, banking on the fact that I'll be able to grab my robe and at least get some mouthwash before she can shuffle to the side of the bed and plummet to what I'm sure would be some form of paralysis.

I do it with inches to spare.

Small victories.

We head down to the kitchen but not before I stub my toe on the damn baby gate at the base of the stairs. I put Jessie on the floor and give her some Tupperware lids to entertain her.

The wind still howls. The *smack-smack-smacking* persists.

The sink is full of cups. So many cups. Cups that didn't fit into the dishwasher. The dishwasher I forgot to run. The coffee pot is in there.

This day is not happening without coffee.

I fish it out of the dishwasher, stack the sink cups to make room, and scrub the pot. I manage to make a full pot of coffee before Robbie appears in the kitchen doorway.

"I couldn't sleep." He walks to the back door and stares out the window. "It's too loud."

"I'm sorry, Bud." I kiss the top of his head. He seems to be staring out the sliding glass door at Fort Lonely. "Have you seen any more shadows in the window out there?"

"What shadows, Mommy?" Robbie says, his voice sincere.

He's a funny kid, and smart, too, but still a little young yet to have mastered the art of messing with me. His face doesn't betray his voice, either—he's not joking.

"Remember yesterday? In your room. You said you saw something."

"What?"

"A shadow in the window of Fort Lonely."

He looks at the fort and pauses for a second.

"You're silly, Mommy." He zooms over to the pantry. "I'm hungry."

Before I can probe deeper, he's whipped out a box of Happy-O's (I'm too cheap to buy the name brand) and proceeds to drop it, a wave of O's cascading over the entire kitchen floor, a chorus of tapping cereal bits filling my ears.

"Robbie!"

He flinches, probably at the crisp pitch of my voice. I'm not much of a yeller, but when I do yell, it's a doozy.

"I'm sorry, Mommy." His face turns red, tears form in his eyes.

Why did I do that?

I can't stand this. I can't stand this. I can't stand this.

I don't want to be here.

I just want to DIE.

"Why don't you go watch some TV?"

"I can help you, Mommy." He steps toward me, his bare feet grinding dozens of O's into a fine powder.

"Go watch TV." My jaw is tight when I say this.

He bolts from the kitchen, leaving a trail of O's behind him, and although I'm being scary and should comfort him, all I can think is: *Great. More to clean.*

I bring Jessie into the living room and put her in the pack-and-play. Robbie's still wiping his tears.

The wind whips; the door smacks. And I can't fucking stand it anymore.

When I run outside—barefoot and braless—rain pelts my face, wind whips my hair in front of my eyes. I wipe the strands away and storm toward the fort.

Some of its siding has blown off, leaving a hole in the wall. The door bangs and clashes, part of the frame beginning to splinter. And my grandmother's doorknob—now cracked in two—lies on the ground.

I grunt and slam the door closed. It bounces back open and clips my knee.

The expletive that leaves my lips is a louder and angrier sound than I thought I was capable of.

Robbie stares at me from the window of the sliding glass door.

Goddammit.

I grab a lawn chair and prop it against the door. As I run back to the house, the cold rain soaks every inch of my body. When I yank on the backdoor, it doesn't budge. How the hell did it lock?

My soggy hand slides and squeaks against the wet pane as I bang on the window.

"Robbie!" *Bang, bang, bang.* "Open the door!"

But he does not move. He does not look at me. Doesn't seem to hear me. His head tilts, the color once again gone from his face.

Then he screams louder than I've ever heard him scream. Louder than the wind, louder than the rain, louder than my banging on the backdoor window.

"Mommy!" He points to a spot behind me.

A dark cloud billows from the doorknob, swift and gray, amorphous and angry. It grows in breadth and depth, becoming taller than me, taller than the fort. My brain screams at my feet to run, but they are not listening, rooted to the ground in fear. The interior of the cloud flashes, the tempo sporadic and unpredictable, like a thunder cloud in a distant storm. A contained tempest inside a soft surface.

A tendril of mist encircles my feet, swirling and rippling, climbing up my legs. It is cold, but in that so-cold-it's-hot kind of way, and when it flashes again, the burning cold intensifies, searing my skin, paralyzing my body. The scent of flesh and anger and cloves surrounds me.

As the circling gray mass reaches my torso, my neck, a second tendril emerges from the doorknob, slipping under the door, into the house.

It heads toward Robbie.

I try to call his name, tell him to run, but no sound comes out.

I'm having trouble breathing.

I can't stand this.

I don't want to be here.

I just want to die.

EVEN IF OUR WOUNDS NEVER CLOSE

ERIC LAROCCA

It's late in the month of September when my cousin Ridley comes to live with us.

I'm never told the exact reason as to why they've arrived puffy-eyed from crying and with their suitcases stuffed with their belongings. It seems so unusual to me for a thirteen-year-old to require more than one suitcase. After all, what could they possibly need that my parents couldn't provide for them? Of course, I'm also more than curious as to why they've appeared so suddenly and so secretively; however, such details and explanations are kept under lock and key by my parents. I know for certain that they wouldn't tell me even if I had the nerve to ask them.

It's not that I dislike my cousin or consider them an unbearable nuisance. In fact, as I watch them unpack their belongings in the guest bedroom, I come to the realization that I know so little about them. More to the point, their very existence confuses me. I find it unusual that my mother never refers to them with specific pronouns. It's always "they" this and "them" that. I don't mind the uncertainty, but it's even more perplexing when my father definitively refers to them as a girl.

Part of me wonders if they truly are.

To me, Ridley is completely genderless, existing somewhere in the ether of what we define as masculine and feminine.

Certainly, there are ways in which Ridley resembles a young girl. The demure way in which they ask for the plate of butter at the dinner table. The delicate way they refer to me when we're speaking. However, there are just as many opportunities to label them as a boy with the hardened, precise way they seem to talk or the confident manner in which they carry themself when addressing adults. Ridley seems to have no difficulty speaking to adults and it makes me so envious. That is until they are forced to interact with my father.

I notice how Ridley seems to curl inward whenever my father is near—the same way a small crustacean tucks its legs inside whenever it's poked and prodded by a prying visitor. Yes, in many ways my dear cousin resembles a small sea creature with a carapace—an outer shell protecting the precious contents within, the fragile guts and innards my father seemed so adamant to expose to the world.

I would listen at the stairwell to the sounds of my parents arguing about Ridley late at night.

"Give me one reason why she can't take the bus like a normal girl," my father would say.

"I already told you," my mother would say. "They don't feel comfortable riding the bus. The other kids are merciless to them."

My father would sulk, clearly exasperated. "Them. *Them.* It's clearly a young girl, Meredith. You're coddling the little bitch."

Perhaps that's true. Perhaps things might have gone differently if my mother had obeyed my father more assiduously in all matters related to Ridley. But how was she to know the horrible things he would do when given the opportunity?

I certainly never expected it.

I never expected to be awakened in the middle of the night by Ridley standing in the center of my bedroom, a blanket draped around their waist, and their eyes swollen from crying.

"What's wrong?" I ask my cousin.

I lean across the nightstand and switch on the lamp. Ridley's standing there without movement, shivering slightly. They keep their eyes lowered, as if distrustful of making eye contact with me.

"A bad dream?" I ask.

Ridley shakes their head. They tremble a little and speak slowly, obviously cautious to part with each uttered word. "Your dad—came into my room tonight. He said he needed to do a thorough examination."

I straighten from my bed, astonished by Ridley's statement. It seems as though it pains them to continue—as if the very words are an acid corroding them from the inside out.

"He—slipped his hand between my legs and felt there," Ridley explains, nearly choking on the vileness of the confession.

I don't quite know what to say. Anything I have to offer seems hollow or inconsequential. Of course, part of me suspected that my father was a monster from the abusive way he treated my mother and our family dog, but I hardly ever expected this kind of loathsome behavior from him.

"Do you want to stay with me tonight?" I ask Ridley.

Their eyes meet mine and, for a moment, they seem to lower their guard. They nod and climb into bed with me.

I'm startled a little when I notice how some of the moonlight passes through Ridley as if they were suddenly transparent like a bereft specter. I shake my head, vision blurring for a second, but it doesn't change anything. Ridley still resembles a hideous thing from a Victorian ghost story—a lovesick wraith doomed to wander the world aimlessly.

How could this have happened? I wonder to myself. *Is this what my father had done to Ridley?*

Although I'm two years younger than Ridley, part of me feels a responsibility to protect them at all costs. They seem quite frail, as if they might crumble to dust if I went so far as to touch them and their ghostly flesh.

To me, Ridley was a rare species—something truly wondrous and on the verge of extinction because such delicate things are incapable of surviving in the cruel world. But to my father, Ridley is nothing more than a hollow vessel to be desecrated and then discarded when their use runs out.

I think about telling my mother what had happened to Ridley last night as she makes breakfast, but my father storms into the kitchen soon after with his briefcase. I notice how Ridley now shudders whenever in his presence. Even more curious, their skin seems to churn in wisps, as if their flesh were a moving current that couldn't be controlled. Ridley seems to noticeably shrink, willing themselves to become smaller and smaller until they're nothing more than a stain on the dining room chair.

I watch as my father is about to peck my mother on her cheek with a kiss when his briefcase snaps open, and papers spill out everywhere. He cries out and kneels to swipe the papers from the floor. I offer to help him, but he waves me off.

Just as he does, he slices his finger open along the edge of one of the pages, and his face sours. He plugs the bleeding finger into his mouth and sucks gently. Popping his wounded finger from his mouth, he orders my mother to call a private car for him because he prefers not to drive.

"We'd better get a Band-Aid for that, dear," my mother tells him. "It doesn't look like it's stopping."

"I don't have time for this nonsense today," my father says, running his finger under the kitchen sink faucet.

He shrieks and lurches away as the water becomes scalding hot.

It's then I notice how the bleeding won't stop. I think my father recognizes this too and it frightens him. Finally, he swipes a Band-Aid from the medicine cabinet and snatches his briefcase from the dining room table.

"I'll be home late, Meredith," he says, already on his way toward the front door. "Wait for me to eat."

My mother agrees, doing her best to placate him as she ferries him out the door and toward the private black luxury car idling near the front steps of our home.

When she returns, she eyes both Ridley and me seated at the kitchen table. She seems to quietly apologize for my father's belligerence—her shoulders dropping, a defeated look etched onto her face.

It's then I wonder if I should tell her. After all, I don't expect another opportunity to let her know what happened. I had asked Ridley if they wanted to share what my father had done to them, but they said they couldn't bring themselves to say the words. Especially to my mother.

"Mom," I say. "There's something I need to tell you."

"Finish your pancakes, dear," she tells me. "You'll be late for school."

"Ridley came into my bedroom late last night," I say, eyeing my cousin in my peripheral vision, as if expecting them to chime in any moment. "They said that Dad did something horrible to them."

My mother tilts her head at me, as if struggling to understand.

"Something horrible?" she says.

"Ridley says that Dad—touched them," I tell my mother. "They were too frightened to sleep alone so they slept in my room."

My mother regards Ridley for a moment, eyeing them up and down with such intensity, such scrutiny—as if Ridley had just uttered something horrible to her, as if Ridley had hurled an unforgivable insult at her.

My mother turns away from us, scraping bits of food from a plate over the kitchen sink.

"Go get your backpacks," she tells us. "We'll be late."

For a moment, I wonder if she's misheard me. She couldn't possibly ignore my confession, could she?

"But Mom," I say.

"Go out to the car and wait for me," she says, tossing the plate in the sink so forcefully that it shatters. "Now."

I glance at Ridley, hopeful that they might say something. They don't.

Instead, we excuse ourselves from the kitchen table and meander toward the garage. There's a part of me that isn't surprised my mother chose to ignore what I had told her. In her eyes, my father was a specimen of perfection—a paragon never to be questioned. For the first time in my life, I feel unsafe—as if I truly do not know those who have raised me. To me, my mother and father suddenly seem as unfamiliar as primitive species—creatures who went extinct long ago and yet had somehow survived in secrecy all this time.

Once my father has returned home and we're sitting at the dinner table, of course, I wonder whether Ridley will say anything. We sit in silence while we eat, my mother occasionally asking him how his meetings went and my father offering lukewarm answers as he shovels more food into his mouth.

Much to my frustration, they don't seem to notice how

Ridley's skin is becoming dimmer and dimmer—light reflecting from deep inside them and rendering their skin as translucent as a deep-sea creature's. These are things only I seem to be able to see for some inexplicable reason.

Everything seems relatively normal until my father slides a slice of butter across a piece of bread and absent-mindedly stabs his hand. He cries out, the knife clattering against his plate as it slips from his clutches. My mother immediately leaps out of her seat and fetches a damp washcloth to hold against his hand. He winces as she presses it there.

"It looks pretty deep," she says, observing the puckered lines of the wound as it runs from one side of my father's open palm to the other. "We might need to go to the ER."

"Nonsense," my father says. "I'm fine."

It's then that my mother notices the small paper cut my father had made earlier today, the Band-Aid torn off and the small wound exposed. We both notice how the area has not closed and is instead still leaking tiny beads of blood.

"Your paper cut," she says. "Is it still bleeding?"

My father shakes his head, obviously frustrated. "The damn thing has been dripping like that all day."

"Let's dress it again," my mother says. "We'll bandage your hand, too."

As my mother ushers my father out of the room and upstairs to their bedroom, I eye Ridley and notice how they seem to be without expression—a dim, vacant stare making its home across their face. It somehow looks as if they had expected all of this. It somehow looks as though they know exactly how matters are going to end.

Perhaps they do.

But I certainly never expected them to arrive at my bedroom door at three in the morning that same night, blood leaking from between their legs and dripping down their thighs like buckwheat honey.

"What happened?" I ask them.

They pour into my room as ghostly transparent as moonlight. They close the door, lock it, and then scramble toward my bed. I notice how they leave a trail of blood dotting the carpet wherever they walk.

"It was both your mother and father this time," Ridley tells me, sniveling. "They came into my room and laid down in the bed with me. They—took turns."

I shake my head in disbelief. "My mother would never."

"Your father made her watch," Ridley tells me. "She said she liked it."

It's then that I notice there's blood dripping from Ridley's swollen lower lip.

"What's that from?" I ask them, pointing to their bloody mouth.

"I bit your mother," Ridley tells me. "Your father hit me. Can I please sleep with you again tonight?"

Of course, I could never turn Ridley down. But how was I to believe them? Certainly, it was their word against my parents'. But did I even truly know my parents? Perhaps they were the repulsive monsters Ridley had described to me time and time again. It sickens me to think that I hardly know them. Perhaps that's how they've wanted it. Perhaps they've never wanted me to truly know them.

I wonder if that's the case with all parents and their children. I wonder if children are ever supposed to really and truly know the people who raised them, who cared for them.

I also couldn't deny the grim realization that something horrible was happening to Ridley's body because of what they had been enduring night after night. They were transforming into something otherworldly, something ghostlike. I couldn't possibly deny this dreadful fact.

I glare at both my mother and father across the breakfast table as we eat the following morning. I notice how my mother has her right hand bandaged, blood dying the edges of the cloth dark brown.

"Did you hurt yourself?" I ask.

She trembles slightly and slides her bandaged hand beneath the table until it's out of my view. "Just a little accident when I was gardening this morning. Nothing to worry about, dear."

It's then that I notice my father's bandaged hand and how the wounds continue to weep. He can't seem to reach across the table without specks of blood pattering along the tablecloth like oil dripping from a car's engine. He throws his hands in the air, exasperated.

"Meredith, I may need to call out of work today," he says to her. "These bandages won't stop the bleeding."

My mother rolls her eyes at him. "Your body will heal quicker if you keep your stress low."

"I'm bleeding all over the damn table," he shouts, wringing flecks of his blood in her direction as he gestures. "Look at this."

"Do you want me to take you to the hospital?" my mother asks, fussing with her bandages and dripping some of her blood along the table when she moves.

"I don't need to go to the ER," he says. "I need these cuts to heal."

"They will. Give it time," she tells him. But there's something in her voice that trembles slightly and seems to wonder if they ever truly will.

Once again, whenever I gaze at Ridley—they are without movement, without comment, like a ghost in a crowded room. It surprises me, but it looks as though they had somehow been expecting all of this, as if my parents were merely pieces on a small blood-spattered chessboard.

Perhaps that's all we were to Ridley.

It's something I consider as I arrive home from school later that afternoon. For some mysterious reason, my father is already home and waiting for us. It feels so exceptionally unusual to see him in the daytime, as he typically doesn't return from work until late at night. But somehow, he's standing there in the kitchen, greeting my mother, Ridley, and me as we pass through the door.

Even more unusual—he's not alone.

Standing beside him are three older gentlemen from our neighborhood. I forget their names, but I know for certain I have seen them at a few of the summertime parties. The three gentlemen seem to immediately eye Ridley with unreserved intent, as if they were predators who had finally cornered their helpless prey.

"Why don't you go play in the living room, son?" my father says to me.

I'm about to leave, but I'm far too stubborn to be so obedient, especially when Ridley's safety is at hand.

"Who are these people?" I ask.

"Some friends," my father says. "We're going to go upstairs with Ridley. We won't be long."

I glance at Ridley, and they appear to be frozen in their tracks. Even if they had the will to move, they couldn't. Instead, they merely stand there—mouth hanging open in disbelief—and gawk at my father and the three leering older gentlemen.

Before I can oppose, my father snatches Ridley by the arm and drags them up the stairs. The three gentlemen follow close behind with my mother joining them as well.

I stand at the bottom of the stairwell for a moment, listening. It's then I begin to hear the sounds of Ridley pleading with them, begging for them to stop. The pleas soon turn to screams. I cover my ears at the horrible sounds of poor Ridley howling at the top of their lungs. Their screams slowly subside and it's not long after that I begin to hear the creaking of the bed frame as it's slammed against the wall again and again.

Finally, after an hour or so, I watch as my mother and father lead the three gentlemen down the stairs and toward the front door. Several of them are buttoning their dress shirts and zipping their pants as they wipe the sweat from their brows. As soon as they skirt outside and down the front path where they lead their guests, I move up the stairwell and drift into the guest room.

There, I find Ridley sprawled out on the bed. They're lying face-down on their stomach, their jeans around their ankles and fresh excrement and blood sliming the back of their legs. I tremble as I approach them, fearful they might already be dead. They stir slightly, moaning as I draw closer.

"You—said nothing," Ridley whispers to me, the agony firming in their throat. "You—let it happen."

Perhaps they're right, I think to myself. *I did nothing. I let it happen. I let my father and his friends have their way with my poor cousin and I did absolutely nothing to stop them.*

"I didn't know what to do," I tell Ridley, the words clogging in the pit of my esophagus. "If I had known what they were planning to do, I would've—"

But I suddenly stop myself. The horrible truth is I wouldn't have known what to do. What could I have done? They were my parents. They never hurt me. They were supposed to protect us.

I clean Ridley and pull their pants up around their waist so that they're covered. They shiver slightly whenever I touch them. It feels curious to press my skin against theirs as it continues to become more and more transparent like a phantom's.

What will they become at the end of this? I wonder to myself. *Will they disappear completely? Will they be worn down to a mere stain?*

"Are you the reason why my parents' wounds won't heal?" I ask them.

Ridley glares at me—as if suddenly distrustful of me, as if I should somehow already know the answer.

"They don't deserve to ever heal," Ridley says to me. "You, too."

I look at them with surprise. I think I've perhaps misheard them for a moment.

"Me?" I say.

"You're going to loathe me in time," Ridley tells me.

I shake my head in disbelief. "That could never happen. You know how much I care about you."

But Ridley turns over on their side, facing away from me and continuing to dissolve like a neglected apparition. "Not enough to help me."

I think to respond, but there's nothing else I can say. I climb off the bed and meander from the guest room into the bathroom.

I stare at myself in the mirror for what feels like hours even though it's probably only a few seconds. It's then I notice a pair of tweezers abandoned on the bathroom counter. I snatch them and hold them in my hands for a moment.

Then, before another moment of hesitation, I stab my palm. A little bubble of blood forms there in the crater of my open hand and begins to drip as I hold my hand over the rim of the sink. I regard the small wound I've opened, and I notice how the edges seem to widen, as if a pair of invisible pliers were stretching the skin farther and farther apart to reveal more sinew and muscle, to expose me completely until I'm completely threadbare.

It's then I make the horrible realization that these wounds will never heal. None of us will ever heal from Ridley after what we had done to them.

Perhaps that's for the best. Perhaps they are well suited to be permanent reminders of our atrociousness, our wickedness. Even mine.

I think for a moment how strange it was for Ridley to confess that I would loathe them in time, as if I would detest them when I finally understood how my body would never completely heal.

It couldn't be further from the truth.

Because the actual truth is—even if our wounds never close, even if dark crimson rivulets spout from me like whitewater rapids and I'm swept away by an unforgiving current so merciless and so cruel—I will always remember Ridley and I will always love them even if I could never save them. Ridley would go on to haunt me and I would be forever grateful for such a reminder because I know in my heart that I have truly earned that anguish.

THE CAMPSITE

ELIZABETH MASSIE

I found the "Barking Up the Right Tree" geocache in a tall ironwood tree near the crest of a densely forested mountain, a good mile and a quarter from where I'd parked my car by the log cabin ranger station. The ranger—a bearded, elderly gentleman with a slight limp—met me outside the station and smiled when I told him what I was up to. "Good luck up there," he said. "I've heard from some of the geocachers who've tackled it that it's a tough one."

Yes, on Geocaching.com, this particular hide had been rated highest possible for terrain and difficulty. My favorite kind.

Or I should say *was* my favorite kind.

A geocache, for those who don't know, is a container of varying sizes, hidden so players can use their GPS devices to locate them. Once found, the player signs a paper "log" and replaces the geocache for the next person who comes looking. Some are easy to spot while others are cleverly disguised. It's tons of fun; you visit places you might not otherwise visit, see sights in places that are crowded or isolated, ordinary or odd, peaceful or even a bit unnerving. I've made 2,457 finds over six years. A lot, but hardly anywhere near a record. My geocaching username is "Mighty Gal." I prefer tricky finds. Lots of geocachers ignore those, preferring easier ones. The wimps.

It was late afternoon, later than I'd usually be geocaching, and chilly. I climbed the mountainside with my phone in my hand, following the GPS coordinates. My backpack was on my back (duh), stuffed with two water bottles, an extra hoodie, gloves, granola bars, bug spray, and some other standard geocaching shit. I was determined to find this last cache before calling it a day, and I hoped there would be enough daylight to do that. I never hunted at night. Okay, I might be Mighty Gal most of the time, but I'm a wuss in the dark. Don't tell anybody.

After nearly an hour hiking up steep slopes, dodging thorny patches, resting, and banging my ankles on hidden stumps, and resting, my phone told me I was within three hundred feet of "Barking Up the Right Tree." I slowed and followed the indicator until I was twenty feet from ground zero—where I saw a tall, gnarly ironwood tree with lots of snaking branches. Yes, it looked like the perfect hiding place! The geocache wouldn't be near the ground, not with a high rating for difficulty. It had to be up the tree. Dropping my backpack and stuffing my phone and an ink pen into my pocket, I jumped up and caught the lowest branch. Wriggling and wrangling, I got my body up and around it. Then I climbed several branches higher. There, holding tightly to a limb over my head, I began searching for the geocache.

It wasn't as hard to find as I would have guessed. It was a small bison tube, wedged deeply into a crack in the bark of the trunk. I pulled it free, twisted it open, and dumped the little rolled paper log into my hand. I unrolled the log, balanced it on my knee, took the ink pen from my jeans pocket, and quickly signed my name and the date. Then I rolled it back up, returned it to the tube, and replaced "Barking Up the Right Tree" in the crack in the bark.

I made a quick descent back to the ground, where I picked up my backpack and reached for the zipper so I could retrieve water and a granola bar, my reward for finding number 2,458. My watch warned me that was already 5:38 p.m.. It was time to head back to my car.

Then it screamed.

It was close by, in the trees.

Damn!

It screamed again, close by.

I grabbed my backpack and took off, tripping on a stone and nearly falling to my face. Coughing, I clawed my way back up again and went barreling through the pines and the oaks and the poplars, jumping fallen logs and cutting my face on a vicious green briar vine. The thing was behind me, definitely gaining on me.

Shit!

The backpack banged crazily back and forth in my grasp.

It screamed. Piercing, high-pitched.

Nearer.

I rounded a maple, skidded in dead leaves, and stopped. I put my head against the trunk, panting, shaking, hoping whatever it was would pass the tree and not see me.

I waited, listened. Silence.

I listened.

No more screams.

I gulped air, still afraid to look around the tree.

The only sound came from the wind-rattled branches overhead.

Then I heard muffled fluttering and glanced up to see an owl settling onto a maple branch. It preened its feathers for a moment. And opened its beak and screamed.

It was a fucking owl. All this time, I'd been running from a goddamn owl! I burst into a painful laugh. "I hate you, you asshole!" I shouted through my laughter. I leaned over, letting it pour out.

At last my laughing and shaking eased. I wiped stray tears away and spit the sour from my mouth. My face stung from the briar scrape, but I ignored it. It was past time to get down the mountain. I reached into my pocket for my phone. It was gone.

No, no, no, no!

It had been thrown free during my owl escape. I had to find it, and I had to hurry. The sun always set more quickly in the forests than anywhere else, it seemed.

Shouldering the backpack, I started back in the direction of the "Barking Up the Right Tree" tree. Looking left, right, left, right, kicking at leaves and brush with my feet, watching for the green plastic casing in which the phone was secured. Green. . . what a stupid idea. Should have been bright red or purple.

I walked longer than I should have and realized I was no longer going in the direction of the ironwood tree.

Damn!

I walked back, taking it slower now, cursing louder. Darkness began to melt across the forest, a darkness reserved for wilderness.

My phone was lost for good.

I had to get to my car. But I had no GPS. And since I never geocached at night, I had no flashlight in my backpack.

Stop whining! You're Mighty Gal. You can find your damn car. Just fucking do it. Just go down.

I squinted into the pewter gray of the landscape. It sloped away in several directions. Which way was right?

I couldn't just stand there. I had to pick a way and go. I began walking, picking my feet up so as not to get tangled in any vines. Bugs, visible during the day and invisible now, hummed in my ears and around my cheeks and forehead. Leaves crunched. Owls screamed.

The assholes.

The land sloped down but then began to rise again.

This was definitely the wrong way.

Fuck!

I turned forty-five degrees, continued walking. The moon was rising now, a half-moon offering its half-assed bit of light.

I reached a sheer drop that I could in no way descend.

The forest was becoming truly dark now.

Oh, God, I am so lost!

I will not cry; I will not cry!

Then I spotted what looked to be a clearing to my right. I pushed through the tangle of undergrowth to enter what was not just a clearing, but a former campsite. A blackened circle indicated where a fire had been. A huge pile of firewood was stacked to the side. I didn't have a flashlight and I didn't have a phone, which sucked big time, but I did have matches. No way I could find my way back down the mountain to my car now. But I could make a fire to keep unknown, unseen creatures away.

I didn't think I'd be able to sleep.

It was going to be a long damn night.

Shaking away furious tears, I salvaged dry leaves and various-sized sticks from the wood pile, dropped them onto the charred spot, and, crossing the fingers of my left hand, struck a match. Leaves caught fire, followed by the sticks.

It wasn't long before a decent fire was burning. Night was fully on with a smattering of stars visible up beyond the trees. I pulled out my hoodie, slipped it on, zipped it up. Sitting as close to the fire as I could without singeing my eyebrows, I tried to ease my still pounding heart. The fire was my friend, my protector, I told myself, and I'd keep awake and keep it burning until it was daylight once more.

Can I do that?

Shut up. Yes, you can.

I drank from a bottle of water. I thought about the granola bar—but what if an animal should smell it and come looking? Would the fire be enough to deter a bear if it wanted a snack? I left the granola bar in the backpack. Holding my watch to the fire's glow, I could see it was only 8:24 p.m.. It was going to be one fucking long night.

I closed my eyes and tried to fold into my hoodie as much as possible.

I'm Mighty Gal. I can do this. I'll have a story to post on the geocache website once this is all over. How not to run from owls and lose your phone.

A breeze whipped up. A sudden curtain of smoke and ash was thrown into my face. I inhaled, choked, gagged. I scooted around out of the direction of the breeze, blowing my nose onto my sleeve to get the smoke out.

Goddamn it, I hate this!

The smoke burned my nostrils, raked my throat, singed my lungs. I leaned over and waited for it to ease. Counted to ten. Twenty. But as the seconds passed, the burning, sickening sensation inside didn't lessen. Instead, it began to twist, to swell. My chest extended like a helium balloon. What the hell had been in that smoke? I gasped, coughed, tried to vomit.

I'm going to suffocate! I'm going to die!

It then felt as if the smoke were crawling up my throat into my mouth. I swallowed desperately while attempting to breathe. The smoke reached my mouth where it forced my jaws apart and poured out into the air.

Help me! God!

It was free of me now, though I wasn't free of it. I gasped and tried to scoot away, to get up and run into the night. I could not look away. A frozen wave of terror cut through my body.

The smoke that had left me was translucent and gray, hovering there over the fire. Then it began to take shape.

It looked vaguely like a woman, with arms, a neck, a lump that was a head.

I'm hallucinating!

It opened its mouth and screeched. Not an owl's scream. A human screech of pain and anguish.

I stared bug-eyed at the wailing, floating figure above the fire.

This is insane! My mind is playing...

"Please!" cried the figure. Its eye slits flashed, black as tar and glistening wet.

I scooted back farther.

"Please no! NO!"

I'd never heard an anguished voice quite so real.

"Go away!" I cried, realizing in saying that I was giving in to the idea that this was not a vision, not a dream. *It can't be real; it can't be real!*

"Me! Help me! Meeeeee...!"

I stared at the figure as it wriggled back and forth as if it were trying to free itself.

Then the extension that looked like an arm flew away as though it had been lopped off. The figure released an agonized howl. Then the second arm was then removed, and, with a gurgling grunt, the head was slowly torn off.

The figure faded and drifted into the sky with the rest of the smoke.

I sat shaking, staring up, wrapped in my hoodie. I had a great imagination; I'd written lots of stories for fun, even ghost stories. This had to have been my mind playing with me. It had been an intensely stressful day. This could not have been real. It could not have happened.

I counted again to calm myself. It took me to over two hundred before my heart had slowed enough to stop trembling.

I sat for over an hour, staring at the campfire, singing old Girl Scout songs to myself to pass the time. I finished the water in the bottle and threw the bottle into the woods. So, sue me.

By nine fifteen, the fire was dwindling, and I was freezing. I got up reluctantly and gathered several arms full of firewood—large stick, small stick, it didn't matter—and tossed them onto the low blaze. It took a moment, but they caught fire, and I welcomed the heat.

I had to get some sleep. So, I curled up on the ground, tightened my hood once more, and closed my eyes. I heard an owl in the distance and hoped he would break his neck on a tree and shut up. I counted again until I fell asleep. . . I have no idea how high I counted.

I was awakened when the wind shifted, and smoke slammed into my face a second time. I inhaled, bringing the burning, ashy air into my lungs. I rolled away, coughing, cursing as the smoke singed my airway. Again, I felt something more than smoke. It grew, puffing out my chest, tearing my nerves, and forcing its way up my throat. I knew I would suffocate. I bent over, growling and trying to cough it out.

I didn't need to. Like the other, it pushed through my mouth with a most foul taste, opening my jaws and oozing out into the air. It felt as if my lungs slammed shut as it exited. I dragged my arm across my lips, spit, and spit again. I did not want to look up; I knew what I would see.

And, of course, I looked up.

It was another figure, similar to the one before though a bit smaller. A wavering, translucent woman, with thrashing arms and a head that wobbled back and forth. The eyes opened and closed rapidly; the mouth was open impossibly wide. And, like the first, it began to shriek.

"Burning! Burning!"

The figure twisted, flailed, as if, indeed, burning there just above the flames of my fire.

"No! Noooo! Please!"

I put my hands over my ears, but the pitiful cry pierced right through. After a moment, the figure seemed to melt, and it, as the other, became part of the smoke that rose into the starless sky.

"Damn it!" I scrambled up and began to kick and claw dirt over the fire. I had to put it out; there was something burning there that was giving me hallucinations, visions, whatever the fuck they were. I didn't care if I froze before morning. I couldn't stand to go through that again.

At last, the fire was out.

I lay down on the cold ground in the utter darkness and began to count. And count.

And count.

And. . .

I awoke to a sound of birds nearby, overhead. The sky was brightening. I rubbed my face, spit out grit that had found its way into my mouth, and looked at my watch. It was 6:02 a.m.. Morning.

Thank God! I made it! Mighty Girl made it!

I ate my two granola bars and found the second water bottle near the bottom beneath a handful of geocaching trade items.

My legs and arms were stiff with the cold. Standing, I shook and rubbed them vigorously, then looked at the charred remains of the fire.

I stopped. I blinked. I stepped over and looked more closely. There was a thin, partially charred bone protruding from the remains. It looked odd, curved like no stick I could think of. I picked it up, turned it over.

It was part of a rib bone.

Someone had a barbecue up here. It's a pig rib or a cow rib.

I went to the wood pile. Last night I'd gathered and dumped wood on the fire without paying close attention to what I was picking up and tossing in. Maybe I could find a deer skull as a souvenir of my dreadful night on the mountain. That would be kind of cool. I could make it into a windchime. I started tossing hunks of wood off the pile. The light was bright enough now to see what I was doing. I caught a huge splinter in my right hand and pulled it out with a gritting of teeth, then sucked the blood away.

I found another rib bone. It was larger than the other, and complete.

More wood off the pile, flung aside.

Then I stopped.

There, crushed a bit, was a jawbone. It was human.

Fuck!

I caught my breath. I stared. I didn't want to look deeper, but I wanted to look deeper. I picked up a long stick and started pushing chunks of wood out of the way. And I realized some of the wood chunks weren't wood at all, but bones. I had burned bones last night. Was that what had caused the figures. . .?

I shook my head. *No, no, don't think that. That's crazy.*

But the jawbone was real, and so were the smashed human skulls I discovered at the bottom of the pile. Two dead people, turned into fuel for a campfire.

I backed away, my arms prickling, my mouth dry. I had to get down the mountain. I had to find someone, to tell someone. Should I take a skull with me as proof? My mind was spinning. *No, leave it. This is a crime scene!*

Shoving my arms through my backpack straps, I pushed through the trees and vines. I found a steep slope and took it. I didn't know how close I would be to my car once I reached the road at the bottom, but that didn't matter. I slid on wet leaves and moss, tripped and stumbled and slammed into saplings, rocks, logs. My hoodie caught and ripped on a thorny branch, and I kept on going. Down, down. Skidding. Sliding.

Down.

At last, I fell out onto the road. I dropped to my knees, wheezing, holding my heart, rubbing my fist against the dirt in my eyes. I think I was crying again but wasn't sure. I counted... *one, two, three, four, five, six, seven, eight, nine, ten, eleven, twelve...!* as I tried to calm my nerves. It didn't help. I knelt there on the gravel, replaying the wailing, ghostly figures in my mind. I was terrified and sadder than I'd ever been before.

Standing at last, I pushed my hair from my face and studied the road. This section was recognizable, as its guard rail was tagged with a large drawing of a penis in red spray paint; I'd driven past on this my way to the ranger's station. And so, I walked.

A car passed me but didn't slow to offer me a ride. That was okay. Walking felt oddly therapeutic. I took slow breaths, deep breaths. Around a curve, shadows cutting the pavement. Around another. A rabbit ran across in front of me. Down a slope, around another curve.

There was the ranger's station. I picked up my pace. Reaching the rough wooden door, I pounded with my fist.

It took a moment for the ranger to answer. He brushed sandwich crumbs from his lips. "My goodness, you look like you've seen a ghost!"

Truer words could not have been uttered. "I—" I began. I swallowed, started again. "I found a murder scene. Up on the mountain."

The ranger, whose nametag I could see now identified him as Bill Harris, blinked and frowned. It took a moment before he could speak. When he did, his voice was slow and patient.

"Young lady, you're that geocacher who went up late yesterday afternoon, aren't you?"

I nodded.

"Did you spend the night up there?"

I nodded.

"Why on Earth would you do that?"

I didn't want to explain. I didn't need to explain. I wasn't the problem. The dead women were the problem. "Mr. Harris, I lost my phone which has my GPS app," I found myself explaining anyway. "I was lost, to be honest. It got dark really fast. I found a campsite, and I—"

Bill held up his hand. "Ah, the campsite. I can see your confusion. That's a hunters' site. There are a couple months a year when folks are allowed to hunt this mountain, these woods. They can shoot bear, deer, turkeys. Not supposed to kill bobcats, though."

"Listen to me! I found skulls of—"

"Deer, maybe? Bear possibly. The hunters who use this area cook and eat what they kill. They don't eat the bones, though, that would be silly."

"Don't interrupt me!" My fists clenched. This old man had no idea. "I found human skulls. A human rib bone, buried in the campsite's wood pile. I'm no idiot! I know what I saw, and you need to call the police!" I almost told him about the ghostly women but knew he'd dismiss me for certain if I did.

Bill sighed loudly and shook his head. "I'm sure you're mistaken."

"I'm not!"

Bill said, "Huh." Then he pointed to his open-topped Jeep, which was parked beside the station house. "I know the campsite you're talking about. I know this mountain very well, it's part of my job. Let's go up there, and I can prove to you that your fears are unfounded, stirred most likely by the darkness and night noises."

"Okay." *You'll see, you old shit!*

We rode in silence, up a narrow and rutted dirt roadway, then turned off and drove through winding, narrow clearings, the Jeep bouncing, me bouncing, Bill bouncing. I ducked as we passed under low-hanging branches, my breathing fast, furious that Bill didn't believe me, ready to prove him wrong, ready to see him flush with embarrassment or apologize at the very least.

We pulled into the campsite.

There was the charred fire area. There was the woodpile.

I climbed from the Jeep and hurried over. At first, I didn't see the skulls—*oh, fuck! It really was my imagination!*—but there they were, partly hidden beneath some thick sticks that had fallen on top. I knelt and gingerly lifted one of the skulls.

Who are you? Who killed you? Who dismembered you?

I turned to show Bill.

And he stood there by the Jeep with a pistol aimed in my direction.

I dropped the skull. "What the fuck—?"

"You nosy little bitch," Bill said. "But it was time for a third, and here you are. Mmm-hmm."

I backed up and he shot me in the knee. The pain in my leg beyond description. I dropped to the ground, groaned, tried to crawl away.

Get away, get away, get away, Mighty Gal! God, please let me get away! Help me!

"They were about your age, too," said Bill. "Lovely young things. And such a barbecue they made! Lip-smacking delicious!"

I forced myself up and Bill shot me in the other knee. I went down again, the pain unfathomable, blood spewing. *I can't die here! No, no, fuck this shit, I can't die!*

Bill put the pistol in his belt and withdrew an axe from the Jeep. He walked over and stood with the axe on his shoulder. "Let's see. You have nice, plump haunches. I'll start with that. Got my Bic to start the fire. Plenty of wood. This will be just right."

He lifted the axe. He grinned, his beard twitching. "Yum."

And as it fell, all I could think was that difficult geocaches weren't my favorites anymore.

Nope.

Not anymore.

THE MURDER WAGON

LARRY BLAMIRE

"Is he that fella grows beets?"

"No, Morley, that's Lem Chandler. This fella Jayston grows turnip. Anyway, the vegetable does not matter."

"It does at market," quipped Hoxey, followed by his usual abrasive *haw-haw,* as he grabbed another mittful of crackers from the big barrel. Gilroy, the general store proprietor, went on unperturbed.

"Well, seems this fella Jayston was sellin' a cow over in Sundry and he run into that assayer William A. Stemm. And Stemm told Jayston the Murder Wagon was spotted over in Stiles just one week prior." Gilroy's tone went hushed and conspiratorial. "Sure enough. . . several folks in Stiles up and went missing. Just like it always happens."

Hoxey snorted, spraying cracker dust. *"Missing!* Gilroy. It's called *movin' on,* and it's what folk do when they get itchy. They pick up and move on, hopin' for someplace better."

"Maybe you should try that, Hoxey," Morley smirked. "Likely a mite less poachin' would go on around here."

This brought a laugh at Hoxey's expense from the little crew of regulars gathered about the wood stove in Gilroy's store. "Haw-haw," sneered the heavyset market hunter derisively as he grabbed more crackers.

"Hey, Hoxey, wouldn't it be easier if you just sat right *in* the barrel?" offered another wag to a fresh round of laughter.

"You lunkheads go right ahead, have your laugh. I'll be laughin' last when that ol' Murder Wagon proves to be a tall tale, showin' you all up for a bunch of fools."

The door to the general store snapped open and several loafers jumped a smidge, proving the Murder Wagon story was having some kind of effect. The newcomer was flashy, from his checkered suit to his mustache and derby.

"Why, hello there, Mr. McKenzie," Gilroy said, immediately going to attend what he knew to be an actual paying customer.

"Afternoon, Mr. Gilroy. Wonder if I might trouble you for some tobacco," McKenzie requested in the sharp tones of an Easterner.

"Right in that case, just take your pick." Gilroy gestured towards a display, then looked around importantly at the others observing the newcomer. "Boys, this is Mr. McKenzie. Mr. McKenzie is a newspaper fella from back east."

A ripple of acknowledgment circled the stove. "Oh, well, perhaps you'll find this of interest, Mr. McKenzie," Hoxey offered with a slightly manufactured air of intelligence. "We were just speaking of that old wives' tale folks have come to call *the Murder Wagon."*

"Murder Wagon," repeated McKenzie as he turned with his choice of tobacco. "I'm sorry, I'm not familiar with that."

"And better you are for it, sir, as it's a load of gossipy hokum squirreled with horse manure," Hoxey opined as he raised another handful of crackers.

"Now, Mr. McKenzie might just want to write about this," Gilroy said defensively. "It *is* news after all."

"I'm all ears, Mr. Gilroy," replied the newspaperman, leaning against the counter, tamping some tobacco into his pipe.

"Murder Wagon's been seen in a whole wash of towns, nigh on three years now, and that's a fact," offered Morley.

Gilroy picked up the story. "Wherever it's sighted, folks go missin', never to be seen again. And so does the *wagon*. Gone like it never was there in the first place."

"Which it never was," scoffed Hoxey.

Gilroy ignored him, his excitement building. "Now... here is the extra troublin' part I was just gettin' to before this tub o' crackers butted in. The Murder Wagon was spotted in Stiles, some two weeks ago. Before that, it was seen up in Rock Bend. Before that, Walkersville. Now, I looked at a map, and if'n you was to track them towns, you would see that they make an almost perfect straight line direct to. . ." The general store man paused for effect.

"Colby?" suggested the newspaperman, lighting his pipe.

Gilroy looked surprised to have his thunder taken.

McKenzie tossed the match. "Forgive me for putting the period on your entertaining yarn, Mr. Gilroy, but it was quite obvious you were breaking the overly dramatic trail that most legends and superstitions find themselves on. Which is to say, inevitably, and sometimes tiresomely, back to the teller of the tale, who then discloses the imminent threat of danger. Without that danger, of course," McKenzie grinned, gesturing with his pipe, "there's nothing to scare the toddlers back to bed."

It was questionable whether all the stove listeners grasped what the Easterner had just said, but Gilroy certainly got the gist, and he was none too pleased.

"Mr. McKenzie, I am a mite surprised that you, seeker of... of knowledge that you are. . . would shrug off somethin' that could be of such interest to your readers."

McKenzie raised a hand. "My friend, forgive this jaded newsman, I meant no offense. It's true, unfortunately, many legends *are* printed. But that's not for me. Those yarns travel not on paper, but through the loose lips of ignorance, in a hush that travels on wind. I, however, am compelled to seek out facts."

Hoxey looked like the fox at a hen dinner. Gilroy was disheartened, but Morley tried to console him. "Look at it this way, Gil. If there *is* a Murder Wagon, we'd be in a right fix. Must be. . . oh. . . twenty, thirty wagons come through here every day."

The clatter of pots and pans stood apart from the noises of the grain and delivery wagons trafficking Colby's ambitiously wide main street. It emanated from a plain peddler wagon; one of those long narrow boxes with a canvas flap on the back, not unlike the ones used by medicine shows, though not nearly as fancy. In fact, there was no indication on its side it even *was* a peddler wagon; no name, no sign selling wares, nothing to even attract attention. Naught but the wear and tear of long miles of dust and wind.

The woman driving it was, for all purposes, invisible. Which is to say, unremarkable to the point that she was hardly there. Her colorless, drawn-back hair and age-defying face looked etched by prairie winds, not unlike her sorry wagon. Her expression would have been called "hard" had there been any. . . that is. . . if anyone actually noticed her amidst the day's traffic.

One did. A wisp of a girl of eighteen.

Match looked at strangers. That's what would have been said of the girl, by the few who chose to acknowledge her. Found as an infant in a settlement with no name, she made her way, by various means (that one might call scrappy or resourceful), to Colby, which was becoming something of a hub now, fueled by freight lines and cattle. It was on this journey that she was christened, if one can glorify the simple act of a stranger saying, "Hey, match." He merely wanted to buy some matches, which is what she sold and how she thrived, if a person can thrive on matches. The name "Match" became conversationally useful, so she stuck with it, and then she never had to think about it.

But Match looked at strangers. And she looked hard, peering into faces, particularly the eyes, searching for. . . she knew not what. But she'd know it when she saw it. At least, that's what she felt, that's what she told herself. And she had to feel *something,* had to believe *something,* or else why go on? Match had purpose. And that, perhaps, was more than some had.

Since arriving in Colby, Match had looked into hundreds of eyes. Sooner or later, everyone came here. And right now, she tracked that hard-faced woman as the drab anonymous wagon clinked and clanked past her on the busy street.

"Don't bend your neck there, Match," chuckled the affable young man observing her. Horace was what might be considered an admirer of sorts. Not particularly good-looking, maybe what was generously called a "pleasant" face. But he'd taken to Match.

"I like lookin' at faces, Horace, anything wrong with that?"

"Tell me what you're lookin' for, maybe I could help you," the lad offered.

"Look, you're a nice fella, Horace, and I appreciate that but. . . well. . . I dunno, ain't you got any woodcuttin' to do?" With that, Match walked on after the peddler wagon.

The persistent Horace tagged along. "Always do. Gosh, I'm mighty busy! Right now, gotta clear some land for old man Banner. Says I can sell it all for firewood, all I can carry. You know, I make a pretty good living—"

"Told ya, I ain't interested. I got—I got somethin' I gotta do and *you ain't part of it.*"

Horace dropped back as she walked on. "Trying to find your name?" he called after her. Match gave no look back, no acknowledgment of what she considered a lucky guess.

* * *

Wagons were lined up a section of the street at midday, as the regular crowd gathered to see what they might buy cheap. Match scanned the crowd, the wagons, the various farmers, tinkers, and pretend doctors. Many she'd seen before. Not that hard-case woman. That face was new.

The unsmiling peddler woman had set up an impressive array outside her wagon; pots and pans, cups and plates, knives and forks, furniture like stools and tables, washboards, coal oil lamps, even some old photographs, which she variously hung on things or leaned against the wagon. It looked for all the world like the life of a person laid out. Or several persons. A bad feeling wormed up Match's back, but only for a moment.

The woman seemed to be doing a brisk business, but the immobile mouth in that stone face never opened. All her barter was done by hand, with fingers for dollars or sometimes pennies, and the crowd seemed to have quickly caught on, making deals in strange silence.

Match was fascinated by this peculiar show and by the woman who moved through it like a flinty wraith. Then she noticed something not immediately evident, something perhaps only *her* searching eyes could pick up. As the peddler woman interacted with the steady flow of people, she keenly looked into each and every face, as though first locking eye contact was a kind of admission price, a passport to proceed with a transaction. Only after that brief frozen acquaintance, that grasping of eyes on eyes, would the peculiar woman proceed to the commerce at hand. It occurred to Match with awkward discomfort that the peddler was looking for someone. Was she looking for family too?

If not... then what?

So rapt was she observing this ritual that it startled her when the woman's eyes suddenly landed on her. And locked. And held her there. Match had the illusion she was unable to move, and time seemed to stop. And she could see now that the woman's eyes were so dark that they appeared to be concave. Something predatory—

"I said I'd like some matches, miss."

The man's voice broke the spell, and Match saw that the woman had moved on, tending to customers. If Match had been anyone the strange peddler was seeking, she gave no hint.

Match turned to the well-dressed man who'd spoken; McKenzie, the newspaperman, pipe in mouth, waiting patiently. She gave an apology and sold him a handful of matches from the pouch around her waist. McKenzie lit up, and his gaze returned to the peddler's wares. "Like so many lifetimes spread out there," he observed, noting Match's fascination. "I understand pioneers were often forced to discard items to continue on their way. Many a difficult decision, I'll wager."

He wandered away, and Match saw now that the crowd was dispersing, moving on to other wagons, and the woman was loading the remaining items back into hers.

"I like your wares, ma'am," Match said abruptly, surprising herself. The woman hesitated, almost turned to her, then went on with her work. It was then that Match spied a photograph she had not noticed before, a formal family portrait with husband, wife, two boys and, most notably, a baby girl. Her gaze stuck like glue to that image resting there on a small table.

Match moved closer, anxious for a better look. Something

seemed to alert the peddler woman, for the stoic face turned just a fraction toward her, and, without looking at her, she snatched the photograph from the table and deftly secreted it behind the canvas cover at the back of the wagon.

Match wasn't sure what to make of that. All she knew was she desperately wanted another look at that family in the photograph. The one the peddler seemed so anxious to hide.

"Could I buy that picture?" Match was fairly certain she didn't have enough coin to do so.

The woman ignored her, stuck the last of her wares into the wagon, and then climbed in herself, drawing the canvas behind her. Match felt opportunity slipping away and rushed forward.

"Ma'am? Could I just—?"

That stone face jutted out through the canvas and those dark holes bored into her. Then the face flashed back inside, and gnarled hands whipped the canvas shut.

* * *

Hoxey liked a moonless night. But only when poaching. His poaching was one of those accepted sins, a secret everybody knew, like the mayor's wife working saloons in a mining camp.

The man was a fair hunter, and he managed to peddle a good amount of stew meat to the cafes and saloons and restaurants up and down Colby's main street. So, perhaps for that, he was forgiven his trap-filching hobby. Plus, he came up with a clever trick to make it look like the work of coyotes, making it tough to prove otherwise. Course, everybody and the coyotes knew about that too.

Right now, he skulked along with his shotgun in hand and two skinny rabbits hanging from his belt. He could tell the clouds were breaking, and that meant time to call it a night.

Hoxey knew the woods around Colby like the inside of

Gilroy's cracker barrel. Even in the dark, he knew he was edging along where the trees tapered off and cleared land began. For a big man, he moved like a great cat.

The moon peeked through, and pools of light woke up around him. Hoxey froze.

A perfect patch of moonlight had spilled onto a clearing, a place he knew quite well. And in that clearing sat a wagon. A boxy old peddler's wagon.

It sat silent in the chilly light, and Hoxey noticed that a wet mist played about it at ground level, like the wagon was in a soup of some kind. He stared at the oddness of it. The team was not there, and he heard no horses. Not a soul stirred.

And then it slapped him like a bucket of ice water. *This* was how that dad-blamed Murder Wagon foolishness started. An innocent sight like this abandoned wagon and folks get all het up. Sure, he admitted, it was a mite peculiar, and the sight of it sitting there made even him a touch uncomfortable. But when all was said and done, it was a damn wagon, like any of a hundred such clatterboxes.

Hoxey looked around a moment then proceeded towards the wagon. He would like nothing better than to sit in Gilroy's store, spouting off to the others how he had singlehandedly busted wide open that lamebrained spooky notion. The big man seemed to grow smaller as he strode into that mist, into the silence of that moonlit clearing. But he went right to the back end of the wagon and, with another quick glance around, reached for that closed canvas cover.

* * *

It took several days to notice Hoxey was missing. Not that folks didn't care. It was just that, with a character like that, there could be any number of reasons. But to miss that midday at

Gilroy's with its bottomless cracker barrel—what Hoxey used to call his free lunch (except for the entertainment he provided of course)—that was something to raise some eyebrows.

Naturally, Gilroy climbed on that soapbox before anyone, the general store man being what you might call an alarmist, with all his worries about Murder Wagons and such. But his uneasy feeling seemed genuine and proved contagious as a murmur of fear seeped through Colby like an oily river. The general store proprietor went so far as to offer free goods (up to a limit) to anyone who delivered word of the missing market hunter.

Match, meantime, haunted the streets, not looking for the larger-than-life Hoxey, but for that peddler woman. Many times she was told, by this or that person, that they had just spotted her here, or just down the street, or they coulda' swore she was over yonder a minute ago. That plain woman and her plain wagon were as slippery as bait worms. Match cussed herself for making such a big deal about the stranger with strange eyes, and about that family photograph in particular. That was just silly. By what half-brained notion did she leap to such a conclusion that it had any connection to her? Based on nothing but some kind of sense.

Or lack thereof.

But she was certain the woman did not want her to study that picture. Why? What about it would she want to hide? There it was, put on prominent display, spied by everyone who stopped by, only to be snatched away when Match showed interest.

The frustrated match girl made Colby her "hunting ground" because it was bustling with people. But that very fact now hampered her efforts to locate this one nondescript woman with coal-black eyes.

Match paused to sit on a crate, part of some freight being

loaded on a heavy wagon. Her eyes didn't rest though; they continued to scan the builders and bankers, seamstresses and cowboys, preachers and drunks, who went about their day.

Then something stuck in her eye like a mote of dust. It annoyed her because it made no sense. She rubbed her eyes. But it was still there. She squinted.

One person in the crowd across the street, one face in the many, appeared to be clouded over in some way. It was like she was looking at them through the bottom of a glass of milk. How could that be? Maybe they were wearing something. Like a veil of some sort.

The features were just not discernible. And though it had no bearing on her personal quest, she found herself eager to satisfy herself that her eyes were working and not playing tricks simply because she was using them too much. If not, if they were working fine, and someone who looked like that did exist, then. . . that would be something to see also.

Match was up and crossing the road, almost getting run down by two fancy women in a buggy, and a horse and rider who were really anxious to get somewhere. But when she reached the wooden sidewalk on the opposite side, there was no sign of the figure.

* * *

Two more people went missing. Mary Fitzhugh was the beloved wife of bank teller Carl Fitzhugh. And Salinas was a stablehand and odd-job worker who never said much. Now, Gilroy appeared a genuine prophet, and it was to his credit that he never boasted, merely tried to sway folks to be careful, helping to put up signs seeking information on the missing. The town marshal was taking it seriously, though he attempted to tamp down the collective murmur that this was not the work of human agency, instead insisting that some traveling band of cutthroats was to blame. The icy claw gripping the town seemed to tighten. The Murder Wagon was all too real.

Saloons and other places of business closed early, but the opposite happened at the general store. More folks than ever huddled by that stove and the Hoxey commemorative cracker barrel (as it became known), holding that there was safety in numbers. Gilroy himself let them stay the night if they wanted. Oil lamps burned well into the morning, while outside, cold weather rode the streets on stiff winds.

It was late when Match entered the general store and proceeded like a will-o'-the-wisp, unnoticed by the stove crowd, to her tiny lodgings off the back storeroom. She lit a candle and slumped on her cot, exhausted. In her singular quest, Match was almost oblivious to the Murder Wagon talk, as though her world and that one never quite overlapped. The peddler woman remained elusive, even though Rebecca Mayerling swore she just bought a comb off her. She showed the comb to Match, but it meant nothing.

Spotty moonlight tried to scratch its way through the small dirty window above her cot, and it was the last thing she saw before her heavy lids closed, lulled as they were by the comforting murmur two rooms away.

Match wasn't sure if she had slept, or for how long, when her eyes drifted open in a haze. The small square of moonlight was now blocked by something. As her eyes adjusted, she realized it was a face in the window. And it appeared to be staring right at her. *Appeared*, since it was hard to tell exactly *where* it was looking. Perhaps by a trick of darkness, dirty glass, and dying candle flicker, the apparition's features were unclear, as though coated by shifting fog. Or like the smudged face in a photograph when the subject moved. Eyes, nose, mouth, cheeks, chin, nothing wanted to resolve or assemble correctly, as though it were not a face at all. . . but the dim memory of a face.

All this, in the space of a single inhale. Now it was gone. In its place, the same dirty window. The tail end of a dream?

Match was up, snatching lantern and matches and unbolting the rear door that led directly to the alley behind the building, where a person, if any, would have to stand to peer inside.

The chill in the air stung her immediately and she pulled her shawl tighter. There was no sign a soul had been there, so she headed to the closest side alley. The moon swam behind the clouds, and she lighted the lantern as she walked. Her trepidation at such an impossible face was swept aside by a peculiar urgency. If this strange woman, this phantom peddler, had the answer to Match's very existence, then no cost was too great.

Her blood rushed as she stalked back alleys between houses and stores, and she felt an otherworldly tingle that she now associated with the apprehension of a truth of some kind. She knew there was somewhere she needed to be. Above all, Match felt deep pride. Those less resolved might have missed this opportunity, missed the signs. Hope raised itself like a flag as Match wondered if the peddler woman might be her own grandmother?

She was on the main street now. Some lamps were lit, an ongoing project for the chamber of commerce. An occasional window glowed with lantern or candle. She felt the wind now, fighting her progress, unobstructed as it was on the wide street. But it was not about to turn her back. Not Match, who clutched her shawl and her swinging lantern that now spilled light into nooks and alleys at a dizzying pace. But for wind, the fearful town was silent.

A wicked laugh cut the breeze and Match stopped. It came again and she lurched towards an alley, raising her lamp.

Myrtle, from the Hock Street Saloon, in a friendly tussle with Rudy Johnstone, wrangler from the Bar-C. They protested, but Match had already spun away down the street.

She was nearing the edge of town. What if she was heading the wrong way? It was frustrating to think of starting over, all that time wasted. The peddler woman could be long gone to wherever she holed up at night.

As Match stumbled past the small outlying buildings, she was considering turning back when a sound stopped her dead. As she listened, she turned in a quiet circle, lantern raised, in what looked like a bizarre ritual.

There was nothing now. But she was sure she'd heard it. The slight rattle of a wagon coming to a halt, somewhere beyond the edge of town, beyond its meager lights. Match shone her lantern in what seemed the right direction with a pathetic plea for it to reach into that dark fold. She squinted as she walked, eyes randomly plucking clues where there were none.

When the clouds moved it was like the answer to a prayer. Moonlight burst through like water from a dam held back too long, marking the earth with stingy spots and streaks.

There it lay, as though prearranged, in its very own private patch of blue light. That plain old wagon with the canvas back.

Match doused her lantern and walked toward it. Her plan was clear. If the woman was there, they would talk, once and for all. If she wasn't, Match would search the wagon, find out what she could, and look at that photograph.

She was well beyond the town's grasp, entering the cool of the moon's domain. Match pictured the elusive and unhappy woman sleeping in the back of the wagon. Or maybe camping in the woods. She could identify with that after all her searching; to be off on one's own, no longer swimming against human current.

She had just reached the yoke of the wagon when the clouds

inconveniently rolled and took the moon with them. She stood very still, then began to feel her way in utter darkness, first finding the small front left wheel, then feeling along the side of the wagon, finally coming to the larger left wheel at the rear. Her hands gently danced over the heavy web of spokes, and she worked around the corner until she touched rough, hanging canvas. To this point, she had successfully avoided making any sound.

But it occurred to her that the woman was not young. How old was anyone's guess. The last thing she wanted to do was startle someone who might be her grandmother into a heart attack. Not when it had taken so long to find her.

So, she gently whispered, "Ma'am?"

She waited a moment. No sound came from within. Had her thoughtfully considerate timidity even penetrated the canvas? She whispered again, slightly louder. How sound a sleeper was the peddler woman? *If* she was there. No light leaked from the heavy, well-worn canvas.

Match barely heard the faint snap behind her. A single twig. She turned, but there was nothing to see in the void of night.

She slightly lifted a corner of the canvas. "Excuse me, ma'am? It's okay. It's me, Match." She immediately felt foolish. The peddler woman didn't know who Match was.

The hostile odor struck her as a physical blow. It was foul, escaping through the raised corner of the canvas. With rising panic, she wondered if the woman had died. Perhaps days ago.

Sudden familial concern propelled her to fumble with the lantern. It took three matches—very unlike her. She was already climbing the closed tailboard, spilling light in as she lifted the canvas higher. Match had not seen the inside, and as she climbed in, her eyes were first struck by the brilliant colors of the peddler's wares, dizzying in the jumping shadows cast by the swinging lantern.

Match moved the lantern, painting the insides with light, bringing the wares into focus. Her breath sucked up into her head like a skyrocket. Bones. Bones and skulls, human skulls, decked out with trinkets, hanging and staring. Bright meat of indeterminate origin, red as hell, draped on hooks. And there was Hoxey. His head, anyway. Good ol' Hoxey, staring at her with that look when he couldn't wait to pontificate. It swung a little now, that head. The wagon was rocking.

Someone was climbing in the back.

Match whipped around, cold with shock, as the canvas yanked violently aside. A figure danced to the swaying lantern. As she always did, Match looked to the face, right to the face, to the eyes. But there was no face. Just that clouded visage, that elusive blur. The vagueness of its non-features seemed to wiggle and float like a fresh yolk, a skill perhaps of the bearer. But as she stared, they began to assemble. And lo and behold there was Horace. Good old Horace, the charming woodcutter. Her amiable but not handsome suitor, his pleasant boyishness now twisted by some bloody need. It flashed in her mind that the various axes and cutting tools hanging in the wagon were *his*.

And one of them flashed before her as monstrous Horace raised a well-maintained axe. Match had just thought to shatter her lantern on its face when, with a loud *boom*, Horace's upper chest exploded. The ruined body lingered for a frozen second before whatever passed for its brain realized it no longer had the stability to remain upright.

Clouds decided this was the moment and moved, bathing the rear of the wagon in blue. Match surprised herself, boldly rushing to the now-open canvas and gazing down at the grotesque tableau.

The peddler woman stood there, face etched in frozen light, right arm curled about an enormous eight-gauge punt gun with two smoking barrels—a shotgun of formidable prowess—as she impassively observed the heap of corpse on the ground before her.

The head had been completely severed from the body. No longer clouded by whatever arcane knack the thing possessed, it was now plainly and simply a monstrous unknown with wildly hideous and predatory features. And best left that way.

For two years the woman had tracked the beast, this beast that had taken her family—the family in the photograph. With one horrendous act, the thing had made her life a solitary hunt. Packing her belongings, painfully selling them along her way as a peddler, as though her memories bought her passage. All the while searching, tracking the Murder Wagon, her dead eyes boring into every stranger, looking for the reaction, the *recognition* triggered by her belongings.

By the photograph.

She had seen it. Seen it in the young man Horace's eyes, that animal fear of being found out, the traveling young woodcutter in a plain wagon with no markings.

And with that, as in a dream best forgotten, the peddler woman dropped the smoking shotgun, turned, and walked off to wherever she'd hidden her wagon.

A SHADOW, SLOWLY SHIFTING

HEATHER DAUGHRITY

Mack Harrington paced throughout the hours of the early morning. One step at a time, one foot in front of the other, he made his way again and again through the echoing rooms of the house he had once shared with his wife and son. The house he had come home to every day for nearly thirty years.

The house he was now afraid to be alone in. Afraid to sleep in.

Afraid to stay, afraid to leave.

Mack Harrington made his way slowly, exhaustedly, from room to room. Every room except *that* room.

He paused at the doorway, let his eyes drift over the familiar shapes of the furniture. The sofa where William, as a child, would lie sprawled and surrounded by toys, watching cartoons on Saturday mornings. The chair where Emma, hair pulled back in a severe ponytail, hands twisting, always twisting together and over each other, would sit watching William.

The bookshelves covered in dust. The old TV, the same. No one had used this room in nearly a year.

Mack's eyes fell to the floor, though his conscious mind warned against this.

The shadow, the impossible shadow, slowly shifting across the rug's faded flowers.

For the hundredth time, Mack lifted his gaze, scanned the room, searching in vain for the source of the shade.

If only he'd listened when Emma first told him. If only he'd believed her. If only he'd been able to see it then.

Mack ran his fingers through his hair, rubbed the heels of his palms against his tired eyes.

If only he'd listened.

* * *

One year earlier:

Emma Harrington first noticed the shadow on a crisp and sunny afternoon in late October. She had finished her daily chores (the house spotless, just the way Mack liked it). She had dinner in the oven (a hot meal, homemade, just the way Mack liked it). She had stopped off in the upstairs bathroom to make sure her hair was smoothed back, her dress unwrinkled, her minimal makeup reapplied (pretty but not trashy, just the way Mack liked it).

The clock in the hall chimed the half hour; Mack would be home in roughly forty minutes. Emma sat in the chair near the living room window, careful not to rumple her skirt, her back perfectly straight. In her lap, her hands clasped each other, twisting together, as she settled in to wait for her husband's arrival.

Ten or perhaps fifteen minutes passed, the house silent except for the sound of the heater cycling on and the occasional sizzling drip of the pot roast in the oven. Emma's eyes were pointed in the direction of the driveway just beyond the window, but her vision was unfocused, her mind gone to that soft blank space that had become a refuge from the life she had lived these past twenty-six years.

So lost was she in this floating place of non-existence that, at first, she did not register the shadow's movement. After a few moments, her head turned away from the window and toward the something-not-quite-right that she could not immediately place. Slowly her pupils focused, and the slightest pinch of a wrinkle appeared between her brows.

The shadow—for that was surely what it was—appeared amorphous in shape, its edges blurred and indistinct.

It moved.

The shadow drifted across the floor in a slight arc from left to right and back again. A few seconds elapsed as it made each pass; at one end of its path, the shadow's edge grazed the spot where the worn floral rug ended and the hardwoods shone beneath; at the opposite end, it stopped a few inches short of the old wooden TV cabinet. In all, the shadow moved across a space roughly six feet wide, but slowly, so slowly that Emma narrowed her eyes as she stared at it, trying to discern whether it was actually moving at all.

She looked around the room, attempting to locate the source of the shade. Her gaze fell on the walls and the furniture, moved up to take in the exposed beams of the ceiling, then flicked to the world beyond the window. Nothing stirred, inside or out.

Nothing except the shadow.

When Mack's truck pulled in the driveway, Emma pushed the curious anomaly from her mind, smoothed her skirt, and arranged her face into a pleasing smile, just the way Mack liked.

* * *

The shadow remained.

Though it was harder to see in some lights than others, Emma took silent note of its existence. Days passed, days of sunlight, days of cloud cover, the nighttime darkness arriving a little earlier each evening, and still, in the day and to a lesser extent in the night, she took in the shadow's gradual swing, left to right and back again, across the surface of the living room floor.

She noted it, but she did not give it much thought.

Emma Harrington had grown used to not thinking over the years. Her ideas had been met in the first years of her marriage with a sort of patronizing amusement. This was followed by a studied indifference, and finally by a few months of unmistakable derision. Mack, accustomed to barking orders to his construction crew during the day, had no gentle affection reserved for his wife, no kind words or patience left when he arrived home each evening.

Emma had learned the importance of routine, to maintain every part of her life in a certain way (just the way Mack liked), and to keep her mouth shut and her thoughts to herself, until the time came when she had no thoughts of her own left to keep.

Which, had she thought about it, was also just the way Mack liked it.

* * *

But by the first week of November, when she woke each morning to patterns of frost traced along the windows and went to bed each night wearing an extra pair of thick, warm socks, even Emma Harrington's mind demanded that she ponder the mystery of the shadow.

She watched silently as Mack walked through the living

room—through the shadow itself—without seeming to notice it. She invented excuses, sly ways to draw him into the room and to try, without being too obvious, to draw his attention to it.

Finally, one dark and chilly evening while the wind whistled in shrieks and starts around the sharp corners of their house, she asked the question. They were sitting together in the living room, Mack's eyes trained on the six o'clock news, Emma's hands wringing nervously in her lap, when the words escaped her mouth before she could think to stop them.

"Can't you see it, dear?"

Mack glanced at her, rolled his eyes, sighed. "See what? What am I supposed to see?"

Emma gestured vaguely at the shadow, which swung languorously back and forth not ten feet in front of him, dark against the amber light from the old wall sconces that lit the room. She watched as Mack's eyes swept the area she indicated, then turned toward her.

"What, woman? It's the floor. Am I supposed to be excited about that?"

Emma, fighting against the tongue-taming that she had instilled in herself for over a decade, forced herself to speak. "The shadow, Mack. The shadow that moves across the floor, just there. Can't you see it?" She pointed once more in the direction of the drifting darkness.

Mack glanced once more along the floor. She felt certain he must see it. For a moment her heart sped up within her chest, and she leaned forward in anticipation of an acknowledgement she barely dared to hope might come.

Mack gave a loud, huffing sigh, rolled his eyes, and spoke: "I don't see nothing. Maybe you've finally gone crazy in your old age, woman."

And that was the end of that.

* * *

The holidays approached, the one time of year in which Emma dared to feel any kind of happiness, for this was the time when William came home. Their son had been Emma's one joy in life, her one purpose. For eighteen years, her only goal had been to raise him, to love him, and to shield him from his father's sharp tongue and neglectful indifference.

But then William had grown up, and as much as he loved his poor put-upon mother, he could not stand to live another day in the same house with his overbearing father. So, as soon as his eighteenth birthday rolled around—exactly one month after high school graduation—William had packed his life into a few cardboard boxes and moved out to room with three other young men.

He had done well enough for himself, Emma was proud to say. He had received a small scholarship and worked to pay the rest of his way through college, although the art degree he had earned had caused his father to snort in derision. After college, William had taken a job at a design firm, but his real passion was devoted to the paintings he worked on at night in the small studio set up in his garage.

The one dream Emma had left in life was to become a grandmother. She tried her best not to chide William about finding a nice girl to settle down with, but the thoughts circled in her mind just the same.

Thanksgiving week arrived, and Emma set to work giving the house a thorough cleaning. She paused in the living room, her shoes mere inches from the shifting shadow, before reaching out quickly and grasping the corner of the rug, pulling it quickly away from the shadow's path, and taking it outside to beat clean in the cool November afternoon.

* * *

Turkey sizzled in the oven, potatoes boiled on the stove, a pumpkin pie sat in pride of place on the dining table. William was due for dinner at seven o'clock sharp, and Emma counted down the minutes until his arrival while Mack snored in the recliner, the TV volume turned low.

At 7:03 p.m., the doorbell rang, waking Mack from his nap and sending Emma running to the front door. She flung it open and wrapped her arms around her son's neck, breathing in the scent of him and reveling in the warmth of his body, her mind for a moment flashing on memories of William as a baby, asleep in her arms as she sat in the old rocking chair singing lullabies.

The three of them sat down to dinner shortly after, and then father and son retired to the living room for drinks while Emma washed up in the kitchen. All the dishes cleaned, dried, and put away, she joined the men, wiping her hands on her apron. Mack sat in his chair, William on the corner of the couch farthest from his father. Both had glasses of whiskey in their hands, and both seemed to be sipping at the drinks with a kind of barely restrained resentment. Emma sighed. All she wanted was a happy day with her son, but his father was always sure to ruin that. She didn't even bother to ask what they had argued about this time.

The next hours passed with strained conversation and long periods of silence during which Emma found herself watching the shadow drift slowly from one end of the room to the other. At one point, she was almost sure that William had seen it too, for his head jerked suddenly in the shadow's direction, and his eyes narrowed for a moment before glancing around. But then he threw back another mouthful of liquor and stood, somewhat unsteadily, to fill his glass again.

When the hall clock rang out ten times, William stumbled into the kitchen to deposit his glass in the sink and then made his way carefully up the stairs, kissing his mother on the cheek and whispering a quick *good night* as he passed. Emma had no doubt that he'd be passed out in a drunken slumber within minutes, his adult body looking disconcertingly large against the small frame of his old twin bed.

She sighed as she heard his bedroom door close and turned to face Mack, who was probably so drunk himself that she'd have to support him up the stairs to their own room. But Mack was not slumped in his chair already half-asleep when she turned around. He was up, standing hunched over the spot on the couch that William had just vacated. He was looking intently at something in his hand.

Emma stepped closer and realized that Mack was holding William's phone, scrolling slowly through what looked like a series of messages. She opened her mouth to say something, thought better of it, and remained silent, watching her husband.

Mack's face grew redder as he scrolled, his whole body beginning to shake furiously. Finally, he turned and glared at his wife. "I knew it," he said, forcing the words out through his teeth. "Our son is a fucking homo."

Emma was so taken aback by this accusation and the vile way Mack spat out the words that, for a moment, she simply stood in shock. Mack thrust the phone toward her; she took it with trembling hands. Slowly she scrolled through the messages that he had just finished reading. The exchange seemed to be between William and a young man named Kevin, and it was certainly the kind of back-and-forth that only occurred between two lovers. Emma let this realization sink in. It had never occurred to her before that her son might be gay, but looking back she supposed there had been signs, if she had been smart enough to notice them.

The thought did not bother her, only surprised her for a moment before a sort of maternal happiness surged through her. Her son had a lover, a boyfriend; from the messages the relationship seemed to be longstanding and committed. She wondered what their life was like, what kind of places they went together, whether they lived together already or just spent the night at each other's place now and then. She would sit William down with a plate of leftovers the next day and ask him all about it.

But then her eyes raised once more to meet her husband's, and a stab of fear sliced through her.

Mack was furious, disgusted; he would never let this stand.

Before Emma could say a word, before she could try in some way to defuse the situation, Mack was standing at the bottom of the stairs, one hand on the banister, one foot lifted to the bottom step. His angry voice bellowed up through the house as he shouted for William.

Mack yelled his son's name five times before the door at the end of the upstairs hall finally creaked open. William, in a pair of baggy shorts and an old T-shirt, stepped groggily into the hall, rubbing his eyes. "What the hell, Dad?"

Mack then let loose a string of vulgarities, insults, and accusations that made Emma dizzy with panic. Mack took his son's phone in one hand and threw it up the stairs, his strength and aim surprising considering how much liquor must be coursing through his veins. The phone hit the wall a few feet in front of William and shattered on the floor.

"Out! Out of my house! I won't have it. I want you out! Now!"

William stared at his father for a long moment, his chest heaving, hands balled into fists at his sides. He opened his mouth and Emma, watching in horror from the bottom of the stairs, thought he was about to begin shouting right back. But he didn't. William's voice was low and controlled as he spoke: "Fine, Dad. I'm leaving."

William turned and went back into his childhood bedroom. There was a flurry of activity, stomping about and things being tossed around, then he reemerged, shoes on, a jacket thrown over his T-shirt, his overnight bag in hand. He stooped to pick up his broken phone and nearly pitched forward face-first onto the floor. His hand gripped the banister tightly as he made his way carefully down the stairs.

Mack stood aside, glowering at his son as he walked past.

Car keys in hand, William reached for the doorknob. Emma, finding her voice at last, cried out. "You can't go right now, William. He can't go, Mack! He's too drunk! He can't drive. He can barely walk!"

Mack turned his hateful stare from his son to his wife. "He will go. I won't have it in my house."

Desperate, Emma ran for her own car keys. "I'll take him, then. I'll take him home."

Mack's beefy hand caught her across the cheek as she tried to pass him. The force of the blow knocked her backward against the wall. "You'll bloody well stay put, woman." Mack's voice was a low growl.

"Stay out of it, Mom." William sounded tired, resigned. "I'll get myself home, or to a motel for the night. It'll be fine."

Then he was gone, out into the night, closing the door behind himself with a calm and quiet click which seemed to signal such finality that Emma burst into tears.

Mack glared at his wife one last time before ascending the stairs, dragging himself up with his arms. He stumbled into their bedroom and Emma heard the creak of the mattress as he fell into bed, still fully clothed. She sat down in her chair by the window and settled in for a night of worrying, her hands twisted together in her lap.

It took exactly forty-seven minutes before police officers knocked at the door to tell the parents of William Harrington that their son was dead. He hadn't even made it out of the neighborhood.

* * *

The days ran together. Emma was so heavily medicated for her son's funeral ("Get that doctor to give you something to shut you up already," Mack had growled) that she barely remembered being there. The crisp, sunny days of November disappeared, and December dragged itself slowly toward winter with dark skies and storms of ice and hail.

The house remained dim even when the sun was high in the sky, banks of slate-gray clouds hiding any weak light that might have reached the windows.

Yet even in the dimness, the shadow made its presence known.

One afternoon, a week before Christmas, Emma found herself sitting on the living room floor, directly in the center of the shadow's path. It seemed to her that she could feel it as it moved across her, as if the darkness had a weight that was not at all frightening but instead offered a strange comfort. She rocked back and forth with its slow rhythm, her arms wrapped tightly around herself, hands gripping her bony elbows.

As she swayed, she hummed bits of old lullabies, imagining the feel of her precious baby boy in her arms.

She was still there in that spot, stretched out on the rug, snoring softly, when Mack came home. He squatted beside her and shook her. Emma's eyes fluttered open.

"Good." Mack snorted. "You're alive. When's dinner? I'm starving."

Each day after that, Emma woke in the morning, stumbled down the stairs, and made herself comfortable beneath the shifting shadow. It brushed across her skin like a lover's touch: gentle, warm, inviting. She stopped eating, stopped cleaning, stopped brushing her teeth or her hair. Her only desire was to sit in this one spot as the shadow slid slowly and peacefully over her.

At times, she felt the breeze it created lifting up stray strands of her hair.

At times, she heard it speak.

There were only sighs at first, soft breaths that swept over her and left trails of goosebumps along her arms. Then the whispers started, low murmurs that resolved themselves into words. They spoke to her of all the dreams she'd once dared to dream.

They reminded her of the lovely girl she'd once been.

Of the innocent, hopeful young wife and the devoted, protective mother.

They reminded her that she was now old and worn out. Childless. Loveless. Hopeless.

They reminded her that she had missed her chance, let life pass her by, that nothing remained for her now but decades of empty numbness.

They reminded her whose fault it all was.

Mack came home two days before Christmas to find his favorite dinner waiting for him, still hot, on the dining table. The kitchen was empty. He glanced around downstairs but did not see his wife, so he shrugged and sat down at the table. He devoured his meal in silence, deposited the plate in the sink, and settled in to watch the news.

From the corner of his eye, he thought he saw something,

some movement just beyond his line of vision. He turned his head quickly, expecting to see Emma walking into the room, and prepared himself to question her about just where she had been. She was not there. Mack's brows furrowed for a moment, and he stared at the walls and floor where he could have sworn he'd seen something. Then he shrugged and turned back to the TV. It must have been a shadow.

Later that night, after Mack had gone up to bed, the front door opened quietly and Emma entered the house, holding a bulky object wrapped in a brown paper bag. She sat down at the dining table and silently prepared Mack's Christmas Eve gift. She hid it away in the hall closet, and then she waited.

Mack woke the next morning to find Emma's spot in bed still empty. He showered and shaved, dressed for work, and thundered down the stairs. He came to an abrupt stop at the bottom. There sat Emma in her usual chair, hands held primly in her lap, clasped tightly together. Her eyes rose slowly to meet his, and a strange smile spread across her face. Mack found himself unnerved by the smile. A stream of demanding questions and demeaning remarks ran through his mind, but these faded away before reaching his tongue. He looked at his wife curiously for a moment, then drew a deep breath, making himself look taller, bigger, before pointing a finger at her and saying, "You and I are going to have a talk when I get home."

Then he was out the door and off to work.

Emma's eyes followed the path of his truck down the street and around the corner. Her smile did not waver as she murmured, "Yes, dear."

Emma took a deep breath. She slid from the chair and crawled across the floor until she lay beneath the shadow's sweeping caress. Her fingertips stroked the worn carpet where the darkness passed across it. For a few moments, she closed her eyes, a look of blissful peace upon her face. Then she pushed herself to a sitting position and spoke: "Yes. Yes, of course. Soon enough. But first, to prepare."

Over the weeks that Emma had spent distraught, depressed, and finally distracted by the shadow, the house had reached a state of disarray over which Emma Harrington now clicked her tongue. This was not the way Mack liked it at all. She tied on an apron and set to work, straightening, dusting, scrubbing the house from top to bottom with the energy of a woman much younger than her own forty-six years. She ignored the clock when it chimed the lunch hour, for she felt no need for sustenance.

At three o'clock, she put away the last load of clean laundry, gave the house a quick once-over, and went upstairs to soak in a hot bath. When she was finished, she used her towel to soak up the water droplets in the tub and then hung it neatly on the rack to dry. She dressed in her nicest skirt and blouse, brushed her damp hair back into a ponytail, and applied the barest hint of makeup—just the way Mack liked it.

She went downstairs and started a pot of soup on the stove, full of large chunks of vegetables and meat. She gave it a stir and tasted a bit from the end of the wooden spoon. Yes, with an hour or so to simmer, it would be exactly the way Mack liked it. She turned the fire beneath the burner to low and set the spoon in the ceramic spoon rest, careful not to drip anything on the stovetop or counter.

Emma stopped in front of the hall mirror to run her hands over her hair and her skirt, smoothing both out. Then she pulled the brown paper bag from the closet and removed its contents. She deposited the bag in the trash before slinging the rope up and over the exposed rafters of the living room ceiling.

It took her a few tries to get it just right, but by the time the hall clock chimed three-quarters of the hour—roughly twenty-five minutes until Mack would be home—she had the rope secured and hanging at just the right height.

She sat quietly in her chair until the clock's gong rang out five times. Ten minutes until he was home. Now was the time.

Emma positioned a small stepladder beneath the noose. She climbed to the top step. Carefully, lovingly, she draped the noose around her neck. Her eyes roamed over the rooms she could see from where she stood (everything spotless, just the way Mack liked it). She breathed deeply, filling her nostrils with the tantalizing scent of the soup bubbling away on the stove (a hot meal, homemade, just the way Mack liked it). She made sure her ponytail was not caught in the rough fibers of the rope and smoothed the front of her skirt one last time (pretty but not trashy, just the way Mack liked it).

A brilliant flash of lightning lit the darkening sky beyond the windows.

The ladder clattered to the floor.

A booming roll of thunder shook the house.

The ceiling beams groaned with the new and unexpected weight.

At 5:10 p.m. exactly, Mack Harrington came bustling through the front door, his hair and coat dripping from the sudden downpour. In the time it took him to drive from his office to the house, the sky had turned from a lovely sunset orange to pitch-black. Lightning now painted the sky with intermittent flashes of purple-blue light, revealing a lashing deluge of icy rain mixed with hail. He was glad to be home but in a foul mood just the same, what with the strange way Emma had been acting lately and the never-ending fires he'd been putting out all afternoon at work.

He hung his still-dripping coat on the hall rack and stepped out of his muddy boots. Something smelled good; perhaps he'd save the talking-to he had been preparing for Emma all day until after he got some food in his belly.

The living room was dim, the light from the back hallway casting everything in a sickly yellow glow.

Mack had just crossed the threshold of the room when movement caught his eye. He took another few steps in, his eyes lifting slowly to the horrible scene that awaited him. Strung up from the rafters, Emma's body still swung gently back and forth, her neck twisted at an impossible angle, her eyes bulging, skin horribly pale. A terrible sight.

But it was the shadow Mack could not look away from.

Beneath her, the shadow of her body swung slowly back and forth across the living room floor, stopping short of the spot where the rug ended and swinging back to stop again just before touching the television.

* * *

Eventually, Mack had the presence of mind to tear his eyes away from the sight and call 911. The firetruck arrived within minutes, the first police car shortly after. Mack was led gently to his chair and surrounded by officers and medics; they seemed to speak a language he did not understand, full of codes and times and words he did not want to hear. The crowd swelled through his house and crammed into the living room, blocking his view as Emma's body was lowered and taken away. Finally, only two police officers remained. They asked Mack questions in gentle voices. He gave answers that he forgot as soon as the words left his mouth, until at last the officers seemed satisfied and stood to leave. One placed a hand on Mack's shoulder in a gesture meant to be consoling. Then they were gone, out into the storming night, and Mack was alone in the house.

Someone had been kind enough to turn off the heat beneath the soup, but Mack now found himself wandering into the kitchen to turn it back on. In spite of everything, his stomach growled as he mindlessly stirred. He ladled a large helping into a bowl and sat down at the table to eat it.

From his seat, he could see down the long stretch of the hallway into the living room. At some point in the evening, the lights in there had been switched on. With the room now empty of the crowd of emergency responders, Mack could see it clearly.

The shadow of his wife's corpse still swung across the floor. Back and forth. Back and forth.

* * *

Months passed. The shadow stayed. Mack began to hurry along the downstairs hall, always passing the open doorways to the living room with his eyes focused straight ahead, toward the back of the house. When he did glance into the room by accident, the shadow still swung there, left to right and back again, slowly, always slowly.

A few times, buoyed by liquid courage, Mack had dared to walk into the room, sit in his chair, and stare the shadow down. On those nights, he saw not only Emma's shadow, but Emma herself, swinging with her shoes three feet off the floor. Her bulging eyes would turn upon him suddenly, and her purple-tinged lips would curl into a sinister smile.

He stopped going in the room at all.

Some evenings when he came home, his eyes turned toward the room, though his mind pulled away. It seemed that he could see the pale outline of his wife sitting there in the darkness, in her favorite chair, her hands twisting, twisting together in her lap. A few times he opened his mouth to speak, found his feet turning toward the room where logic told him not to go, but then the cold sweep of the shadow would swing toward him, and he would step quickly back. When he glanced at the chair, Emma's shade would be gone.

Time went on. Winter turned to spring which turned to summer. Then, as if no time had passed at all, autumn descended once more, all blustery wind and scurrying leaves. Mack turned the calendar on the kitchen wall to November—a picture of a fat turkey above a grid of dates. For a moment, a pang of loneliness and guilt shot through him, but he pulled himself up to his full height and spoke unconvincing words of disdain to the empty air.

Thanksgiving arrived. Mack sat at home, alone, drinking first wine and then whiskey straight from the bottle, eating a prepackaged turkey dinner, the potatoes still partially frozen. He sighed, wishing he could go into the living room to watch the game on the television there, but he would not dare to enter that cursed space. He pushed the remains of his sad feast away and laid his head down on the table, cradled in his folded arms.

Mack awoke hours later from another nightmare, the house already submerged in darkness around him. A nervous, jittery feeling danced in his stomach, a feeling of anxious expectation. He did not trust the darkness, did not trust the house, did not trust himself to sleep.

Mack paced. Up and down the downstairs hall, up the stairs and in circles around the bedrooms. He paced while the hall clock chimed away the hours, while the people in the houses around him slept soundly, while the growing sense of dread gnawed at his stomach.

He paced until the sky beyond the windows faded from black to blue and then a somber gray. Finally, when the rays of the rising sun began to reflect off the neighbor's windows, Mack made his decision. He could not stay in this house a moment longer, not with the shadow, not with his guilt, not with *her.*

He stepped into his shoes, shrugged on a jacket, ran his fingers once more through his wild hair. He stopped one last time and forced himself to look into the living room, to stare his fear in the face in a desperate act of bravado before fleeing. The shadow was dark, distinct against the rug and the floorboards. Overhead, the ceiling beams groaned.

Mack ran for the front door, slammed it shut behind him, and stumbled down the front steps and to his truck. His fingers fumbled with the keys before finally managing to insert the right one and unlock the door. The truck rumbled to life as Mack checked the rearview mirror. His vision swam in and out of focus, a day of lonely holiday drinking and a night of nervous pacing beginning to catch up with him.

He backed out of the driveway, pointed his truck eastward, and maneuvered along the neighborhood streets until he merged onto the small highway that would take him speeding toward his office. The rising sun lit the sky in front of him in a brilliant and beautiful flash of light, blinding him just long enough for him to drive directly into the oncoming semi at seventy miles an hour.

* * *

The sun was well into its path across the sky when two uniformed officers climbed the steps of the Harrington house. Their faces were serious and sad; it was never easy delivering the news of a death to the loved ones left behind. They knocked and rang the bell several times before giving up. No one was home. The poor old guy they'd scraped off the highway, maybe he didn't even have anyone in his life to tell.

The officers climbed back into their cruiser and drove away.

In the living room of the Harrington house, the shifting shadow slowed, its arc growing smaller and smaller, until one last swing brought it to rest directly over a patch of morning sunlight. With a final breathy sigh, the shadow dispersed and floated away like the dust motes that swirled and danced in the sunbeam's glow.

I WAS GOING TO TELL YOU TONIGHT

DAVID NIALL WILSON

The pendant Nicolas wore was a blood-fattened tick sealed in acrylic. It was his own blood, of course. For that matter, it was his tick. He'd hunted it himself in the woods near the edge of the swamp. He also had leeches and had spent a solid month on the Internet learning to collect mosquitos and their eggs. The glass of their enclosure was a magnifying lens, so he could watch them. There was an opening at the top where, by driving his arm in through a rubber gasket, he could watch them land and feed on his skin. When he did this, he made me try to catch the ones who fed on him with a tiny net, but it was impossible.

He saw the whole setup on an ancient TV commercial on the Internet. In the advertisement they showed how to prevent bites. Nicolas wanted to be sucked dry. All of that was before.

I met him on the job. I'd spent three boring, interminable months training for my North Carolina Pest Control license. What to spray, when to spray, what *not* to spray, and whatever you do, don't poison the children or the pets. Wasps sting. Hornets sting harder. Always smile. Rinse and repeat.

Nicolas took that job to heart. At first, I thought it was a joke. He showed up for work dressed all in black. His one nod to corporate policy was a black T-shirt with the company logo on the breast—BUG-GONE. They would have fired him for sure, if they could, but not many people want to be exterminators and he was too good. He didn't just know pests, he knew their varietals, which poison took them out most quickly, where they bred, how long they lived, if they spread. It was eerie, and just like some kind of insect serial killer, he kept trophies. Only the hematophagous ones. Only things that fed on blood.

"It's a matter of permanence, Paulie" he told me my first day on the job. "Sure, you can save your semen at a medical clinic or have unprotected sex with a bunch of randos but think about it. Your blood? Your DNA? What they get from that isn't a kid who might not care about you one way or the other. With DNA they can get *you*. You can come back, reincarnation through cloning. Your *code* is available. You never die. You can *spread.*"

I didn't care about any of that, but I should have listened. As things started to get worse, and more serious at the same time, I should have worried. I should have stopped him. I should have left.

I did none of those things. I was a skinny kid with dark eyes and no friends. I had felt a part of something exactly one time. That was my family prior to my junior year in high school, when I told my parents I was gay and they tossed me out on my ear. My older sister took me in while I finished school, but she had a different world, and I wasn't a part of that. She supported me but like with a long stick and some serious protective walls in case I was contagious. I know she loved me, but I also know I made her uncomfortable to the point of being sick. That was my early life.

Nicky, despite his full-on goth wardrobe and strange habits, was beautiful. He was pale, but surprisingly well built. He didn't care about sports, never worked out, but he was always moving, always working. It was only three weeks after I started the job that I left my relieved sister and her perfect family behind and moved into the one-story ranch-style house he'd inherited from his parents. He said they'd been killed in an accident. I have seen and read enough horror to know not to ask for details. I didn't care.

And he wanted me. He was the first. My family was happy to have me gone, even my sister. In school, I'd been mostly ignored, but the times I wasn't were bad, and there had been no one to support me. I'd resigned myself to loneliness out of naïve, adolescent angst. Nicky changed that.

He accepted me into his world as if I had always been there. He talked constantly, sometimes about bugs, sometimes about DNA and sequencing and advancements in cloning. And he included me. He explained it, brought me gifts, made me laugh. It wasn't until he dove into darker research that things started to go so far south the compass broke.

I make no apologies. My life, up to the point when I met Nicholas, was a long string of unkept promises and people who abandoned me. Many of them claimed to love me but he was the only one who listened. Who held me in the middle of the night. Nicky was the most private man I'd ever met, but when he looked at me, it was like a window or a doorway. He seemed self-contained, but it was a sham. He needed me too.

I hated when he let the mosquitoes bite his arm. That was just the start. He brought in terrariums and kept mice and small rodents in them, but they weren't pets. He also kept ticks, lice; any creature he could find that fed on blood consumed him. He spent hours watching them, taking notes, and scribbling odd designs; not really sketches, but more like mathematical sequences. I only knew that word from what he'd taught me about DNA, but I knew that was what he was drawing.

I lived with it and worked around it until one night when he'd been working too late, and I finally coaxed him to bed. I was kissing his throat, moving down his chest, and I felt something wrong. Something I didn't recognize. Nicolas was not shy about making love. We explored one another constantly. I knew the tiny bump I felt below his nipple wasn't supposed to be there, even as his skin hardened, and he gasped. I pulled back.

"Don't stop," he said.

I should have listened. I should have made love to him and rolled over and counted black bloody sheep leaping off a cliff until I passed out, but I leaned over, yanked the cord on the lamp beside the bed, and I saw it. It was brown and ugly, attached so tightly the skin around it had puckered. I drew back and only barely managed to choke back a scream.

"What the fuck, Nicky?" I said, backing across the bed. "What the actual *FUCK* is that thing. And. . ."

I knew, of course. It was one of the leeches, and it was swollen with his blood. He held up a hand.

"Wait," he said. He gripped the thing, worked it back and forth a few times, then ripped it free, like removing a Band-Aid. There was a bloody welt on his chest, but he managed to free that thing without crushing or killing it. I couldn't take my eyes off it. Its underbelly was red with his blood.

He held it out to me.

"I was going to tell you tonight," he said softly. "I want to share this, all of this," he swept the room with a quick glance, then turned his gaze on me. Those eyes. I wanted to reach out and stroke his cheek. I wanted to tell him to throw that goddamned thing away and we could find another place, another job.

"I have so much to show you," he said. "So much to share. But this," he waved the squirming leech absently. "This sharing. We have to be joined."

He reached out then, and before I could bat his hand away, or scream, he pressed the leech to my chest. I felt its sudden grip, felt it settle and dig, but Nicky's fingers were stroking my cheek at the same time, and he leaned closer. I tried to pull away, but his breath was sweet, and close. His hand slid down my hip and all thoughts of blood and leeches vanished.

When I woke, and the memories flooded back, I reached quickly to my chest. Nothing. I glanced down. There was a red, sore spot directly below my left nipple. Near my heart. Nicky was nowhere to be seen. I tried not to think about it, but my skin burned, and I was suddenly afraid I'd vomit. I ran to the bathroom, closed the door behind me and ran cold water over my face. Then I showered. I turned the water so hot it scalded. I rubbed soap across the puckered skin, rubbed harder and harder. The water was too hot, and I felt layers of skin falling away. The soap felt coarse and I couldn't stop myself from scrubbing until it seemed like I would scrub my bones.

Then the panic broke and I was able to breathe. I scrabbled for the faucet handle, stopped the water, and rested my forehead on the tiled wall of the shower. I closed my eyes and slowly ran back through the events of the previous night. When I reached that moment, that dark moment, tears flowed down my cheeks, but I felt myself stiffen.

I dried off, returned to the bedroom, and dressed quickly. I told myself I was going to leave, but I knew better. I found Nicky bent over his workbench. We had about an hour before we were supposed to report to work. He looked like he'd been up all night. He had something in a glass bowl, and I knew what it had to be. I didn't get close enough to see.

"Hey," I said.

He turned and smiled, and my reserve crumbled.

"We should get breakfast," I said.

"One minute. I just need to preserve this properly."

He rose and dragged a vial from a rack above the bench. He lifted something from the bowl with a pair of large tweezers. I turned away. I knew, but I couldn't look. I heard the clink of glass and liquid pouring. A moment later, he was at my side, one arm around my waist.

"Shall we execute some roaches?" he asked, pressing his hip into mine and pulling me close. I bit my lip, tried to form a protest, and then, I followed him out of that dark place.

That day he stopped telling me things. He'd explain in vague terms, but he was up late every night. New specimens and terrariums appeared and disappeared. Strange books that I opened but couldn't read littered his workbench. There were diagrams on the wall above the bench. Jars and vials lined the shelves, but they weren't labeled, and I couldn't imagine their contents, or could and chose not to. Some of them held specimens from his collection, suspended in various liquids.

It wasn't that he wasn't attentive. He was—obsessively. It was the disconnected segments of his life, growing more numerous and complex. The way his skin grew even paler, and he lost weight. He ate as much, if not more, than he ever had, but I knew that meant nothing. I'd had a friend who ate like a starved animal and left every drop in the bathroom when she thought no one was looking. She died not long after they locked her up "for her own good," but I never forgot that lesson. Appearances deceive. People deceive. Pain is a powerful mistress. So, I watched him waste away. His color faded until he could have passed for a mime without using makeup.

His energy never wavered. His eyes blazed with...something. Sometimes, when he stared at me too long, I felt that heat drawing me to him. I tried to answer but he diverted me. I know he felt my need. Sometimes he drew me close and used his body to shift my mind from the questions that were eating me alive but mostly, teasingly, he kept me wanting him to the point of distraction.

There were no more leeches. No ticks. He neglected the mosquito habitat, and the few times I glanced at it, I saw no movement. No life. With nothing to feed on, they'd died. We still went out daily, sprayed basements and yards, excised hornets and wasps, and even on a couple of occasions re-homed hives of honeybees. He went through the motions, but I felt him withdrawing from that world. From my world. I should have let him go.

And I should never have looked under the bed. A dropped quarter that rolled beneath and me thinking I might need it to help pay for my coffee. An odd sound, so slight I nearly passed it off as nothing caught my attention. Then I saw the case, long and slender, reaching to the bottom of the box springs and the ends of the frame. The second time the sound came, I was sure. It was a strange sound, wet, but like a scratch. There was something there.

I tried to move the case, but it was heavy, and I knew Nicky was waiting for me outside. I suddenly very much did not want him to know what I'd seen, so I abandoned the quarter, dropped the blankets back over the side of the bed, turned, and ran.

It was a busy morning and I lost myself in the work. I spoke as little as possible because inside I was screaming, and I knew if I tried to make small talk I'd fail. He would know. Nicky had a way of reading the tone of my voice or even the way I walked.

"You okay?" he said.

We'd just rooted a stubborn nest of hornets out from under a hedge a little too close to a farmhouse. He was wearing the safety hood, and I couldn't make out his features. I felt queasy and weak. I couldn't concentrate, and it must have shown.

"No. My stomach is a wreck." I went for it. "Is there any way you could drop me home and finish without me? I need to lie down."

He only hesitated for a second, then nodded.

"Let me get rid of this nest. The house is on the way to the last stop—some problem with spiders. I can manage that."

"Thanks." I didn't try for more words, and I wrapped my arms around my stomach and hunched over. It was only partially an act. Fifteen minutes later, I was climbing out of the truck.

"You sure you'll be, okay?" Nicky asked. "Should I bring anything?"

"I'll be okay. I just need to rest."

My imagination? Did he stare at me a little more carefully? Did he hesitate a little longer? He turned away. I counted to ten slowly, then turned and shuffled to the door. I heard the truck pull away but kept my pace slow until I was sure he was gone.

I'm not a big guy. The frame of the bed Nicky and I shared was wood and not heavy, but I still struggled. I grabbed the headboard and slid it to the side, then the footboard. The final leg banged into that tank, or whatever it was. The sound was like a deep-toned gong, or one of those singing bowls. It vibrated up through my feet, and I thought, *no, that's not possible,* and started pulling on the bed frame again. It took several minutes to scoot the bed far enough to make out what was beneath.

Except, even after I'd uncovered it, I couldn't see. The base was dark metal, almost black. The top—the lid?—was thick glass, but it was either black, or smoky, or whatever was inside was too dark for my gaze to penetrate. I knelt and put my hand on top of the thing and there was a tingle, another vibration, as if it had reacted to me. I jerked my hand away and dug in my heels, scooting across the room so quickly my back came up against the dresser on the opposite wall. My head caromed off the middle drawer and I cried out.

A new sound emanated from the tank. I reached to rub my head where it had hit the glass knob on the dresser drawer. Then the pain shifted. That sound, that vibration blended with it and dissipated it. I shook my head, and that brought the pain crashing back.

"What. . .?"

The sound came again. It wasn't as much of a shock, but I still wasn't prepared. I rolled forward and crawled back across the floor. Fascinated, I pressed my palms to the glass. There was an instant shiver of energy. My back arched, just for a second. The pain disappeared again. Everything, really. Everything I knew, or thought I knew, was sucked into another place. I shivered and I swear my bones caught the frequency. They hummed, branching out from my fingertips, up my arms through my shoulders, and then down my spine.

Deep in my mind was a place where I was screaming, where I wanted more than anything to pull free and run, run until that tank and that room and everything associated with it was nothing but a bad memory. I barely noticed when Nicky slid down behind me. He pulled me against him, careful not to dislodge me from the tank. I leaned into him and felt him harden against me, but that only seemed a part of the greater whole.

Nicky leaned forward, reaching around me to the tank to place his hands beside mine. Then, slowly, he slid his fingers past mine and down over the side. There must have been hidden clasps, something I'd missed. A moment later he lifted the lid slowly. The weight of my hands and my arms opposed him, but he was strong, and as he lifted, my fingers slid off and down. They rested on the edge of the tank. Something wet, soft, and smooth pressed against my fingertips.

That touch triggered the last of my willpower. I yanked my hands back. At the same time, I brought my knees up, planted them against the tank, and pressed back into Nicky. Somehow, he was carrying the signal, that vibration, and transferring it to me through his touch. I screamed and kicked. The connection, whatever it was, broke with an audible snap, like a shorted light switch.

Nicky lost his grip and tumbled backward. I saw his eyes, so wide and full of shock, and I tried to rise and reach out to him, but far too late. His head slammed into the same dresser I'd hit earlier but not on the flat wood. The knob caught him right at the base of his skull and he hit hard, hanging there, mouth open and arms suddenly flopping about as if disconnected from his brain.

The sound grew louder, and I clapped my hands over my ears. No good, it was reaching up through the soles of my feet, calling me back. I turned and saw something dark sliding over the edge of the tank. It was fat and swollen. My mind flashed back to Nicky and the leech, and I shuddered.

Nicky had managed to pull loose from the dresser. His eyes were unfocused, but he was gathering strength from that thing as it drew nearer to him. His lips moved, but no sound came out at first. Then, softly, like whistling through a broken flute, "We were... joining. I was going to tell you... show you. I..."

The leech, that's what it was, what it had to be, reached his legs and gripped, drawing itself up and over him like a giant, blood-gorged inchworm. Nicky's body stiffened but his eyes cleared. He lifted an arm, not quite in control of it, and reached for me. "We can be together forever. She will spread us across the world to gather others. Come back."

I turned, and I ran. I didn't close the door behind me. I didn't call the police. I'm sure they are looking for me. My things were there, all my things—my life. But I can't go back. I have to keep moving. There are times when I'm trying to sleep that I'm certain I hear that sound, that it's growing closer and louder. Sometimes I dream, and Nicky whispers in my ear, so close I can feel his breath, but I awaken to nothing.

It's only a matter of time, I know. The part of me that responded to that vibration, that energy, is calling out to them. I can't make it silent. I don't always want it to be silent. They are spreading across the world and a part of me, the blood stolen that single night of passion, spreads with them. One day, we will be one.

But not today.

THE IVORY BED

JESSICA AMANDA SALMONSON

I remember a sable beauty
I met at Shelley's Leg
Clad in silken violet laces
Oh, her languid gaze.

She might have been
Lilith's most privileged daughter
Princess of the Esoteric Night
Goddess of ghosts in violent places.

She kept watching me
And there was that shy smile
Such as helped me find the nerve to say
"You are by far the loveliest woman
here."
She so quickly quipped
"And you're a Botticelli angel."

All these long years later

Having become a cynic and ill-humored
Well-worn or corroded,
Hunched like a savage satirist's
Parody of Vice,
I recall those first quick moments
Of our meeting,
Then condemn myself, or Time,
For having so defaced
What she had consecrated.

But then I recall
What I had forgotten until now:
This was the one, the only night I
performed
In Shelley's Ivory Bed, so rarely seen
That I had heretofore regarded it as
legend.

We writhed, we murmured, with
Cameras clicking overhead,
So that I know somewhere, to this day,
In a private collection
Someone yet possesses
The photographic evidence
Of the carnality of two angels,
The Sacred, the Profane.

BLOODY ROOTS

BRIAN KEENE

Doug Kent stood frightened and waiting, hands stuffed into the pockets of his jacket. The night was unseasonably cold for early September. His breath fogged in front of his face. The sounds of a television came from across the street—the home of the Stackpoles. Their curtains weren't yet drawn, and he saw Jim and Bonnie sitting together on their couch, laughing at whatever they were watching. Only then did Doug notice that their windows were open. So, too, were the windows of the family who lived to the right of them. And on this side of the road, he heard the quiet mechanical hum of the air conditioner in Morty Adams's window.

The only place it was cold was here in his front yard. The rest of the neighborhood was enjoying normal temperatures.

He felt the house behind him, a looming and insistent presence, but he did not turn to face it. Doug hadn't been inside since they'd left. His wife, Marissa, and their son, Doug Jr., were at a Days Inn up on Route 30. They'd been staying there nearly a week now, ever since fleeing in the night after their German Shephard, Pikachu (named so by Doug Jr.), got turned inside out and smeared—still living—all over the walls, ceiling, and floor of the family room. One minute they'd all been sitting together, just like Jim and Bonnie Stackpole were doing. The next? Well, the next minute Bosco had whimpered. Then there was a squelching implosion, followed by a wet *expansion.* And then the family room was covered with the dog like peanut butter and jelly across a slice of bread. Pikachu had still been whimpering and yelping—his mouth situated up near the light fixture while his tail was down by the electrical socket on the other side of the room—when they'd fled, screaming.

That hadn't been the first thing the ghost had done, but it was definitely the worst.

Doug wondered if Pikachu was still alive, even now. He hated himself for abandoning the dog. Hated his cowardice. He'd told himself that it hadn't been so, in the heat of the moment, and technically, he was right. His only thought at the time had been to get Marissa and Doug Jr. to safety. But he hadn't gone back for the dog. Hadn't wondered if there was some way to reverse what had happened. Hadn't returned to put poor Pikachu out of his misery. Hell, he couldn't even bring himself to turn around and look at the house. Just standing here in the yard, and knowing it was there behind him, filled Doug with a deep and abiding dread. If that wasn't cowardice, then he didn't know what was.

Doug Jr. was worried about his hermit crabs. He had two of them, obtained last summer during their family trip to Ocean City, Maryland. Like the dog, he'd named them after various Pokémon characters, but Doug couldn't remember what those names actually were. If he was any sort of father, he'd march inside right now and rescue the damned things and take them back to the Days Inn tonight. He'd get the fish, too, although they were more Marissa's than they were the boy's, and she hadn't mentioned them since the escape. Of course, who even knew if they were still alive? They hadn't been fed in a week. And there was a possibility that whatever was inside the house had done the same to them as it had to the dog.

He heard a soft clopping sound coming from farther down the street, just audible over the other noises. He peered into the darkness, frowning. A horse appeared, pulling an Amish buggy behind it. The driver was in his late thirties or early forties. He had a full, black beard, and was dressed modestly—black shoes and pants, a white button-down shirt, black jacket, and black hat. Doug took an involuntary step backward, felt the house's presence push against him, and then moved forward to the curb again.

The horse neighed softly and stopped in front of the house. Curiously, the driver didn't pull back on the reins or seem to give any sort of command. He stared down at Doug, touched the brim of his hat, and then smiled.

"Mister Kent?"

Doug nodded. "I'm sorry. I don't mean to stare. It's just that. . . well, Nelson said you were a ghost hunter. I guess I wasn't expecting you to be Amish."

The man's smile remained. "Nelson was correct in that ghost hunting is one of the services I can provide, although I tend not to think of it in those terms. But I'm not Amish."

"Oh?" Doug blinked. "Mennonite, then?"

The man shook his head. "No, I'm not Mennonite, either. If it helps, just consider me nondenominational."

"I'm sorry," Doug repeated. "I saw the buggy, and your clothes, and your beard. I just assumed. . ."

"I was Amish," the man explained, slowly climbing down onto the sidewalk. "But that was a long time ago. I like the clothes and the beard, so I kept them. The buggy? Well, have you seen the price of gas lately? Plus, old Dee here likes to get out of the stable."

"Pretty horse. Pretty name."

"Thank you." The man gently patted the horse's neck. "Dee and Crowley—he's my dog—have been with me a long time. I don't know what I'd do without them."

The mention of the dog made Doug think about Pikachu again. He imagined him still smeared across the house, tail thumping against the wall. Tears welled in his eyes.

"You may call me Levi." The man stuck out his hand. "And it's going to be okay."

Shuddering, Doug began to sob. He shook the man's hand, but it was all he could do not to collapse to his knees in front of him. "T-thank you... I... I'm s-sorry... it's just been..."

Levi stared at him with a sympathetic expression. Then he gestured to the street. Still holding Doug's hand, he led him to the other side of the buggy, putting it between them and the house. Through his tears, Doug noticed that the horse was eyeing the house warily. It stomped one hoof and snorted.

"Easy, girl," Levi said. "All in good time."

Doug let go of his hand and wiped his eyes with his knuckles.

"Mr. Kent—"

"Please, call me Doug. And I am so sorry about all of this."

"There's no need to apologize. From what Nelson has told me, you and your family have been through an ordeal."

Doug heaved a heavy sigh. "We have. My father died back in August. And then... all of this stuff started happening. It's been a bad four weeks. Nelson told you what's been going on?"

"He did. Furniture and other objects moving by themselves. Strange noises. Temperature fluctuations. A ghostly figure. Your dog."

"Yeah. All that, and more. Although, it wasn't a ghostly figure. I mean, I guess it was a ghost. I don't see what else it could be. But it wasn't transparent, you know? It was solid."

"What did it look like?"

"It was. . ." Doug paused. "It was like an old wooden man and an old wooden woman, fused together. Like two wooden people in one body. Does that make sense?"

Levi nodded, stroking his beard.

"Do you know what it is?"

"No. At least, not yet." He looked up over the buggy and stared at the house. Then he turned back to Doug again. "My condolences on your father. Was he a religious man?"

Doug snorted. "No. He was about as far from religious as you can get. Why? You don't think this is him, do you?"

"Not necessarily. But judging by what you've just said, the haunting began shortly after his death. They could be connected."

"So, you believe me then?"

Levi reached out and clasped his shoulder. Doug was surprised by the strength in the man's grip—and the warmth.

"I believe something sinister is happening inside your home. I can feel it from here. So does Dee. She's very sensitive to these things. Plus, Nelson has been a good friend to me for many years now. He vouches for you."

Doug's lip quivered as he fought back tears again. This time, they sprang from relief and gratitude. "Can. . . can you help us?"

Levi offered a tight-lipped smile. "I intend to try."

"D-do I have to. . . come with you?"

"No! Not at all. I work better alone. Where are you parked? I don't see a car in your driveway."

"I parked down at the end of the street."

"Good. Why don't you go wait in your car? I'll come find you when I'm done. It may take me a while."

"Can you just leave your buggy parked here? Will it be safe?"

"Oh, yes. Whatever the presence is inside your house, its power doesn't extend this far. Its malevolence does, but that's nothing more than. . . well, it's like a skunk, spraying the air. The actual manifestation is inside your home. But even if it could get to us out here, both Dee and the buggy are well protected. As am I. No worries."

Levi clambered up into the back of the buggy, knelt, and opened a wooden box at the back. Doug saw him remove a small brown book and place it inside his jacket, presumably in a hidden pocket. Then he removed a black cloth bag, opened it, and placed several other items inside. In the gloom, Doug couldn't make out what they were. Levi stashed this inside his jacket, as well. Then he closed the box, locked it, and climbed back down to the curb.

"Okay, I think I have everything I need. I'll go inside and check things out."

"Don't you need my key to unlock the door?"

Levi winked at him. "No, that's okay. I've got my own."

Doug stood gaping as the ex-Amish ghost hunter strolled across the yard. His pace was leisurely and nonchalant. He whistled a tune that Doug didn't recognize. Shivering, Doug turned away and hurried to his car as Levi approached the front door.

* * *

Levi heard a car door close down the street and knew that the homeowner was now safely out of immediate harm's way. He finished humming the old Susquehannock blessing tune and stood staring at the home's front door. The energy boiling out of the house was unlike anything he'd ever felt before. He couldn't identify it, but he had a sense that it was very old and of the earth. He'd hoped that it might react to the magic of this area's indigenous peoples, which is why he'd whistled the melody, but instead, that feeling of malevolence continued unabated.

"Okay," he whispered. "So maybe you're older than that. Maybe you were here before the Susquehannock people."

He stared at the house and felt something staring back at him. The blinds and curtains were drawn tight. Lights were still on in several rooms. He assumed that was because the family had fled in a hurry. He cocked his head, listening. There was something. . . undefinable. A whimper, maybe? A cry? Perhaps the Kents had left a television on in their rush to leave.

"The cross of Christ be with me," he prayed aloud. "The cross of Christ overcomes all water and every fire. The cross of Christ overcomes all weapons. The cross of Christ is a perfect sign and blessing to my soul. Now I pray that the holy corpse of Christ bless me against all evil things, words, and works."

Again, there was no reaction from the house. That air of menace seemed to just hang there.

Levi's free hand drifted to his coat, patting the bulge over his left breast. A battered copy of *The Long-Lost Friend* lay snuggled in his inner pocket. It had been his father's and his father's before him. The front page of the book held the following inscription: "Whoever carries this book with him is safe from all his enemies, visible or invisible; and whoever has this book with him cannot die without the holy corpse of Jesus Christ, nor be drowned in any water, nor burn up in any fire, nor can any unjust sentence be passed upon him."

If the force inside the home was of Judeo-Christian origin, surely there would have been some reaction to his prayer. He made a third attempt, reciting a benediction against evil.

"Ut nemo in sense tentat, descendere nemo. At precedenti spectaur mantica tergo. Hecate. Hecate. Hecate."

Again, there was nothing.

"Hmmm. . ."

Levi's neighbors knew him as a woodworker. On weekdays, he made coat and spoon racks, lawn ornaments, decorations, and other knick-knacks in his garage. On Saturdays he sold them from a stall at the local flea market. But he also had a second occupation. Levi worked powwow magic, as his father and his father before him. Patients, mostly the elderly, who remembered the old ways, or the poor, who couldn't afford healthcare, came to him seeking treatments for everything from the common cold to arthritis. Farmers called upon him to heal their livestock. Occasionally, he dealt with more serious matters like stopping bleeding or mending a broken bone.

And there were also times when he was charged with doing more than helping the sick or curing livestock.

Times like now.

Levi wasn't just versed in powwow. He'd studied a multitude of magical and occult disciplines from all over the world—and some other worlds, as well. It was this that had led to his excommunication and banishment from his church and family. But Levi was of a mind that the Lord had given him the knowledge and ability to learn these other ways and use them to glorify Him and do His will upon Earth. Thus, in addition to being a folk doctor, he was also sometimes an exorcist, medium, occult detective, slayer of monsters, killer of vampires, and even a ghost hunter, as Mr. Kent had referred to him.

But before he could deal with whatever was inside the house, he first had to investigate and identify it.

Sighing, he pulled the small bag from inside his jacket pocket and opened it. He selected a sprig of chicory root and shoved it into the keyhole. Then he clasped the doorknob in his hand and directed his will at the door. Slowly, he turned the knob. The lock clicked and the door opened a crack. Finished, he removed the chicory and returned it to the bag.

"Okay," he whispered, "let's learn more about you."

He pushed open the door. It swung back silently, revealing a small foyer with a tiled floor and a lovely hickory end table. Atop this sat a glass bowl with several pairs of keys and some loose change. Framed photos of the family hung on the wall. Beyond, there were openings to the left and right, as well as a staircase leading to the second floor. Light emanated from what he assumed must be the living room or family room.

Then, it went out, plunging the house into darkness.

Levi rummaged through his pockets, pulled out a compact flashlight, and turned it on. He shined the beam about. It occurred to him that just moments before, he'd seen lights on in other rooms, as well. Now, there were none.

On the street, Dee whinnied nervously.

Hoping that the inscription in his copy of *The Long-Lost Friend* would once again hold true, Levi crossed the threshold and stepped inside.

The door slammed shut behind him.

He jumped, startled, and nearly dropped the flashlight.

"I enter freely and with the permission of those who live here," he said, hating the tremor of fright in his voice. "I ask that you show yourself to me, spirit, and give me your name."

Footsteps padded softly above his head, on the second floor. Judging by the sound, it was either more than one entity or something with multiple appendages. Levi pointed the flashlight at the ceiling, following their path. When the footfalls reached the top of the stairwell, they stopped, and then retreated, going back the way they had come. The sound stopped, as if whatever was making the noise were now standing still and waiting.

He heard another sound then, that same whimpering that had caught his attention while he was outside. It was louder now, but still muted.

Levi sniffed the air but found nothing amiss. Certain entities had a smell, but all he detected was the faint hint of cleaning products and potpourri. Nor did he see anything out of the ordinary. There were no misplaced objects or moving shadows or angles where angles shouldn't be. No pools of ectoplasm or clouds of dark matter. No vortexes or discernible doors to other realities. Indeed, other than the sounds above, and the overall feeling of oppressive malignance, there was no sign of anything out of the ordinary. That psychic malevolence, though—so heavy and encompassing—left no doubt that something dark and powerful had been loosed in this space.

Levi traced his beam across the wall, studying the family photos. He'd purposely not asked Doug Kent a lot of questions because he'd wanted both his conscious and subconscious mind free of influence and suggestion. His only knowledge of the overall situation was what the homeowner had told him on the street, and what Nelson had told him when asking Levi if he could help. The photos revealed more of the story—a smiling family, happy and joyous in every scene. Mrs. Kent was beautiful. Their son was adorable. He spotted an older man in a few of the photographs. He assumed this was the grandfather who had recently passed away. There was also a dog in several of the photographs—a beautiful, large German Shephard. Levi glanced back over his shoulder to see if there were any photographs that he might have missed on his way in. His eyes widened.

The hickory end table now hung upside down from the ceiling. The glass bowl was next to it. The spare keys and change remained inside, defying the laws of gravity.

"Can you reveal yourself to me entirely?" He struggled to keep the tremor out of his voice. "What is your name, spirit?"

The whining sound came again.

Levi turned around to find that the light was back on in the room to his right. Slowly, he clicked off the flashlight and approached the doorway. When he rounded the corner, he stopped, gasping.

He'd found the Kent's dog.

The walls, floor, and ceiling of what had once been a family room were now wet and red. The dog had been stretched across them, with horrific spacing round each window, the light fixtures, and electrical outlets. The furniture sat atop the mess. Still functioning organs glistened obscenely. A heart fluttered rhythmically amidst the offal. Feeling his gorge rise, Levi traced the circulatory system, gaping as he watched blood visibly flow through the intricate network. The animal whined again. He turned his head upward, following the sound. A pair of dark, soulful eyes stared back at him, full of pain.

Crying out in despair, Levi muttered the curse of B'nath—a powerful spell that brought instant death with just a touch. The words felt like sawdust in his throat. He prodded the moist, living wall with his index finger. The dog fell silent. The heart stopped in mid-beat. In the silence that followed, he heard his own pulse hammering.

Then the room erupted with noise. Simultaneously, the big-screen television, video game console, fish tank pump and filter, and the household's voice assistant all clicked on in an abrupt cacophony of sound. Startled, Levi dropped the flashlight. The television blared a sitcom he didn't recognize. The voice assistant speaker chimed and glowed, and then a voice that sounded both male and female issued forth from it, speaking in what Levi thought was Vietnamese.

"Ninh Hòa," it said. *"Khánh Hòa."*

Frowning, Levi fought down his panic and pondered the situation. This was no ghost—no poltergeist or run-of-the-mill haunting. The dog, the voice, the overall malice—these were signs of something demonic. Yet the activity didn't align with any demon he knew of. He stood up straight and puffed out his chest.

"I, Levi Stoltzfus, son of Amos, demand that you show yourself to me! In the name of—"

He choked as digestive acid burned his throat—an aftereffect of the spell he'd just used. Eyes watering, he rubbed his neck and coughed. Then he bent over to retrieve the flashlight. As he stood back up, the water in the fish tank began to roil and bubble. Inside, the fish frantically darted back and forth in obvious distress. The water churned faster and louder, and the sides of the glass tank began to fog. Steam rose from the top. The smell of cooking fish filled the air. Perversely, Levi's stomach grumbled.

"Enough," he rasped. "Enough of this cruelty! These creatures did no harm to you. They were innocent!"

"Quay lại," said the voice on the home speaker. Again, it sounded like two people speaking in unison.

"I don't understand. I demand your name. I demand that you reveal yourself to me! Your true form!"

"Quay lại."

"Give me two minutes," said a woman on the television. "And meet me upstairs."

The program's live studio audience laughed at this. Levi did not.

"Quay lại. Quay lại va nhin thay toi."

Levi's stomach cramped again as he slowly turned around, intent on exploring the rest of the house. He faltered, nearly dropping the flashlight again when he realized that he was no longer alone in the room. The entity had manifested itself behind him, blocking the doorway. It was difficult for him to comprehend its form. The thing stood tall, stretching from floor to ceiling. It resembled a tree, but one made out of people—specifically, two humans: a man and a woman. Both were naked, and made of wood, with bark for flesh. No faces or heads were discernable, but their bodies made up the bulk of the trunk, twisting and intertwined.

Tensing, Levi gestured with his hands, preparing for battle. Instead, the entity simply raised one branch and pointed at the stairwell.

"What are you still doing here?" the woman on the television asked. "I thought you were going to meet me upstairs?"

The audience laughed again as Levi cautiously slipped by the manifestation and made his way to the stairs. He gripped the banister and peered upward. A light flicked on above him.

Shuddering, he began to ascend. The psychic presence grew stronger with each step. When he reached the top, it seemed to hit him like a wall. But he realized now that it wasn't evil he sensed. It wasn't malice, so much as it was anger. A deep and abiding resentment almost physical in its intensity. He felt as if he were wading through it as he made his way down the hall, like dog paddling in a swimming pool filled with vexation.

The light led him to the child's bedroom. The rage was strongest here, and Levi had some difficulty entering. Breathing became difficult. Unlike downstairs, nothing was amiss. As far as he could tell, all the toys and furniture were in their right places. Nothing levitated or moved.

Closing his eyes, he drew a deep breath, held it, and exhaled. His chest ached with the effort. He waited until he felt a tug at the edges of his consciousness. Then, eyes still closed, he allowed himself to be pulled until the psychic anger grew so loud that he thought his head might burst. He opened his eyes and found himself standing in front of an eighteen-gallon terrarium. Several dead hermit crabs lay inside atop bedding made from sand and shredded coconut husks. There were a number of enclosures and vines for them to climb. In the center of the tank stood a piece of dried wood. One end had been thrust into the bedding. The other scraped against the screened top. The shard's aura was completely black—something that was impossible since only living things possessed auras.

Head pounding, Levi fumbled with the top of the terrarium. His fingers felt numb and swollen. He finally managed to lift it up and grab the wood. When he did, the sensation abruptly vanished. It was as if the entity had left the home. But Levi knew better. Even if he couldn't sense it, he was certain that the thing—whatever it was—remained, lurking. He released the object and let the lid fall closed. His ears rang. He worked his jaw back and forth to relieve the pressure until they popped.

"I don't understand," he said, addressing the empty room, "but I want to. I have given you my name as a warning, but now I give it to you in good faith. I am Levi Stoltzfus, son of Amos, and I will help you if I can. But I will need time. I wish to leave this place now, unmolested, and unimpeded."

He made his way back down the hall, flinching when the light in the child's room flicked off behind him. He resisted the nearly overwhelming urge to run, and instead focused on slow, deliberate footfalls. When he reached the foyer, he tensed again. Then, he grabbed the doorknob and turned. The door opened freely.

"I'll be back," he promised.

He closed the door behind him, walked halfway across the yard, and then collapsed, shivering, until Doug Kent eventually came to check on him.

"Mr. Stoltzfus? Are you okay? Are you hurt?"

Levi raised one arm and weakly waved him off. Then, panting, he clambered to his feet. Both men hurried for the safety of the street.

"What did you do? What is it?"

"I don't know," Levi gasped, trying to catch his breath. "This is something I have never encountered before."

"Like a demon or something?"

"Possibly," Levi admitted. "As I said, I just don't know."

"What happened in there? Did you. . . our dog was. . ." Doug choked, unable to finish.

Levi reached out and grasped the grieving man's shoulder. "I took care of the dog. It was quick and painless. He suffers no more."

Sniffling, Doug whispered, "Thank you. I couldn't. . . I just couldn't."

"It's okay. And that's normal and okay. Nothing to be ashamed of. Most people couldn't. That's why God brought me to you. Because I can, when needed."

"That's no way to go through life."

Instead of agreeing, Levi changed the subject. "The hermit crab tank in your son's room. There was a piece of wood in the enclosure."

Doug nodded. "Yeah. My father had a cedar chest with stuff from the war—one of his old uniforms, a bayonet, some photographs. It was in with them. I figured it must have had sentimental value to him, but I don't know why. My father never talked much about the war. After he died, I gave it to my son for his crabs. He likes watching them climb it."

"The Vietnam War?"

"Yeah. He and Mom had me late in life. Why? Is it important?"

"It might be," Levi mused, "but I don't know yet. Did your father ever experience anything like what you've been through?"

Doug shook his head. "Never."

"You're sure?"

"Positive. None of this started until after he died."

"After he died, or after you took the wood?"

Doug hesitated. "After we took the wood."

Levi stroked his beard, thinking.

"What's going on," Doug asked. "It's just a piece of wood,

right? I mean, it's nearly petrified. How could it be causing all of this?"

"Again, we can't assume anything yet."

"I'm sorry. It's just. . . we want our lives back."

Smiling sympathetically, Levi hoisted himself up into the back of the buggy. "I understand. I'll do my best to return them to you soon."

"So, what happens now. Are you going to do an exorcism or something?"

"Not quite." He rummaged around inside the large wooden box and pulled out a cannister of table salt. Then he waggled it at Doug. The homeowner frowned.

"Salt?"

"Got it at Sam's Club," Levi said. "I use it in bulk."

He crossed the yard again and stooped over, sprinkling a thick line of salt across the front doorstep. Then he continued pouring, making an unbroken line all around the perimeter of the house. When he'd reached the front door again, he thrust the index finger of his right hand into the line. Finished, he returned to the buggy and tossed the empty container in the back.

"Is that it?" Doug glanced at the house in confusion.

"That will help contain things for now," Levi explained. "I don't think it can leave your home. But just in case, the salt will make it think twice."

"What will you do in the meantime?"

"Research. I'll be in touch."

Doug blinked. "Research?"

Levi nodded. "That's the part those paranormal reality television programs never show. Ninety percent of any investigation is spent in libraries or on Google."

"They should make one of those shows about you."

Levi climbed up into the bench seat and took the reins in his hands. "Trust me, Mr. Kent. Nobody wants to see the things I've seen.

* * *

It was nearly midnight before Levi reached his home. He parked the buggy in the driveway, unhitched Dee, and led her into the stable. After feeding the horse and changing her water, he walked toward the house. Crowley, tethered in the backyard, crawled out of his doghouse, and wagged his tail enthusiastically. Levi frowned, noticing not for the first time how much slower the dog moved, and how he favored his rear hips.

"Hey buddy." He patted the dog's head and scratched his ears as he unfastened him. Then the two made their way to the front door. It was unlocked, as per Levi's custom. A series of mystical wards and circles of protection formed an invisible barrier between the edge of the yard and the door, each one stronger than the last. Perhaps only two dozen people on the planet would be able to pass through them all unmolested and without triggering an alarm. And any who did would then have to face the invisible guardian lurking just inside the foyer. Levi himself felt it now, as Crowley darted ahead, and he closed the door behind them. The guardian loomed; a length of darkness coiled amongst the shadows where the wall met the ceiling. Like the dog, it too was happy that Levi was home.

Crowley danced, tongue lolling and nails clicking on the kitchen floor, as Levi prepared his supper—a can of dog food supplemented with herbs from the garden to ease the animal's hip pain. While the dog ate, Levi spooned some ham and bean stew out of a crockpot left simmering at low heat on the counter. He carried the bowl down the hall. Crowley scrambled after him, expression hopeful.

"This is mine. I've told you—you need to savor your dinner,

rather than gobble it down. And besides, this has onions and garlic in it. Those aren't good for you."

A room at the end of the hall served as a combination den and library. Levi placed his bowl on the coffee table to let it cool, balancing it next to a marble chess set, and turned to the bookshelves, which occupied all four walls and stretched floor to ceiling. These were overloaded with old, unabridged esoteric and occult volumes—Frazer's *The Golden Bough*, the collected works of John Dee, Francis Barrett's *The Magus*, the *Book of Soyga*, the *Cipher Manuscripts* (including the Johannes Trithemius cipher), all of Aleister Crowley's occult writings, the *Theatrum Chemicum*, a translation of the *Alexandria Codex of Sofia*, and even a scattering of loose pages from the *Necronomicon*. There were also countless research books and indexes on things like parapsychology, cryptozoology, cults, ancient peoples, and more. His eBook reader sat on a nearby desk. It held digital copies of most of these volumes in case he needed to refer to them when traveling, which was often. But it also held countless more.

It took Levi fifteen minutes to scan the shelves and find anything having to do with Vietnamese folklore, magic, or paranormal legends. In total, there were six books he thought might be helpful. He carried them over to an armchair, took a seat, and began to read, smiling to himself as he did, thinking back on his conversation with Doug. Research was the bulk of any paranormal investigation. Knowledge was power—and a weapon. To force a confrontation with any sort of supernatural entity without having first done one's research was like standing unarmed on the beaches of Normandy during the D-Day landings.

Crowley turned in a circle three times, lay down beside the chair, and fell asleep almost immediately. Soon, the only sounds were the dog's soft snores and the flipping of pages.

It was nearly dawn before Levi finished, and his uneaten stew had long since cooled. He looked up from his studies, pinched the bridge of his nose, closed his eyes, and sighed.

There were many mentions of demonic trees in Vietnamese folklore. The legend of Lac Long told of an old tree possessed by an evil genie. Reading up on that had led him to something called *cây quỷ*, which—according to the source—was Vietnamese for "devil tree." He couldn't be sure, of course, and therein lay the danger. It was folly for him, a Pennsylvanian who was raised Amish to take a crash course in Vietnamese occult folklore and become an expert overnight. There were people far better suited to tackle this than he was. A shaman from the Ruc people, who lived in the high mountains of Vietnam could have handled this haunting easily, but Levi knew no one among them. By all accounts, they eschewed modern technology, so it wasn't like he could send an email. He could do his best to replicate the *bùa chú* magic incantations and amulets, or fashion some *bùa ngải* potions based on the instructions before him, but it wasn't lost on him that he wasn't even sure how to correctly pronounce those things. Finding a Ruc shaman or another expert would take time, and time wasn't something that Doug Kent and his family had.

Despite his misgivings, Levi thought the most likely culprit could be found in the myth of Tinh Cây Ráy—an ancient ayurvedic tree that had originated in the forests around Ninh Hòa, a small city in Vietnam's Khánh Hòa province. Tinh Cây Ráy was said to have absorbed the essence of heaven and earth to gain its supernatural power. Having past experience with Ayurveda, Levi was familiar with the five principles—that the entire universe was composed of five elements: air, water, earth, fire, and the ether (which some considered space or the Labyrinth). Those five elements formed the three basic humors of the human body. Tinh Cây Ráy was said to have absorbed the ether and the earth and manifested those two elements as a naked man and a naked woman, with both forms intertwined. He'd witnessed an entity in that shape, as had the Kents. That had to be what he was dealing with. Of course, it was also possible that those forms were simply a demonic trick by the entity, intent on disguising its true identity and name. If that was so, then there was a very real chance Levi would lose the next time they met. While his faith was strong, powwow and Judeo-Christian magic would be useless against such an opponent.

"Tricky," he murmured, closing the book.

Crowley stirred at the sound of his voice, opened one eye, and yawned. Groaning, the dog stood and wagged his tail expectantly.

"Time for a walk?"

Crowley's tail wagged faster.

"Okay." Levi winced as he stood. His legs had fallen asleep during his time in the chair. "But not too far this morning, buddy. I suspect that before this is over, I may have a long way to travel, indeed."

* * *

That afternoon, Doug Kent stood unsteadily in front of his house, swaying back and forth. He'd never been one for drinking during the day, particularly during the workweek, but given that he'd lost his job earlier that morning, he didn't think it mattered anymore. His employer's sympathy had been steadily ebbing over the past week, so Doug wasn't entirely surprised things had ended this way. It wasn't like he could tell them his house was haunted.

His house. Was it even his house anymore? Or did it belong to the thing inside now?

He coughed, snorted, and then spat a wad of phlegm on the curb. His eyes were drawn to the lawn. The last time he'd mowed had been two weeks before they'd fled. The high grass was speckled with dandelions, and weeds had begun to run rampant. The shrubs needed trimming, as well.

His attention returned to the house, and he decided that no, it wasn't his home anymore. The motel was their home now, although he didn't know how they'd continue to pay for that now that he was out of a job. He clenched his jaw in drunken anger.

"All our stuff is still in there."

What the hell was wrong with him? How had he let things get this bad? Pikachu dead. . . abandoned because they'd fled. No job. No home. No belongings save what they had back at the motel. His wife and son would probably have PTSD from this for the rest of their lives. All because of his cowardice. All because he couldn't face up to what was inside. Oh sure, he'd needed to get his family to safety, but after that? He hadn't been back inside. Not once. Levi strode up to the door all sure of himself, and what had he done in the meantime? Hid in his fucking car.

"No more," he slurred. "I want our stuff back."

He opened the passenger door of his car, snatched the bourbon bottle from where it sat on the seat, and took another swig, draining it. He wiped his mouth with the back of his hand and tossed the bottle to the floor. Then he closed the car door and turned back to the house.

"You hear me, you motherfucker? Gimme our stuff back!"

Determined, Doug marched across the yard. When he reached the front door, he fumbled his keys out of his pocket. Squinting, he leaned forward and inserted the right one in the lock.

The door swung open before he could turn it.

"Damn Amish guy must have left it unlocked."

Steadfast with drunken resolve, Doug Kent stepped inside.

The door slammed shut behind him.

* * *

Levi sensed something was wrong immediately, even as he guided Dee to a stop behind Doug Kent's car, which was parked alongside the curb, directly in front of the house. Dark psychic energy rolled out of the dwelling in pulsing waves, unseen but undeniably felt. His head throbbed in time with his pulse, and his breath caught in his throat. The horse whinnied, stomping her foot.

"I know," Levi soothed, hopping down to the street. "I feel it, too."

He quickly checked inside the vehicle, but it was empty. His eyes were drawn back to the house. It seemed to glare back at him through the windows. As he watched, dead leaves and other detritus erupted from the gutters, soared into the air, and then floated back down. It was as if someone were blowing compressed air through the gutters. A muffled scream came from somewhere inside the dwelling. Levi couldn't be certain, but he thought it sounded like Doug.

"I told him to meet me outside. Why would he have gone in?"

Hurrying to the rear of the buggy, he leaped onto the back and gathered some tools he'd brought along for this particular job. There were two bamboo tubes, fresh cut just a few hours ago from a small cluster along the Susquehanna River near his house. One length was an even three feet. The other tube measured about half that length. Next to these lay a smooth, flat rock about the size of his palm that he'd plucked from the river. He set the three items aside and opened the wooden box at the rear of the buggy. He selected an empty wooden bowl, a bottle of purified water, a plastic cigarette lighter, a piece of white chalk, and a beeswax candle he'd made himself. Stuffing all of these into his vest pockets, Levi jumped down onto the street and hurried toward the house. He clutched a length of bamboo in each fist, and his knuckles were white against them. Making his way across the yard was like walking through quick-drying cement. Each step was a struggle. Wave after wave of anger and malevolence crashed against him. Gritting his teeth, he fought back, exerting his will.

As he plodded toward the front door, it swung open, and the sensation vanished. Clearly, the entity realized it couldn't hold him at bay. Now it was inviting a confrontation. Rising to the challenge, Levi squared his shoulders and marched inside, hoping that the crash course he'd given himself on the magic of the Ruc people would be enough. Once again, the door slammed shut behind him, but Levi barely noticed. His attention was focused on the two figures at the end of the hall, next to the stairway.

Doug Kent hung plastered to the wall, his head brushing against the ceiling. His arms were stretched out to his sides. It was clear the man was struggling against whatever unseen force held him in place, but to no avail. His eyes widened when he saw Levi. He tried to speak but couldn't. Standing before him was the figure Levi seen before—the treelike thing shaped like an entwined man and woman. One half faced Doug. The other glared balefully at the magus.

"Let him go," Levi warned. "He means you no harm and I only wish to talk."

The entity turned. Now the male face stared at him, while the female studied Doug. Not taking his eyes off it, Levi slowly transferred both bamboo tubes to one fist. He stooped low and, with his free hand, pulled the chalk from his vest pocket. The house shrieked. Something slammed into him suddenly, knocking him backward off his feet. Framed photographs flew off the walls, pelting him. He quickly drew himself into a fetal position, trying to protect his face and head from the broken glass and splintered wood. He clutched his tools in desperation, using them as shields.

"I can get you home," he yelled during a break in the barrage. "I can return you to where you came from!"

The entity responded by exploding a nearby electrical outlet. The wall began to splinter and crack, and then, slowly, electrical wires snaked out of the fissure.

"Ninh Hòa," Levi shouted. "I can return you to Ninh Hòa!"

Levi had the sensation as if a great breath had been drawn. The wires slumped to the floor. A second later Doug Kent did the same, sliding down the wall with a groan. The entity loomed over Levi, rotating slowly. Rising to his knees, he quickly drew a hasty circle around himself with the chalk. Then he stood.

"Ninh Hòa," he said. "I'm starting to suspect you don't understand the rest of my words, but you understand that. Ninh Hòa. Khánh Hòa. Yes?"

The air seemed to vibrate at the words.

Levi dropped the chalk and held up both hands, displaying his palms in a gesture of peace. Then, he slowly crouched down again and produced the bowl and the bottle of water. He filled the former, plucked a hair from his head, and placed it atop the water. The entity watched, unmoving. Moaning, Doug Kent propped himself up on his elbows.

"Doug," Levi murmured, "are you injured?"

"I. . . I don't think so."

"Good. Stay very still. But when I tell you, run upstairs and get that length of wood from your son's hermit crab cage."

"W-why?"

"Because we need it, and because this thing is between me and the stairs."

The psychic energy began to build again.

"Ninh Hòa," Levi soothed. "Just be patient."

Levi lay the rock at his feet. Then, gripping the bamboo tubes in each fist, he began to rub them against the smooth surface, producing a series of low, droning sounds. Taking a deep breath, he chanted, matching their cadence, and phonetically sounding out an incantation he'd memorized on the way to the house. The entity shivered.

"Now, Doug." He fought to keep his voice calm. "Hurry."

The terrified man lurched to his feet and stumbled toward the stairs. The entity shrieked, the multi-voiced cry screeching simultaneously through the home's A.I. assistant, television, stereo, and other devices. The banister twisted and coiled, wrapping around Doug's wrist. The stairs turned to liquid beneath his feet, sucking him down.

"No," Levi said, trying to draw the creature's full attention. "Let him go! Focus on me. I'm the threat here. Not him."

He rubbed the tubes against the rock again and repeated the incantation. The stairs solidified once more, and Doug wrenched his feet free. The banister splintered and cracked. Doug stumbled upward. Levi heard him sobbing, even over the cacophony of the entity's electronic Vietnamese threats and demands.

"Ninh Hòa," Levi promised. "Khánh Hòa. I give you my word."

The walls shuddered, breathing in and out. The house creaked and groaned.

Levi pulled out the candle and the lighter, crouched, and lit them. The noise subsided as the flame flickered and danced. When the thing spoke again, it was with a plaintive, pleading tone.

"Ban se dura toi ve nha?"

"If you're asking me if I'll take you home, then yes. Yes, I will. You have my promise."

Doug returned to the top of the stairs. He crept down halfway and then hesitated, staring with caution at the creature.

"W-what's it doing?"

"Waiting. Do you have what I asked for?"

Swallowing, he nodded.

"Good. Bring it here. But slowly. Very slowly."

Doug descended to the bottom, clutching the piece of wood in his right hand, and gaped again at the thing between them. Then he faltered.

"I can't. I'm afraid."

The entity turned, watching them both. Levi felt the energy building again.

"It's growing suspicious, Doug. Hurry."

"I can't!"

"Then throw it to me!"

Blinking, Doug took a step backward and then tossed the shard underhanded. Levi waited, careful not to extend his arm beyond the protection of the circle. When the wood breached the diameter, his hand shot up, snagging it from the air. The entity reacted savagely—lashing out with all limbs and smashing into the walls. Levi quickly snuffed the candle, jammed the wood into the softened beeswax, and muttered another incantation. There was a low, rumbling groan that terminated in a heavy sigh, and then the thing disappeared. The house grew silent again.

Slowly, Levi bent and picked up the piece of wood. He held it close to his face and whispered, "Ninh Hòa. We'll leave today."

"W-what just happened?" Doug took a faltering step forward. "Is it over? Is it gone?"

"Not gone." Levi held up the shard. "But it has retreated back into this last piece of itself. It no longer occupies your home."

"Piece of itself?" Doug inched closer, staring at the shard in wonder. "Wait... you're saying what? That this was the ghost of a tree?"

Nodding, Levi wrapped the shard in a silk handkerchief embroidered with a series of symbols from the Sixth and Seventh Books of Moses and carefully placed it inside his vest pocket.

"Will those symbols bind it or something?"

"No," Levi explained. "They have no power over what we just faced."

"Then why use that handkerchief?"

Levi shrugged. "Because I had it in my pocket."

Shaking his head, Doug surveyed the damage to his home. "A ghost did all this. A ghost of a tree..."

"In a sense, that's what it was, yes."

"I still don't understand."

"Neither do I," Levi admitted, "At least, not entirely. But based on what you've told me, what I uncovered during my research, and what happened just now, I can make some educated guesses."

He then told the homeowner about the myth of Tinh Cây Ráy. When he was finished, Doug still appeared confused.

"But my father never mentioned encountering anything like that. If he had, he would have told me."

"Most likely, he didn't even know. The tree lived in the forest around Ninh Hòa, which is in the Khánh Hòa province. During the Vietnam War, that area was a hub of military activity for the ARVN."

"Those were the bad guys, right?"

"No, we fought against the Viet Cong. The ARVN were our

allies—the Republic of Vietnam's soldiers and sailors. Khánh Hòa was also the headquarters of our own Green Berets."

"Dad was a Green Beret."

"My guess is that the tree's physical form was destroyed during the war. At some point during his deployment, your father came across this piece of wood. For whatever reason, he took it as a memento. A souvenir. Maybe the tree's spirit lulled him into doing so. Or perhaps it was benign on his part. Maybe he just thought that it looked pretty. Regardless, he brought it home."

"But he was never haunted. None of this ever happened when he had it."

"Your son's hermit crab cage was lined with sand and shredded coconut husks—an earthy combination. I think Tinh Cây Ráy lay dormant all those years while your father had it inside his cedar chest. Placing the shard in that organic material is what woke it up again."

"So now you'll what... destroy it? Burn it?"

"On the contrary," Levi said, packing up the rest of his gear. "I'll leave soon as possible for Vietnam. I promised the entity that I would take it home, and that's what I intend to do. I'll go to the forests it came from, reinsert it back into the soil from which it first sprang. And that should be the end of the matter."

Doug snorted as he opened the door. The two stepped outside.

"That seems like a lot of work. Flying all the way to Vietnam? And if you put it back in the dirt there, won't it just haunt those people the way it did me?"

"No. You and your family called me because you wanted to return home, right?"

Doug nodded.

"Well, so did Tinh Cây Ráy."

THE RUNNING PEOPLE

MAURICE BROADDUS

Every day, you wake up as both gazelle and lion. Each morning, a gazelle wakes up and knows it must outrun the fastest lion or be killed. Just as a lion knows it has to run faster than the slowest gazelle or it will starve. This is the secret knowledge of survival.

Puttering about your room, you double-check its fortifications, entrusting your daughter to it for another day. A literal cabin in the Eagle Creek National Park. You need to be out of the city, but only just. Near enough that you can scrounge for supplies as needed, but still retreat from because *they* overrun its streets.

"Mommy's off to play the running game." You shuffle out the door with a nod, your last words to your daughter whispered, to not wake her up more than you have to. You hope to be back before she fully stirs from bed, around noon these days. It isn't like either of you have a strict calendar to keep these days. Not since before the shadow fell and the black door opened.

The cabin stands on a bluff, not too far from a bridge, on a trail rarely used except by tourists who seek it out or are directed there by park rangers. It was once a tourist attraction for the park. A historic recreation of how life used to be, with its rustic appearance. Thankfully, it was built from modern materials. Cement walls, concrete ceiling, like living in a cinder block —the "logs" of the cabin walls strictly decorative—it shields you from the worst of the elements. With no network access, you are cut off from the outside world, in your own little pocket universe without electricity or running water. But the cabin is safe. Fortified. Home.

Closing and locking the door behind you, you stretch for a few minutes under the thin light of the late morning sun. Your muscles already ache, each movement testing your old tears and stiffness. You tie a leather thong around your ankles, high onto your calves, and fasten a tire tread into place as a sandal. You snap your goggles into place and wrap a bandana around your mouth. Not being able to put off the run any longer, you slip on your backpack and set off.

When you first moved here, you were thirty pounds heavier and had fallen out of the practice of running. Walking the trail nearly did you in. Now you run them with an ease—a lightness and looseness—that leave you anxious to run more.

You push aside memories of your brother.

Shortening your stride, you bend your knees, your legs absorbing the shock of the jarring path. Leaves and dry branches crunch under you, your feet caressing the ground. Each foot circles back around to catch the next step as you lean into the trail. Impact shock shoots up your legs into your spine. Each pounding step adds to the relentless grind of your bones, breaking down your muscles. Running breaks down your bones, the way a hammer does stone, eventually reducing even the sternest rock to dust. The instant you get sloppy, pain shoots up your shins like a crack spiderwebbing a car's windshield. Your body is reduced to a ticking time bomb of what will give out first, waiting for the inevitable pop of cartilage, the rip of a hamstring, the burn of a torn Achilles tendon. Knees, shins, hips, heels, or ankle.

When you were in high school, your brother, who was in college, introduced you to the joy of the run. You used to beg to join and train with him early in the mornings, recalling the simple jubilation of a child barreling at full tilt to kick a ball or chase down a friend. Barefoot, your feet skittered along the rocks and twigs of a creek bed, the pain of running teaching you how to run better. Eventually, he quit, but you kept on.

Running is life, the lessons of how to be free. The rush of endorphins that come with the runner's high make you smile, a demented euphoric rush that curls your lips.

Just over an hour later, you exit the last copse of elm trees at the westernmost point of the park. Despite your goggles, your eyes burn. The air a low-lying cloud of smog—you are unable to afford a medical-grade re-breather—you layer your bandana with material cut from an industrial filter. You almost long for the days when the most difficult calculus of environmental management was what kind of car to buy. Now, climate stresses have displaced millions of people. In a just and moral universe, victims of other peoples' messes would be given justice by those who made the mess. But in this unjust and immoral universe, the wealthiest one percent co-opted the most susceptible into their Zero White Effect narrative.

You want to grieve for your brother, but now isn't the time to dwell on that kind of conspiracy nonsense. Slowing, you all but creep through the winding grove of thick foliage. Lots of bad things can happen in the woods: dogs, snakes, wolves, a thousand-foot drop-off. People.

Styling themselves an eco-fascist group, ZWE feared the apocalyptic countdown to the supposed death of the white race. An actual apocalypse wasn't good enough. Once the door opened, the world teetered on the verge of complete ecological collapse. Locust plagues in East Africa. Droughts. Floods. Pandemic protocols as the new world order. The earth itself shuddering in birth pains. Naturally, brown people had to be the problem. Ecological breakdown only stoked the flames of that fear, stirring hatred as rationalization for failing to live responsibly. They called it a plague, leaving so many of their people dead or missing. Their apophenia drew connections between intense events that weren't there. The only consistent element was fear, of all the things they couldn't control. The dangers were the same in any direction. Trusting your honed instincts, at the sight, sound, smell of trouble, you ran.

The Indianapolis suburb of Brownsburg stretches out, an ocean of abandoned storefronts. Following Green Street, past the purple "Welcome to Brownsburg" sign—the image of the high school mascot bulldog glares down from it. The population count of 26,397 has been spray-painted over, as has the replacement figure of 9,003, leaving the bright red number of 3,108. Now is one of those times you are glad you chose this sleepy suburb. The days fresh and uncertain, small towns have sealed themselves into conclaves of their own. Muttering to their people while not saying anything to the outside world.

Early after the door opened, you heard talks of people suffering from downtown fever, the freak-out brought about by the eeriness of empty, neglected buildings. Desolate monuments to a life that once was. The parking lots a sea of sizzling black pavement as the sun slides toward its mid-morning apogee. Even as you cling to the side of the buildings, an ocean of abandoned store fronts and parking lots, you sense the press of eyes on you.

A ghost along the street, you approach the rear of the services building. The former city courthouse has an "auto-services area," a bay of lockers little more than a receiving dock with supplies dropped off by drones. No one wants to go too deep into the city of Indianapolis for services. Communities have had resources rolled out to them to fortify themselves against extreme weather, clean tech with the promise of a return to the way things used to be. You just have to survive long enough, week by week on government-provided ration drops, until they can be deployed. The suburb is close enough to suckle from the municipality's teat and this building close enough to Eagle Creek National Park that you can make the supply pick up with relative ease. Still, you eye the streets with caution, not letting their emptiness lull you into a state of false security. They are lawless, feral, and full of secret things.

Raising your mask, you drizzle spit onto your finger and drag it across the gene-ident pad. The light flashes green and a lock clicks free. Cognizant of the airborne parasites and such, you slip your mask back into place. You open the locker door and haul your box to the counter. Flicking open your utility blade, you cut it open. You plop your backpack onto the counter. Your face drips sweat as you transfer the goods to your backpack. Medical supplies, batteries, seeds, tablets to purify water. Whoa. . . a pack of frozen meat. You've grown your own food, living on meals of beans and yams, and you've forgotten what meat tastes like. Deliveries are only large enough for you to carry. Any more than that makes you a hoarder, and the rule of survival is that hoarders are killed, their cache hauled back as bounty.

You fasten your backpack and test its weight. Not too bad. Not enough to slow your run.

A low, throbbing headache begins at your temple. You take a swig of water to stave off dehydration. You slip out of the building but pause, rattled by the feeling of invisible eyes again. A shadow splits from the building across the way. It may have been a trick of the light, a heat mirage of the baking concrete.

Taking no chances, you run. Cutting between the next buildings you curse yourself for an idiot. A figure waits at the end of the alley. You know before turning that more men seal off the way you came. Unkempt men with sullen faces, they smile without joy or mirth, only quiet desperation. Hyenas closing in on easy prey, they shuffle toward you, confident and clumsy.

"We just have a few questions for you." An emaciated stoop-shouldered man. Youthful and repugnant, deep creases thicken his neck. A dull, expressionless face except for the empty fear that dances in his watery, blue eyes. A red bandana covers his face, and his dancing eyes dart about, fixing on nothing. A robed figure with an excess of weird jewelry, as if styled from foraged metal. The clergy for the lost and forgotten, his shaved head sears his grayish skin to a deep red. You recognize the familiar, ancient glint in the eyes that study your skin, the color of burnished leather.

He is ZWE.

A scheming virus of humanity. The wealthy and their rituals. Convincing the poor and desperate that, without them, the world as they know it will cease to function. That the tacit promise of wealth one day trickling down to each of them will be snuffed out. Instead, they need to worry about a conspiracy of agents of their social destination. The list is as endless as it is absurd, created by ZWE just to keep their followers spinning desperate and hopeless. They fancy themselves a group of rebels, protesting curfews and restrictions on movement, for such safety measures are an assault on their freedoms—as though there is an Oppression Olympics they are eager to get in on. Their manifestos a weird amalgamation of railing against population growth and an environmental welfare state. You always get the feeling they still need to sound out all the words they are using.

"I don't want any trouble. Just come for my supplies and I'm on my way." You angle your body to position both groups in sight.

"You're a long way from wherever you stay." A red-bearded man comes up from behind you. His hair grows in thin patches across his splotchy face. His white tank top, streaked with a dark grease, shows off his knotted muscles. His weathered blue jeans frayed nearly to threads, patches of flesh peek through the stretched fabric.

"You're on the wrong side of town, looking all suspicious."

"At least the system's making you work for your welfare these days. But it's all still coming out of the pockets of real citizens." Gesturing back toward the subdivision, the hoary character's fingers are disproportionately short compared to the rest of his hand.

I have the right, all people have the right, to move and seek safety. The words take shape in your mind, but you decide to not waste the breath or effort. This isn't debate club. Conspiracy theories are the great unifiers of his people. There is nothing scarier than privileged people defending spaces they see as theirs. You hitch the backpack higher onto your shoulder. "I think I'll just be on my way."

"Why don't you go back to where you came from like the others." The red-bearded man raises his voice, not sure if he means to ask a question.

"All we want to know is why you're here, and how did you get a code." Their leader steps nearer. "Scratch that, we just want your code. For future drops. All we need is a gene sample. A finger or two should do."

The walls of the alley close in, a coffin lid threatening to fall shut. Shadows spread like a blood pool. The strange acoustics produce phantom whispers. His menacing scowl deepens into a scornful snarl. He wears a sliver of tire rubber for soles, each fastened into place by a Velcro strip. His companions wear expensive athletic shoes you guess were probably raided from the stores for which you and your people have been blamed. He turns away from you, his back a tortured contortion of bones aligning at odd angles preparing to spring. You can only surmise that the gesture must be a signal to the rest of the pack. They are about to pounce.

You dash down the trash bin-lined thin gap between the two buildings beside you. Scampering around or over them as best you can. The leader hesitates before committing to your chase. When you chance a peek behind you, a sinister grin crosses his face. This is part of his sport.

"Run her down!" He twirls his fingers for the others to circle around the buildings.

Predator packs often split into smaller groups while in pursuit. One initiates the chase while others bolt ahead of the prey along possible escape routes to trap them. This is a kind of persistence hunt, dogs running down a gazelle. To run one to death, all you have to do is scare it into a gallop on a hot day. If it darts into the grove, one of the pack breaks off to drive it back into the open. Their way of picking one from the herd if they can't just scatter the herd to isolate a single antelope.

Behind you, your pursuers pant and grunt in slavering chase. They chant things. Nothing in any language you are familiar with. Soon their barking is reduced to unintelligible vocalizations. Nothing human, embracing whatever possesses them from the other side of the black door. If you can't outrun them, you outthink them. Make their weakness your strength.

You just have to figure out what it is.

Protests and lootings had erupted amid frustrations from lockdowns. The houses of the subdivision across the street, half of them boarded up, left more abandoned properties than people. Now the blacked-out windows gape from deserted houses in an empty, spectral stare. Weeds overgrow doorsteps, their lawns brittle and brown. You embrace the existential dread of running from death, focusing on the discipline of form. From the waist up, you keep your body serene and still, your legs and feet pistoning in a fast dance over the uneven pavement and ruts. The nerves of your toes as finely wired as those in your lips and fingertips, each foot-slap against the pavement brings the strange mix of fear and pleasure. Your chin held high, your thoughts and breaths merge into a symphony of stream of consciousness. Your jumbled thoughts drift to the opening of the black door.

On that day, a long black line split the sky, a lateral malignancy which tore through space leaving only an afterimage of intense, unaccountable horror, the object of it coalescing into a large dark rectangle. You could only perceive it as a door.

The door opened.

Kaleidoscopic darkness, swirls within darkness. Its patterns hinting at elder secrets, unimaginable abysses of time and space. The raging blackness. Other shapes emerged, aqueous proportions of no known geometry. And other nameless horrors.

The sheer nothingness peered into you, sifted your soul.

* * *

The landscape of abandonment shifts from the concrete glare of empty storefronts to ramshackle sheds. Sliding and scrambling down the final concrete embankment, you escape the walls of soaring brick and plaster.

The trail snakes through the thickening copses of trees, the stands merging together in new growth where civilization has crumbled and retreated. You scamper, sure-footed along train tracks with the ground dropping away on either side and prepare to enter Eagle Creek Park. Another world. *Your* world.

Ringed by hills, the massive reservoir bottles up heat and drops an oppressive weight on the heads of any who enter. The overhead sun broils the ground beneath your feet. Sweat drenches your body, the pangs of your headache slamming your skull like an ancient drumbeat calling you home. Your elbows pump for power. Your footfalls unsteadily clump along the concrete. You sluice sweat, but when you focus on the run, you push past your limits, never realizing that you are at the point of exhaustion. Your heart pounds, your dry eyes blur.

When you glance over your shoulder, the ZWE leader's head bobs about like it's loose on a swivel, his arms slashing back and forth, wild and undisciplined. You take what the trail gives you, learning the stones, the ones that help you spring forward, the ones that roll out from under you, the ones that lie in wait like traps set to take you out. Your arms float, your hands find their rhythm next to your ribs, working the air like a frantic row man. Your stride reduces to a short choppy motion, tiny quick steps, your back straight and tall. You embrace your fatigue, not giving into it, not fearing it, not avoiding it. Fatigue means death. Such is the secret knowledge of the gazelle.

You run the ZWE members through a series of hairpin turns and gentle switchbacks—the trees dissolve into runes of bark—using the terrain to carry you. Each step a well-timed drop, allowing your legs to go loose and let gravity do the work. The pace risks snapping your ankle with a bad misstep, but you trudge along. A stinging itch grates your feet, but you can't stop to check your socks. You throttle back to save your quads, keep your toes pointed down, trailing from the gut.

The strange entanglement of the thickets among the copse of trees causes you to blink twice. You fear illusions even when you know you are hallucinating. Your brother lies there, bedridden. His eyes bloodshot. Mouth open in a soundless scream, accusing you of abandoning him. You shout about having no choice as you back away from him, knowing the things without shapes—whatever slipped through the black door—have worked their way through his system. Liquefying his insides, he slowly drowns from the fluid buildup in his lungs. Each wet, wheezy breath too loud, too strained, too difficult to listen to. Unable to help yourself, you shout his name.

The image dissolves into heat shimmers.

Committing the cardinal sin, you take your eyes from the path. Your feet misjudge the stones, and you slip. Your arms pinwheel trying to catch yourself, but you tumble down the hill. A gentle slope, not like the steeper plunges deeper into the park. The ground jolts you, each hard bump banging against you as you roll. When you stop, you hesitate to move. Checking for anything broken or out of place. At last, you drag yourself over to the creek and vomit what little food remains in your belly.

Drawing your legs under you, you don't chance standing just yet, not confident they won't give out from under you. Your teeth chatter despite the near noon sun. You slump into a pool of sweat and spit. It is all so hopeless, each day a pointless trek. There has to be more to life than just survival in their world, the hell they've created with their selfish ambitions and fears. That voice alarms you, too. The one that wants you to quit, to give up. The run isn't about you. Someone else depends on you, and you refuse to fail her like you did your brother.

Along the path you catch glimpses of figures bobbing along. Uncouth shapes, charging forward with uncertainty with their crouching, shambling strides. A wave of absolute despair washes over you, like nothing since the door opened. Your hands grope past your knees, fixing at your sock. Blood has soaked through it. Running your finger along your numbed skin, you find them. Blisters. The leather thongs have chafed against your leg despite the protections of your sock. Twisting your body around, you unstrap your shoe and soak your wounds in the icy creek and lie on the matted grass. You fear the ZWE jackals lying in wait by the watering hole. For a moment you consider it worth it: a quick death, much better than choking on a thirst-thickened tongue, dying by inches in the heat by thirst or hunger.

For ten minutes, you drink in the silence with corpse-like rest. Finally, you stand. You visor your hand over your eyes, squinting at the sun. You lace up the leather straps. You test your weight on your ankle. A gazelle catching a scent, you lope off along the trail, uncertain whether you can get your stride right again. Your weight distributed on the outside of your foot, its movement rolls from little toe to big until your foot falls flat. Then comes the next step. And the next.

Cutting down the meandering path, you scrabble over a scree of rocks. You relax, your feet flexed along the hard surfaces of the jagged stones, molding themselves to them. Leaning back, you keep your feet spinning under your body, easing into the pain until your body stops fighting it. You relax into the rhythm, unaware you are even moving. Studying the trail, your feet fall into the meditative pace of the run. The only thing that matters is finishing.

A shallow gorge runs along the base of the hill. A figure lies sprawled along it. The red-bearded man. You slow your approach, wary of the possibility of a trap until you notice the side of his head bashed in from a vicious fall. You try to judge how long he's been dead because death is only part of the circle, especially in the woods. Already his belly swells, and the thin mesh of skin undulates. Abscesses erupt on his skin. Three-foot long worms taper from them. And one from his eye socket. One of the worms rears. Its eyeless head casts about, sensing you. It lunges toward you. Dodging to the side, you scramble for a stick. Images of your brother flitter through your mind. You stab the worm, its gentle flesh splitting with the first wound.

"There you are," the ZWE leader shouts, his attention locked onto you with an odd tilt of his head, like he wants you to repeat a question. "The rest of my men gave up the chase. I almost did, too."

You study the terrain with a hunter's squint, appraising and dissecting at the same time. You allow your pace to slacken, appreciating the sight of the cabin in the distance, determined not to allow any of these shamblers anywhere near your home. Your daughter. Trapped by your own pace, he sucks air, his chest shuddering with each breath. He runs the city; you run the woods. You ran these few miles faster than you've ever run in your life, not allowing him to think about his course or to focus his vision on you.

You pick up your pace again. The sunlight has difficulty reaching you through the overhead smog, haze, and foliage. This stretch of the White River forms a basin with isolated pockets. The winding path corkscrews along the steep hill's edge, then falls off the sides. Wobbling in the soggy Indiana air, thick and cloying in your lungs, each breath becomes a struggle. You note every trickle of sweat trailing down your back. Scrambling up the steep trail, on a path only you can see, you begin the thousand-foot climb. At the peak, the view is spectacular, but below it is certain death. Breath, mind, and muscles unite into a perfect engine. Your muscles tighten as they approach that critical threshold. Faster and faster your feet pedal, a wheezing gallop at a pace you know he can't maintain. Each leg pounds into the earth, propelling you forward, your mind an insensate swirl until it hits the endorphin high. You turn around enough for the ZWE leader to see your smile. From the grim contortions of his face, his head swims in a woozy glare, his hamstrings scream, knots riddle his calves. You cut back along a hidden switchback. He dogs your path, frantic to not let you out of his sight again. He misses the slight veer. Too late, he realizes the path drops off. His arms over-correct, and the earth continues to fall away. His screams echo until cut brutally short by the ravine bottom.

Easing into a trot, you slow to a walk as you turn back toward the old cabin.

The blankets on the small camp bed lie crumpled and empty. Your heart lurches into your throat. What if one of the ZWE hasn't abandoned the hunt but found your daughter instead? A soft flip of pages draws your attention. Perched on the ledge of the back window, her foot dangles down while she reads, a stack of books piled under her.

"Dishes?" You drop the supplies on the table.

"Done. Even gathered firewood."

"Were you seen?" You regulate your voice to keep any rising alarm from creeping into it.

"C'mon now. I'm like a ghost in the woods. You taught me how to run." As if sensing something wrong, she hops down from the sill. "What took you so long?"

"Got hung up at the gas station."

She stares at you, studying your face for unspoken stories, and—catching a glimpse of them in your eyes—reconsiders probing any further. "You're home now. That's all that counts."

"Yeah." You give her half a squeeze, as much as her teenage mood will allow, apocalypse or not.

Smiling, you risk dreaming of a better world. It falters, and you fix your lips.

Tomorrow is another run.

THE DISAPPEARED

KASEY LANSDALE

Crack of thunder. Spark of lighting. And then the skies opened, and the rain came down in sheets. I pumped my little legs hard, working overtime to catch Crystal already halfway up the big hill at the end of our road.

"Wait up!"

She looked back over her shoulder, bright, dyed red hair plastered across her brown face with sweat and rain. "Hurry up, Eve!"

Then I watched her bike crest the hill and disappear.

The air was full and sticky, and the trees on either side of us vibrated from the wind. Thunder rolled as the rain poured from the darkened sky like a round of applause. The trailhead was just beyond this hill, where the blacktop turned into gravel, and the gravel turned into red clay dirt.

Crystal and I had spent a lot of time out there, especially in the summers when the days were long and the idea of going outside to play was still in favor.

We had a secret spot back in the woods that wasn't all that secret. A sinkhole where the creek ran off and made a cavern of sorts underground. We'd go fishing or swimming, hunt crawdads, or just hang out and talk about nothing in particular. Crystal said that when she was my age, all the kids in the neighborhood used to go back there to play until it was made off-limits by the landowner after some kid had drowned. Crystal always tried to act like she was grown, but she was only a year or so older than me. I'd heard the rumors at school, but the story and the "No Trespassing" sign did little to deter us.

By the time I got to the top of the hill at the end of the road, Crystal's bike was already propped up against a tree near the entrance to the woods. A car sped by as I placed my bike on top of hers, forgoing the kickstand like she had. Water splashed up from the wheels of the bright red Corvette and into my face, causing me to cough and gag.

"Slow down, shithead!"

But they couldn't hear me. Probably best. A few steps inside the treeline, and I could see the creek in the distance, the water sloshing up against the gravel shore. I wandered into the woods and called out her name, even though I knew she wasn't far ahead.

It grew darker from the trees that kept us sheltered from the brunt of the sudden storm. A hot breeze rustled through the leaves and limbs and shook them something awful. They rattled and swayed, flinging water droplets from their edges like a shaking dog, and then they were still. I didn't mind the rain; it kept the mosquitoes at bay. I zigzagged my way across thick roots and through damp cobwebs until I finally saw Crystal stopped, leaning against an old pine tree up ahead. When I caught up to her, she turned and grinned, her white teeth luminescent against her sable skin.

"You good?" Crystal asked. "Would hate to lose you next."

I was thinking the same thing.

We walked a few more minutes through the maze of underbrush until we reached the water. The rain had blown through, but the steam from the heat had started to rise and wrap around us. The bugs were coming back in force, ravaging my exposed skin. Crystal stripped down to her underwear, seemingly untouched by anything. She tossed her pants across a tree branch nearby and shed the rest in a snakelike trail as she jogged towards the slippery bank. I followed a few steps behind, scooping up thick mud and smearing it down my arms to act as a barrier, like I'd heard the Indians did.

At the water's edge, Crystal eased her way across the slick, mossy rocks until she reached the rim of the underwater cavern. The water was dark green, with not much to see beyond a few leaves floating across its surface. She looked over at me, made sure I was watching, took in a deep breath, squeezed her eyes tight, then jumped.

Water splashed my already rain-soaked body as she disappeared into the dark. Bubbles floated up towards the surface, and the leaves danced across the ripples for a moment. Then things were still. My eyes stayed fixed on the depths of that water as I waited for Crystal to resurface.

I waited and waited. Then I waited a little more. Enough time had passed that I was getting awful damned uncomfortable. I'd just squatted down closer to the water to see if I could make something out when I felt a tap on the back of my head.

Startled, I toppled over into the water, splashing and thrashing, fighting to stay above its surface.

When I looked up, treading water now, there was Crystal staring down at me and laughing with glee. Way she was grinning, you'd have thought it was all her birthdays and Christmases rolled into one.

"You're an asshole," I said between coughs.

"Don't be a weenie."

I used my arms for leverage, slipping a few times on the

thick moss until I managed my way up and onto the damp clay rocks. I lay there, the stream of water running over my body as I caught my breath.

"You scared the dogshit out of me," I said.

"Come on now. It's funny if you think about it."

I thought about it. It was a little funny. I peeled myself up to standing, squeezed some water out of my long hair, and walked over next to her.

"How'd you do that, anyway?"

"Was out here the other day," she said, "just me, messing around, and you know what? Some tunnels in there. You keep going down in that little cave, it comes out the other side, just there." My eyes followed her finger to the dark spot beyond a fallen tree.

"Well, I got that, genius, but why would you do that in the first place? And alone at that?"

Crystal shrugged. "I guess I wanted to know how that kid could have drowned. Didn't make sense. Drop-off's not that deep, but if they got stuck under the surface, or sucked into one of those little pockets down there, and didn't make it over to the other side in time, well. . ."

"Yeah," I said.

"Yeah," she said. "Anyway, I was just having fun with you. You mad?"

"Little," I said. "But I'll get over it."

For the next half hour, we took turns swimming out over the sinkhole, treading water and the like, but opting not to go under to the other side. Crystal was a great swimmer, and in another life, she could have done something with it.

By now the sun had dipped low enough that Mama would be waiting for me at the door when I arrived home. There was a plopping sound and we turned to see a water moccasin had slithered into the water. It didn't take long for Crystal and me to be out of there and onto our feet, far away from that snake.

We heard a sound in the distance across the water. Someone was laughing. A girl. A thin smear of pale skin against the dark brown of the tree trunks, her foot propped up on a rotting stump like a pirate who'd spotted land. She was somewhere around our age. Older than me I figured, and younger than Crystal. That would put her around thirteen. She wore a long black rain slicker with the hood pulled back, and shiny, tall black rain boots. Her long black hair hung in a low, loose ponytail.

I didn't recognize her from the neighborhood, but that didn't mean much. The trailer park at the far end of the road had provided a regular rotation of occupants throughout the years. Fingers spread wide, the girl raised her hand in a wave. I smiled and waved back at her.

"What's your name?" I said. She didn't answer. Instead, her wave grew faster and more frantic.

"What's her deal?" Crystal said quietly. I shrugged my shoulders and tried again.

"What's your name?"

Still nothing. Instead, she turned, and in one fluid motion, disappeared back into the woods from where she'd come.

"That was weird as shit," Crystal said. "You know her?"

I shook my head from left to right. "Maybe she's from the park up there."

"If she is, that's news to me."

We stood there contemplating, the snake now far from our minds. It wasn't like she'd been unfriendly. She had waved after all. Hell, maybe she was deaf. Whatever the case, it was time to get home.

* * *

Once home and cleaned up, I sat around the table with Mama and Gary, my stepdaddy, and my little brother Billy. We ate a good dinner Mama had prepared and made small talk about our day against the backdrop of the radio. I had a mouth full of mac n' cheese when Gary shushed us all, went over and turned up the sound of the radio DJ's voice.

"This weekend, expect severe scattered thunderstorms across the southeast. And in local news, still no sign of Timothy Daniels, reported missing since last Thursday."

"Isn't that Derek's boy?" Mama asked.

"Yeah," Gary said. "It's been all over the news of late. Derek didn't show up for work again today."

Mama made a clicking sound with her tongue. "Shame. First the Reynolds girl, now this."

"And Nelson's boy."

She swiveled her body towards me as though about to tell me something, took a deep sigh, then turned back towards her plate. "Turn that off, would you?" Mama asked. Gary plodded back over to the radio and turned the dial all the way down until we heard the subtle click. "In other news," Mama said, a little too cheerfully, "Gary and I have been invited to the Lewis's Luau up the road, and this year, we've decided to go. Eve, you're old enough now to be home alone and watch Billy for us, aren't you?"

I groaned. A night at home with my little brother—on a weekend no less—whose idea of a good time was eating boogers he'd piled atop a fire truck did not strike me as how I wanted to spend my evening. Not that I had great plans otherwise.

"We anticipated that might be your response," Mama said. "So, to sweeten the deal, Gary and I have decided to let you rent up to five scary movies this weekend."

Now she had me. That meant the whole *Halloween* series would finally be at my disposal for back-to-back viewing.

"Fine," I said. Secretly, I was thrilled.

"Alright now," Gary said. "It's getting late. Finish up so we can all get to bed."

* * *

It was the end of the week, and the main talk of the town was the Daniels boy. Though Mama did her best to keep me and Billy in the dark, the kids at school had plenty of theories. I sat in the cafeteria, drinking my carton of milk and blotting grease off my personal-sized pizza as the other kids proselytized.

"Maybe he was kidnapped. Prolly being held in a basement somewhere?" Ronnie said.

"Dipshit," the other kid said, "nobody has a basement around here. Too much rain. That kid is worm food. Just like the others."

"Says you."

I dodged a rogue french fry intended for Ronnie, aka Dipshit, downed the last swallow of my chocolate milk, and got up from the long table. My classmates weren't exactly Mensa members, but they weren't exactly wrong, either. There'd been rumors of missing kids throughout the last year, but they'd been just that —rumors. And all from the trailer park up the way until now, so no one seemed to be in a hurry to verify if they were true or not.

Once school was out, I caught up with Crystal in line for the bus home.

"You wanna come over tomorrow night? Mom and Gary let me rent the whole *Halloween* series. I'm gonna have a marathon."

"You know I'm Black, right?" Crystal asked.

I brought an open palm to my chest. "Well, I'll be," I said. "Why, yes you are. I hadn't realized. . . . So?"

"You ever seen a Black person make it out alive in any of them scary movies?"

I thought on it for a moment, "I guess not."

"There's your answer. I'll see you on Monday."

"Fair enough."

"You girls getting on the bus or what?" I followed the soft voice to the mild man sitting behind the steering wheel. He looked unnaturally small behind the wheel of that big bus, like he might need a telephone book to see over the dash and a pair of platform shoes to reach the pedals.

"Yessir, Mr. Eddy," I said. "She's coming. My mom's picking me up." I looked at the line building up behind us. "But you can go first," I said, and gestured to Nancy from math class to go ahead of us. The driver nodded his head in approval.

"Can't say as I blame her," Mr. Eddy said.

We waited for Nancy to board, then I watched Crystal from the sidewalk follow her up the short metal steps.

"See ya," I said after her.

"See ya."

* * *

I shoved a handful of popcorn in my mouth as "Tonight, he's back," flashed across the small screen in the family room near the front glass door. By now, Billy was asleep in his room, and I was three movies into the *Halloween* series.

A fierce crack of lightning ripped through the sky and caused me to jump. The room went bright, then dark just as fast. In that moment, I thought I saw something move on the front porch. Then a snapping sound caught my attention as a tree branch broke, splintering against the glass and the windowpane outside before landing on the porch with a thud. The TV flickered, so I put down the popcorn, paused the movie, and got up to get a closer look outside. Another flare of lightning followed by darkness. And that was it. The lights were out, the movie gone from the screen.

I moved through the dark to the phone mounted against the wooden beam at the room's edge; picked it up and held it to my ear.

No dial tone.

Mom and Gary would likely ride out the storm at the Lewis's place anyway. I put the phone back on the receiver and felt my way to the window, eager to investigate the carnage outside. Once at the door, I flicked the porch light on out of habit, but of course, no light shone down. I gazed into the deep black, able to make out the tree limbs scattered across the porch and the patio furniture blown askew. As I surveyed the scene, a sharp movement caught my attention outside. For a moment I thought it could be Billy. No. A tower of giraffes could roam through the house and Billy would sleep through it.

This was different. More delicate. More graceful. I cleared my throat, pushed my face close to the door, saw the heat from my breath fog the glass as I spoke.

"Crystal, that you?"

The wind roared and walls shook in response. Then suddenly the house hummed with electricity as the lights flickered back on and I found myself nose to nose with the dark-haired girl from the woods.

Startled, I took a step backward and stumbled over a leg of the coffee table, sending both myself and the cold popcorn flying into the air, and crashing against the floor. Warm blood oozed from my right kneecap and trickled down my shin. There was a hot flash up my arm as little kernels of popcorn embedded into my palm like concession stand road rash. I scrambled to my feet, brushed the popcorn from my front, and looked around the room to survey the damage. Mom and Gary would not be pleased.

I rushed over to the front door for another look. She was still there. Only now, as the rain fell ruthlessly and the soft glow of the porch light emanated behind her, she looked smaller and paler than before. Her long, dark hair, no longer loose, was instead slicked back into a tight, unforgiving bun. Water bounced from the hood of her rain slicker, which rested atop her head like the garb of Death. From where I stood, she seemed to be floating there.

"You okay?" I said, unsure whether I was talking to her or me.

She didn't answer. Instead, the wind died down and the rain ceased. The little girl was gone within the mist.

* * *

Sun shining down on us like it had always been there, we stood outside at the bus stop, waiting on Eddy the bus driver to pick us up for school.

"She looked like that girl from the woods," I said.

"That Wednesday Addams-looking girl?"

"Yeah, but more. . . I dunno know. . . off."

"Not sure how that's even possible," Crystal said. She shifted her backpack to the other shoulder, then looked at my knee swathed in bandages. "What happened to yo' leg?"

Before I could answer, the big yellow school bus came to a rolling stop in front of us. Eddy honked the bus horn, saving me the embarrassment of the story, for now.

* * *

The day seemed to drag on until, finally, school was over, and it was time to meet at our spot in the woods like we'd agreed. Crystal was already there waiting on me by the time I arrived.

"Sorry," I said and approached her from behind. "Had to wait for Mama to get home before I could leave Billy." Crystal didn't move, just stood there staring at the shoreline beyond.

"The hell you doing?" I asked and stepped closer to her side, sliding in the mud as I did so.

Never had I had a feeling like I did in that moment. The woods swelled with a cacophony of birds and bugs; water filled my ears with a hum that paralyzed my entire body until it was one long drawn-out vibration that shook me from head to toe.

The body was lying there, swollen and bloated, twisted up in the roots of an ancient cypress, the ebb and flow of the creek water washing over it, scattering sticks and leaves atop the remaining flesh. His head rested gently across a jagged stack of rocks, covered in flies and rot, the white of one eye exposed. The rest of his face was covered in insects and dried mud. In a way, he didn't look so bad. Not dead so much as sleeping and dirty. But I knew better. I watched a beetle travel from the corner of his mouth and across his skull, then disappear underneath the weight of his body.

Then came the smell. A rancid, gag-inducing odor that traveled into my lungs on beads of wet air. My throat tightened and I tried to swallow, certain I would be sick. I turned away. I didn't need to look anymore; I already knew it was Timothy Daniels. The retching sounds from behind brought me back into the moment, and when I turned, there was Crystal wiping the corner of her mouth with the back of her hand.

"Shit," I said. "What do we do now? We can't leave him here. Critters'll take what's left of him by morning."

The thought was sickening.

"Makes no sense." Crystal said. "Where'd he come from?

Couldn't have washed up, the dam's just yonder, and there's no sign he walked here, or we'd see the tracks in the mud." I hadn't thought about it, but she was right. I started scanning the earth for some sign of his arrival, but there was nothing. "How long he been missing?"

I thought on it. Thought about the news on the radio and the kids at school. The few days before when everyone expected he might come home after running away, and the few days after when he didn't.

"Over a week," I said.

"Ain't nobody been out here but you, me, and that weird girl."

"How can you be so sure?"

"Just 'cause I don't come with you all the time, don't mean I don't come. I prefer the trees to the men Mama brings home."

"You ain't seen nothing, I don't know, different?" I asked.

"Well. . . that day I was out here, swimming around on my own, there was something off. I didn't think much about it at the time, but it happened again when you and I was out here swimming."

"What do you mean?"

"When I went down the other day and came out the other side, I tried to dive to the very bottom but couldn't."

"Well, you're not exactly training for the Olympics out here."

"No shit, but I can dive to the bottom where the silt is and have done so, but this last time and the time before that, it was like someone had piled up a bunch of rocks and I couldn't get down there. . . I just thought things had shifted with the rains we've been having, but now I'm wondering if someone put them there on purpose."

"You don't think this was an accident?"

"Maybe."

"We gotta do something," I said. "Tell the law."

"I knew you would say that."

"Well, what else can we do?"

"All these kids gone missing lately, you hear any news stories about suspects? The law don't care. They want peace and quiet, not justice. And trust me, in the news, you're only hearing about the white kids. Not the kids who live in my neighborhood. There's been others."

"What do you mean?" I asked.

"Nobody wants to say it, but yeah. It's been happening. They can't all be runaways." She wiped her face with her sleeve, and I realized she was trying not to cry.

"I didn't know," I said.

"Yeah, well. Now you do."

"What now?"

"We catch him in the act."

* * *

We covered him as best we could before we left, before the daylight disappeared completely. I didn't feel good about it, but if Crystal was right, then we couldn't be too careful. Crystal stayed at my place that night. I was glad Mama didn't make a fuss about it. She didn't mind Crystal, but I knew she worried about our friendship. Worried it might make things harder on me. She never said it, but she didn't have to.

I stared up at the popcorn ceiling of my bedroom without so much as moonlight across the pines, listened to the whir of my best friend's breath by my side. I thought about Timothy Daniels. Of his mother and father. I thought about his body lying out there under a foot of forest debris. No matter how tight I closed my eyes, I could still see it, the image of his face fresh in my mind. I didn't think I could, but I dozed in and out—

felt myself slipping into the darkness and eventually into a dream.

The threat of dawn crept in through the window as the early morning shadows tumbled across the foot of the bed. I yawned, then climbed over Crystal to let in some fresh air. Before I could, I heard a noise just outside my bedroom window, soft at first. So much so that I thought maybe I was still dreaming. But then Crystal sat up and I knew she'd heard it too. My heart was pounding hard against my chest, my legs trembling. Then it grew louder. No longer a gentle vibration but a sharp, rapping sound against thick glass. I was having a hard time making it all make sense, but I forced myself over to take a look.

There was the girl, mist-like and pale as ever staring back at us, waving like she'd done that day in the woods. Only this time, she wasn't alone. Timothy Daniels and a dozen others I didn't recognize stood at her back like a tiny, ethereal army. I heard a scream. A low, rumbling howl that hung in the air and then burst like a cloud above us. Then I realized it was coming from me.

Mama exploded into the room with a baseball bat hoisted high above her head, Gary hot on her heels with a leatherbound Bible at the ready. The New Testament, though, so I had my money on Mama and the bat. Crystal slung her body back and tossed the covers over her head as though they were an invisibility cape.

"What in the hell are y'all doing in here," Mama said.

"Sorry," I said. "I had a bad dream. That's all. It was just a dream." Mama lowered the bat and Gary dropped the Bible to his side. They both let out sighs of relief.

I did too.

"You scared the daylights outta me," Mama said. "Now get back to bed and go to sleep. There's still a few hours before school. I have to go in to work today, so you better not miss the bus. Billy's catching a ride with little Stevie's mom. He'll stay at their place tomorrow night."

"Yes ma'am," I said.

"You too, Crystal. Go to sleep."

"Yes ma'am," she said from underneath the blanket.

Mama closed the door behind them, and I laid back down next to Crystal. Neither of us said another word. I felt the pull of my dreams take me down into the darkness, deep below the surface of the rippling, cold black waters.

"Come on. Get up," Crystal said.

"Get your elbow out of my face, brat." I pulled the covers up over my head and turned onto my side. "I just got back to sleep."

"Come on. Let's go! Got an idea."

"Don't hurt yourself," I said softly. Crystal cut her eyes towards me. I stopped talking, rolled out of bed and onto my feet. But I wasn't happy about it.

We ate a quick breakfast and were out the door before Mama or anyone else was up. We were crazy to be doing this, but it didn't slow us down. I'd formulated some ideas of my own last night, my subconscious putting pieces of the puzzle together as I slept. Crystal and I were on the same page.

By now the creek bed was dry from the morning heat, the storms seemingly millions of miles away. Beads of sweat rolled down my back and across my face as we arrived next to where we'd left Timothy's body. Still there, in spite of this morning's sighting.

I had thought, hoped maybe, someone else might find him and this whole thing would be over with.

Sometimes I think back to that moment when we first found him, wonder why we hadn't gone to the police right away.

I wish we had.

Wish that the memory of what came next was someone else's. Wish that Crystal was around today to talk about things. Things that didn't involve death and sadness and disappointment. That she'd been able to see who I'd become. That she'd been able to become somebody. But no, that's not how things went down.

Standing on the creek bank, I looked over at Crystal, her face shiny from the dampness. We both knew what had to be done.

And so she did.

Clothes piled on the bank next to where I stood, she dove down deep into the murky water like a mermaid, swift and effortless, feet pressed together like a long tail. I wasn't sure if she did it for her or for me, but I was grateful all the same. As I waited, my heart pounded hard inside my chest. I felt as though the silt beneath me might swallow me whole and take me down into its depths, absorb me just like it had the rains.

I waited longer than I would have liked, even though it was less time than before, when a body floated lazily to the surface like a budding flower in spring.

Then another.

And another.

And another. Until I lost count.

"Jesus," I said.

I hadn't pictured it like this. I didn't move. Didn't breathe. Just stood there, surrounded by this macabre garden of dead kids, floating atop the surface of the water we played in. Then Crystal breached the surface and made her way to land.

If the discovery of Timothy Daniels had not been enough to shake me to my very core, this memory would haunt me forever.

* * *

Crystal and I didn't say much on the walk back to my house, though we agreed to tell Mama and Gary after school while Billy was at his friend's place. We'd left everything as it was. Not much else we could do. This whole thing had gotten too big for just us, and if I never saw another dead thing again—human, animal, or otherwise—it would be too soon.

When we finally loaded onto the bus later that morning, Eddy seemed to sense something was wrong.

"Everything okay, kid? Look like you've seen a ghost."

Before I could answer, Crystal said, "She can't stop watching them horror movies, Mr. Eddy."

From the sound of her voice, you wouldn't know we'd spent the morning mining for corpses out in the woods. The little man laughed, slapped at his leg. I couldn't help but think he looked like a kid wearing his dad's clothes on Bring Your Son to Work Day.

"Got one just like that," Eddy said and pointed to a photo I'd never noticed before taped to the dash. "Isabelle. She can't get enough of that stuff."

I studied the photo for a moment. My knees turned to rubber and I had to catch myself on the back of the vinyl seat ahead to keep from falling down. I glanced back to Crystal on reflex.

"I didn't know you had a daughter Mr. Eddy," I said. "How come we ain't never seen her at school?"

"You kidding me?" Mr. Eddy said. He leaned in close like he was telling us a secret. "After everything I hear on this bus, no siree Bob. She's homeschooled."

"She looks like you," Crystal said.

Mr. Eddy laughed. "Everyone says that. But that long dark hair? Porcelain skin. No, that's her Mama, but I'll take the compliment. Now go on, load up now."

We headed to our seats, and Mr. Eddy turned and winked as

the folding doors closed behind us. Then he put the bus in drive, and we all lurched forward.

At that moment, I knew we were in for worse trouble.

* * *

I barely made it through the school day. Even tried calling Mama to come and get me, said I didn't feel well, but she was having none of it. Usually at lunch period, I bumped into Crystal, but today she had detention. Today, it was just me, alone with my thoughts.

When the time came, we skipped the bus and instead hitched a ride with another kid from the neighborhood we were friendly with. We arrived back at the woods just before dusk and were greeted by the crickets singing, as pleased as we were with the slight drop in temperature. The squirrels chittered about as they bounced eagerly around us from limb to limb. By all accounts, it was a nice day.

As we reached the water's edge, I steeled myself for what waited just beyond the banks.

The shock of nothing was almost as intense as the shock of everything. Almost.

All day I'd been mapping out what to do. Running down every thread of what if and what could be when we returned that evening. Never, not once, did that scenario include the bodies already gone.

"Well," Crystal said, "it ain't the cops that moved them, or there'd be tape everywhere. It's got to be Eddy."

"Really think so?"

"How else can you explain it? You saw the photo, same as me. Saw the way he was acting. And he's seen us come up from these woods."

We sat down on the boggy earth, unsure of what to do next. A half hour passed before either of us said another word.

"What now?" I said. "We can't tell Mama and Gary. We got no proof. They'll think we made it all up. Especially after I called her at work today. She'll think it's for attention."

"If nobody's gonna believe you, they sure as shit won't believe me."

I heard a rumbling sound in the distance I thought might be thunder, but the evening sky was clear through the tops of the trees.

"You're right, Crystal," I said. "We're fucked."

"Maybe it's better this way. Not getting involved and all."

I swiveled towards her. "You think we're not involved? You think that won't be the last thing I see every night before I go to bed and the first thing I see when I wake up every morning? We're involved all right. Whether we like it or not."

Crystal sucked at her teeth, followed by a clicking sound which I took to mean agreement. She stood up, walked over to where Timothy Daniels' body had been only hours before. Then she squatted down next to the dirt, studying things as the sounds of running water echoed around us.

"What are you doing?" I asked.

"I don't rightly know," she said.

* * *

I had hardly noticed when the sun slipped away, but I could see her silhouetted against the moonlight, looking beautiful, silver strands reflecting across the water, landing at her feet. And then a branch cracked behind us. I glanced back over my shoulder, and though I couldn't quite see at first, I knew we weren't alone.

Within moments, Eddy emerged, partly hidden by shadow,

which made him appear all the more threatening. We started running, me a few steps behind, Crystal already over the water and on the other side like a goddamned gazelle. Eddy moved like an ape, closing in on us with ease. We darted up sloped earth and made a beeline through the trees off the beaten path. Continued through the brush, maneuvering our way to the blacktop we knew waited for us in the distance. The creek sounds had disappeared behind us, but there was another rumble; louder, more visceral than before. Eddy stayed tight on our heels. It was like we were clearing the way for him more than anything.

Eventually, we found ourselves at the bottom of the paved hill, closer to the trailer park than to the creek. Crystal and I paused just for a moment at the edge of the road, laboring to catch our breath. Across the street, I could see a drainage ditch with a metal tunnel connecting to a maze of pipes and stones beneath the surface. If we could get down in there, we might manage to lose him. We didn't talk about it, just darted across the street and towards the ditch in time to feel the air behind us swell and Eddy's hot breath and outstretched arms graze across the backs of our necks, missing us by inches.

At that moment, I saw a streak of red—and then understood the sounds I'd heard before had not been thunder, but the low rumbling engine of the 1989 Corvette that lived at the end of the road at the top of the hill. It came barreling through, striking Eddy and lifting him away from the earth like a cloud.

Stunned, Crystal and I watched from the trenches as his head jerked back, rolled, then snapped clean off, landing in the grass like a baseball in the outfield. His body crumpled and collapsed, a puddle of blood and goo and excrement spreading beneath him like rising dough. I looked over to Crystal, who trembled like a chihuahua. Her mouth opened and closed repeatedly, but no sounds made it out. I didn't think the driver of the Corvette had seen us. He didn't seem to be looking for anyone when he got out of the car. Just stood there, staring at the pile of what used to be Eddy.

To this day I don't know how it happened so fast, but sirens were screaming towards us as we ducked down into the tunnel, still hidden from view. It was all I could do not to scream and vomit, run over there to kick Eddy's head like a soccer ball—maybe all at once. Instead, I said, "We gotta go."

* * *

We followed the underground tunnel maze until we were sure we were far enough away from it all. Tired and damp, starving but unable to eat, we parted ways and headed home. The whole night had turned into a blur. All we could do now was let the cops look into the accident, and it *was* an accident.

When I read about it later in the news, they found Eddy had made a cemetery out back of his house and buried all the bodies there at some point. Had put them next to his wife and daughter. What happened to his wife was still up for debate, but according to the article, his daughter had been the one who'd drowned all those years ago. Rumor was some of the other kids had held her under as a practical joke and things had ended poorly.

That was why Eddie became a bus driver, to find out who had done such a thing and seek revenge on those kids. Yet revenge turned into something else, and he started after kids who had nothing to do with what had happened to his daughter. I hoped he was wandering in some purgatory somewhere, head detached, struggling to keep his guts in his belly.

Over twenty years, the world changed, and the further away from it things got, the crazier it sounded in my head. I never could make sense of it all, and eventually, I just stopped trying. Crystal and I stayed tight for a few more years, but in time, she did what her Mama did, then had her own little girl to care for, and then another. And like it sometimes does, it became too much for her. She started using meth and hung herself from the ceiling fan while her kids were at school.

We'd fallen out of touch a little before that, but she'd named me in a note painted in red across the wall of her bedroom. The note didn't say much else. Just a list of names that meant nothing to anyone but her, and probably never would. In the end, I couldn't save Crystal, but at least we'd gotten some justice for the others, if indirectly. I try to check in on Crystal's kids from time to time, but they don't really know who I am. Every year, I leave a message on a memorial blog they made for her birthday. From the looks of things, I'm the only one who does.

I hoped Crystal—unlike Eddy—was somewhere peaceful. Someplace with an ocean nearby full of fish and plenty of space to swim and dive. She never got to see one in person when she was alive... the ocean, that is.

* * *

Tonight, when I lay down, I dreamed of all of them for what would be the last time—the lost and forgotten, standing in the woods alongside Isabelle as she waved her long, frantic goodbye.

* * *

Crack of thunder. Spark of lighting. And then the skies opened, and the rain came down in sheets.

DRIVING JAMES COLE

ERRICK NUNNALLY

"I had reasoned this out in my mind: there was one of two things I had a right to, liberty or death; if I could not have one, I would have the other."

— *HARRIET TUBMAN*

Tagley lit a cigarette without cracking a window first, same as he always did on a long drive. It bugged the shit out of Grace. Two years as partners and Tagley still couldn't offer a consistent baseline of respect. Grace didn't smoke, and he hated the way his clothing smelled whenever he got off shift. The senior detective wouldn't entertain being thoughtful of his partner; he considered being "a nail in the steel coffin"—riding in the police-issue gray Caprice—a right granted by God Himself. And Tagley outranked Grace, so that was that.

Grace cracked the passenger-side window.

It rolled back up with an electronic hum.

"Too fuckin' cold," Tagley said, breathing smoke through

nose and mouth. His slim lips were surrounded by a thick rat's nest of a beard. Rarely seen without a worn watchman's cap pressing his wild curls down, the detective cultivated a look that convinced criminals he was just as dirty as they were. Sometimes they were right.

"Too much fuckin' smoke," Grace said, cracking the window again.

"Y'know, you're no better than that piece o' shit in the back."

Grace glanced at their prisoner, cuffed in the back seat of the unmarked car.

"I'll try to do better next time I'm assigning you shit duty, Detective Tagley," Grace said. "Oh, wait, I don't assign shit duty. I get assigned shit duty 'cause I'm partners with a shithead."

"Fuck you, Grace."

Grace nodded and put his head back to catch the fresh air sluicing through the open window. "Yeah, fuck me, all right."

Tagley danced on the far side of dirty too often, and lately his behavior was threatening to drag Grace down with him. The cop may have been Grace's senior in rank, but he smeared dirt wherever he went. If you're going to skim, be smart about it. Instead, Tagley played in a field of fire, and now they had the ignominious duty of shuttling one of Tagley's mysterious collars to the next county.

It serves Tagley right for being a cowboy, but not me, Grace thought. *I wasn't even present for the arrest.* It wasn't entirely clear how Tagley even knew James Cole—a perp he described as an accomplished burglar.

Trees whipped by in the dark as they hurtled north. The only thing visible ahead of them was the double-yellow line fading into the night.

Grace said, "You been dodgy for the last two weeks, Tag. Real nervous. Why?"

"How the fuck would you know that, rook?"

"I think we're way past that 'rookie' shit. I ain't blind, and I'm sick to death of covering for your ass when you want to slink off and fuck up. That ends tonight."

"You didn't answer my question, but you got that last part right."

Grace sighed. "You've been smoking more, answering fewer questions than usual, and—believe it or not—you're even more of an asshole."

"Ah, the master detective. You think I'm stupid, like I don't know what the fuck is going on?"

Grace said, "I do think you're stupid, but not in the way you think I do."

Tagley cleared his throat, pulled the cigarette from between his lips, and said, "Listen, I got some business that needs to be taken care of soon. Since I'm the generous type, what I can tell you is that it's worth ten Gs o' your time." He stared at the Marlboro for a few seconds before putting it back to his mouth.

Grace sneered and said, "Aboveboard?"

"Money," Tagley said, "is money."

Grace stared at his partner and swallowed once before answering. "I'm listening."

"Our boy here is a slippery one. Flexible, knows how to get into trouble. He's seen things he shouldn't have."

Grace said, "Like what?"

"Like things he shouldn't see, things that are now inside his head that don't need to come out of his mouth."

Grace tried not to bristle at Tagley's condescending tone and glanced at the prisoner, whose attention was now focused entirely on the detectives' conversation.

Tagley looked into the rearview mirror and said, "Hey, you want a cigarette, Cole? Jonesin' fer some tabaccy, blacky?"

The prisoner, James "J-Bone" Cole, looked into Tagley's face and then away into the night before he said, "I don't smoke."

Grace shook his head and rolled his eyes.

"You sure, now, buddy? Not much time left on the ride, J-Bone."

Grace furrowed his brow and said, "We've got at least another fifty minutes on the road. What the fuck are you talking about?"

"Jesus fuck, Grace, put two and two together."

"Do the math for me, Tagley."

"Ten Gs is plenty fuckin' math, Grace. You're a detective. So, sort it out."

Grace sat back and sighed, "You want to, what. . . take 'care' of this kid?"

From the back seat, Cole said, "Hey, what—"

"Niggersaywhat?" Tagley cackled.

Cole ground his teeth and choked back a response.

Grace said, "Knock that shit off, Tagley."

"Calm down, Mighty Whitey, just passin' the time." He exhaled a long plume of blueish smoke.

"Oh, this again. You think me calling you out for making racist, shit-the-bed comments is some noble quest? You gonna give me shit about blond hair next, about how I should grow a mustache to prove I'm as dumb and ugly as you, maybe get someone killed?"

"Easy, big man, take it easy. That clean-shaven all-American look suits you. Climb down from that high horse before you hurt yourself. Y'all think I'm some dumb racist, right? Well, guess what, I know more shit about race and history than you two fucks ever knew."

"Oh, really?" Grace cocked his head and watched Tagley with theatrically wide eyes. "Do tell."

"I bet neither of you know jack shit about this forest we're drivin' through." Tagley smiled and glanced at each of the men in turn. "My daddy used to take me huntin' in these woods. This road right here is next to a network of trails that were part of the Underground Railroad. Runaways from our county were escorted to the next by an escaped slave named Abraham. This son of a bitch was one of the biggest, meanest niggers around. This buck carried a fuckin' axe to make his point, and his murderous ways stirred up the local posse—know what I mean? Patrols around here were actually afraid of this guy. They couldn't catch him. He was happy to kill whites, *and* he was providing inspiration to the workers."

Cole issued a derisive snort and muttered, "'Workers.'"

Tagley glanced in the mirror and shook his head. "Anyway, a posse of twenty men goes into the woods, sure-as-shit they're going to skin this motherfucker." He grinned, savoring his own dramatic pause. "Only four of them make it out. The only thing they could do was contain this guy, keep him trapped in the woods, cut off the routes in and out. You tellin' me you never heard of this?"

"No, Tagley, never heard of him."

"How 'bout you, J-Bone?"

Their prisoner scowled at the night and the engine hummed while the three of them held their tongues for a few minutes.

Tagley grinned and said, "That's 'cause it's bullshit, J-Bone. A mythical blip in history, dead and gone forever, just a story. You got no hope, just like that black bastard they allegedly trapped in these thick-ass woods."

"Fuck's sake, Tagley," Grace said, exhausted with his partner's behavior.

"Look, Grace, all I'm sayin' is if our boy here managed to get the door open and run into the woods and not make it out, there's a win for us both."

"This's bullshit, Tagley."

"And now it's eight Gs, Grace. How low you wanna go? Take the fucking deal, and let's get this shit done."

Feeling trapped and heated, Grace took a breath to answer when the car lit up from the outside. Bright lights bathed the interior in a blazing white wash.

Tagley squinted and raised a hand to shield his eyes. "Fuck! What stupid-ass is this? You ain't got friends this dumb, Cole, do ya? Naw, they don't even fuckin' know where you are, right now."

The vehicle behind them ran up to the tail of the Caprice. When Grace looked back, all he could see was the silhouette of Cole's thick hair, sculpted into a wooly flattop. He reached under the dash and pulled out the red bubble, opening the window to affix it to the roof.

The car backed off and floated into the night, its glare receding along with the growl of its engine.

"Yeah, you better back the fuck off," Tagley said.

Grace swung an arm over the back seat and peered through the night at the headlights. He could hear the low-pitched rumble of the car's engine, could almost feel the muscle in the thing. His heart picked up the pace as he watched the vehicle behind them.

"Here he comes again." Grace glanced at Tagley's profile. The senior cop looked strained and greasy around the eyes. The car lurched forward as their pursuer rushed up to tailgate them again, high beams blazing.

They accelerated for several tense seconds, but the vehicle behind them remained close enough to appear as if it were being towed. None of them could see through the glare.

Cole divided his attention back and forth between the detectives and the car behind them. He'd been feeling the fatigue of fear since he'd been put in cuffs and jailed several days ago. And now a new set of terrors—crooked cops and crazy drivers—rushed in to replace the old ones.

"Enough o' this shit," Tagley mumbled and started applying the brakes.

The car, Grace could see, was some sort of custom job, all black, even the grill and bumper. It slowed as well, maintaining its distance, matching their speed. Tagley slammed the brakes and both cars screeched to a halt.

Cole peeked over the backseat, eyes wide. The longer this went on, the longer he'd stay alive. Only it wasn't clear how this particular problem would end. He didn't dare open his mouth for fear of drawing the cops' attention back to him. With any luck, all this action would derail Tagley's plans long enough for their plot to be abandoned. For now, all he could do was listen to the hammering of his heart, the blood pounding in his ears. He wondered if that was all he was going to be good for. Listening, to his last day, with no one on his side.

"This ain't fuckin' right," Grace said. He hoped that his hunch was correct, that it was some sort of joyriding dare, because what sort of demented fool harassed a cop car like this? He reached for the radio, ready to make a call, run plates—something—but they were in a topographic hole in the landscape, surrounded by hills full of rock. The car's radio was strong, but radio waves were straight-line communication, and no antennae existed out here in these hills yet. For now, they had no backup, no support, and it made Grace second-guess whatever decision they might make next.

Tagley, perpetually high on authority, had no such quandary. He threw the driver's side door open before Grace could say anything. Service weapon drawn and pointed, badge in sight, he shouted into the headlights, "Hey, you wanna play, huh? This something you want to fuck with? Shut the engine off, get out o' that vehicle!"

The car's tires screeched in response. It peeled away in reverse, weaved down the highway, and executed an impressive J-turn. Grace still couldn't make out the plates and caught only a vague silhouette of the car before it shot into the night. He barely remembered popping the door and stepping out of the car to back-up his partner. Tagley hustled back and hopped in, his weight rocking the vehicle before Grace managed to get seated.

"Let's go, let's go! This fucker's gonna pay!" Tagley slammed the car into gear and spun the wheel, engine screaming as they slid around in pursuit. The car fishtailed as Tagley whipped the wheel left and right to straighten out.

Grace yelped, "Hey, easy, easy! Maybe let this go?"

Tagley's only response was to growl and lean into the wheel, looking for taillights in the dark.

The forest, a massive, jagged shadow, whipped by as the detectives strained to see as far forward as possible. Tagley flipped the high beams on and punched the steering wheel in frustration. The engine went from a rising whine to a steady chug as he took in a calming breath.

"Hey," Cole said, "just take me to jail, man, this ain't got to be nothin,' I don't want nothin' to do with y'all. Okay? I didn't see nothing, don't care what y'all do."

Tagley said, "Shut the fuck up, Cole."

"No, man, look: I'm just a burglar, man, I don't want nothin' to do with whatever y'all's doing."

Tagley took a breath to say something when two red lights snapped on fifty yards in front of them.

"Shit!" Tagley pushed hard on the brakes, and the car screeched.

Grace put one hand on the dash and clenched everything he had. For a sick moment, it felt like they were going to rear-end the black car and make pancakes out of everyone. The idling vehicle's tires smoked, and the vehicle shot forward.

Tagley swore and stayed hot on the zigzagging beast.

Grace got a quick look at the license plate and saw only incomprehensible red characters pressed into the white tin rectangle. With every blink, the plate seemed to blur, its type senseless.

"Look at the tags, you see that shit, you ever see anything like that?"

Tagley hissed, knuckles white on the wheel. "No, but once we bust his ass, you can ask him about it."

They lurched around two bends, the rubber tires squealing on asphalt. The machine they were pursuing made a sudden left turn and disappeared into the forest. Tagley jammed both feet on the brakes.

Cole slammed into the back of the seats with a pained grunt and said, "Y'all fuckin' crazy!"

"Shut your goddamned mouth," Tagley said, cranking the vehicle into reverse and craning his neck to see as they backed up.

The engine peaked and the transmission shrieked for a few hot seconds.

"There," Grace said, pointing at a gap in the dense foliage. "Side road."

"Yeah, got it." Tagley spun the wheel, and they plunged into the deep green.

Branches whipped by, scraping the sides of the car. The occasional impact of a thicker branch reminded them that this was a trail, not a road. Tagley leaned on the gas, and the forest responded by getting thicker, pulling harder at the car.

"Hey, slow down," Grace said. As they dove into the unknown, he felt the uneasiness of a civilian, not the authority of the badge. He flinched when another thick branch smacked the passenger side of the car and raked screeching limbs down its side.

"Slow down, damn it!"

Tagley scoffed but eased up. "Look at the tire tracks. Fucker came this way, all right."

The muddy ruts were easy to see in the glare of the headlamps, thick and deep. The car thumped along for an uncomfortable amount of time, maybe fifteen minutes of bobbing in and out of ruts, until the tracks stopped. The trail petered out to nothing in the thick mud.

Tagley leaned forward over the wheel. "What the hell?"

The car they'd been pursuing had vanished.

"That's... that's not possible," Grace said.

Tagley cursed three times, and each time he struck the wheel.

Cole sat in a swamp of his own sweat. As far as he was concerned, every decision these cops made scraped against the grain of common sense.

"Unless, hold on. . ." Grace blinked a few times and said, "Unless he took a switchback or something. Maybe backed up after making these tracks and then took off in another direction. Back up."

"Yeah," Tagley said almost to himself, then he repeated it with more conviction as he put the car in reverse.

They rocked back and forth, snaking backwards down the road, branches scraping the car again until they spotted a fork in the road.

"Oooh, yeah, there we go, that's the shit right there, partner," Tagley grinned.

The smile dropped completely off of his face when the car came to a jarring halt.

"What the shit?" Tagley laid hard on the gas, but the wheels simply spun.

Grace listened to the tires spin and debris ping off the bottom of the vehicle as long as he could stand it.

"We're stuck, feels like a rock or a root."

Tagley snarled, ground his teeth, and gave more gas to the car. The engine whined and the tires spun.

"Hey, knock it off! We're stuck. Lemme take a look." It took two tries for Grace to force his door open against the close-pressing brush. Flipping on his flashlight, he inched toward the back of the car.

Tagley wrenched the car into park. As soon as the door closed, he turned to Cole. "Don't think I forgot about you, boy, we got unfinished business."

Cole licked his lips and decided he didn't have any options left. "Don't seem like your partner's into it."

"Temporary setback, J-Bone, very temporary. You get me?"

Cole sighed, eyes burning, and slumped in the seat as Grace picked his way back, opened the door and stuck his head in.

"Yeah, it's a hollow with a root runnin' through it. We must've popped right over it coming in, but. . ." Grace shrugged.

Tagley cursed, a single sharp syllable.

Grace said, "Yeah, that's helpful. This fucking goose chase, man, you're a piece of work."

"Don't you fuckin' blame me, Grace, you wanted that bastard too."

Grace took a deep breath and expelled it. "*Whatever.* Only way out is to walk. Or push. And this ain't a one-man job, it's slippery as fuck out here."

"I can't drive and push, dickhead."

Grace glared at his partner and decided enough was enough. He'd call in every favor he had to terminate this relationship as soon as they were back in the district. For now, he closed the front passenger-side door and opened up the rear one.

"C'mon out," Grace said, "you're gonna help me push. Unless you want to hike out of here in cuffs?"

"Seems like I ain't hikin' anywhere."

Grace sighed, hearing the hitch in Cole's voice.

The prisoner sucked his teeth before scooting across the bench seat and stepping into the cold, moist air with Grace. The branches on the trail caressed them both. Occasionally, a light breeze sent tree limbs knocking into each other. Cole imagined it as the sound of dry bones knocking together.

"Turn around," Grace said, producing keys.

He uncuffed one of Cole's wrists and then cuffed the prisoner's hands together in front.

Grace motioned for Cole to join him at the car's nose. The only light came from the headlamps, creating an uncomfortably bright bubble of sight. They positioned themselves on either side of the car's centerline and started to push. Tagley worked the engine and all three men rocked the vehicle in a steady rhythm.

As they started to make progress, Cole spoke to Grace. "You can't let Tagley kill me."

Grace glanced at Cole and said, "Shut up and push."

"It ain't right, that shit ain't necessary, I didn't see nothing."

"I said, 'shut up.' Just push, nothin's gonna happen, you'll be fine."

Cole clenched his jaw and committed to a decision. He eyed the back of Tagley's head as he sat behind the wheel, looking backward into the murky red light from the rear lamps. Through the fog of exhaust, it looked as if anything could be out there. They rocked the car and just as it lurched over the root, Cole lunged at Grace and pushed the detective as hard as he could.

"The fuck—?" Grace toppled into the brush and quickly became tangled in the undergrowth.

Tagley missed the action, guiding the vehicle as it jumped

backwards. When he looked forward, his partner was struggling to regain his feet. Cole's figure appeared briefly in the headlights as he rushed down the switchback.

"Son of a bitch!" Tagley had to wrestle his door open against the thick branches before he could leap out and draw his service weapon. Without a shout of warning, he fired three shots where he thought Cole might be.

Grace stumbled up next to Tagley. Incredulous, he said, "You shot him?"

"Assaulting an officer, Grace. You're welcome."

"Jesus Christ. Did you hit him?"

"No. I dunno. Maybe. Why you so worried? The fuck do you care?"

Grace looked away from his partner into the forest. "I'll follow down the switchback, you go the way we came from. He's bound to head for the road. We catch him, we get the fuck out of here."

"You on board now?"

Grace didn't answer and pounded off into the dark. Tagley shook his head and started down the other trail.

It was one thing to navigate a car through this and a whole other to walk it. Branches snagged Tagley's clothing, and wet leaves smacked him in the face. In one hand, he held his flashlight, and in the other, his pistol. The cover was dense enough that the flashlight only illuminated several feet ahead.

After a few minutes of crunching branches and foot-sucking mud, Tagley stopped and listened. Switching off his moonbeam, he cocked his head. An irritating, single-note tone seemed to be building beneath the crunch of the forest and chattering of insects. Branches rattled as the pitter-patter of past rain dripped from leaves. When he glanced up through tangled, black-streaked trees at the nearly starless sky, a thread of primal fear wormed up back of his throat. The mindless tone in his ears turned into a fluted howl above his head, raising the hairs on his neck and causing a chill that tightened his scrotum. It seemed to come from everywhere at once.

A surge of adrenaline crackled through Tagley's body, making his scalp itch. Fast-moving footsteps squished nearby.

"Grace, that you? Grace? Answer me, damn it!"

The rapid steps continued and Tagley didn't bother to think any further. He raised his gun and fired into the dark. Each shot illuminated a circle of light around him. Then he heard a shout and the pop of gunfire that wasn't his. Bullets thwacked into the trees around him.

A wild thought crossed Tagley's mind: *That son of a bitch took down Grace and got his gun.*

Any doubts vanished as instinct took over. He was in danger; his life was on the line. He kept pulling the trigger until the slide locked. He reloaded, clicked on his flashlight, and pushed through branches and undergrowth toward what now sounded like moans in the dark. Hard and slick, bare branches tugged at his clothes and scratched his face. With his pistol in one hand and flashlight in the other, it was nearly impossible to protect himself from the forest.

At close range, his light fell on Grace's pale face. His partner was lying on his back in the brush.

"Oh, shit, shit, *shit.* Grace. I was shooting at him, you were down, right? I thought you were down. Cole got your gun, right? Ah, shit, just hang on, okay? Hang on."

"Tagley," Grace struggled to breathe and speak. "You fuckin' idiot, I called out, you di'n't ans'er, tol' you to stop, G'damn it. Help... me, he'p me up."

"Right, yeah, yeah, we'll get you back to the car real soon. Which way did Cole go?"

"Tagley," Grace said, barely a whisper now, "you fuckin' prick."

Tagley then saw that Grace still had his gun.

Grace pulled the trigger and shot his partner in the chest.

Tagley stumbled, gasping. Grace fired three more times. One of the bullets passed through Tagley's eye, and the senior detective toppled to the ground. His flashlight fell away, its beam pointing out to nowhere.

Grace's breath came slower and more ragged. He struggled to take in air, roll over, call out—anything. His fingers and toes felt cold. The steady pull of death dragged him down until he was gone.

* * *

Cole pushed through the thick blackness, the tangled brush pulling back and cutting him. Welts stung, and blood flowed freely from several slashes on his arms and face. He burst from the forest and stumbled on the raised edge of paved road, skinning his palms and knees. The detectives had nearly cornered him, shooting wild into the forest. He'd started his run frightened for his life, but desperate for freedom. That had changed as the darkness enveloped him, the clicks and whirs of bugs the only accompanying sounds. Unable to see even his own hands in front of him, the unnerving hoot of an owl had pushed him over the edge. He'd nearly gagged in fright and choked back nervous vomit. When the shooting started, he'd curled up in a ball against a tree until the last few shots. He wasn't sure how long he'd stayed that way, but the freezing terror had saved his life, and now he was back on the asphalt of the road.

He paused to gather his breath, relieved that he could see a little better now that his eyes had adjusted to the dark and he was out of the woods. Still cuffed, he swiped both palms awkwardly across his face and pushed himself up off the cold road. The guttural grinding of an engine startled him. He stumbled and, unable to resist turning to look, was rewarded with the blinding glare of headlights too close to dodge. He cringed, clenched his eyes shut, and held his breath, expecting the impact to kill him. The car screeched to a halt and Cole dropped to his knees, sobbing and incoherent.

Warmth boiled off the engine mere inches from his head. If he dared, he could have reached out and touched the hazy black grill through the roiling heat haze. The only light came from the two glaring orbs in the car's grill. Something dry and old poured off the car that smelled like dust, like years of sweat and grief. The door creaked open and, in a few strides, a long silhouette appeared in front of Cole.

Cole said, "Hey, hey. Okay, look, I-I know this looks bad, with the cuffs, but. . ." He cut off with a sob, pitching off balance so that he had to place his hands on the road.

The figure carried an object as long as a man's arm. Cole couldn't make out the details of the axe or the person carrying it. A smoky haze enveloped the silhouette. It raised the tool over its head. Cole flinched and fell facedown, extending his pleading, cuffed hands out in front of him. He didn't see the strike from his fear-praying position, but he could feel the air shift as it came. He heard the dull *thunk* of metal and felt a snap as his wrists suddenly came free. He opened his eyes.

The head of a rough-hewn axe was buried a forearm's length from his nose, neatly bisecting the links of the manacles and resting inches deep in the road. Cole looked up at the figure, a void of liquid darkness. It wrenched the weapon free and pointed down the road, waiting.

Cole nodded, gathered himself onto his haunches, and gulped for air.

The figure retreated to the car with heavy steps, slammed the door shut, and gunned the engine. Cole heard the gears catch. Then the car roared backwards down the road, spun forward, and disappeared screaming into the night.

He sat there for several minutes, listening to his heart thump in his chest. He listened until the pounding receded, and he became aware of forest sounds, and a light breeze that chilled the sweat on his neck.

James Cole stood up straight and began walking north.

DYING RIVER

BRIDGETT NELSON

"Maybe if it had been caught earlier," Dr. Powderly said, the sadness in his voice reflected in his eyes. "Please understand, Ms. Feig, we'll do everything we can. We're not giving up, but bacterial meningitis has the potential to be life-threatening, and River's has progressed rapidly."

"I didn't know," Cynthia said. She dropped her head, stared at her interwoven fingers squeezed tightly together, and whispered. "I. . . I. . . didn't know. It was just a headache."

Beneath the exterior of shock and stoicism, her insides were a roiling monsoon of activity. Adrenaline pumped as her mind raced. Muscles wriggled with tension. Respirations were shallow and swift, causing her under-oxygenated body to feel dizzy and weak. The flight or fight response kicked in, and she stood, tensed for this unexpected battle.

The physician gave her a knowing look, her bedraggled, crazed expression a routine occurrence within the hospital's walls. "I understand. Please don't beat yourself up. It's easy to miss something like this, because the symptoms are so vague."

He gripped her thin shoulder in his palm and squeezed. "This fight isn't over. Far from it." His voice was soothing, confident. Walking out of the room, he shut the door behind him, leaving Cynthia staring at her unconscious son. After several minutes, she sat back down.

Yesterday at breakfast, River had complained of a minor headache. She'd given him some children's ibuprofen and promptly forgot his symptoms after Marlee fell and scraped her knee. Cynthia hadn't seen him again until lunch, where he'd eaten only a few bites of his chicken salad sandwich and asked to be excused.

"Not hungry?" she'd asked.

"Nah." He hadn't met her eyes.

"Is your headache gone?"

"Mostly. Just tired. The light is hurting my eyes, so I think I'm going to take a nap."

That was the moment she should have known something was wrong. River, her boisterous twelve-year-old, never napped. Instead, she'd obliviously loaded the dishwasher and replied, "Okay. Just not too long, or you'll ruin your sleep tonight."

"Yeah, okay." Then he was gone.

At dinner, he'd complained of a stiff neck. "You probably slept in an odd position," she'd reasoned. "I bet that's what caused your headache too. Run and get a couple more ibuprofen from the medicine cabinet. No more than two!" Afterward, she'd driven Marlee to a birthday party and spent the evening socializing with her daughter's classmates' parents. She'd peeked into his bedroom before bed, but he was nothing more than an undefined lump under the blankets.

But the next morning, she'd found him fevered and confused, sitting inside his closet. His glassy eyes stared uncomprehendingly at her, as his body quaked with pyrexial shivers.

"River, buddy. . . you okay?"

"Dirt! Bloody rocky dirt!" He raked his fingernails down his chest. The wounds oozed a pink plasma.

Her mother had arrived to watch Marlee, while Cynthia rushed River to the emergency department. The medical team had immediately drawn blood, taken him for a CT scan, and much to Cynthia's dismay, performed a lumbar puncture. Less than two hours later, River was diagnosed with bacterial meningitis. Based on the doctors' reactions, the prognosis was bleak.

Now, she looked at her son's deathlike pallor and felt a weight growing bigger in the pit of her stomach.

As rain pelted against the window, obscuring the city skyline, her mind drifted back to his birth day—how his father held her hand as she pushed this perfect, tiny human out; her joy at seeing those ten tiny fingers and toes; the way she couldn't keep her lips away from the silky peach fuzz covering the soft skin of his slightly misshapen head—he was her first-born, and she'd known in that moment she'd never love anyone or anything more. She still remembered the way it felt as his small mouth suckled her breast; the way his bright blue eyes stared so intently into hers as he breastfed; the way his delicate fingers encircled trustingly around hers.

Cynthia was startled back to awareness by River's raspy voice. "Mommy?" He hadn't called her 'Mommy' in years.

"I'm here." She placed her hand on his leg. "How are you feeling?"

His chin was lying awkwardly against his chest, hips and knees flexed. He licked his lips. "Weird burnt taste in my mouth. Feels like my feet are asleep. Hurts." Before Cynthia could respond, River's eyes rolled back in his head, and his body began spasmodically jerking. *What should I do? What should I do?* She was completely paralyzed. Finally, she forced herself to hit the nurse's call button. When it was answered, she said in a voice unlike her own, "He's having a seizure!"

Less than a minute later, a nurse was injecting benzodiazepines into River's intravenous line as another rolled him onto his side and repositioned the pillow beneath his head. After what felt like a lifetime to Cynthia, her son's body stopped convulsing. Depleted, her legs gave out, and she slid down the wall she was leaning against.

"Is he okay?" Her voice was high-pitched, child-like.

"When children have seizures following a meningitis diagnosis, it's because the cerebral hemispheres of their brain are damaged due to the swelling and inflammation caused by the infection." The nurse paused. "I'll admit, it's not a great sign, but we were able to control River's quickly, which is reassuring. We'll continue giving him intravenous corticosteroids and antibiotics and, hopefully, that will be the last seizure he has."

Cynthia let out a deep breath. "How long will he be unconscious?"

"It will take his brain a while to reset following the seizure. Why don't you take a walk, Ms. Feig? Stretch your legs. I'll stay with River and call your cell if he wakes up."

Cynthia nodded her head vigorously; a small child being directed by a parent. "Okay. . . yeah. . . all right. I'll do that." She walked out the door without looking back, tossing her mask into the contaminates receptacle, and swallowing bitter bile. Pulling out her phone, she called her mother.

"He just had a seizure." She struggled to get the words out.

"Take a deep breath. You sound like you're hyperventilating." She did as she was told, sucking the cool air into her burning lungs. When her breathing regulated, her mother went on, "Now tell me what happened."

"It's bad. The doctors are talking as though he won't make it."

"One step at a time," her mother gently said. "River is strong, and he's at the best hospital in the state, getting top-notch care."

Cynthia didn't respond. Seconds passed.

"I know you're still there. I can hear you breathing and your footsteps. Let me reassure you that Marlee is fine—we're making peanut butter cookies, and she has zero symptoms—and River is going to be fine too. You'll see."

Again, Cynthia stayed silent.

"I love you and River very much. Please keep me updated." Her mother disconnected the call, and Cynthia collapsed onto a bench that reeked of smoke and nicotine.

Resting her head in her hands, she finally let herself cry. The depths of her fear, her lack of control, her *dread* seeped from her core, as tiny, tear-shaped droplets watered the grass beneath her feet with her pain and loathing. *What kind of mother am I? How could I have let this happen? How could I not have known?*

Cynthia recalled how, when River was three, his father decided his boy needed a dog. They'd researched various breeds, trying to find the perfect playmate for their gifted son, finally settling on a Jack Russell terrier. Cynthia would never forget River's delighted squeal upon seeing his new friend.

"A *puppy*!"

He'd jumped up and down, clapping his hands, unintentionally scaring his new white and tan playmate. Cynthia picked up the shaking puppy, holding it against her breast so it could feel her beating heart. Its tiny body calmed immediately. She sat on the couch, and River had climbed onto her lap, rubbing the dog's silky ears and exclaiming, "I wanna name him Rocky like on *Paw Patrol*!"

Leaning back on the bench and staring up at the stars, a small smile crept across Cynthia's blotchy, tear-streaked face, remembering the pure, unadulterated joy she'd seen on River's that long-ago day. She checked her phone. She'd been away for nearly an hour. It was time to get back to her son.

Standing, she brushed back her hair and wiped the wetness from her face using the sleeve of her zip-up hoodie. She breathed deeply, trying to calm her fried nerves. It didn't help.

Cynthia made her way back to the hospital. Her cell phone vibrated inside her pocket. Worried it was her mother telling her Marlee was now exhibiting symptoms like River's, she removed the phone and glanced at the screen. It read GTL, which she knew stood for Global Tel*Link Corporation, the telephone vendor used by the state prison system. Grimacing, she declined the call, placing the phone back inside her pocket.

As she approached River's room, she noticed several masked individuals on their way out, and broke into a run. "What's going on?" she asked the nurse.

"He had another seizure. A much bigger and longer one. The doctor decided to transfer him to the pediatric intensive care unit so we can monitor him more closely."

"Jesus! Is he okay? When will he be transferred?"

The nurse hesitated before responding. "The doctor will talk to you once he's stabilized. He's already in PICU room five."

Without asking for directions, Cynthia turned and bolted down the hallway, following the various "YOU ARE HERE" signs to lead her where she needed to go. By God's grace, neither she, nor her family, had ever needed the ICU / PICU before this, so she was clueless about its location. She arrived at a colorfully painted wall—trees and flowers and sunshine creating a lighthearted mural—and a sign that read "Pediatric Intensive Care Unit" in rainbow hues. The door was locked, and Cynthia nearly panicked and began pounding before she noticed the call button to its right. She pressed the red disk, and a soft voice responded, "This is Debbie, RN. How can I help you?"

"I'm Cynthia Feig, River's mom. I'm told he's in room five."

The nurse's voice instantly became more sympathetic. "Of course, come right in." The door clicked open. Cynthia entered and was immediately struck by the eerie silence. These weren't children who were on the mend and ready to be discharged—this place felt more like their graveyard. Faint beeps came from the rooms she passed, but the lack of human chatter and laughter seemed funereal. Parents sat with their children, perhaps silently pleading, or bargaining with their chosen deity, to just let their son or daughter live.

Cynthia reached room number five and glanced inside. Her son had wires protruding from nearly every orifice of his body. An oxygen cannula nestled within his nostrils. His body looked small and insignificant in the big hospital bed. Trying desperately to breathe, despite feeling like she had an elephant sitting on her chest, she took the seat beside River. Within five minutes, Dr. Powderly made an appearance.

He smiled warmly at her, but she could see the worry reflected in his eyes and in the lines etched on his face. Her stomach clenched and acid formed in the pit of her stomach.

"Ms. Feig, River is currently stable, but I made the decision to bring him here for closer monitoring. This last seizure was such that we're worried about possible hypoxic brain injury." He nodded, acknowledging her confusion, and explained, "The seizure was sustained. During the peri-ictal stage of a seizure, or during the midst of it, rather, breathing can become very shallow or sometimes cease all together. Despite using every trick in our arsenal, we couldn't get the seizure stopped. River's body seemed impervious to the medications. So, between the inflammation caused by the meningitis, and the potential hypoxic injury, the concern now is that your son may have brain damage."

"But," Cynthia choked out the words, "what does that mean?"

"We won't know right away. River's brain may be perfectly intact. Or, he may have physical limitations with his speech or vision. Maybe some extremity weakness or paralysis. Possible memory issues. There's really no way to say at this point. Until the inflammation decreases and we can run some tests, it's all just speculation."

"He was a healthy little boy hours ago. I can't. . . I just. . . he'll live?"

"This infection is vicious. We don't yet know the strain we're dealing with, but based on what we've seen so far, and the rapid progression, I'm inclined to believe it's not a good one. I feel I should also warn you that River might develop a meningitis rash. Basically, because the bacteria are multiplying at such a rapid rate, they're creating toxins that circle through the body, potentially injuring his blood vessels and organs. As the damage progresses, the blood vessels leak, causing bruise-like spots to appear on the skin that looks like a rash. It's not something we want to happen, but it's not a death sentence either. It can look scary, so I want you to be prepared." He cleared his throat and ventured to the doorway. "None of this is your fault, Ms. Feig. I think you need to hear that." He turned and walked out of the room.

Cynthia stared at the screen recording her son's heart rhythm, blood pressure, heart rate, even his oxygen saturation levels. She looked at the catheter draining the urine from his body, the pale, gold liquid clear. She gazed at the bags of medications and fluids hanging from the IV pole and dripping into his veins. . . and she knew she had to get out of that room. Nearly running to the nurse's station, she told the woman behind the desk she was going to get some coffee and that she'd be back as quickly as possible.

She knew she wouldn't. She needed time—time to process, time to rationalize that she may have a very different version of her son at the end of this, time to comprehend she may leave these walls without a son at all.

She wasn't sure she could do this alone. She needed someone to talk to. . . someone who wasn't a cheerleader like her mother. But there was no one. She trudged slowly to the cafeteria and paid for a black coffee that tasted like battery acid. Then she sat at a booth and willed her phone to ring. Seventeen minutes later, it did.

Glancing at the screen, though she already knew what she'd see, she accepted the call and said, "Hello, Toby."

"Hey, Cyn. Long time, no talk."

Cynthia tried to remember the last time she'd talked to her husband and couldn't. He was a part of her life she preferred to not dwell on, but tonight, just this once, she was grateful to hear his voice. "Yep. It's been a while. How are you?"

"As well as can be expected." She heard a sharp inhalation and knew he was smoking one of his beloved Marlboro cigarettes. "Listen, it's been a weird day. I've been anxious as fuck since the moment I woke up this morning, and I just wanted to call and make sure everything was okay."

She gave a bitter laugh. "Funny that you're so perceptive now, Toby."

"Cut the shit, Cynthia. I don't need your guff. I just want to know if my kids are okay, and then I'll be on my merry way, all right?" When she didn't respond, he repeated, *"All right?"*

Cynthia choked down a sip of her coffee. When she finally spoke, her voice was raspy. . . haggard. "We're not okay, Toby."

"What's going on?" he asked, fighting for a calm tone but not quite succeeding.

"River is in the pediatric intensive care unit with meningitis." She took another drink of the toxic sludge the hospital labeled 'coffee.' "It's not looking good."

Toby sucked in a breath, but this time, she knew it wasn't

smoking-related. "What do you mean, 'it's not looking good'? Is he going to die?"

"I don't know, Toby. I just don't fucking know."

"Tell me what you do know."

As Cynthia relayed the day's events to her soon-to-be-ex, she felt part of the momentous weight being lifted from her shoulders. It was nice to share the burden. Despite everything Toby had done, the *truly awful, vile* shit Toby had done, he'd always been a good father, and she knew he'd help as much as he could, given his limited means.

"Jesus," he said when she finished.

"Yeah." She hesitated. "Toby, I don't know what to do."

"There's not much we can do, except trust them to give him the best care. . . and pray."

"Pray? That doesn't sound like the Toby I lived with for ten years."

"Things change."

"Clearly."

"I'll call back for an update. Try to get some sleep." The phone disconnected.

"Thanks for nothing, asshole," she muttered under her breath, sticking the phone back in her pocket.

After all they'd been through, after all she'd learned about the man she'd married—the man she thought she'd known—she still let him crawl beneath her skin and wedge himself there. And it needed to stop.

Tossing the undrinkable coffee into the nearest trash receptacle, Cynthia headed back toward the PICU. She walked slowly, unable to garner any enthusiasm for the sterile, unnaturally silent unit. Hospital visiting hours were long over, but those rules didn't apply so much here, to the parents of gravely ill children.

No matter how much the man annoyed her, she couldn't

help but remember Toby at his best. As she shuffled down the darkened corridors, she recalled how excited he'd been the first time River had invited his friend, Dylan, over for a sleepover. He'd planned all sorts of activities for the boys—fishing at the local pond, sleeping in a tent in the backyard, and roasting marshmallows over the firepit. His disappointment was profound when the boys had shown no interest in his ideas. Typical preteens, they'd wanted only to play video games, eat junk food, and watch scary movies.

Toby had left the house that night in a sulk, and she hadn't seen him until the next morning. If only she'd known then what she knew now.

Shaking her head to clear *that* memory, Cynthia got buzzed into the PICU and ventured to room five.

River's room.

He looked the same—purple smudges beneath both eyes, crazy bedhead spikes in his thick, dark hair, freckles stark against his pale skin. The bed seemed to swallow him whole, the outline of his body barely visible through the white cotton blanket. New, nearly full bags of medication hung from the IV pole and were slowly trickling through his intravenous tubing. She lifted the bedcover to pull it up around his shoulders, glanced briefly beneath, and gasped in stunned disbelief. River's arms and legs were covered in ominous purple, bruise-like splotches. Pain stabbed from behind the orbs of both bloodshot eyes as her sight blurred. Tears poured, creating crisscrossing swaths of moisture across her flushed cheeks.

Cynthia glanced one final time at her son's struggling body and calmly tucked the cover around his scrawny shoulders as she'd originally intended. She then sat in the chair beside his bed, rested her head against the stiff faux leather, and allowed her emotionally overwrought brain to shut down.

* * *

She awoke in the cold, clinical vacuum of the PICU to the annoyingly cheerful chirping of her phone. Pulling it from her pocket, she saw it was nearly eight o'clock in the morning. . . then noticed the Global Tel*Link Corporation name on her screen. Accepting the call, she said, "Well, if it isn't my fucked-in-the-head husband, federal prison inmate number 04470-061!"

"Quit being a bitch, Cynthia, and tell me how River is doing."

"No."

"No?" She could hear anger penetrating the single word.

"I don't have to tell you anything. I needed you last night, despite everything, but you offered nothing but generic platitudes. You may have been a decent father, but you sure as hell sucked balls as a husband." She lowered her voice, which had grown louder as she'd talked. "If you want to know how River's doing, call the fucking hospital and see if they'll give information to a serial killer, you lousy fuck."

"What the hell has gotten into you? Jesus Christ, he's my son too!"

"Yeah, well, you should have thought about that before you raped and dismembered all those men." She heard a loud thud and knew he'd punched something, though she couldn't identify what.

After several seconds and some heavy breathing, he said, "I'll just call your mom."

"I haven't spoken to her in hours. She knows nothing."

"Cynthia, don't be like this. I love him, and I'm worried."

"Do you have any idea in that depraved brain of yours how much I've worried about River and Marlee since you went away? Do you, Toby? Because the last few years have been hell. *Hell!*

And I'm tired of being the nice guy. If you want information about River's condition, go charm somebody else, because I'm done." She let out a sob. "I'm just so fucking done."

She disconnected the call, placed her face into the palms of her hands, and cried, remembering.

That goddamned morning. . .

. . . that horrible Saturday morning when two detectives arrested Toby in their driveway as he washed their decrepit minivan.

. . . that horrible Saturday morning when they'd pushed her husband face-first to the ground and cuffed his hands behind his back.

. . . that horrible Saturday morning when they informed her he was being charged in the rapes and homicides of four men.

. . . that horrible Saturday morning when they'd forced him into the back seat of the awaiting police car and driven him to the station to question and book him.

. . . that horrible Saturday morning when Toby was taken from them forever as their two innocent children watched every moment from the front window of their home; when she'd seen the defeated look on their father's face and knew their lives would never again be the same.

The day-to-day was hard.

Trying to keep River's abhorrent secret, without Toby's reassurance that he was just a typical boy, was impossible.

The puppy—Rocky—had been dead within a month of coming to live with their family. River had cut off his paws and left him crying piteously in the backyard, unable to move on the bloody stumps. Toby had shot the poor creature in the head to end his suffering, then spent the next year trying to convince her River's behavior was normal.

Fuck that.

Her dear son's first sleepover had ended with a wailing

ambulance careening down the street, hauling his friend Dylan. Who had, according to River, accidentally fallen out of the tree-house and broken his leg.

The next day, Cynthia received an irate call from Dylan's father, claiming River had tried to sexually molest his son, and had pushed him out of the treehouse when he wasn't receptive to River's advances.

Again, Toby had tried to convince her that sexual exploration in young children was perfectly normal. Hell, maybe it was.

But then she'd found an aroused River standing over his sister's bed, watching her sleep.

She'd grown to hate his father.

And, though she'd never admit it to anyone, she hated River too. Even worse, she feared him.

Now, here her son was, gravely ill, and what she felt most was intense relief. Though she could never harm her own child, perhaps God had bestowed mercy on her suffering and was doing the job for her.

God help her, she hoped River died. She'd prayed for it every day, and now it might actually happen.

Her attention shifted as she heard rustling in the bed. She turned to look at her son.

River was awake and alert. His eyes were bright, his cheeks a healthy pink.

Cynthia's blood ran cold as he smiled and said, "I feel a lot better, Mom."

ROADBLOCK

TONY TREMBLAY

Parked on the shoulder of the road, Susan gripped the steering wheel.

The astonishing sight before her almost swept away images of her best friend screwing her husband. *Almost.* Those visuals of Karen and Tom didn't entirely fade away. They lingered like autopsy photos on a television true crime show.

She had stopped by her husband's business to surprise him with an invitation to lunch. Without bothering to knock, she'd opened the door to his office, and there was Karen, flat on her back, draped over his desk with Tom between her legs. Karen's head had turned toward the door to discover Susan staring at them. She'd made no attempt to push Tom off. Instead, with her eyes half closed, Karen had grinned. There was no shame in that crooked smile, no guilt, no remorse. If anything, it projected triumph, satisfaction.

Susan had turned on her heels and walked out of the building.

She'd spent twenty-five years married to that man, devoting her love and life to him. They had two daughters, who had grown up to be as perfect as any parent could wish for. She was now on her way to see one of them.

Despite the anger and sorrow battling within her, Susan managed to focus on her driving. She was a safe driver, always taking notice of the traffic—easy enough now because hers was the only car on the road. After cresting a hilly curve and coasting on a flat section, she reflected on the lack of traffic.

Unusual for this time of day.

Then shock seized her when she spotted something ahead.

Something incredible.

What looked like a huge, black wall blocked her way.

She blinked a few times, unsure of what she was seeing. Her disbelief mounting, she pulled onto the shoulder, shut off the engine, and got out of the car.

At this close range, she could now see that the wall had the appearance of fog—though unlike any she had ever seen. Its leading surface was flat, suggesting a strangely dark mass of vapor pressed against a large sheet of glass. But jutting from this smooth surface, countless smoky fingers wriggled, curled, and spiraled into misty threads that quickly dissolved in the warm air. From what she could tell, these wispy tendrils extended less than a foot before they disappeared, only to be replaced by others. She thought of macabre weeds, sprouting from areas where nothing else could take root.

The wall of fog was, for the most part, dark as ink and almost as opaque. The density of the darkness, however, varied. Layers of ebony hues drifted lethargically in all directions, like shadows searching for corners to hide in.

The wall stretched into the sky as far as she could see. To her left and right, it appeared to extend endlessly through the trees, hills, and countryside.

What the hell is this?

A notion tugged at her: get closer, have a better look. While she didn't reject the idea outright, she managed to temper it with caution.

I'll go far enough to see it better, but no way am I going to touch it.

She took a few steps forward, but the sound of squealing brakes stopped her. She turned and saw a car—old, with faded paint and a license plate hanging by one screw—slewing to a stop on the shoulder in front of hers. The driver, a young woman, maybe in her late teens, sat and stared at the wall for maybe half a minute before shutting off the engine and getting out.

"Holy shit, lady! What is that? Some kind of fog?"

Susan's guess as to her age seemed right enough. Bright red streaks accented bleached blond hair. She wore pre-torn jeans and an untucked T-shirt with a photo of Billie Eilish. Big black boots enveloped her feet. A nose ring completed the ensemble.

"I—I don't know," answered Susan. "I've never seen fog that color before."

"Damn," said the young woman, her voice a combination of awe and anxiety, "I don't need this right now. I need to be out of here."

"You in trouble?"

The young woman looked down at her boots. "Yeah."

"Looks like we're both running from something."

When Susan received no reply, she turned back toward the wall's shifting, seething face.

Is it closer?

She couldn't be sure; maybe it was an optical illusion. All that black was distracting, disorienting. She looked around for an object to mark its location. There—a speed limit sign a few feet from the wall. She locked the visual in her mind before the young woman's voice broke her concentration.

"Let's get closer. Maybe we can see into it, tell how far it goes. If it's not too thick, I'm gonna drive through it."

She's really itching to get out of here. I wonder what she's running from.

"Okay," said Susan, "but if I were you, I wouldn't touch it. Notice there are no cars coming out of it?"

"Yeah, I did notice. It's creeping me out, too."

"My name is Susan, by the way. Yours?"

"Becca."

"Okay, Becca, let's have a closer look."

They moved hesitantly toward the wall. Becca remained close to Susan, near enough so their elbows brushed. Her eyes were wide, her mouth stretched taut. Susan wondered what Becca was more nervous about—what they were walking toward, or what she was running from.

She's just a kid.

Susan's maternal instincts kicked in. She placed a hand on Becca's shoulder and smiled. Becca gave her a weak smile back. When they were a yard or so from the wall, Susan stopped and released her grip.

"That's far enough. We'll look from here."

As Susan peered at it, she half-expected to see a milky, distorted reflection of herself in its flat, smooth surface. Her nerves settled a little when, up close, she saw no reflections of any kind.

Not quite sure what to make of that, she decided to try something. Since the sun was behind her, she lifted an arm to see if it would cast a shadow. It did not. Confused, she lowered her arm and studied the wall further.

Why is it so dark?

As if moving a few extra inches closer might reveal an answer, she leaned in.

She noticed now that pale, yellowish patches swirled and

shifted in the inky mist. These seemed to move through the wall's ebony layers almost as if with purpose.

"You see them, too." Becca's comment wasn't a question.

"Yeah. Something about them. . . ."

Mid-sentence, Susan focused on the pale, flaxen patches. They were almost mesmerizing, yet she understood that she *could* look away. She *could* turn and leave. However, her choice was to keep looking. To try to understand what she was seeing. A sense of calm gradually replaced her nervousness. The longer she stared at them, the more soothing their gyrations became. It couldn't hurt to inch a little closer. . . .

"Hey! What are you doing?" Becca's hand clutched Susan's blouse and pulled her back. "Don't get too close!"

Susan shook her head in confusion. "I—I wasn't. I just wanted to see better."

It was Becca's turn to shake her head. "You were almost touching it!"

What the hell?

"Okay," said Susan, "I don't remember doing that. I'm not sure what happened, but I think *something* about this wall messes with your head. Becca, we've got to leave. Turn around and go back—"

"No!" Becca's voice was loud, pleading. "I'm not going back!"

"Look, we can go to Page Hill Road. It's only half a mile or so, and it forks toward Concord. We'll just go around this thing! Do you have your phone on you?"

Becca's eyes shifted to the side. "No. I left it."

If she's telling the truth, maybe it's because she doesn't want to be located.

"Okay, mine's in the car. You take off while I call 911. That will give you time to get to Page Hill Road before the police come. But they should know about this!"

Relief washed over Becca's features. "Thank you, Susan. I hope whatever you're running from turns out okay."

Susan nodded. "I hope the same for you."

They each headed for their cars. When Susan reached hers, she opened her purse and removed her cell phone. The screen was blank. She hit the wake button—with no result. Turning it on and off had the same effect. Frustrated, she tossed the phone onto the passenger seat. The battery *couldn't* be low—she'd charged it this morning before visiting her husband.

Her husband.

Well, he won't be for much longer. There's no way he's talking his way out of this. And as for that bitch Karen. . . .

Susan lifted her gaze to the windshield. To her surprise, Becca's car remained parked in front of hers.

For someone who wanted to get out of Dodge so fast, she's sure taking her time.

She got out and walked over. Becca was slouched forward, hands on the steering wheel, shoulders jerking in rhythm with her audible sobs.

"Becca, what's wrong?"

The girl glanced up. Her face was red and puffy, her cheeks damp. "The car won't start. The dash lights won't even come on. I had no trouble with it before I got here."

Susan's back stiffened. It was just like her phone. "Come on, let's take mine. I'll drop you off wherever you want."

As the two hurried back to her car, Susan's gut clenched. It remained tight as she settled in the driver's seat and turned the key.

As she feared, hers wouldn't start either.

Becca's moans echoed in Susan's ears.

"What's going on? I'm scared."

Susan had no answer. She sat quietly behind the wheel, attempting to put everything into perspective. There *had* to be a rational explanation for all of this. A weird weather pattern, a magnetic field. *Something—*

She sat up straight. Sucked in a breath and held it.

The speed limit sign. It's gone.

Urgently, she turned the ignition again.

Not so much as a click in response.

"W—what's going on?" Becca asked, her voice catching.

"The wall. It's closer."

"Shit, shit, shit. What do we do?"

"We walk. Let's go."

As Susan grabbed her purse, Becca rushed to her car, removed her handbag, and looped its strap over her shoulder. She cradled the handbag as if it held something precious.

I wonder what she's so protective of?

They'd gone no farther than ten feet when they heard a vehicle approaching from the direction of Goffstown.

"Oh, my God, someone's coming," Becca said.

As the car came around the curve, Susan waved both hands in the air and jumped up and down to get the driver's attention. Becca lifted her free hand and screamed, "Hey, hey, over here!"

It was an almond-colored car with a logo from a security firm Susan had never heard of. Overjoyed, she turned to Becca and hugged the girl—only to be confused when Becca's body stiffened.

"What's the matter?" she asked.

Becca did not respond. Instead, she tightened her hold on the bag as the security car pulled alongside them and stopped.

"No!" Susan cried. "You turned off your engine!"

The driver, a brown-uniformed man, glanced at her before swinging his gaze back to the wall. "Yeah, I did. Why? But what the hell is *THAT*?"

"Turn it back on." With pleading eyes, she added, "Please."

He regarded her for another moment, then obliged. His car

wouldn't start. When he tried his radio, not even static crackled over the speaker. Same went for the remote radio strapped to his chest.

"What in the hell is going on here?" he asked, getting out of the car.

Susan filled him in, finishing with, ". . . and we were about to walk back to town when you drove up."

While Susan was talking, the man kept looking at Becca. His continued appraisal of the young woman, with an occasional glance to the wall, had Susan wondering why he was so interested in her. He hadn't driven toward them with his amber lights flashing. But that didn't mean he wasn't searching for someone.

Also concerning, Becca avoided eye contact with him.

"You two, stay here," he said. "Don't move. I'm going to check out whatever this thing is. I'll be right back."

Susan marveled at the man's demeanor.

He's a professional. He's paid to remain calm.

She did notice that his hand clasped the handle of his holstered gun as he approached the wall. She also realized the wall's leading edge now stood only a few feet from the front bumper of Becca's car.

"Officer! The wall! It's moving. It's closer to us than it was before!"

He lifted his hand to acknowledge her warning but then waved her off.

Just before he reached the wall, he stopped. His gaze roamed over its surface—up, down, side to side. Then, his body went still. His hand dropped from his holster to hang by his side.

He sees those pale shapes inside.

She and Becca stared at him. Neither of them moved or said a word.

A chill descended upon Susan, and a violent shiver racked

her body. Images of frost and sheets of ice entered her mind. With every exhalation, a cloud of vapor escaped her quivering lips.

But the assault on her body was brief, and she lowered her head in relief as it passed.

When she raised it again, she saw the man at the wall, standing stiff and immobile, as if frozen in place. Suddenly, with an audible crack, his arms flew out behind him. Another sound, like gears crunching against one other, and his head ratcheted backward, his neck stretching to the point Susan could see his face, his mouth wide open, his eyes huge cavities that swirled with the darkness of the fog itself. The officer's body rose into the air. With another crack, his legs bent violently behind him.

Becca's shrieks pealed even louder than Susan's.

What the hell. . . what the hell! He's bent like a fucking Ken doll. I told him not to get too close. Oh, my God, please, don't let this get any worse. No, no, I take that back, I didn't mean. . . .

A shape emerged from the wall. Susan's first thought was of a black snake with suction cups before a more precise term came to her. *A tentacle.* It curled and arced through the air like a sentient live wire enjoying its newfound freedom. It took her a moment to realize that those wild movements weren't as random as they appeared.

It's hunting. Searching for purchase!

The tentacle found its prey.

The black arm wrapped itself around the man. It squeezed, and patches of blood soaked through his uniform. With its hold secure, the monstrous *thing* withdrew into the wall, still holding its prize.

Susan's focus had been on the gruesome spectacle, but after the officer disappeared, she turned to Becca. The young woman was on the ground, her arms around her knees, head buried between them. Her moans were soft, whiny, like a puppy begging to be held. Susan placed a hand on her shoulder.

"Becca, come on. We have to go. Now!"

Becca's head rose. The look of defeat on her face melted Susan's heart. But there was no time to wallow in pity.

"Come on, get up!"

The girl remained on her ass.

Susan took a handful of Becca's hair and pulled.

"Ow! Okay, I'll get up!"

Once she was on her feet, they faced each other. Susan wrapped her arms around Becca, who did not protest.

"Are you ready?" asked Susan.

"Yeah. Let's go." Becca squeezed her handbag tight to her body.

They turned to make a fast retreat but got no further than one step.

Another wall, jet black—every bit as imposing as the first—blocked the road in the other direction. It, too, reached for the heavens, and its sides extended forever.

"It's not going to let us leave!" Becca's body hitched as she sobbed.

Susan didn't have the emotional strength to comfort her this time.

It? Is it an "it," or a "they?" There are two walls, they don't appear to be joined. Whether it's one entity or more, though, she's right; something doesn't want us to leave.

But WHAT?

Susan tugged at Becca's sleeve and led her to the rear of the security man's car, where they hunkered down behind the bumper. She needed a moment to think, to put some logic to this mess. Looking side to side, she saw only woods and hill-sides, with no impediments. But the length of the walls seemed to be unending, closing to form a perspective point in the farthest distance. And the way they seemed to be coming together. . . .

She looked back at the first wall and found it now just inches from the front of Becca's car.

How could that be? We were just looking at it a minute ago. How did it move that fast when we weren't watching it?

Wait. WHILE we weren't watching it. . . .

"Becca, the wall, the first one, it's closer. I think it moved when we weren't watching it. . . *because* we weren't watching it."

"What?"

"Maybe it only advances when we aren't looking at it."

Confused, Becca asked. "You're saying we have to watch it all the time?"

"Yes. No. I don't know."

"What do we do?"

Susan took a deep breath. "We sit back-to-back, each keeping our eyes on the wall in front of us."

Becca pointed to her left. "We can't go through the woods?"

"We'd be looking at the ground while we're walking. And the trees would block our view. If I'm right, those walls would close in on us in no time. Besides, they stretch as far as my eyes can see. We'd still be trapped between them no matter how far we go."

With sagging shoulders and downcast eyes, Becca stood and trudged to a point on the road about midway between the walls. It could have been invisible hands pushing her to the pavement, but Susan knew it was the weight of resignation. Of helplessness.

Susan sat down with her back against Becca's. She had no idea how much time had passed, or how much more time passed once they took up their observation positions. The sun crept ever on across the sky until the shadows faded, absorbed by the waning light.

Dusk.

They had spoken very little and moved only slightly—mostly for reasons of comfort. They'd had nothing to drink or eat, so the pressure to relieve themselves had not yet reached a critical point. At least the walls had not moved any closer.

"Susan?" Becca asked.

"Yeah?"

"Can they see in the dark?"

"I—I don't know."

"I'm so tired. I'm trying to fight it, but I'm falling asleep."

Susan wanted to reply, to give Becca a pep talk, but she was tired, too. The frightening notion that the worst *would* happen if they fell asleep had occurred to her earlier, but she had chased it away.

Now, there was no ignoring it.

How about it, you big black pieces of shit? Do you see in the dark? Do you sleep? Are you going to grab us when we nod off? Because we will sleep. Maybe it won't hurt as much if you take us then.

If the walls *could* read her thoughts, they offered no answers.

Susan fought like hell to stay awake. When her head bobbed, she would snap it back up. She sang songs in whispers but struggled to remember the words. Eventually, her eyes closed, her chin fell to her chest, and sleep staked its claim.

Dreams—nightmares—invaded her slumber. Scenes of monsters chasing her traded places with those of her husband's betrayal. Sometimes, the two were intertwined. In every dream, a black wall stood in the background.

A pain in her neck woke her—the result of her lowered head stretching her neck muscles. How long had she been out? Her vision was so blurry she couldn't see a thing. As the grogginess of sleep slipped away, the recollection of what she and Becca were doing took its place. Leaning back, relief washed over her when she pressed against the young woman.

She rotated her head to work out the kinks. Above, she saw blue skies, without a cloud.

She had slept through the night. And she was alive!

The walls!

Preparing herself for the worst, Susan took a deep breath and looked around.

Her gaze got as far as her own feet before she screamed. She shook and cried out until her throat was raw. Her fists pounded the pavement until the pain proved too much. She drew her knees up to her chest and wrapped her arms around them. Tears distorted the image before her, but they didn't obscure it.

Just in front of her, Becca's severed head lay in the road. The flesh of her neck was ragged where it had been ripped from her torso. No blood pooled beneath it. Her eyes and mouth were open, filled with black, swirling voids.

Susan drew away from the dead thing. Her back contacted Becca's again—

What?!

Adrenalin pumping, she sprang up and whirled.

Becca's legs were still crossed, boot heels pressed against her thighs. Her relaxed-looking hands rested in her lap. The remaining flesh of her neck hung limp over her top.

It took her in her sleep. It looks like she didn't even know it was happening.

Enraged, Susan spun toward the wall. "You..."

The words caught in her throat.

The wall was gone.

The road stretched on as it always had. Trees, scrub, hill-sides, and rocks dotted the landscape. A quick glance revealed all three parked cars. Turning, she saw the other wall was also gone—she could see the short straightaway before the road curved out of sight. Her eyes roved back and forth, making sure she wasn't imagining it, but the views didn't change.

They're gone, they're really gone. I'm getting the hell out of here.

The car. Check the car!

Susan ran to her car, inserted the key in the ignition, and the engine turned over. Picking up her phone, she found that it worked. She was tempted to call for help, but her fingers wouldn't move.

The date on the phone was yesterday's. The time displayed was 1:30 p.m..

That's. . . that's impossible.

She gathered her wits and dragged herself back out to the road.

These things that happened here—I'll never be able to explain them. I'm not even sure if I WANT to know what this was all about. But there is one mystery I can solve. . . .

Susan approached Becca's body.

"I'm sorry, Becca," she whispered, as she slid the handbag from the dead woman's shoulder.

She heard the rumble of an approaching vehicle.

God! I'll never explain any of this.

She rushed back to her car, threw the handbag onto the passenger side floorboard, shoved the transmission into drive, and sped off. When she passed the approaching car, the driver, an elderly man, did not so much as acknowledge her with a glance.

Her eyes on the road, a whirlwind of thoughts kept her company as she drove.

What the hell was that thing—or things? How come I was the only car caught up in it until Becca arrived?

Becca.

She was right behind me after I got there. Were the walls waiting for her the whole time? Was I just collateral damage? That man from the security agency—was he after her, or was he after what she had in the handbag? Now, they're both dead and the walls are gone.

Is that it? Is it over?

She stole a glance at Becca's handbag on the floor.

Do I want to know what's inside?

Susan pulled over.

To steel herself, she rolled the window down and inhaled the warm air. After a few moments, she pushed her seat back as far as it would go and reached for the handbag.

For a time, she only stared at it as it sat on her lap. At last, she reached into it.

Her fingers brushed on something small, thin. She removed it.

This answers one of my questions.

She held a nametag with a picture of Becca on the front. Rebecca Forth. Becca appeared bored, staring straight ahead from the picture. To her right was a duplicate of the logo on the side of the security man's car and, underneath it, a company name:

Dunwich Scientific.

The nametag indicated that Becca was a lab technician, but there was no further information other than her start date. Susan couldn't suppress a shiver. Then she tossed the nametag out of sight onto the backseat.

She dug through the personal items in the handbag and dropped them on the passenger seat. When she reached the bottom, her fingers fell on a hard, smooth surface. She withdrew the item: a small box, darker than coal. Despite the smoothness of its surfaces, the object did not reflect light. She searched it for any markings but came up empty. However, to her puzzlement, the box had no seams.

How in the world do you open this thing? Is it solid?

Then, with an audible click, seams appeared along the box's sides. A lid that wasn't there seconds ago slowly swung open.

A wisp of black fog slithered from the darkness within and rose toward her face. Gasping, she snapped the box shut and drew back in panic.

The wisp, like a little puff of black smoke, floated until it was even with her face. It wafted to within inches of her quivering lips and hung there.

It—it's studying me.

She stiffened, closed her mouth, and held her breath. She pressed her head harder against the headrest. Her hand crawled toward the door until it contacted the handle. A portion of her brain commanded her to pull the damned handle and jump out of the car. But dread held her fast in her seat.

Please, God, don't let me breathe that in!

The black wisp drifted closer. She clamped her mouth tighter and forced air out her nose.

GO AWAY, DAMN YOU!

The wispy horror retreated far enough for her eyes to focus on it. It remained stationary as if watching. Listening. Then, after a moment, as if propelled by a powerful gust, it flew out the open window.

Susan closed her eyes and inhaled. With every corresponding exhale, her fear and stress dissipated.

"What the fuck?" she whispered.

The box!

To her surprise, the box again revealed no seams. She returned it to the handbag, which she deposited back on the passenger-side floorboard.

What to do with the damned thing? She couldn't bring it to her daughter's—what if it should open *there*? Leave it on the side of the road? What if someone came along and found it? She finally settled on buying a shovel and burying the box—the whole handbag, for that matter—where no one would ever find it.

Satisfied with this idea, Susan pulled back onto the road. She would find a hardware store in the next town and—

She slammed on the brakes.

A huge wall of seething black fog blocked her way.

NOTHING BAD CAN EVER HAPPEN TO YOU HERE

PATRICIA LEE MACOMBER

Brie and Cameron's courtship had been epic, the proposal even more so. Cameron had taken her to Griffith Observatory and given her a first look at the star he'd named after her. When she turned away from the telescope, he was on one knee, holding a shiny diamond ring. While the stone was less than impressive, his presentation was perfect. Brie's parents had gone all-out for the wedding and though it was a gray and rainy day when they exchanged their vows, it didn't dampen their spirits. Everyone at their ceremony agreed that they would make beautiful, blond-haired, blue-eyed babies. . . if they could successfully run the gauntlet of marriage.

The honeymoon in Hawai'i was sheer bliss and, before either knew what had happened, they'd returned home to begin building their together-lives. Cameron, ever attentive and thoughtful, kept Brie as happy as happy could be.

Since life is not composed of just happy moments, there eventually came hardship. First, Cameron was demoted from his job of six years when errors in his data compilation led the astronomers and astrophysicists to a series of wrong conclusions. Cameron was promptly demoted to data entry and, in an ever-increasing state of stress, lashed out at one of his bosses. Cameron would work at the observatory no more.

What followed was a succession of tedious and meaningless jobs, jobs that were nearly as trivial as Cameron felt. Brie, lovely Brie, adored him, though, and she was sure he would come out of it. Each day ended with Cameron returning home, glancing a kiss across Brie's cheek, and heading straight for the liquor cabinet. Whether it be beer, whisky, or wine, he dulled the pain of his meaningless existence with the liberal application of alcohol and the occasional gruff rebuke of Brie. Things in the apartment grew tense and their lives joyless.

And that's when the really bad thing happened.

Deep in the night on October 12, Cameron's phone rang. Good news never comes in the wee hours of the morning, those hours being reserved for bad news and death. Sure enough, it was Cameron's father.

"What's wrong, Dad?" Cameron asked, trying to rub the sleep from his face and regain some form of coherence.

"It's your Nana, son," his father began quietly and then told Cameron everything he needed to know.

Beside him, Brie rolled over and rubbed his arm, concerned but waiting for Cameron to sort things out for himself. "Oh no," Cameron sighed. "Is she. . .?"

"She's in the hospital, son. She's had a stroke. The doctors say it doesn't look good. If you hurry. . ."

"I'm on my way."

Under Brie's watchful and very concerned eye, Cameron threw on some clothes and grabbed his keys. Already, he felt the hot sting of tears and a lump in his throat. Nana was ninety-four and had had a good life, but she was Cameron's favorite person in the whole world, and he was her only grandchild.

"Do you want me to come?" Brie asked as he shoved his feet into his loafers.

"No. They won't let you see her. And it's apt to take a long while. You have work..."

"So do you..."

". . .and they'll understand. I'll call when I know what's happening." He dropped a kiss on her soft cheek and hurried out.

Cameron spent the entire day, and half of the next night at the hospital, sitting right at his Nana's bedside and holding her hand. Sadly, she never regained consciousness, but, happily, she passed without pain.

What followed was a flurry of arrangements. There was a funeral to be planned, papers to be signed, and the minutia of an old woman's life to be gathered and dealt out. Cameron was devastated.

After the funeral, there was a wake at Nana's house. She had collected a large group of friends over the years, and the house was filled with people ranging from her dog walker to her attorney. The latter stayed until everyone had left and then gathered the family for the reading of the will.

"I'm sure it doesn't matter a whit to any of you, but Grace left behind very little of worth." The attorney cleared his throat and nodded an affirmation. "Neither did she leave behind any debt beyond the as-yet unpaid monthly bills. I'll handle those since I already have the information."

The family listened quietly and nodded.

"The only thing of real value that Grace had was this house, which I'm sure you're aware isn't worth a great deal, but it is paid off. So, her wish was to have Cameron live in the house, with the stipulation that he only sell it or bequeath it to another family member."

Cameron teared up and shook his hung head dolefully. "Agreed," he said and shook the attorney's hand.

"Well, I'll get out of your hair now and let you all get some peace. I'll have the deed transferred, and I'll call you when it's done. If you need anything else, don't hesitate."

They all shook his hand and saw him out. When the door was closed, Cameron turned to his father.

"Are you upset?" he asked.

"About what? The house?" He chuckled. "Naw. We already have a house that's nearly paid off. Besides, you have a ton of memories tied up in this place. I'm sure you'll take good care of it."

Cameron hugged his father long and hard, and together they fought back the tears.

His parents left soon after that. Brie and Cameron remained to clean up the mess from the wake.

"Don't worry," said Cameron, out of the blue. "We'll make this place our own."

"I'm not worried at all," Brie responded, slipping into his arms and looking up at him. "Besides, it will be good to have a house with no mortgage. We won't have to worry about money so much."

Over the coming weeks, Brie and Cameron signed the deed to the house—in both their names—and moved their worldly goods from a tiny apartment in the city to Nana's house in the suburbs. All was well.

Because of Nana's death and their new home, Brie figured there would be no better time to start a family. She wanted a girl first, so she could name her Grace after Cameron's Nana. Then a boy and one last girl. She was sitting on her new-to-her sofa and dreaming of babies when Cameron came home from work unexpectedly. She looked up just in time to see him slam the door.

"Cameron, what's wrong?" she asked frightened.

"That son of a bitch Maxwell is what's wrong. I spent weeks compiling data and putting together that report and then Maxwell took the credit for it."

"But how?"

"I was out for three days, dealing with Nana's funeral and all. He swooped right in." Cameron dropped onto the sofa and hid his face with his hands. "That isn't the worst of it."

Brie scooted next to him and rubbed his back, waiting for him to be ready to tell the tale.

"I lashed out at him. And when he lied straight to our boss's face, I lashed out at him, too."

"Oh, no," said Brie.

"Yeah. They fired me on the spot."

Brie sighed. Her dreams of having a baby poofed into the wind. "Well, at least we don't have to worry about paying the mortgage."

Cameron leaped off the sofa, out from under Brie's soothing hand, and went to the liquor cabinet. There, he found solace in three fingers of whisky and the classified ads.

Over the coming months, as Brie tried to keep the faith and Cameron tried to right his own ship, they ran through almost half their savings and a slew of menial jobs. After four unsuccessful starts, Cameron finally landed a position as a clerk at an all-night convenience store. He considered the job beneath him but figured it might offer him some peace and a chance to regroup.

It took Brie at least a month to be able to sleep without Cameron in their bed. His shift was from eleven at night until seven in the morning. More often than not, Brie was in bed right after sending Cameron off to work. She would be in bed, but sleep would not take her for several hours.

Cameron came home one morning, just as he always did.

Brie was in the kitchen, fixing him a large breakfast, just as she always did. She waited until they were both seated in front of their plates before she said a word.

"How was work?" she began, without looking up from her food.

Cameron's fork fell to the plate, and he gawked at her. "A damn sight better than this breakfast. Seriously, Brie, could we please have something other than bacon and eggs?"

Brie shrugged and stuffed a bite of bacon into her pert little mouth. "You don't give me much money for food. It's the best I can do."

Cameron sighed and picked up his fork again. He poked at his food and made a face, then threw his fork down again. "Honestly, it wouldn't be so bad if you weren't such an awful cook. The eggs are runny and the bacon's burnt. You're the worst cook in the world, and if I had known that in the beginning, I might never have married you."

He stood up so suddenly that it knocked the cheap little wooden chair over onto the floor. He watched Brie's eyes tear up, and for some reason, it infuriated him.

"Oh, don't start crying!" he hollered, his face reddening. "Can't you at least take a little constructive criticism?"

She came at him then, not as a show of retaliation or defiance, but out of hurt and disappointment. "That wasn't criticism, Cameron. That was just mean. Now, come on. Let's just finish our breakfast and—"

"I'm not eating this shit!" he spat and snatched up his plate. He flung it across the room, where it should have shattered and sprayed the wall with egg yolk. Instead, it stopped an inch from the wall and hung there.

Brie's mouth dropped open. Then she covered it with both hands, staring at the floating plate. Her eyes went from the plate to Cameron's face, which portrayed irritation rather than surprise. Then she gaped at the plate again.

"Fuck!" Cameron yelled and went to retrieve the plate. He dumped it into the sink and turned, targeting Brie with his swollen, red eyes. "And don't you say another fucking word. In fact, just stay away from me for the rest of the day."

Then he stomped out of the kitchen.

Brie remained motionless until she heard his steps on the staircase. Then she went to clean up the breakfast mess and load the dishwasher. Something weird was happening and it scared her. Her husband was frustrated, angry, and scared over his rapid descent from the top of his career ladder. She understood that. What she didn't understand was the plate's antics and Cameron's lack of shock over it. That dish should have hit the wall. It should be broken. So many questions swirled through her head that she ultimately abandoned them all.

She went to work an hour later, and all those questions came rushing back at her. She tried to focus on work, but there was no hope for it. She was too distracted. By the end of the day, she hadn't even planned anything for dinner, so she let herself into the house and went straight to the fridge to figure it out. There was a pound of ground beef and some canned tomatoes that had been left over from the chili she'd made and ultimately thrown out because it was too spicy. Once she found a box of macaroni, she had everything she needed to make dinner.

Proud of herself, she had dinner all ready when Cameron came downstairs. She heard him stop at the bar on the way to the kitchen and she sighed, wishing he hadn't taken up the habit of drinking throughout the day. . . and possibly night.

Cameron hit the kitchen, freshly showered and dressed for work, a whisky in one hand and his phone in the other. "They want me to work on my day off," he growled. "My day off."

"What did you tell them?" Brie asked as she set down his plate.

"I told them no. I worked eleven straight days, I'm into overtime, but I've got to have some time to myself."

"What if they fire you?" she asked demurely.

"What if they do?! You think I'm worried about keeping this shitty job? Think again. . ." He paused to look down at his plate and made a face. "Oh, not this again! How much fucking Beef-a-Roni can one man eat?" He shoved the plate away. "Just make me a sandwich instead."

"Maybe you could make your own sandwich," Brie countered without an ounce of venom in her voice. She set down her own plate and was prepared to sit down when Cameron stood.

In a million years, she would never have guessed what came next. Nor could she have foreseen the outcome. In a lightning-swift movement, Cameron drew his hand back, cocked and ready to strike. He put every ounce of force into slapping her and, even if she had seen it coming, she couldn't have avoided the inevitable. His hand cut through the air, bound for her face, then just *froze*.

At first, Brie thought he had changed his mind but then it seemed almost as if he were struggling, trying to complete the slap or trying to pull back his hand. Either way, his hand wouldn't move, and his eyes went wide as he increased his struggle.

Frightened, Brie ran away, out of the kitchen, up to the bedroom, and into the bathroom. The next sound she heard was Cameron slamming the door on his way out to work. Then she made her way slowly to bed, where she wept for nearly an hour.

And that's where she was for her twelfth consecutive night when she met *him*.

"Brieeeee," came the soft call.

Brie ignored it at first, figuring it was the wind or some sort of house noise.

"Oh, Brieeeeeeee," said the voice again. It was surely a voice.

Brie sat up and clutched the covers under her chin. "Hello?"

"Helloooo," it said, definitely from the left corner this time.

"Who are you and what are you doing in my house?" She took in a deep breath and gathered her courage. "I'm calling the police."

"Please don't do that," said the voice, a bit closer this time, but still lacking a source.

"Then show yourself."

Slowly, shadow separated from shadow, and the darkest part of it came just to the edge of a patch of light in the window cast by the streetlights. "I am the Guardian," it said. "And as long as you live in this house, nothing bad will ever happen to you."

Brie swallowed and squinted, trying to separate darkness from darkness. "The Guardian? Have you always been here?"

"Alwayssss," it returned. "I served Grace before you, and I serve this house still."

"It was you, wasn't it? In the kitchen this morning."

"Yessss."

"You kept the plate from breaking, and you kept Cameron from slapping me." She smiled to herself.

"I cannot allow harm to come to any in my charge."

Brie thought for a moment and smiled again. "Thank you for that. Now, let me see you. All of you."

"Do not be frightened by my appearance. I mean you no harm." It moved, slowly, and slipped from the shadows like silk.

It was tall, nearly brushing the ceiling with its. . . head? It wore a black cloak with the hood pulled up and when finally Brie's eyes came to gaze upon its face, she gasped. It had a skull for a face, but not a human skull. It was more the skull of a bird with an elongated beak and exaggerated teeth. There were no eyes in its sockets.

"Well, then, there you are." Finally, Brie let her hands drop and the covers with them. "So, you protect this house. . ."

"And the owners of it. Yesssss."

"And nothing bad can ever happen?"

"Neverrrr."

"No plumbing leaks?"

"No."

"And if I drop a glass. . . ?"

"It will not break."

"And no one can break in?"

"One did. He did not get past the foyer."

Brie smiled. "Well, then. I think I find that comforting." She thought for a moment, her pretty little brow creasing with the effort. "You're always here? Always watching?" There was mild concern in her voice.

"Alwayssss."

"When I'm in the shower. . ."

"Oh no! I would neverrrr!"

"And when Cameron and I are. . ."

"Never." It shook its beaked, hooded head rapidly. "People deserve privacy. Alwayssss."

Brie nodded and sank into the pillow. "In that case, I haven't a worry in the world and will sleep like a baby."

Brie rolled over and fell asleep immediately.

Over the coming weeks, incidents increased, both with the house and with Cameron. There was a grease fire that extinguished itself almost as soon as it started. A neighbor boy hit a baseball, and it drove straight at the kitchen window—only to bounce off. Cameron's criticism of Brie became faster and more furious as time wore on, with him blaming her for everything, right down to the price of gas.

Once, in the middle of a heated argument, Cameron threw a heavy metal vase at her head, which stopped inches in front of her face and then floated harmlessly down to the floor, unmarred.

Yelling and throwing things became the norm. When that wasn't satisfying enough, Cameron moved on to other things, such as trying to strangle her to get control of the remote. He found his hands simply wouldn't work anymore—and she simply laughed in his face.

More and more, Brie found herself looking forward to the times when Cameron was out of the house.

And then it happened. One sunny day in August, Brie looked at her calendar and realized that a pregnancy test was in order. She waited until Cameron had gone to work, but she already knew what the result would be. The little plus sign only proved that she was right. Brie was with child.

As she sat on the bed and contemplated the wide ramifications of this new development, she found herself increasingly scared.

"Guardian, are you there?"

"Alwayssss."

"I'm going to have a baby." She swallowed hard. "Will you protect my child?"

"Only so long as it issss in your belly, missss. After that, I only protect the owners of the house. Even guests are outside my reach."

Brie frowned. She placed both hands on her belly and thought. So far, Cameron had not been able to hurt her because of the Guardian. If that didn't hold true of her child, then it was very likely that her baby would be the focus of all Cameron's rage and frustration. There had to be some answer, she thought, some way of keeping him from hurting the baby.

She called her mom with the news and cried to her for half

an hour. Through the tears of fear and joy, she managed to convey her concerns without putting them into words.

"Don't you worry," said her mother. "You bring Cameron here. Come for Christmas. We'll take care of everything."

"My parents are so excited to have us for Christmas," Brie said as she tucked her best dress into the garment bag. "Seriously, it's been years, and I really want to thank you for agreeing to visit them."

Cameron said not a word, simply zipped up his suitcase and set it on the floor. "Don't flatter yourself. Ever since you got pregnant, your parents have gotten more insistent. It's almost like they care more about seeing the baby than they do us. Your father was downright threatening about us coming this year."

"They just want to feel a connection to their only daughter and their future grandbaby... and you, of course." Brie smiled to herself and zipped up her own suitcase.

Sixty miles lay between Brie's house and her parents', and she and Cameron made the drive in silence. Lately, they hadn't anything to talk about except the baby, the nursery, the birthing plan, the expenses... any one of which led to a fight. Now that they were out of the house, Brie didn't have the Guardian to protect her and her unborn child. She also didn't have the Guardian to protect Cameron from her. So, she sat quietly until they reached her folks' house and then made her way quickly up the walk.

"Mama! Daddy!" she bellowed, launching herself through the door and hugging them each in turn.

"Oh, baby! We're so happy to have you with us this year." Her mother took her hand as she turned, leaving Brie's father to hug Cameron and slap him hard on the back.

"Your old room is ready for you both. You've got plenty of time to get settled before supper if you want." She hugged her daughter and smiled.

Brie and Cameron went straight to their room to stow their things. Brie's old room was like a shrine to her childhood. The walls were hung with trophies, medals, and certificates. Her shelves were still lined with dolls. In the corner sat a teddy bear nearly as tall as Cameron, his goofy face smiling out over the room.

"It's creepy," Cameron said, "how they just keep everything like this even though you've been gone for ten years."

"They love me. I think it's sweet."

Cameron grunted.

He stayed on his best behavior the rest of the day, making sure to put up a good act as the affectionate, loving husband and doting father-to-be. And Brie was careful not to trigger him.

At around eleven, Brie and Cameron said their goodnights and headed for their bedroom. They took turns in the bathroom, then slipped into the queen-sized bed with the flowery, ruffly comforter and sheets. Cameron grimaced as he did so, reluctant to pass a night in her old room, with her parents just down the hall.

They had been in bed about five minutes when Cameron rolled over and slipped his hand over her waist. He slid his hand down, over her rounded belly and slipped two fingers under the elastic of her underwear.

"Cameron, no! Please! My parents are just down the hall. They'll hear."

"You think they don't know how that baby got in your belly?" He sneered at her. "We are married after all; not a couple of teenagers groping in the dark."

"I don't feel like it anyway. The baby's all up on my bladder and everything's so uncomfortable down there. . ."

Suddenly, Cameron flipped her over and scooted on top of her. He grabbed a wrist in each hand and with it a handful of her hair and pressed her head as deep into the pillow as it would go. “You’ll shut up and take it because if you struggle and your parents hear, you’ll regret it. And here, you don’t have any protection.”

She felt his hot breath on her face and his hips pressing her down. She giggled into his face. “How long have you known about the Guardian?”

“Always.” He reached down to tug at her underwear. “Now shut up and give me what I want.”

“No,” she said simply.

At that moment, Cameron made a strangled sound deep in his throat. A large hand had reached out and wrapped its bony fingers around his neck and squeezed. It hauled Cameron off of Brie and held him in the air, inches from its pointed beak.

Cameron thrashed and grunted, his engorged member now just a memory. Then he slapped at the Guardian’s arms and tried to free himself.

“You can’t hurt me. You’re supposed to protect me. You’re the Guardian.” Cameron tried to swallow and found that he couldn’t.

“Yessss. But I am not your Guardian.” He tossed Cameron to the floor like a sack of rice and grabbed one ankle. “I am herssss.”

Cameron managed to flip over and tried to dig his fingers into the carpet, but to no avail.

The last thing Brie ever saw of Cameron was his red, blood-splattered face as he was hauled backward, scratching and clawing, into the closet.

An hour later when her parents came to check, nothing remained of Cameron, not so much as a drop of blood.

“Thanks for this, Mom and Dad,” Brie said. “For putting my name on the house and for not trying to talk me out of it.”

“Our pleasure, honey,” her mother said as she sat down and gave her a hug. “Nothing bad can ever happen to you here.”

RIPPLES IN A POND

RICHARD THOMAS

Jessica's apartment was on the top floor of a six-flat, and she stood looking out her windows upon the world with both glee and aching horror, the clanging of the heaters pushing acrid scents into the room. She was both hyper-aware of the subtle vibrations of the universe and filled with black holes, light years away from any human connection. She felt invisible—winking in and out of existence as if a light switch was being flicked on and off and then on again. Her cell phone vibrated on the quilted blanket that covered her bed, a gift from her grandmother. She had a difficult time moving, a single tear streaking down her left cheek, slowly freezing in place. Her body was dusted in white, a glow wrapping around her flesh, a spark of yellow motes dancing in her eyes. She was both comfortable and empty, molasses and anxious, shimmering and a dull flat presence.

Outside the window, snow fell in fat flakes, tires hissing on the wet road, patches of ice slick and shiny, every action a solitary moment that both comforted and distressed her. There was life in every corner of this diorama of a city—a couple laughing over a cup of steaming coffee, a mother dragging her child towards a bus stop, a man shivering under cardboard and filthy blankets. And right next to them was death in many forms—snapping at ankles with sharp, yellowed teeth, lurking in a hunched shadow at the edge of violent intersections, flipping a coin in a bony hand that fated bad decisions. She had been ready for this for a long time—had brushed up against this trembling reduction in the shape of a sharp blade, in the rumbling of traffic, in the gusting winds of a rooftop gathering—and now it was finally here.

She turned her long neck toward the door of her humble abode, the pulsing gold outline reverberating around the edges. A clock ticked loudly from her bedside table, as a dishwasher ran in quiet swooshes from the kitchen, a lingering smell of ground coffee, oranges, and lemon cleaner. She knew that she had to get moving, as the walls had already started to sweat, the aubergine wallpaper with gold fleur-de-lis peeling off at the edges, a black swirl of buzzing agitation over every sink, toilet, and shower drain. This space would not hold forever. While she did not know all of the rules, or exactly what was required of her, she shifted her arms and legs as if guided by an unseen puppeteer, her limbs aching in rusty resistance. When she looked down at her iridescent frame, it blurred around the edges, swirling eddies and throbbing white paste, causing her vision to swim, her equilibrium gone. Taking a gulp and a breath, she exhaled cinnamon and sour milk, roses and rotting meat, and it gave her pause, a flicker of melancholy rippling across her gooseflesh.

She took one hesitant step after another as if walking underwater, an incredible amount of effort required to lift each leg, to open her mouth, to release a plume of buzzing houseflies into the air, black beetles skittering out over her bottom lip, falling to the floor between her feet.

She moaned in pain, in pleasure, in distress as her bones shattered and splintered and knit back together with each lumbering movement, shards of glass scattered throughout her skeleton, her head churning with wet cement. There were several places she had to go, each space a part of this apartment building, a person and emotion that she longed to embrace, to chastise, a longing that felt rife with purpose and turmoil. It both thrilled her and deadened her, adding weight to her already heavy existence, while simultaneously sprouting wings upon her aching back, lifting her slightly off the ground.

With her hand on the doorknob, she took one last look around her apartment, still clinging to yesterday and what might have been a different outcome. On the bedside table, a candle had been snuffed out, leaving only a single strand of smoke rising to the ceiling, a last puff of red currant and regret. Beneath it was an ashtray overflowing with cigarette butts, some of them still holding smudged lipstick kisses. A glass of water sat in silence, still sweating droplets, as the cold water within it glistened in its potential. On the floor there was a pair of jeans, white socks turned inside out, black panties, and a matching lace bra with the underwire pushing through. The mattress held a slight indentation in the shape of her body, curled to one side in the fetal position, the blanket pulled back to reveal dingy white sheets.

Nothing was perfect, no, but it was hers.

It had *been* hers.

She closed her eyes and turned the knob slowly to leave. And in that moment, a series of choices added up to this, a pattern of decisions looping back to itself, a nagging sensation that the wrong path had been taken, again and again, and that now, there was no turning back. It was done.

She dissipated in a puff of smoke, in a rippling of stardust, meat falling off her bones, as the apartment now truly sat empty and alone.

Not for the first time.

Not for the last.

3A

Jessica stood in the corner of Amanda's apartment, hunched over in the shadows, watching her sleep. It was a similar layout to her own rental, and so she knew it quite well. Amanda slept in a fitful state—rolling this way and that, trying to get comfortable, coughing, and then turning over, fluffing her pillow, lying back down, clearly uncomfortable—not quite awake and not quite asleep. She wore an old Cure T-shirt that Jessica had given her ten years ago. Seeing it brought back fond memories of music and drinks, dancing with strange men, laughter and perfume, gentle hands on her hips, firm bodies pressed up against each other.

On the bed, Amanda's cat, Leo, sat staring at Jessica, eyes glowing gold in the darkness, its fur fluffed out and electric, a purr turning into a growl and then back into a purr. In better days the cat had slept between the two of them, as they blissfully drowsed in a state of spent energy. But now, at this moment, the cat flattened its ears, a hiss building in its mouth. Jessica saw Amanda not as everything she wanted to be, no, not some image of perfection and peace and success but more as a presence that shifted in color, as so many memories ran over her flesh. A series of black and white photos fell from the ceiling, scattering over the bed. Jessica frowned from the corner, pushing herself back deeper into the shadows, glimpses of moments they had shared together, as well as secrets that she had hoped were false paranoias.

Looking back, Jessica watched Amanda with her blonde bob

and button nose lean against a kitchen counter at a party they had attended, next to Jessica's then-boyfriend Gordon—both of them laughing, both holding glasses filled with amber liquid, both standing a little too close to each other. A hand was placed on an arm, a shoulder, then the bump of a hip, then the bared flesh of a waist. Their mouths and lips twisted together in a wet kiss, his hand on the small of her back, her hand placed on his muscled bicep. The door to the kitchen swung open, Jessica's own laughter filling the space, still talking to somebody in the other room with her back to them, as they pushed apart, eyes on her, drinks consumed. And then she turned, rushed over, and hugged them both, oblivious to their intimacy.

Later she would hike up her skirt in the alley behind the party and take everything that Gordon had to offer her. They would tremble under a brilliant moon, skin slick with sweat, a violent peace thrust into her, a glow and glory shattering over her body as she became one with the universe, stars exploding in her eyes. Later, after he went home, she and Amanda would lie in bed, trading stories of the evening, eventually holding each other, eventually kissing, bodies and minds charged with an electricity that could not be extinguished. It was both familiar and entirely different, a moment they had both been working towards for some time, and yet a secret they would bury in the morning behind fresh orange juice and the tuck of a stray strand of hair over an ear, the bashful blush of something they weren't sure they should forget. Or could forget.

Jessica leaned over Amanda's sleeping frame and kissed her on the forehead, prompting Amanda to wake up screaming, her hands flying in all directions, scratching and punching at the shadows over her bed. The cat leaped into the empty space above her owner, claws extended, its bravado disappearing in the expanding darkness that had descended on the room. Amanda pushed her back up against the headboard, kicking off her blankets, scrambling for purchase, trying to move away, hands and fists still pummeling the air, eyes open wide, scanning the room, and yet not really seeing, no, not seeing at all.

She muttered something under her breath—perhaps I'm sorry or more likely, get out. Fear wrapped in certainty dipped in betrayal and dusted with hope. And in that moment, Jessica saw all of Amanda—the deeper parts that could have been something, a chasm filled with friendship and desire, a heady confidence in what path might lead them out of their despair and into the light. Those few veins ran all the way to her core, and they pulsed with possibility, throbbed with potential. But the rest of Amanda, she was diseased—a sickness that spread throughout her body in a sporadic pattern made of jealousy, bourbon, selfishness, and obsession. Amanda was as broken as Jessica—it was part of what drew them together, to this apartment building, to this tainted space.

Misery loves company, after all.

Except at this moment. As a realization washed over Amanda, the walls went up around her heart, her veins filling with ice, her eyes two black dots of coal, hands pushing away and back with elevating desperation in the darkness.

Not her.

Not now.

Not ever.

And so, Jessica stepped back into the shadows, this moment nothing like what she had hoped it would be—doors slamming, dogs barking, the shattering of glass on the sidewalk below, the whimper of truth from the skinny blonde in the bed, a cacophony building up to its inevitable conclusion. As Amanda screamed again and again, the room filled with a vibrating static, something burning, something breaking, the windows rattling in their frames, voices underwater, violence unfolding in the street with a gunshot slap, the dull thud of a fist on flesh, crying and screaming, more dogs barking, a siren in the distance, coming closer. Jessica disappeared into the darkness, nodding her head as she wept with despair, losing one more thing today than she had planned on, for sure.

And then with a pop and a greasy sizzle, she was gone.

2A

Gordon lived one floor down. And now that certain things had been revealed, it made a lot of sense. Too much sense to Jessica, and so the end of their relationship months ago started to come into focus—late-night phone calls and hushed conversations, slammed doors and footsteps on the fire escape, phantom knocks on her apartment door.

She stood in the corner of his room—the same spot she had occupied a moment ago, one floor above. Her eyes shifted to the ceiling where the screaming had finally stopped. A long time ago, perhaps. Her gaze turned to the window and the shade filled with light, and then back to darkness, everything shuffling forward, and then standing still. It was a minute, an hour, a day, a week. She was not entirely sure. A thousand days and nights unfolded in fast-forward before her very eyes. Gordon was in the bed, and then he was gone. The bed was made and then unmade. He was alone, and then not alone.

After what happened with Amanda, Jessica would have preferred to not be here at all, and yet, she could not move, this moment permanent, fated, destined to be part of this equation. And so, with a deep breath filled with razor blades and cotton balls, she slowed her heartbeat down to a barely recognized tremble. Outside, a car passed with the bass pounding so loud that Jessica wasn't sure whether her heart was still beating or if she was merely reverberating with the music. As it drove off, everything went still.

The same windows rattled in their frames, the same built-in armoire squatted in the corner, the same placement of the bed in the center of this room. The French doors opened to a wooden table with a bowl of fruit in the middle, a splash of color in an otherwise drab space. On his nightstand, there was a hand-carved Buddha, the peacefulness of his intricate expression washing over her like a cool dip in a murmuring stream. The room smelled of garlic and onion mixed with patchouli, and at this moment, she relived a dozen evenings filled with food and film and endless conversation. A television set flickered in the darkness of the living room, and Jessica was holding hands with Gordon on the couch as they laughed and gasped, cried and rippled with fear.

Though they had been apart for months now, she was still surprised to turn back to the bed and see it writhing with pleasure and desperation. The sheets barely covered their ghostly undulations—open mouths moaning as they gasped for air, the arch of a pale back, the curve of glistening ass, hands grabbing at her neck, her pushing back to meet him, slick flesh slapping against each other as the tempo increased. And while Jessica wanted to be angry, she could not. He was no longer hers. He hadn't been for some time.

The television set buzzed with static, and then a slightly different version of an event played out on the screen. Some of it was the same—he was in that kitchen, leaning on that counter, drinking and laughing with Amanda. But in this version, she placed her hand on his bicep and he removed it, gently and without fuss. She leaned in closer, and he took a step back, still talking, still sipping at his bourbon. The third time, she slipped in fast and kissed him with violence, grabbing his hand and dragging it down to her waist. And then the door opened, and Jessica saw herself walk in, laughing while looking back into the other room, still not facing them, a scowl on Gordon's face as he gently pushed Amanda away, putting some distance between them.

This was a little bit different.

Later, not that night, but at a future party, after an oddly coincidental coffee shop run-in, a meeting on the L-train, and a moment in the hallway of their apartment building, Gordon will have multiple conversations with Amanda and straighten her out. She will nod her head, and act as though she understood and heard him, but that was not true. She wanted him and would do everything in her power to break them up.

And she succeeded.

In the quiet afterglow of the coupling, Jessica sensed something was wrong. Nobody had moved. Gordon was on his back, eyes open wide to the ceiling, the girl sitting very still against the headboard—no cuddling or conversation, no offer of a drink of water, no rubbing of her back. Only silence in the miles between them on the mattress. And then she slipped out of bed, navigating the dark space under the soft glow of a candle and the glow of a waning moon. Water ran, first from the bathroom sink, and then the shower.

In the blink of an eye, the new girl was back in the bedroom, getting dressed quickly, and Gordon had still not moved. His hands were pressed together, and if Jessica didn't know any better, she'd say he was vibrating, shaking maybe—barely containing the subtle sobs of a crying jag held at bay.

The girl had something to say to him as she buttoned her jeans and pulled on her coat, boots laced up, gloves pulled on. She told him that there was a presence in the room, and it was upsetting, distressing to her. She couldn't see him again, not like this, as he was obviously thinking about somebody else, fixated on another woman, hardly there at all. In her accusations he faded in and out, entirely gone and then blinking back into existence. She told him to get help, that he couldn't move on, couldn't give of himself until he dealt with these emotions. Don't call me until this is dealt with, she said. It's like fucking a corpse, she reiterated, shivering though she was bundled up, a sheen of sweat on her forehead, her hands cold as ice.

And then she was gone.

In her absence—a minute, an hour, a day—Jessica walked to the bed, and placed her hand on his bare shoulder, and he immediately quieted, falling into a deep, satisfying, heavy sleep.

With a bang and a shower of ash, Jessica disintegrated.

1A

One more floor down, and Jessica appeared in the kitchen of Mrs. Johnson. A single bulb over the sink provided the only illumination in the tiny apartment. Outside the open window, the world was quiet, the moon swollen and bright. The old woman stared into a swirling cup of tea. Jessica assumed she was pondering the mysteries of the universe, and perhaps she was, to some degree. Kept mostly in shadow, over in the corner, Jessica pulled the gaze of the old woman, who shivered before rushing to finish her tea in hopes of curbing her sudden chill. She turned the cup over and pushed her fingers through the leaves, a frown bringing creases to her face, as her eyes welled with tears.

The elderly woman sat at a blue-and-gray Formica table with glistening chrome around its edges. The swirling pattern of the table and chairs was hypnotic in its antique, retro vibe, something she and her husband had bought brand new some fifty years ago. What Jessica knew about Mrs. Johnson was that her husband worked in the furniture industry, running a store up the street. It had been around for a long time, but quickly closed after his passing—sold by Mrs. Johnson, as it was his thing, and not hers. It was a source of pride with him, and yet, a thorn in the side for Mrs. Johnson.

"Ethel," she said to the room.

Directed at Jessica, or the universe, who knew.

Her eyes raised up to take in Jessica, slowly absorbing her presence, nodding her head, and then slowly shaking it back and forth.

She pulled a deck of Tarot cards out of her housecoat pocket —the light blue flowers of the fabric matching the kitchen décor —and dealt out a quick pattern, forming a cross, with several cards to the side. For a moment, Jessica saw the same card appear each and every time one was flipped over—the Tower. But then she rubbed her eyes and the cards changed—the ten of swords, Death, the Devil, and finally, the Tower.

Jessica only knew Mrs. Johnson—Ethel now—from their encounters in the halls and on the street. Many a night Jessica had helped her upstairs with her groceries, taken a bag of garbage back out to the alley, or brought in a heavy box that had been delivered outside as a gesture of goodwill. They were not friends, but they were not enemies, either. Now and then, there would be a knock on Jessica's door, and the old woman would hold out a tin of cookies, fudge, baklava, or cupcakes. They were always accepted with a smile, and a bit of guilt, feeling that she could have done more for the woman.

It was true. She could have done more.

In a few instances, after the husband had passed, Jessica had indeed sat with Ethel and had tea—Lady Grey—notes of bergamot and orange filling the air. Jessica quickly tired with the questions about a husband and babies, a raised eyebrow at the clothes she might be wearing that day, short skirts and torn stockings not what Ethel would have suggested.

When Jessica took a step forward out of the shadows and into the dim light of the kitchen, Ethel held a hand up to halt her movement. The lightbulb fizzled and went out before shattering with a startling pop, sending glass shards flying like shrapnel. A gurgle bubbled up from the metal innards of the sink below it, a thick, rancid tar pushing its way up out of the drain. Ethel murmured something under her breath as she stood, her voice rising into an unintelligible chant as she walked across the kitchen—bowls of fruit on every surface, sticks of earthy incense lit, a smudge of sage smoking on a plate surrounded by black pillar candles. The woman ran her gnarled fingers over a rosary she pulled up from the neckline of her blouse, working the wooden beads with a fevered urgency, her eyes shut tight in concentration.

Later, Jessica would understand that when Ethel said get out, she wasn't angry, or scared, or sad—she was trying to help her. But at that moment, it felt like the woman had turned her back on Jessica, lashes of pain striking her flesh.

Ethel opened the back door to her apartment, tears in her eyes, unable to speak, her tongue tied by powers beyond her control, pointing out to the alley, to the horizon, to anywhere beyond the footprint of the apartment complex, and the hold it had on its tenants.

If Jessica could have known what Ethel was truly thinking, she might have understood. Like the television set and photos from the apartments above her, Ethel had secrets, misunderstandings, regrets, and remorse. There were so many nights that the old woman had sat at the kitchen table as the food got cold, waiting for her husband to come home—meatloaf and mashed potatoes, pierogi and kielbasa, lasagna from the old country—so many recipes handed down through her ancestors. The resentment that grew, the ways that she tried to end her husband's business, the jealousy she had for any woman that walked into that store—it undid her. He had always been a friendly man who enjoyed helping others, but

Ethel could only see his smile toward another woman and hate him for sharing himself with anyone but her. She could only see his helpful advice as some sort of flirtation. She could only see his late hours as time he didn't want to spend with her.

What didn't she see?

She didn't see that with every sale, he went back to his office, to kiss their wedding picture. She didn't see the music he sang to himself as he squirreled away secret money for their return trip back home to Europe. She didn't see the exhaustion as he'd collapse in his office chair, longing to go home to her, but terrified of going broke—a distant memory of his parents losing everything, homeless and without a country, feeling violence and persecution.

Jessica couldn't see any of that, and instead of following the direction of the long, crooked finger that Ethel pointed out beyond the bubble that was their building, she instead turned inward, and downward, missing the clues.

THE BASEMENT

When Jessica shakes back into focus, pixelating into a whole entity again, she appears outside the mailboxes in the front hall of the apartment building, by the basement door, with its rusty lock clamped shut.

In her mailbox slot, there is a bent piece of orange paper, and she tugs at it, pulling it free. It is a message—one she has been hearing her whole life—one she has repeated to herself in the long, dark hours of depression and loneliness. Today, the note is from Amanda, folded over and over. Yesterday, it was a tiny scroll tied with a purple ribbon, from Gordon, scrawled in ink, the paper dotted with his tears. The day before, it was a torn piece of parchment from Mrs. Johnson—Ethel if you prefer

—in her delicate calligraphy, one word looping gracefully into the next.

For a moment the world trembles, and she telescopes up and above it all, looking down on the apartment complex from a great height. As she rises, the building changes—a new coat of paint here, a fresh red door there, some tuckpointing for the bricks, a new roof. And then it crumbles to the ground, reborn as a tower of metal and glass which then crumbles again into a parking lot, from which rises a garage. This is torn down and replaced by an advancing black void of darkness that murmurs and chuckles in its abstract, intangible form. And then it reverses. Dialing backward, the building is brick. The building gone, replaced by a small A-frame house. The house gone, replaced by a dirt road winding all the way into the city. The dirt road framed with trees and wilderness. An open plain bisected by natives on horseback, by an empty expanse, by a frozen tundra.

And then her hand is on the doorknob, the lock popping open with a resounding *click*, and she descends, called to the darkness by a pull and power she no longer tries to resist. There in the gloom, a tapestry covers the walls. At first, there are threads, and patterns rippling in the dark, the only glow her body, descending, a luminescence that fades and then pulsates back into life. Upon closer inspection, the walls are not cloth, linen, thread, or ink. They are flesh—mottled shades of pale white and sickly milk; a leathery tan and mottled brown; a scarred black and glistening pitch. Around her, there is an encroaching presence, the sensation of compression, limbs bending and unfolding, and unfolding, and unfolding. There is a great chittering of mandibles, a clacking of beaks, and gnashing of teeth. It closes in, this pressure, as a thousand eyeballs snap open, yellowing from their disease, rife with red veins, bulbous in their gaze—searching for, and seeing everything. And then darkness, the sensation of being held by rubbery appendages, suction cups with barbed tips, a stench filling the space—rotten meat, sour milk, vomit, waste, disease, and death.

Jessica cannot breathe, not for some time now, but at this moment, it is all-consuming, filling her with a sticky, heavy weight that pulls her to the ground. As her eyes turn to the wall, she tries to understand what she is seeing—men, women, and children with Slavic features, and then African faces, Nordic noses, and then Cro-Magnon foreheads—all of them in rictus, in horror, dotted with metal spikes, and strips of fabric, buzzing flies, and tiny, swarming mites.

In a moment of horrifying clarity, Jessica realizes that she is broken, and has been for some time. This building is not a building, the people are not people, and the basement is not a basement.

This building is a wound—a seeping mass of pain and desperation that houses one lost, empty soul after another. In their selfishness and depravity, they continue to infect each other, dragging each other down, where they can wallow in their filth.

The people are stains on society, each a series of choices and actions that could easily have been turned around, out of the darkness, back up into the light, if only they had been willing to put in the work, to truly change.

The basement is a trap, a ripple in a pond that has reverberated out into reality for as long as there has been life. It is only visible to those that want to see it—the depraved, the sick, the users, the thieves, the manipulators, the liars, the vampires, and the dead.

If a single ray of hope, a glimmer of kindness remains, then the occupant can resist, move out, and move on.

A series of images flickers in front of Jessica's eyes once again, her version of certain moments, her truth finally revealed. She is betraying a friendship, lying when she knows she will get caught, rolling her eyes, bad-mouthing in secret, making phone calls, and false references, to employers, banks, and men. She is denying intimacy, stealing and gaslighting, undermining and cheating, leaving clues to certain discoveries. She is ignoring a knock, laughing in the face of sadness, taking what is not hers, seducing those who are committed, slandering and deceiving, reminding the meek of their place.

Up to this very moment, she could have resisted, changed, and fled.

She could have been forgiven.

Now, she will be punished, and the suffering will be eternal.

In the darkness, a door closes, as a lock snicks shut.

There is a vacancy in the building now, an empty apartment to fill.

It is a cold space, filled with sadness and longing.

Ten people will be shown the two-bedroom flat, with its French doors, and vintage appliances in a shiny turquoise blue.

Five couples will grasp for each other's hands, and quickly back out of the space.

Four single women will take a spin around, eyes glittering, then tearing, a sour taste filling their mouths, hands to throats, walking slowly away, looking over their shoulders for confirmation.

One man will step inside, take a deep breath, exhale, and relax.

He is home.

For how long, nobody knows but him.

And in the basement, something stirs.

THE DEVIL'S BOUNTY HUNTER

JEFF OLIVER

I know I'm marked.
I've seen the beastly scars.
Burning patterns upon my skin formed
from years of a broken heart.
The patterns are not in the shape of stars.
The patterns are carved.
They are carved from the shards of a
broken mirror that was once a piece
of art.
It's still art in a sense.
It's not the kind of picture you'd want to
paint.
It's not the kind of reconstruction you'd
want to come your way.
When it comes, it comes masked by the
thunder.
Its only goal is to pull you under.
Blinding you through each storm is The
Devil's Bounty Hunter.

It picks out each flaw to use beautifully
against you.
It makes you hit walls as it controls
everything you do.
It wants you to stay lost while forever
confused.
The Devil's Bounty Hunter is gunning for
the soul you've abused.

You can try to run, but it will always
find you.
You can hide in the dark, but it will
always come through.
Tearing out your emotions one by one.
Tearing out your dreams as you try to
reach them.
It pours gasoline into your wounds as it
strikes a match.
When you start to scream, it begins to
laugh.
You're floating on a never-ending ocean
with holes in your life raft.
The Devil's Bounty Hunter will find you
no matter where you are.
Its eyes are as black as that void you fell
into.
Its claws are curved so they never come
out of you.
Its teeth are hollow like a venomous
snake's.
It only cares for your soul to take.
It has one mission.
It has one purpose and instruction.

It is to collect your soul and deliver the
destruction.
You should stay silent now....

The Devil's Bounty Hunter is coming.
Start running!
You'd better move fast.
You'd better not scream when you hear
the shattering glass.
The ghosts in the mirror were always
there.
They were planted in your soul while you
were having those nightmares.
It was all a plot.
It wants you to rot.
It wants you out of your mind at all costs.
It doesn't matter how hard you have
fought.
Your lungs are filling up followed by an
uncontrollable cough.
You've been marked.
You've been singled out.
The Devil's Bounty Hunter has come to
tear your soul apart.

Your open wounds are its entrance.
Your screams are its essence.
You are exposed and do not have
protection.
It is over for you now that you are in its
presence.
The Devil's Bounty Hunter has come to
collect.

PRAYERS FROM THE MOUTH OF HELL

RONALD KELLY

Grandma's room had that smell to it. Like a nursing home room. . . a room reserved for failing health and dying. It was a difficult smell to describe, but it was there. Thick in the senses, heavy on the mind.

Miss Lurlene—Grandma's hospice nurse, or "transitional companion" as she liked to put it—lingered at the doorway as Ben Griffin stood at the foot of the big cherrywood bed. "Don't be very long," she told him. "She's had a rough day."

"Yes, ma'am."

The door closed behind her and then it was just the two of them. He simply stood and stared at her, startled at her frailty and lack of color. She stared back through weak eyes, equally disturbed at her grandson's appearance: gaunt, hollow-eyed, sickly.

"You look a few steps closer to the Reaper than I do, boy." Her voice, once robust and commanding, was a low, dry rasp.

I've had a hard few years, he wanted to say, but didn't. She already knew that and had set her opinion of him because of it. He looked over at her nightstand. Amid a dozen prescription vials lay her Bible. The book she lived and preached from. . . judged and condemned by. "It wouldn't hurt me to gain a few pounds," he admitted. "Haven't been taking care of myself like I should."

The old woman shook her head slowly. Disapprovingly. "How long have you been off the drink?"

"A little over two months, Grandma." It was something to be proud of.

Not to her, though. "Two months." She made a gruff noise of dismissal. "You really think that's going to last, boy? You've been on a binge for seven years."

"I'm going to try. I'm doing my best."

Grandma launched into a coughing fit that raised the color in her face a couple of shades. Ben started for her nightstand, but the elderly woman's spidery hand reached the tumbler of water before he did. She brought the plastic straw to her mouth, took a couple of swallows, and returned the cup to its rightful place.

Then she started. Ben knew that she would. That was why he was there, wasn't it? To speak to her after all those years. . . probably for the last time. . . and hear exactly what she thought of him and his wasted life?

"My only grandson," she said. "My only *grandchild.* Grandma's pride and joy. I had such high hopes for you. College, then an upstanding trade. . . doctor, lawyer, businessman maybe. But you chose to pull a cork and drown your ambitions. Pickle yourself and abandon everyone who loved you. Me. . . your poor mama and daddy." A pained expression crossed her shriveled face, not bodily pain, but emotional. "Both of them dying in that tornado last year. . . swept off the face of the earth with their house and all. . . and you didn't even show up at the funeral."

"I was in a bad way," he told her. "I wasn't in any condition to make it here from California in time." There was a weakness in his voice that he'd sworn not to let slip past. But it had and it seemed to fuel her resentment even more.

"And me lying in this bed even before that," she continued. "I thought you loved me, Ben. Was sure you'd come and be with me. . . share some closeness like we did when you were a young'un. I prayed for you, boy. Every morning when I rose and every night before I went to sleep. Prayed that you'd abandon the bottle and come back to us."

And don't you think I prayed, too? he wanted to say in defense. *Locked up in that damn rehab. . . my guts twisting. . . head aching. . . aware of everyone I'd ever hurt or let down?"*

"But did my prayers do any good?" she continued. "No. You stayed out west and ignored us. Kept right on tearing yourself down, one drink at a time."

Ben closed his eyes. "Grandma. . . I don't know what more I can say."

"Me, either," she said. The old woman turned her head on her pillow, looking away from him. "I reckon I've said all there is to say."

"I'm sorry I disappointed you."

If his words affected her or altered her opinion of him in any way, it didn't show. "Where's that wife and child of yours?"

"Out in the car. Would you like to. . . ?"

"No. Leave them where they are. No need for them to come in and act like they know or pity me. Best they remain strangers."

He knew then that his visit had been a futile effort on his part. Ben turned to leave. When he reached the door, he laid his hand on the knob and paused. "Grandma. . . if I could go back and do things differently, I would in a heartbeat."

She refused to look at him. Her eyes grew moist and red with grief as she stared at the wall beside the bed. "I'm tired, Ben. You'd best go and let me get some rest."

"Yes, ma'am." As an afterthought, "I love you."

If she reciprocated the affection, she failed to express it in words.

Ben thanked Miss Lurlene for calling him and setting up the visit. Then he left the old farmhouse and walked to the road where his Ford station wagon was parked with a U-Haul trailer hitched to the back of it.

When he climbed into the car, he simply sat there and stared through the cracked windshield. His time with Grandma had pulled the rug from beneath him, threatened to undo all he had accomplished since March. *Damn. I could really use a...*

His grip tightened on the steering wheel. *No.*

"How did it go?" asked Candy.

"It didn't." He looked over at his wife. Pretty, good-hearted, infinitely better than anything he deserved. It pained him that his kin had never taken to her, never accepted her into the family circle. Likely it had been her tattoos, or the ring in her nose. Stupid, little, petty things. For people who put so much stock in the soul, they had been terribly blind to how beautiful hers was. "Let's go see our new home."

Candy nodded, but she didn't look very happy about it. "Okay."

"Does it have a backyard, Daddy?" Dustin asked from the back. The six-year-old was the spitting image of his mother.

Ben winked at the boy in the rearview mirror. "It does. With a swing."

Then he started the car and left the two-story farmhouse and the expanse of acreage that engulfed it. It was a place he had once loved; he had practically grown up there as a child. But now it seemed distant and out of reach, like ground he was trespassing on, rather than revisiting. Driving away, he wondered if he would ever lay eyes on it again.

* * *

"Oh... Ben."

Candy's tone caused his stomach to sink. She and Dustin deserved so much more.

"It's just until we get back on our feet," he told her. "Mr. Lewis was willing to let us have it for twice as cheap than anything else in town. You can't find a deal like this anymore... not renting a place."

"Yeah, it's a deal, alright," she said, but he knew she was thinking *dump*.

The single-wide trailer was old and weathered, probably a sixties model, or older. Two-toned. . . white and aqua green... but actually tri-colored, if you counted the amount of rust that was on it. The windows were narrow and cloudy, and dirty plastic skirting concealed the frame and wheels underneath. There was no porch at the front door, just a set of rickety steps constructed of scrap lumber.

"Let's go look inside," he suggested. He dug a key from his pocket and, together, the three walked across the yard. When they mounted the steps, he unlocked the door, and his wife and son went in. He lingered a moment longer and looked around the trailer park. The neighboring dwellings seemed to be of similar caliber, with the addition of broken-down cars and a few abandoned washers and dryers here and there. The only person he saw in the vicinity was an old woman directly across the road, sitting on her porch, snapping beans and eyeing him curiously.

Ben ignored her and joined his family inside. The living room was dark and dingy, the green carpet filthy and in need of cleaning... or replacing. On the far side of the room was a kitchenette with table and chairs, and a long, narrow hallway leading to the bathroom and two bedrooms.

"It stinks in here," said Dustin.

"It does," agreed his mother. "Badly."

Ben looked over at Candy. She was trying to be positive, she really was, but her resolve was slipping. "I'm sorry. It's the best we can do right now."

"For what. . . $750 a month? I know it's cheaper than an apartment, but, dammit!"

The boy backed a couple of steps toward the door. "I don't like it here."

Candy suddenly knew she'd said too much. She turned away for a long moment and stared at an ugly brown stain on the wall next to a back window. Then she crouched next to her son, all smiles. "Hey! You know, I think we could clean this place and make it really nice. We'll all pitch in and turn it into a home we can be proud of!"

Ben caught her eyes, grateful. *Thank you.*

"Can we go out back and see the swing set?" Dustin asked excitedly.

"Sure, we can!" said his father, doing his best to match the boy's enthusiasm.

Together, the two exited the rear door into the overgrown yard out back, leaving Candy to survey the dismal job ahead of her.

* * *

"I'm sorry, baby."

Candy rolled onto her side on the air mattress and looked at him. "What have you got to be sorry for? We're doing great. *You're* doing great."

"If I'd tried a lot earlier. . . a little harder. . . we'd still have the house in Santa Cruz. You'd still be a manager at Starbucks and Dustin wouldn't be going to a new school and making new friends. And we wouldn't have ended up in this damn trailer."

His wife reached out and took his hand beneath the covers. "We'll make it work. Maybe a new place in a new town will do us all some good. What time do you start at the plant on Monday?"

"Gotta be there at eight o'clock for orientation," he said. It was a position in the shipping department. "They say we'll have health insurance in sixty days. That's a good thing."

"It certainly takes a load off my mind." She paused for a long moment. "And AA?"

"Friday night at seven-thirty."

Ben lay there and looked up at the dark ceiling above them. The light was off, but he could still picture the cracked plaster and outdated light fixture. He thought about the last seven years, and even before that. His alcoholism. It had started in high school. Bad friends pressuring him into bad choices. Then even worse friends in college, with wild parties every weekend. He thought he could handle it, but it was a lie. His grades began to suffer, and he had ended up dropping out. He had started working minimum wage jobs just to keep a roof over his head and buy his booze. Things had gotten better when he'd met Candy—in a grocery store check-out lane, of all places. They'd started dating and got married. A year later, they had Dustin. He tried his best to remain stable, to be a good husband and father, but. . . the drinking. Things had gotten increasingly worse, and he'd ended up losing his job, and then the house. He had reached a critical point and Candy and Dustin had stayed with her mother while he was in rehab for ninety days. When he got out, they packed all their possessions and left California. Ben's motive for moving back to Tennessee was partly to leave old haunts and influences behind. The other part was to try and smooth things over with Grandma. To make amends for the sorrow and trouble he had caused over the years.

"Let's get some sleep," he suggested. "We've got to start the big clean-up tomorrow."

Candy laughed. "Yippee! I'm certainly looking forward to that."

The two leaned toward each other for a kiss, when a scream echoed shrilly from down the hallway.

"Dustin!"

Ben was up off the mattress and feeling his way to the doorway. "I'll check on him. Probably woke up and forgot where he was."

He stepped into the hallway and groped along the wall until he found a light switch. A single sixty-watt bulb revealed his son, running down the hallway in the direction of their bedroom. When Dustin saw him, he launched himself into his father's arms and clung to him, burying his face tightly into his shoulder.

"What's wrong, buddy? Did you have a nightmare?"

Dustin shook his head violently, dampening Ben's T-shirt with his tears. "N—n—no!" he blurted. "There. . . there was a *man* in my room!"

Ben smiled and gave his son a reassuring hug. "Dustin, it was just a bad dream. There's no one in your room. Come on and we'll take a look."

The boy wrapped his legs around his father's waist. "No! I ain't going back in there!"

Suddenly, Candy was there with outstretched arms. "Come here, baby." Dustin released his hold and, leaning past his father, fell into his mother's embrace.

"I'll tell you what. I'll go and check it out. Will that make you feel better?"

"Maybe," mumbled Dustin. "But I ain't going back...not tonight!"

"Alright," cooed Candy, turning and heading back into the master bedroom. "I believe there's enough room on this trampoline for all three of us."

Ben walked down the hall to the bedroom at the very end. He reached through the open doorway and snapped on the light. The room was empty except for the little twin mattress, a box of toys that Dustin had been playing with before bedtime, and a rolling suitcase holding most of the boy's clothes. He reached for the light switch, then, as an afterthought, walked to the room's only window. It was securely locked.

He was crossing to the bedroom door when he paused. He thought he had caught a whiff of something. . . or maybe a couple of things. One was the faint skunky scent of body odor. The other was distinctive and disturbingly familiar to him. It almost smelled like. . .

No, he thought. *That's impossible.*

Ben stood there for a long moment. Gradually, the odors dissipated, leaving only the smell of age and neglect.

He turned off the light and walked back to his and Candy's bedroom. He left the hallway light on and closed the door, leaving a narrow crack to provide a little illumination, just to comfort his son.

Dustin was snuggled in the crook of his mother's arm. "Did you see him?"

"Sorry, partner. There was no one there. You just had a bad dream."

But the boy was adamant. "He *was* there, Daddy! I woke up and he was standing at the end of my bed. . . just looking at me."

"What did this man look like?" Ben asked.

"He was *big*! A lot taller than you and heavier. I couldn't see his face very good in the dark, but he was bald like Uncle Stan back in Santa Cruz."

The mention of Stan sent a jolt through Ben. Stan hadn't really been Dustin's uncle; he was just a drinking buddy of Ben's that he spent way too much time and closed way too many bars with.

"And he smelled kinda funny," continued the boy. "Like you used to, when you were... well, you know."

Ben looked at Candy. His wife frowned and shrugged, as if saying *Just ignore it. He didn't mean anything. He was having a bad dream, that's all.*

"Well, if he was there at all, he's gone now. Do you feel safe now?"

Dustin grinned and snuggled closer to his mom. "Yep."

As Ben turned off the light and made his way to the big king-size mattress, the guilt of how his addiction had affected his son lodged in his mind like a thorn that couldn't be extracted. But, as they all settled in and prepared for sleep, Ben was sure he smelled the lingering stench of raw liquor that had hung faintly in the stale air of his son's bedroom.

* * *

Dustin never would go back to his bedroom.

For the next three nights, he was camped out on the big air mattress in his parents' room before they came to bed. Ben wanted to put his foot down, but Candy urged him to give the boy some time. "Maybe he'll change his mind once we paint his room and fix it up for him."

Ben's job was going well. Mundane and unchallenging, but not bad. At least it was a steady paycheck and some semblance of security. Candy stayed home with Dustin until she could find someone who would watch him, or a daycare that didn't cost a fortune. It was summer, so there was no school to worry about. Dustin spent most of his time outside, swinging or attempting to climb a maple tree out back. That or playing with his action figures in the living room while his mother cleaned.

It was Thursday afternoon when Ben returned home to find Candy waiting for him on the front steps.

"There's a leak under the house," she said, concerned. "I hear water running. There may be a busted pipe."

Ben opened the door to the crawlspace and looked under the trailer. He shone the beam of a flashlight into the gloom and saw standing water. He could hear a steady gush of water somewhere beneath the bathroom.

"Damn!" He dug his phone out of his pocket and tried calling their landlord, Harvey Lewis. There was no answer, only his voice mail. Ben left a message, then went in the house.

"I can't get a hold of him," he told Candy in aggravation. "Even if I did, who knows when he'd get out here to fix it. I better go under and see if I can at least find the problem and patch it until he shows up."

Taking the flashlight, a roll of duct tape, and a couple of tools—pliers and a screwdriver—he crouched before the open door of the crawlspace, then began to crawl through the mud toward the sound of the water.

As he expected, the problem was directly beneath the trailer's bathroom. The water pipe leading up through the floor to the sink had ruptured. He looked around and found a bigger PVC pipe with a red cut-off switch on it. It took some effort, but he finally turned the lever clockwise until the water ebbed to a trickle and then went off completely.

Awkwardly, he set to work on the split line, wrapping it tightly with the silver tape. *Let's see what this does*, he thought. He gave the red lever a turn, then went back and examined his work. It was still leaking a little, but not nearly as bad as before.

"Did you get it?" Candy asked from somewhere above.

"Yeah," he hollered. "It's not perfect, but it'll do for a while."

He was about to turn to leave when he heard a sound behind him.

A whimper.

He froze and listened. It came again, but this time it was more distinctive. A quiet sobbing. Like the crying of a small child.

Ben turned and regarded the far end of the trailer. Sparce sunlight shone through cracks between the vinyl skirting, but it was pitch dark at the very end. He directed the beam of the flashlight in that direction and. . .

Startled, his heart leapt in his chest. At first, he thought his eyes were playing tricks on him. Crouched between two columns of cinderblock supports was a small girl.

She was three or four years old in age; blond, slight, dressed in a dingy pink nightgown with a Disney princess on the front. She clutched a Barbie doll dressed like a veterinarian to her chest. She was scared half to death, that was plain to see. Her sky blue eyes were wide and full of panic, and fresh tear tracks ran down her dirty cheeks.

"Who. . . " Ben attempted to speak again; his throat was bone dry. "Who are you?"

She simply stared at him at first and said nothing.

"What are you doing down here?"

Her lips trembled as she whispered. "Hiding."

"From what?"

She raised her frightened eyes to the jousts of the floor above her. "He's mad. *Really* mad."

"Ben?" called Candy from above. "Did you say something?"

He shifted his gaze for a moment while answering. "Honey, I found someone down. . . "

When he looked back, she was gone. The space between the

two supports was dark and empty. All that occupied the space was a few old cobwebs.

Ben crawled to the spot and swept the beam around. Still no sign of her. No sign of anything. . . living.

When he turned to crawl back to the access door, Ben put his hand down on something. The beam of the flash revealed it to be a Barbie doll. It was covered with dirt and black mold. Like it had been there for a very long time.

Taking it with him, he left the crawlspace. He found Candy waiting for him.

"What were you saying a minute ago? I couldn't make it out."

He thought about mentioning the girl but didn't. He tossed the old doll into the grass. "I found this."

Candy picked the toy up, then dropped it when a roach skittered out of the Barbie's waterlogged outfit. "Yeech!" she said, flinging it away. "How long do you think it's been down there?"

He didn't answer. Just stood up and looked at the amount of mud he'd collected on the way to the water leak and back. "Candy. . . do any children live around here? A little girl, maybe. . . three or four years old?"

"As far as I know, Dustin's the only kid in the trailer park," she told him. "I talked to our next-door neighbor this morning. . . asked her if there was anyone around for Dustin to play with. She said there haven't been any kids around here for a couple of years." She looked at the moldy doll on the ground. "Acted kind of funny about it."

Ben crouched down to close the crawlspace door. "What's for supper?"

"Hamburger Helper and green beans."

"Again?" He instantly regretted his reaction. They were on a shoestring budget, especially grocery-wise, until he got his first paycheck. "I'm sorry. That's fine."

"Like you're so fond of saying, we're doing the best we can." Then, a little peeved at him, she stomped around the corner to go inside.

Ben stared through the square of the little doorway leading under the trailer.

He directed the beam of the flashlight inside again, but saw nothing but spiderwebs, plastic drainage pipes, and a few tatters of dirty insulation hanging here and there.

What the hell did I see? he thought to himself, before pulling the door firmly shut.

* * *

Every couple of days, Ben would call and check on his grandmother.

"She's holding her own," Miss Lurlene would tell him. "She's getting weaker, won't eat but a bite or two. I don't think it's going to be very long." As an afterthought, she would always add, "Would you like to stop by and visit?"

"No," he would tell her. "I don't want to upset her."

The next few nights were rough ones.

Living in the rundown trailer seemed to plague their slumber with dreams, none of them good. Sometimes Dustin would wake up screaming about the big man with the bald head standing over him. Sometimes the man's hands would be empty. . . other times he held things. A bottle in one hand, a belt in the other.

More than once, Candy thrashed around on her side of the air mattress, moaning, her hands outstretched, as though fending off something. . . or someone. Once, Ben reached out and gently stroked her shoulder. *"Don't touch me!"* she had screamed and sat up in bed, crying. Her reaction had disturbed him. Even during his drinking days, he had never wrongfully laid a hand on his wife.

And he had dreamt, too. About the little girl beneath the trailer. Eyes wide, lips quivering, clutching Barbie like it was the only barrier between her and disaster.

"He's mad. Really mad."

Sometimes, Ben didn't have to dream at all. He would get up in the middle of the night to take a piss and, cutting on the hallway light, catch a glimpse of something just within the darkened doorway of Dustin's bedroom.

A large form wearing boxers and a V-necked undershirt. A *wife-beater*... wasn't that what they called it?

Then he would take a step forward and it would recede into the night and was gone.

* * *

They had been living there for nearly a week and a half when he woke up one night to the sound of shattering glass.

Ben sat up and stared into the dark. "What was that?"

His son slept between them, dead to the world. Candy only mumbled something and turned over.

He got up and walked to the bedroom door. There was an aluminum baseball bat leaning next to the door frame; a precaution as the nights became increasingly troublesome. Ben took it and quietly started down the hall to the living room. He found the light switch and turned it on.

There was nothing or no one there. He searched the living room floor and the little kitchen but saw no sign that anything had fallen or shattered.

Then he smelled it. Strong and pungent. . . and hauntingly familiar.

Before he knew it, Candy was standing in the hallway staring at him. It was apparent that she smelled it, too.

"Ben?"

The cloying odor dredged up old memories. . . as well as guilt and regret.

"Oh, Ben. . . you promised!"

"What do you mean?"

"Where is it?" Her face was livid, her eyes hurt.

He took a step toward her. "Where is *what?*"

"The whiskey!" she nearly screamed. "I'm not stupid! This place reeks of it!"

"Candy, I swear, I haven't. . . "

Tears bloomed in her eyes. "I trusted you! I thought you wanted to do the right thing. . . for all of us!" Then she turned, ran back to the bedroom, and slammed and locked the door.

With the stench of Jack Daniels in his nostrils, Ben sat heavily on the ratty sofa they'd bought at the Goodwill. Candy cried in the bedroom for nearly an hour, while Dustin kept asking "What's wrong, Mommy?" over and over again.

The odor of spilled liquor hung in the air of the living room for a long time, before finally fading away.

* * *

That Saturday, Ben mowed the front yard, partly because it needed it and partly to clear his mind.

Things had not been good between him and Candy since the night of the shattered glass. He swore adamantly that he hadn't taken a drink, while she practically called him a liar and said that he'd betrayed them. As if that wasn't enough, Grandma wasn't doing well at all. Miss Lurlene would call and tell him maybe he should stop by if he wanted to see his grandmother one last time. He promised that he would, but he never did. He was afraid and ashamed of how she might react, seeing him again after their last uneasy parting.

He cut the motor on the push mower and took a sip from a water bottle that sat perched on the mailbox. He was capping the bottle when a voice called out.

"Hey! You!"

He looked across the road. The elderly woman sat on the porch of her trailer, beckoning to him.

Reluctantly, he walked over and mounted the porch steps. "Yes ma'am?"

"Have you seen them?"

Ben frowned. "What?"

"Have you seen them yet?"

He didn't understand. "Seen *who*?"

Exasperated, she motioned to a second folding chair next to her. "Sit down."

He didn't really want to, but he did as she asked.

The old woman stared at his face, as though searching for something. "You really don't know... do you?"

"Know about what?"

"Are you folks from around here?"

"No, from California," he explained. "Well, I used to be from here... I've just been away for a few years."

"Then you wouldn't know." She looked at the trailer across the road, then back at him. "And, of course, that asshole Lewis wouldn't tell you."

"Tell me *what*?" Ben was starting to grow weary of the old woman's cryptic question and answer session.

"About the killings."

Ben felt like someone had just sucker punched him in the gut. "Killings?"

"People died over there. A man, woman, and their daughter. It was a murder-suicide."

"Shit!" he said beneath his breath. "Uh, sorry. When did this happen?"

"A couple of summers ago. A fellow named Jake Peal." A grim sadness seemed to creep into her aged eyes. "His wife was named Terri. They had a pretty little daughter. Bethany."

"He killed them? Why?"

"Because he was a no-account, drunken son of a bitch, that's why. That poor woman and her young'un didn't have an easy moment with him in the house. Many a night I heard him hollering and her screaming." She shook her head sorrowfully. "And that little girl's cries. . . it just broke my heart."

"Why did you ask if I'd seen them?"

"Because that place where you're living is haunted."

Ben considered her words for a moment, then laughed. "Really! Mrs.. . . ?"

"Garfield. Virginia Garfield."

"Mrs. Garfield. . . you can't actually be serious."

"As serious as a heart attack!" she declared. "Since that awful night, things go on over there that you can't rightly explain. Noises and sights. Three shots a quarter after one in the morning. Lights blazing and shadows passing by the windows when no one lives there and there's no electricity on. Fussing and screaming and crying in the dead of night. . . only the place is empty and no one's there."

Ben tried to digest what she had told him. "But Mr. Lewis has rented the place before, hasn't he?"

"Yes, but he shouldn't have. . . the bastard! Six families have lived there since the night Jake shot his wife and young'un, and then put a bullet through his head. But none of them stayed more than three or four months. A decent man would have had the place hauled off and destroyed after what happened. But he's far from it. He cleaned the place up the best he could and kept renting it out."

"Still, Mrs. Garfield... ghosts?"

"Believe it or not," Virginia told him flatly. "But if I were you, I'd get your wife and little boy out of that dump as fast as possible."

"I can't do that," Ben said, feeling helpless. "We're having a hard time. And we've signed a year's lease with Lewis."

"To hell with the lease!" the old woman said. "Pack up your things and drive away from here. I'm telling you for your own good!"

Ben thought about her warning, then stood up from his chair. "I appreciate your concern, Mrs. Garfield," he said. "I really do. But leaving... that's impossible."

The elderly woman sank back in her chair, defeated. "Well, I've done all I can do. Take my advice or leave it. It's up to you, I reckon."

As Ben left and walked across the road to his mowing, he stared at their new home. It seemed even less desirable now than it had before. *Crazy old lady,* he thought as he cranked the mower and finished cutting the grass.

But, considering what he'd heard, seen, and smelled during the past few days, he couldn't help but wonder who the crazy one really was.

* * *

"He swears he hasn't had a drop, Mama," Candy explained, cradling her phone in the crook of her neck as she toted a clothes hamper to the trailer's little utility nook. "No, I'm not coming out there with Dustin. I'm going to stick it out." She paused and closed her eyes, taking a deep breath. "He's not lying! At least I don't think so. He's my husband! I'm supposed to do the right thing and help him, aren't I?"

She listened to her mother for another minute, then said,

"Listen, Mama... I'll call you back tonight, okay? I've got housework to do. Alright? Bye!"

Candy hung up and slipped her cell phone into the hip pocket of her jeans. She loved the woman dearly, but, Lord, she could get on her last nerve!

She dumped a load of towels in the washer and added detergent and fabric softener. Outside, in the backyard, she could hear the shrill squeak of unoiled chains as Dustin played on the old swing set. She closed the washer lid and stood there, listening. It was about the only normal thing about a stressful, abnormal week.

Is Mama right? Are you lying to me, Ben? Have you started that crap all over again?

She sighed. Remembering that she'd left dish towels in the kitchen that needed washing, she took the empty laundry basket and headed down the hallway. When she got there, she stopped in her tracks. Her fingers grew slack, letting the basket fall to the floor.

A woman sat in a chair at the little kitchenette table. She was slumped, her head in her hands, crying silently. She was dressed in a T-shirt and pair of pajama pants, both stained and speckled with blood. Her thin arms were scratched and mottled with ugly splotches of purplish-blue.

Candy cried out in alarm when she saw her.

In response, the woman lifted her face. It was battered and bruised. Her left eye was swollen shut, her lips split and bleeding. Beneath her chin, Candy could see a necklace of fingerprints encircling her pale throat.

The stranger's single good eye, wild and desperate, settled on her. *"I'm doing the best I can!"* she screamed shrilly.

Terrified, Candy ran past the woman at the table, through the living room, and out the front door. She crossed the front yard and paused at the mailbox, trembling, not sure what to do.

The old woman across the street, stood up from her chair. "Dear? Are you okay?"

Fortunately, at that moment, her husband drove up in the station wagon.

Candy yanked the door open the moment he stopped the car. "Ben! There's... there's someone... in the house!"

Ben climbed out and she fell into his arms. Startled, he held her. His wife was trembling. It was clear to see that something had upset her terribly.

"What do you mean?"

"There's a *woman!*" Candy shrilled in his ear. "I. . . I came out of the hallway. . . and she was sitting at the kitchen table!"

Ben's heart sank. He looked across the road and saw Mrs. Garfield standing there, glaring at him in accusation. *You didn't tell her... did you?*

"Come on and let's take a look..."

"*No!*" screamed Candy. She pulled away and backed up a few steps. "I'm not going back in there!"

"Stay here," he told her, then walked across the yard to the trailer steps. The door was open.

I don't want to go in there, he thought. But he knew he had to.

Slowly, he climbed the stairs and stepped inside. Looked toward the little table and chairs that sat adjacent to the kitchen.

There was no one there.

Ben walked over to the table and looked off down the hallway. Still no sign of anyone. Absently, he laid his hand on the back of a chair. It was cold to the touch.

He glanced down. There were droplets of fresh blood on the table top.

He glanced out the kitchen window and saw his wife pacing, back and forth, next to the station wagon.

When he looked back down, the blood was gone. The surface of the table was clean.

Numbly, he walked to the open door. "Candy, sweet-heart... come here please."

She shook her head vehemently. "No!"

"Please... honey, there's no one here."

She paused in indecision, then joined him. Together, they looked at the kitchen table. Then tears bloomed in Candy's eyes. "Ben... I wasn't lying. I... I saw..."

"I know, baby," he said, pulling her into his arms. "I believe you."

As he held her, he felt an oppressive mixture of guilt and fear. *You should tell her.*

But he did the best thing for her—or so he thought—and said nothing.

* * *

That night, Ben and Candy slept restlessly.

The incident in the kitchen had frazzled Candy's nerves. After seeing the battered woman, she was afraid to stay in their new home. She had practically begged to leave and spend the night in a hotel, but both of them knew they couldn't afford to.

Ben turned every light in the trailer on, except their bedroom. Dustin had complained about it at first, but soon fell asleep. After tossing and turning for an hour or two, so did Candy.

He lay there thinking of the story Virginia Garfield had told him. He wasn't a man who believed in such things, but so many disturbing and unexplained occurrences had taken place that he couldn't help but doubt his own skepticism.

Just settle down and go to sleep, he told himself. *You've got work tomorrow. You don't want to be dead on your feet.*

A few minutes later, he must have dozed off. Then, all of a sudden, he felt the air mattress sag near his feet, and he woke up.

Someone was sitting there, silhouetted in the light of the open door.

"Forgive me."

Frantically, Ben reached over and turned on a lamp that sat on the floor next to the bed. Illumination filled the bedroom, revealing who sat there.

It was an elderly woman; tall and robust, dressed in her Sunday best. She was no longer the frail, cancer-ridden octogenarian that had lain, bedridden, under patchwork quilts, waiting to die.

"Grandma?"

She turned and looked at him. Her eyes were gravely serious and full of regret. "I shouldn't have judged you so harshly. It wasn't a fitting thing to do, shunning my own flesh and blood the way I did."

A chill ran through him. *Am I dreaming this?*

"No," she said, as if answering. "I'm here."

"I. . . I don't understand. . ."

"All you need to understand is that you've got to take Candy and Dustin and get out of here. Now."

Again, that awful sensation of hopelessness. "I can't. We have no place else to go."

Grandma smiled gently. "Yes, you do."

It was at that moment that Ben looked past his grandmother and saw someone standing in the hallway. It was the massive form of Jake Peal, filling the doorframe, glaring at him with murder in his eyes. The big man held no liquor bottle or belt in his hand. Tonight, it was a loaded revolver.

Grandma scowled. With a flip of her hand, the bedroom door slammed violently, blocking the angry apparition from entering. The noise was so loud that it woke his wife and son. They sat up abruptly and stared at the woman perched on the foot of the air mattress.

"Go!" Grandma told them. She nodded to the bedroom's single window. The sash shot up swiftly, with such force that the glass shattered from its frame. "It's time for you to move onward. Just like this fiend and his poor family."

Ben wasted no time. He grabbed his jeans, which held his car keys and cell phone, and then helped Candy and Dustin out the open window. When he was certain they were safe, he climbed through himself. Before he lowered himself to the dark yard below, he glanced back and saw three outlets around the bedroom walls shoot sparks, igniting the dry carpet.

By the time they reached the road, the trailer was completely engulfed in flames.

As sirens wailed in the distance, Ben's cell phone rang. He dug it from his pants pocket and answered. "Hello?"

"Ben? This is Miss Lurlene." The woman paused, then told him. "Your grandmother. . . she passed away about ten minutes ago."

"Yes," he said absently, staring at the burning structure a few yards away. "I know."

It was difficult to tell, through the roar of the flames, but Ben swore he heard the sound of an old woman praying.

As well as a man, screaming long and loud, surrendering himself to a deep and lasting Hell of his own making. Paying just penance for all the pain and evil he had once wrought within those blazing walls.

* * *

Ben stood at the porch railing, watching Dustin chase fireflies through the night. He smiled, for he remembered doing the same as a child, while Grandma and Grandpa sat in their rockers, laughing and cheering him on.

Candy let the screen door of the farmhouse close behind her with a slap, then joined her husband at the edge of the porch. "He's so happy," she said, as her husband snaked his arm around her waist and pulled her close.

"He's not the only one."

Candy smiled. It seemed surreal. . . what had happened in a matter of only a few weeks. "I still can't believe she left you this place. I mean, sure, you were her last living relative. . . but considering the way she acted toward you. . ."

Ben thought of the last time he had seen his grandmother; sitting on the edge of the air mattress, a few moments past her time of death. "Grandma was a proud woman, but she knew she couldn't hold a grudge forever. We came to an understanding at the end."

The night was humid and warm, but his wife shivered, despite the heat.

"Did it happen, Ben? Was she really there?"

He shrugged, feeling a chill of his own. "I like to think she was." Ben also thought of the specter of Jake Peal, standing in the bedroom doorway. "To tell the truth, I'd hate to think of what might have happened if she hadn't been."

"Look, Daddy, look!" Dustin ran up, holding something gently between his thumb and forefinger. The bug's tail flashed, grew dark, flashed again. "Should I keep it?"

"Let it go," he told his son. "Just think of how much darker the night would be without them."

Dustin giggled as he tossed the insect into the air. They watched it take flight and join the other winking lights that filled the yard and the vast stretch of pastureland just beyond.

ABOUT THE AUTHORS

LINDA D. ADDISON is an award-winning author of five collections, including *The Place of Broken Things* written with Alessandro Manzetti, & *How to Recognize a Demon Has Become Your Friend.* She has been honored with the HWA Lifetime Achievement Award, HWA Mentor of the Year, and SFPA Grand Master of Fantastic Poetry. She is a member of CITH, HWA, SFWA, SFPA and IAMTW. Find her in the anthologies *Black Panther: Tales of Wakanda*; *Predator: Eyes of the Demon; Chiral Mad 5*; *Writing Poetry in the Dark*; and *Shakespeare Unleashed.* Visit Linda's website at **www.lindaaddisonwriter.com**.

MEGHAN ARCURI is a Bram Stoker Award®–nominated author. Her work can be found in various anthologies, including *Borderlands 7* (Borderlands Press), *Madhouse* (Dark Regions Press), *Chiral Mad,* and *Chiral Mad 3* (Written Backwards). She is currently the Vice President of the Horror Writers Association. Prior to writing, she taught high school math, having earned her B.A. from Colgate University—with a double major in mathematics and English—and her masters from Rensselaer Polytechnic Institute. She lives with her family in New York's Hudson Valley. Please visit her at **meghanarcuri.com**, **facebook.com/meg.arcuri**, or on Twitter (**@MeghanArcuri**).

LARRY BLAMIRE is a writer, director, actor, artist, and playwright, known for the feature films *The Lost Skeleton of*

Cadavra, Trail of the Screaming Forehead, The Lost Skeleton Returns Again and *Dark and Stormy Night,* plus the audio series *Big Dan Frater.* He has authored two volumes of western horror (*Tales of the Callamo Mountains*), a novel (*Doc Armstrong: Suburb at the Edge of Never*) and the recently released epic graphic novel *Steam Wars.* Larry's play of *Robin Hood* has been performed worldwide and he regularly writes / illustrates for RPGs. A proud recipient of three Rondo Awards, he contributes to numerous horror Blu-rays. Larry is currently developing an absurdist comic *Flapjack Alley.*

MAURICE BROADDUS is an accidental teacher, an accidental librarian, and a purposeful community organizer. His work has appeared in such places as *Magazine of Fantasy & Science Fiction, Lightspeed* magazine, *Black Panther: Tales from Wakanda, Weird Tales,* and *Uncanny* magazine, with some of his stories having been collected in *The Voices of Martyrs.* His novels include the science fiction novel, *Sweep of Stars,* the steamfunk novels, *Pimp My Airship* and *Buffalo Soldier*; and the middle grade detective novel series, *Unfadeable* and *The Usual Suspects.* He's an editor at *Apex* magazine and his gaming work includes consulting on *Watch Dogs 2.*

Learn more about him at **MauriceBroaddus.com.**

HEATHER DAUGHRITY is a writer of old-fashioned horror. She dreams of long candlelit passages and things that go bump in the night. Her writing is influenced by the old Gothic stories that she grew up reading, and the terrifying tales she heard at her grandmother's knee. She released her first book, *Knock Knock,* in 2021, her second, *Tales My Grandmother Told Me,* in 2022, and her third, *What the Dead Leave Behind,* in 2023. Her short stories and poetry have been featured in various magazines and anthologies. Heather lives in a century-old house (likely haunted) in a tiny town in Oklahoma.

TIMOTHY G. HUGUENIN is a hillbilly writer of the strange and spooky, living in the dark Allegheny Mountains of West Virginia. He is the author of the books *When the Watcher Shakes, Little One*, and *Unknowing, I Sink.* His short fiction has appeared in various publications including *Vastarien, CHM* magazine, and *The Saturday Evening Post.* Find out more and get a free ebook by visiting **https://tghuguenin.com/**.

BRIAN KEENE writes novels, comic books, short stories, and nonfiction. He is the author of over fifty books, mostly in the horror, crime, fantasy, and non-fiction genres. They have been translated into over a dozen different languages and have won numerous awards. Keene also serves on the Board of Directors for the Scares That Care 501(c)(3) charity organization. The father of two sons and the stepfather to one daughter, Keene lives in rural Pennsylvania with his wife, author Mary SanGiovanni. Official website: **briankeene.com**

RONALD KELLY was born and bred in Tennessee. He has been an author of Southern-fried horror fiction for 37 years, with fifteen novels, twelve short story collections, and a Grammy-nominated audio collection to his credit. Influenced by such writers as Stephen King, Robert McCammon, Joe R. Lansdale, and Manly Wade Wellman, Kelly sets his tales of rural darkness in the hills and hollows of his native state and other locales of the American South. His published works include *Fear, Undertaker's Moon, Blood Kin, Hell Hollow, Hindsight, The Halloween Store & Other Tales of All Hallows' Eve, After the Burn*, and *The Saga of Dead-Eye* series. Kelly's collection of extreme horror tales, *The Essential Sick Stuff*, won the 2021 Splatterpunk Award for Best Collection. He lives in a backwoods hollow in Brush Creek, Tennessee, with his wife and young'uns.

JOE R. LANSDALE is the author of fifty novels and four hundred shorter works, including stories, essays, reviews, film and TV scripts, stage plays, introductions and magazine articles, as well as a book of poetry. His work has been made into films, animation, comics, and he has won numerous awards including the Edgar, Raymond Chandler lifetime award, numerous Bram Stoker Awards®, Lifetime Horror Award, and the Spur Award. He lives in Nacogdoches, Texas with his wife, Karen, and pit bull, Rudy.

KASEY LANSDALE has been in the fiction world since birth as a writer, editor, audiobook narrator, and creative professional. Based in Los Angeles, Lansdale is an active voting member of the HWA and currently serves as executive editor at Pandi Press. As an author and editor, she has released numerous short stories and anthologies from publications such as Harper-Collins, Titan Books, and more. Lansdale's fiction has been optioned and adapted for television as well as comic books. She has just completed her first novel. Find Lansdale online at **www.kaseylansdale.com**, and check out her music while you're there.

ERIC LaROCCA *(he/they)* is the Bram Stoker Award®–nominated and Splatterpunk Award–winning author of the viral sensation, *Things Have Gotten Worse Since We Last Spoke*. A lover of luxury fashion and an admirer of European musical theatre, Eric can often be found roaming the streets of his home city, Boston, MA, for inspiration. For more information, please visit **ericlarocca.com**.

PATRICIA LEE MACOMBER has been writing and publishing since the age of 15, when she sold her first novel. Since then, she has appeared in such publications as *Cemetery Dance, Shadows Over Baker Street,* and *Best of Trek* #13. She is the author of over 25 novels, a Bram Stoker Award®–winning former editor at *ChiZine,* and currently works as an editor at Crossroad Press. Today, she resides in a modest house, in a modest town, with the love of her life, David Niall Wilson, and twelve cats.

ELIZABETH MASSIE is a two-time Bram Stoker Award®–winning and Scribe Award–winning author of horror novels, novellas, short fiction, media-tie ins, poetry, and nonfiction. Over the years she has been published by Simon & Schuster, Berkley, Pocket Books, Harper, Leisure, Pan, Crossroad Press, and many others. Her novels and collections include *Sineater, Hell Gate, Desper Hollow, Wire Mesh Mothers, Homeplace, Naked on the Edge, Dark Shadows: Dreams of the Dark* (co-authored with Stephen Mark Rainey), *Versailles, Buffy the Vampire Slayer: Power of Persuasion, It Watching, Afraid, Madame Cruller's Couch and Other Dark and Bizarre Tales, The Great Chicago Fire* and more. She is also the creator of the *Ameri-Scares* series of middle-grade novels, which was optioned for television by Warner Horizon in 2021. Beth's short fiction has been included in countless magazines and anthologies, including several years' best publications. She lives in the Shenandoah Valley of Virginia with her husband, artist / illustrator and Theremin player Cortney Skinner.

BRIDGETT NELSON is a registered nurse turned horror author. Her first collection, A Bouquet of Viscera, is a two-time Splatterpunk Award winner, recognized both for the collection itself and its standout story, "Jinx." Her two latest collections, *What the Fuck Was That?* and *Sweet, Sour, & Spicy* are available now! Her work has appeared in Counting Bodies Like Sheep, ***Dead & Bloated***, American Cannibal, A Woman Unbecoming**,** ***The Never Dead*****,** and *Razor Blade in the Fun-Size Candy.* Bridgett is working on her first original novel and has been contracted by Encyclopocalypse Publications to write a novelization of the cult classic film *Deadgirl.* She is an active member of the Horror Writers Association and the co-chair of HWA: West Virginia. To learn more, visit her website at **www.bridgettnelson.com**.

ERRICK NUNNALLY was born and raised in Boston, Massachusetts, and served one tour in the Marine Corps before deciding art school was a safer pursuit. He enjoys art, comics, and genre novels. A graphic designer, he has trained in Krav Maga and Muay Thai kickboxing. His short stories have appeared in several anthologies of speculative fiction, including *Apex* magazine, *Fiyah* magazine, *Galaxy's Edge, Lamplight, Nightlight Podcast.* His novels include *Lightning Wears a Red Cape, Blood for the Sun,* and *All the Dead Men.* Visit **erricknunnally.us** to learn more about his work.

JEFF OLIVER was born in Baltimore, Maryland on April 6th, 1982. A poet by passion and father of eight beautiful children, his dedication to his family and his craft is second to none. Currently residing in Western New York State, he is a writer of intense emotions, having started composing his dark poetry at just eleven years old. His gift for transforming darkness to words shone brightly from a young age. Jeff Oliver's poetry has an ethereal quality. When others may have been destroyed from such a devastating darkness, he manages to weave lyrical justice into an otherwise unfair world. His published works include *Venomous Words, Strange Sounds***,** *Poetic Fiction: Journals of Silent Screams, Scattered Thoughts: Volumes I, II,* and *III, New World*

Monsters, INKBLOTS: A Poet's Perception, and *Infinite Black: Tales from the Abyss.*

JESSICA AMANDA SALMONSON is an American author and editor of fantasy and horror fiction and poetry. She is the author of the *Tomoe Gozen* trilogy, a fantasy version of the tale of the historical female samurai Tomoe Gozen, as well as several short story and poetry collections. She has also edited a series of single-author collections of ghost stories and weird tales, many of them of historical significance to genre literature. She lives on Puget Sound with her partner, artist and editor Rhonda Boothe

RICHARD THOMAS is the award-winning author of eight books—*Disintegration* and *Breaker* (Penguin Random House Alibi), *Transubstantiate, Herniated Roots, Staring into the Abyss, Tribulations, Spontaneous Human Combustion* (Turner Publishing), and *The Soul Standard* (Dzanc Books). He has been nominated for the Bram Stoker Award®, Shirley Jackson, Thriller, and Audie awards. His over 175 stories in print include *The Best Horror of the Year* (Volume Eleven), *Cemetery Dance* (twice), *Behold!: Oddities, Curiosities and Undefinable Wonders* (Bram Stoker Award® winner), *Lightspeed, PANK, storySouth, Gargoyle, Weird Fiction Review, Shallow Creek, The Seven Deadliest, Gutted: Beautiful Horror Stories, Qualia Nous, Chiral Mad* (numbers 2-4), *PRISMS,* and *Shivers VI.* Visit **www.whatdoesnotkillme.com** for more information.

TONY TREMBLAY is the author of two genre short story collections with Crossroad Press (*The Seeds of Nightmares* and *Blue Stars and Other Tales of Darkness*) and two novels (*The Moore House* and *Do Not Weep for Me*) with Haverhill House Press. He also hosted a genre television show called *The Taco Society Presents* (available on You Tube). Tony is the co-editor of three anthologies and the co-creator of the NoCon convention. He lives in New Hampshire with his wife.

DAVID NIALL WILSON is a USA Today bestselling, multiple Bram Stoker Award®–winning author of more than forty novels and collections. He is a former president of the Horror Writers Association and CEO and founder of Crossroad Press Publishing. His novels include *This is My Blood, Deep Blue,* and many more. Upcoming works include the collection *The Devil's in the Flaws & Other Dark Truths,* and the novel *Tattered Remnants.* His most recent published work is the novel *Jurassic Ark,* a retelling of the Noah's Ark story. . . with dinosaurs. David lives in way-out-yonder NC with his wife Patricia and an army of pets. **davidniallwilson.com, crossroadpress.com**

ABOUT THE EDITOR

Stephen Mark Rainey is the author of *Fugue Devil: Resurgence, Blue Devil Island, The Monarchs, Dark Shadows: Dreams of the Dark*, and more.

He was the editor of *Deathrealm* magazine from 1987 to 1997. In its decade-long history, *Deathrealm* won dozens of awards and featured hundreds of short stories, poems, and essays by authors ranging from the most established professionals to young, aspiring first-timers, many of whom proceeded to carve out names for themselves in the horror/dark fantasy field.

You can visit Mark Rainey at **stephenmarkrainey.com**

A NOTE FROM SHORTWAVE PUBLISHING

Thank you for reading *Deathrealm: Spirits*! If you enjoyed this anthology, please consider writing a review. Reviews help readers find more titles they may enjoy, and that helps us continue to publish titles like this.

For more Shortwave titles, visit us online...

* * *

OUR WEBSITE
shortwavepublishing.com

SOCIAL MEDIA
@ShortwaveBooks

EMAIL US
contact@shortwavepublishing.com

Printed in the USA
CPSIA information can be obtained
at www.ICGtesting.com
LVHW090305081223
765818LV00054B/894

9 781959 565178